Knowledge Hurts

Knowledge Hurts

The Nememiah Chronicles, Book III

D.S. WILLIAMS

Copyright (C) 2015 D.S. Williams
Layout Copyright (C) 2019 Next Chapter

Published 2019 by Sanguine – A Next Chapter Imprint
Cover art by Cover Mint
This book is a work of fiction. Names, characters, places, and incidents are the product of the author's imagination or are used fictitiously. Any resemblance to actual events, locales, or persons, living or dead, is purely coincidental.
All rights reserved. No part of this book may be reproduced or transmitted in any form or by any means, electronic or mechanical, including photocopying, recording, or by any information storage and retrieval system, without the author's permission.

CONTENTS

1	Confusion	1
2	Healing	6
3	Heartache is hard, Numbness is easy...	12
4	Explanations	21
5	Awkward	32
6	Confrontation	42
7	Choices	48
8	Transfusion	56
9	Pick-me-Up	63
10	Enchantments Broken	71
11	Rendezvous	80
12	Nightmares	85
13	Speak the Truth	91
14	A Safe Harbor	95
15	Shock	101

16	Distress and Desire	106
17	The Hunt for Zaen	112
18	Nememiah Revealed	119
19	Nememiah's Mark	124
20	Sanctuary	131
21	Negotiations	137
22	Disbelievers	143
23	Attack	156
24	Rally	167
25	Understanding	175
26	Confessions	184
27	Trust	194
28	Demonstrations	204
29	Facing Demons	214
30	Angel Battles	223
31	Aftermath	231
32	Home Truths	236
33	Discovery	241
34	A Quiet Moment	250
35	Getting To Know You	257

36	Round Two	263
37	Requests for Exile	269
38	Fan Club	274
39	Confrontation	283
40	Into the Valley of the Shadow...	292
41	...of Death and Destruction	297
42	Cold, Hard Reality	301
43	Learning to Cope	306
44	Madness	314

Chapter 1

Confusion

I rolled out of the portal, falling heavily to the floor and my arm took the brunt of a rough landing. Pulling myself onto my knees, I fought the wave of nausea which beset me from travelling through the portal - further complicated by dizziness from donating blood to the Tines.

It took a few seconds to gather my senses and I caught sight of Epi waving his hand across the closing portal. "*No!*" Lurching unsteadily to my feet, I watched in dismay as the pentagram disappeared from the wall. "Damn it, Epi! You've got to open it again, I've got to go back..." I swayed shakily and Conal caught me, lifting me effortlessly into his arms.

"Easy, Sugar. You're not going anywhere."

"You don't understand, he's not dead! I saw him as I stepped through the portal! That thing, it's still alive!" I yelled heatedly, frustrated at my inability to make them understand.

Epi was staring at me as though I'd lost my mind and Conal was frowning as he held me firmly against him.

"Put me down, will you? I'm *fine*." I wriggled until Conal lowered me onto the ground, his hand against my elbow to keep me steady. I inhaled sharply, calming enough to make some sense. "Archangelo - the other Nememiah's Child. I thought I'd killed him - but he's not dead."

"I think you're hallucinating, Lottie. He was dead when we left. You threw the Philaris at him, he copped it straight in the chest," Ralph stated uncertainly.

"I thought he was dead, but he wasn't. He must have been faking, pretending to be dead or he was unconscious the whole time we were preparing to come back. I saw him watching me when I went through the portal," I explained bleakly.

Alarm was evident in Epi's wizened features. "Either way, there is nothing we can do about it now. You most certainly cannot go back through the portal again. You're bleeding," he was scrutinizing my arm where the gash had split open, "and you look dreadful."

Wrinkling my nose, I twisted my arm to study the wound. "Guess I hit hard on the way back."

"That should not have made a difference, child. The blood sigil should have sealed it and healed it instantaneously," Epi announced emphatically. He eyed me with open suspicion. "Why do you look so pale?"

"Gee, maybe because she supplemented the vamps' diet with some blood of her own?" Conal announced, intense sarcasm in his tone.

"You did *what*?" Epi apparently couldn't decide whether he was astonished or furious and decided on a combination of both. "That was extremely foolish, child. Unlike your vampire friends here, your blood needs are one of a kind. I'm fresh out of Angel blood to give you."

"That's okay - I'll survive." Glancing around for the first time since returning, I discovered the church had been altered yet again. The bookshelves and shabby furniture had vanished and beds which appeared to have been liberated from a hospital were lined up in two neat rows. The Tines were being settled into the beds by werewolves and shape shifters, while Nonny flitted between them, handing out bottles of blood. "I like what you've done to the place," I stated drily.

"Lottie - for Christ's sake, can you never stay out of trouble?" The sound of Jerome's thundering voice startled me and I turned to discover him limping across the room.

"What are you *doing* here?" I wrapped him in a hug, delighted to see my favorite surly doctor.

Jerome returned the hug and when he spoke, his voice was brusque. "Nick requested my presence and I flew down. He thought I could be of assistance when you returned. Plus," he threw Nick a dirty look, "I've been none too pleased with his behavior towards you recently."

"It's good to have you here." Looking around the room, it was evident that we needed him. We needed all the help we could get.

Lucas caught my eye and smiled, making my heart hammer a little harder. Butterflies twirled in my tummy as I returned his gaze, my feelings for him just as intense now as they had been five months ago. I managed a weak smile before my attention was captured by Katie. She'd been lying with William, held in his arms, but she'd managed to wriggle out of his hold and ran towards me. I dropped to one knee as she threw herself at me, squeezing me forcefully against her small body. "Hey, sweetie."

"You brought William an' Gwynn back!" she announced with a happy grin. "You brought ev'body back!"

"I told you I would," I replied with an affectionate smile.

She pulled away to study my face, the expression on her little face serious. "They is hurt."

I bit my lip anxiously, worried about how this tiny little girl would cope with what she was seeing. I'd never dreamed they would be so badly injured, so hideously disfigured when we rescued them.

Any worry was quickly extinguished when Katie continued on without taking time to breathe, her voice filled with confidence. "You can fix them, you is special. An angel can fix them, no problem." Wrinkling her nose daintily, she sniffed the air around me. "You smell stinky, Lottie."

I couldn't help the chuckle which erupted. "Yeah, it is pretty stinky, isn't it?" A hellish mix of demon blood, dirt and sweat plastered my skin and clothes. "You think I should take a shower?"

Katie nodded, her pixie-like face solemn. "I think so."

"I promise I'll go soon."

"Shower first, Charlotte. You're covered in blood and that arm needs another healing sigil," Conal insisted as I straightened up.

"*They* need healing sigils," I replied obstinately. There were ten beds in the room, five down each side and every single one held a vampire desperately in need of help. Nick and Ralph were gently lowering Rowena onto a bed, keeping their eyes respectfully averted and handling her with the utmost care. Nick carefully drew a sheet up over her still form before he brushed a tender kiss against her forehead. They were all hurting, each and every one of them and I couldn't desert them now.

"They need blood more than anything," Jerome announced, "and we've got that under control." He eyed me with unabashed interest. "What the hell are healing sigils?"

"Hasn't Epi brought you up to speed yet?" I questioned, distracted by the hum of activity around us.

"He's given me a brief rundown on the history of Nememiah's children, but I only got in an hour or two ago. I hit the ground running."

"You and me both, Doc."

Conal rubbed my arm softly. "The healing sigils can come later, Sugar. Right now they need blood and lots of it."

"It's the only thing we can do for them, unless these healing sigils will have an effect on vampires," Jerome said, eyeing his patients with concern. "These injuries…" his voice trailed off and he visibly forced himself to relax, showing a level of professionalism I admired. "They're going to take some healing."

"Trust me, Jerome," Nick said, coming across to join us. "The healing sigils will have an effect. Be prepared to have your mind blown."

"Why am I here, then?" Jerome questioned tartly, raising one bushy grey eyebrow.

"Because they'll need other help," Nick said quietly. "This kind of torture… there are injuries that aren't just physical and you know it. We're gonna need your expertise." Nick inclined his head towards me. "Go have a shower, Lottie, we can hold down the fort for now."

I sought out Epi, found him rushing across the room with a bowl of water and some towels and he rolled his eyes. "The new shower facilities are through the door on the right. Anyone would think I was running a hotel here."

"Terrific," I responded drily. "I'll order room service when I've washed up. Don't suppose you could rustle me up some clean clothes?"

"I keep telling you, Charlotte," Epi called towards my retreating back. "I'm not some two bit magician!"

Waving my hand in recognition, I stomped tiredly through the door which had magically appeared since our earlier departure. True to his word, Epi had created a large bathroom, with a row of showers against one wall and toilet cubicles on the other. The walls were tiled in pale blue, the floor covered in smaller squares of white and blue. A pile of white towels lay on a bench near the doorway. Glancing into one of the shower stalls, I was ecstatic to discover he'd even supplied shower gel and shampoo. I vaguely considered what Epi usually did for a shower and whether these alterations to the church showed on the outside of the building. Might check that out later. I stripped off my destroyed clothes and released my hair from the tight braid. Turning on the faucets, I stood under the pulsating jets of hot water and washed away the filth, easing the pain in my aching muscles. I scrubbed until I felt clean again, then wallowed under the hot water for a few minutes more. Wrapping up in a large white towel, I stepped from the stall and grinned at the clean clothes laid neatly on top of the bench. "Love you, Epi."

I dressed in fresh underwear, jeans and a pink tank top, all of which seemed to have been spirited directly from my wardrobe at Conal's apartment. I retrieved the Hjördis and Katchet from my ruined camouflage pants, kicking them to one side in disgust. Turning on the faucet, I ran water over the blade to remove the demon blood, slipping it into my pocket along with the Hjördis.

Studying myself in the mirror, the first trickle of nerves slithered down my spine in a cold shiver. It had been five long months since I'd seen Lucas and a fierce dose of anxiety gripped me. What if he wasn't interested now? What if he found the changes Conal had mentioned too radical to deal with? Worse still, I needed to explain my actions over the past few months. For a few, brief seconds I considered marking a new fearless sigil, but quickly disregarded the notion. Maybe Conal was right and I was out of control with it. Thinking of Conal led to further consternation. How was I meant to act around him now? We'd become so used to touching one another, hugging and kissing. It was going to be incredibly difficult to stop doing what had become natural after so long.

Hell, what a mess. I was an idiot with a capital I... and D... and... oh, to hell with it. I'd gotten into this mess, now I needed to work through it.

The injury to my arm still seeped blood and a quick glance at the palm of my hand confirmed it wasn't holding together any better. I drew healing sigils against both wounds. A third sigil went against the cut in my forearm where the Tines had drunk my blood. I examined the wound and screwed up my nose at the enormous, plum-colored bruise which had blossomed around it.

For another few minutes I stared at the mirror, deliberately avoiding what would come next. *For God's sake, pull yourself together*, I warned myself sternly. *Stop hiding out in here and go and help them. Don't be such a god-damn chicken - they're badly injured and you're worried about a relationship status? You're pathetic.* Squaring my shoulders determinedly, I shook my head at my reflection and marched towards the door. An hour ago I'd faced off against a fifteen foot tall demon - how hard could this possibly be in comparison?

Chapter 2

Healing

It was a relief to find werewolves, vampires, shape shifters and one lone wizard getting along agreeably when I left the bathroom. At least they weren't trying to kill one another. Nick and Conal's men had spread themselves out amongst the beds, caring for our patients and I saw Nonny and Jerome leaning over Acenith, carefully cleaning the ragged stumps where her fingers had been hacked off. My stomach churned and I looked away. "Shower's free," I called out, stepping down from the altar.

"*Yes!*" Marco shouted gleefully. He snatched up a pile of clothes from the end of one of the beds but Nick stopped him with a pointed glare. "I can wait," he muttered, looking a little disenchanted. "Conal, you can go first."

I knew it was some sort of pack hierarchy at work but I grinned at Marco. "There's more than one shower, Marco. In fact, there's enough for all of you. Go get cleaned up."

Marco joyfully collected up his clothes again after seeing Nick nod his assent and the men exited the room in the race for a hot shower.

Conal passed me at the altar and smiled reassuringly. "You alright, Sugar?" he asked in a low murmur. He knew me too well. Although rescuing the Tines was something we'd talked about repeatedly in the past few weeks, having them here was creating a ferocious apprehension that I hadn't been prepared for. Explaining my relationship with Conal to Lucas was going to be more difficult than I'd ever envisaged. Recreating ties with my friends was going to be complicated.

"Yeah, I'm okay." I swallowed nervously, brushing my still damp hair behind my ears.

Conal brushed a soft kiss against my cheek. "It's going to be fine, he'll understand." He threw me a wink and disappeared into the bathroom.

I stepped down from the altar and approached the beds slowly. The men were tucked beneath the sheets, leaning back against pillows. The women had loose hospital gowns to cover their nudity and give them a degree of reassurance in trying conditions.

Jerome drew me to one side. "They're in a bad way, Charlotte. It'll take weeks for them to recover from these injuries, even if I could set up an intravenous line and feed them blood twenty four hours a day, it'd take weeks to heal the damage they've sustained. Nick tells me a lot of these injuries were caused by silver..." He trailed off, shaking his head in disgust. "Never dreamed it could affect vampires in this way, thought that was a myth, but here we are..." He stared down at me, his expression somber. "Nick says you can help them. If you can, you need to be doing it now. Vampire physiology is different, but they're in serious trouble and their bodies are in shock. I can't suggest what will happen if we don't do something soon."

"Tell me where to start, Jerome. I'll do my best."

He eyed me for a long moment, his grey eyes serious. "Let's start with the ladies first. That's what Lucas will insist on anyways." He limped towards Acenith's bed and Nonny moved to one side so I could see Acenith's ravaged face. Her eyes were wide and glazed, pain shadowing her pretty features. Her hand had been carefully cleaned and rested against a soft pillow.

"Hey, Acenith," I greeted her quietly, brushing my fingers across her forehead.

"Charlotte..." Acenith croaked weakly.

"Don't speak," I cautioned her. "Just let me try to help you."

She nodded feebly and shut her eyes, too exhausted and overwhelmed to do anything else. Nonny had given her a careful sponge-bath, as much as was possible in her current traumatized state. I wanted to cry as I looked at the dreadful disfigurement covering her cheek, where holy water had been dribbled until her face resembled a melting candle.

Nonny patted my arm and gave it an encouraging squeeze. "You can do this, Lottie." She slipped away and headed towards Rowena's bed where Epi waited for her with a fresh bowl of water and clean towels. I watched them for a minute, saw them gently washing the accumulated grime and dirt from Rowena's abused body.

"Lottie." Jerome brought my attention back to the here and now.

Drawing the Hjördis from my pocket, I ran a careful eye over Acenith, trying to decide where to start. "Jesus," I muttered under my breath, not sure how to handle this. They were all so incredibly damaged - injuries which didn't come under a classification of either blood or poison.

Jerome squeezed my shoulder and I nearly snapped at him, until I saw the empathy in his eyes. "I know it's tough, Lottie, but you need to focus. One thing at a time, it's all you can do."

After a quick discussion with the spirits, I began to work, their gentle murmurs soothing. The sigils were ones I hadn't known before, but I trusted their advice. I drew an intricate sigil on the back of Acenith's hand, close to where her fingers had been so cruelly amputated. I didn't realize she'd opened her eyes until I heard a sharp intake of breath and found her staring as the stumps began to glow. We watched as new fingers began to extend from the shattered bone remains. As knuckles and joints were created, a layer of muscle and tendons followed, wrapping around the bone before the skin followed, carefully molding itself around fingers. Then fingernails formed, perfectly shaped and evenly trimmed. The skin glowed for a few seconds more as it knit over itself at the tips of her fingers, then slowly dissipated, leaving us staring at her hand in open-mouthed disbelief.

"Holy mother of God..." Jerome gasped. He lifted her hand, requesting she wriggle her fingers and make a fist to confirm she had full movement. "Did that hurt?"

"Non," Acenith whispered, still staring at her hand as if she couldn't believe what she was seeing. "It was warm and I felt... a tingle, but no pain. Like épingles et aiguilles...pins and needles."

I continued to work, leaning over her arm. The silver burns proved easier than I'd expected - the spirits identified the need for poison sigils because silver acted like toxin to a vampire. On the down side, they were also harder to deal with, because of the sheer number of them. We rapidly discovered a sigil could heal only a small amount of the damage before it faded and required repeating. It was going to be a long, time-consuming haul to repair all the damage. By the time I'd completed the poison sigils on Acenith's battered body, the men had started returning from the showers. Rafe headed towards us and brushed his fingers tenderly across Acenith's matted hair. "How's she doing?"

"Getting there," I muttered, as I conferred with the spirits regarding the holy water burns to her face. "Do you want to sit with her?"

Rafe grinned. "Nah, I'll leave that for Ripley when he's feeling better."

I glanced up. "I thought…"

"Your plan worked," Acenith whispered hoarsely. "Ripley and I," she glanced across the room to where Ripley lay, her eyes filled with affection, "are together."

I smiled happily. "I'm so pleased for you both." Aware this situation might be awkward, I slanted my gaze to Rafe, wondering how he felt about Acenith and Ripley.

Rafe took Acenith's hand and squeezed her fingers, winking at me as he did so. "Acenith's a good friend. She asked me to help out and I did."

A giggle erupted from my chest. "It was all a set-up?"

Rafe nodded. "Somebody needed to give Ripley a good kick up the ass so he'd see what was right in front of him."

Jerome returned from Lucas's bedside, his forehead creased in the almost perpetual frown he'd sported since we'd arrived. "I've spoken to Lucas, I'm worried about how much blood we can get into some of our patients," he glanced at Acenith, who'd lain back against the pillows with her eyes shut, exhausted after our small talk. "I want to intubate those who are struggling to feed from the bottles."

"We can do that?"

Jerome shrugged, the motion non-committal. "Can't feed them intravenously, but a nasogastric tube might do the trick. Intubate through the nose, directly into the stomach and feed them blood from bags. Lucas thinks it should be achievable."

"Okay, let's do it," I agreed easily.

"Charlotte, we won't have enough blood to keep up with demand," Jerome warned. "You obviously didn't know how dire things would be and you don't have enough supplies to last out."

"We'll get more," Rafe announced, releasing his gentle grip on Acenith's hand. "How much do you need?"

"A lot," Jerome admitted, glancing around the room and mentally calculating. "Given their injuries, we're looking at probably... eight to twelve pints apiece over the next twenty four to thirty six hours."

Rafe was already moving, calling to Nick and Ralph who'd returned from the showers and they conferred for a few minutes in the corner. Nick strode over a few minutes later, his gaze taking in the work I'd already done with Acenith. "We're heading out to get blood. Be back as soon as we can."

"You won't..." I began but Nick interrupted.

"We know the rules, Lott." He squeezed my shoulder. "Keep working. We'll get what you need."

Jerome bustled about, preparing to intubate Acenith while I gingerly approached her face. If this failed... I shuddered at the thought. They'd all received injuries from holy water, but to see Acenith's beautiful face so hideously disfigured... I was terrified I couldn't fix it. Would she be scarred like this forever?

Epi bustled across as I wavered in indecision, his owl-like eyes examining her injuries. "You have done well, child, but why are you hesitating now?"

I swallowed. "Her face... if this doesn't work..."

"She will still thank you for saving her life," Epi announced. "Go on with your work and stop vacillating. Others are in need of your assistance."

He hurried off again and I rolled my eyes. "Old bastard," I muttered under my breath.

Jerome snorted and didn't bother to hide the amusement in his gray eyes. "Looks like you've got two of us to deal with now."

Acenith's eyes fluttered open and she gazed at me for a moment, her usually sea-green eyes faded and listless. "Your friend is right," she murmured. "I will thank you, regardless of whether I am completely healed or not. I have faith in you, Charlotte." Her eyes closed again, her lashes creating dark fans against her too-white cheeks.

I licked my lips and did what I'd been told - stopped vacillating. With final verification from the spirits, I drew the sigil they'd recommended on Acenith's cheek, shuddering when my hand came into contact with the wax-like rivulets of skin running down her cheek like a gruesome living candle. Stepping back, I held my breath and watched. I noticed Jerome had also stopped and was watching Acenith's distorted features with undisguised interest.

Her eyes opened and she gasped, inhaling sharply as the damage on her cheek glowed and began to flatten and smooth out, the streams of damaged tissue integrating as though they were being melted into place by a hot iron. It took a few minutes, but by the time the sigil had vanished, so had the damage.

Jerome brushed his fingertips across the smooth skin, as if he couldn't believe it was real without physical touch. "Did that hurt?" he questioned bluntly.

Acenith shook her head minutely. "No, it was... again... a warm, a tingling sensation." With a visible tremble in her fingers, she carefully touched her cheek and her eyes widened in astonishment.

I grinned broadly and whooped with delight, before encasing Acenith in a gentle hug. "Get some rest, I'll be back to visit later."

Chapter 3

Heartache is hard, Numbness is easy...

Walking between the beds, I made my way to where Marianne lay beside Striker. After the success of treating Acenith's wounds, I was feeling more confident, but still far from comfortable. Those of Lucas's Kiss who had the energy to keep their eyes open were watching me cautiously, but it was Striker who broke the awkward silence. "So," he remarked casually, "you left our place as meek little Charlotte and now - you're what? Buffy the Vampire Slayer?"

"Something like that," I couldn't help but smile at the comparison.

"So it's true, huh? Ralph says you really are an Angel," Striker continued. He was coping better than some of the others, with three empty bottles sitting beside him on the bed it was apparent he was regaining strength, but there was worry in his eyes as he watched over Marianne protectively.

"That's the rumor," I agreed easily, settling carefully beside Marianne on the bed. She watched me solemnly, her skin the same stark white as the pillow she lay on. Since I'd last seen her in Montana, she'd added dazzling aqua blue streaks to her hair, but they were muted by the dirt and detritus of captivity. "I'm going to put some marks on your skin, give those wounds a helping hand," I explained.

Lifting her wrist carefully, I drew a sigil against the deep gouge where the silver chain had burnt into her skin, watching with approval as it began to heal. Within seconds, the skin smoothed over, leaving a faint scar.

"That didn't hurt," Marianne whispered.

"Healing sigils don't hurt supernaturals, only the ability sigils cause pain," I explained, placing a second sigil further up her arm.

"So we're supernaturals now?" Striker asked with a wry grin. He shifted on the bed and gasped with pain.

"Lay still, Striker," Jerome growled. "You're not Superman." He began to prepare a feeding tube, his actions belying years of medical experience.

Undeterred by Jerome, Striker continued our conversation. "So tell me, Lott. How'd you get strong enough to kick a vampire in the head and send him flying across the room?"

"The ability sigils give me extra strength." A tiny smiled played on my lips. "And I wear titanium capped boots to stop my toes getting broken. One of Epi's innovations."

"Ahh. That explains a lot," Striker agreed huskily. His voice was hoarse and an octave deeper than normal. If he'd been human, I would have thought he was suffering from a sore throat. As it was, I knew it came from torture and probably screaming for mercy. A cold shiver trickled down my spine.

"How did you know the Consiliului had taken us?" Ben rasped. He was lying on the bed beside Striker with his eyes closed, but obviously he was listening to the conversation.

I worked steadily across Marianne's battered body, marking sigils. "The spirits told me as soon as it happened, then Nick called and confirmed it. The Tremaine pack was attacked by younglings on the same night."

Straightening up, I moved further down the bed to treat the wounds on Marianne's legs. I forced myself to look at the calf which was devoid of flesh. Another quick word with the spirits confirmed which sigil was needed and I marked her skin, close to the edge where muscle and tendon lay brutally exposed. There was a numbness spreading over my body as I worked, a protective barrier against the horror I'd witnessed today. I welcomed it, embracing the numbness and nurturing it to keep me from screaming my frustration and anger and running away from the scene around me. The utter lack of sensation was better than the alternative for now.

"The Tremaines were attacked?" Ben opened his eyes, blinking at me in disbelief.

"Yeah," I responded unhappily. "Lyell Tremaine was murdered, along with half of their people. Conal is Alpha now." The back of my head had started to thump and there was a tremor in my hands which was becoming obvious the longer I worked. The initial adrenaline from having escaped Romania was fading fast, leaving me nauseous and weakened. I glanced over at Ben and Striker, then back to Marianne. "Let's talk about this later, when you're feeling better." I was worried how more bad news would affect them when they'd already suffered so much.

To my utter relief, both men lapsed into an unsettled silence and I moved on from Marianne after pressing a kiss against her cheek, leaving Jerome to set up the nasogastric tube. He directed me towards Gwynn next, who looked so small and vulnerable, her glorious mane of copper red hair matted with dirt. She watched me warily as I approached, pale blue irises washed out. She looked as if she suffered from the milky blindness of cataracts.

"I need to shower," she rasped, fingers plucking nervously at the gown she was wearing.

"Later, Gwynn. For now, we need to heal your injuries," I insisted quietly.

She shook her head wildly, the plucking of her fingers against the material growing more agitated.

Nonny caught my eye and came over to stand at my side. "She won't allow me to bathe her," she whispered, although I knew everyone in the room could hear her. "She won't allow anyone to touch her yet."

Swallowing down the painful lump in my throat, I gazed down at Gwynn. "Please Gwynn, you're not strong enough to shower right now." My eyes drifted across her arms studying the blackened pattern of deep wounds. "Let me heal your injuries first, then we'll see."

"No, no, no," Gwynn chanted hoarsely. "I have to get clean, I need to be clean..." Her pretty, heart-shaped face screwed up suddenly, as she fought to cry tears impossible for her to shed.

Jerome limped over from Acenith's bed and his practiced eye flew over Gwynn's body, shaking his head infinitesimally. "I'd dearly love to give her a sedative, but it's a useless wish, won't have any effect on her."

"What should we do?" I asked in a low voice. Gwynn was obviously bordering on a breakdown and I wanted to avoid it, desperate to stop her from worsening. A bottle of blood sat by her bed, unopened and untouched and her fangs were run out, pressing against her blistered lips.

There was a flurry of motion from the other side of the room and I turned to see Phelan lifting William gently in his arms, carrying the vampire across the room. He laid William at his wife's side and William cradled her in his arms, ignoring the pain it must be causing him with his own grievous injuries. He whispered softly to her, holding her tightly against him and his pain - the agony which was not only physical, but psychological - was apparent in his grey eyes. Gwynn settled in his arms, burrowing her head against his chest and William continued to softly murmur against her hair.

We stood there - Jerome, Phelan, Nonny and I - four outsiders intruding on a moment between a husband and wife which was both acutely heartrending and breathtakingly tender. I wanted to turn and run, get away from this church, these horrific scenes which would be indelibly inked in my psyche forever. Subconsciously I took a step backwards, but Katie appeared at my side, reaching up to grasp my hand as her round grey eyes took in the scene before her. For long minutes she remained still, watching William and Gwynn vigilantly and flashes of emotion filtered across her face as she tried to in vain to comprehend the sight before her. Finally she tugged on my hand and looked up at me. "You gonna fix William an' Gwynn now?"

"Yes, Katie, that's exactly what we are going to do," Jerome announced gruffly. He turned away and wiped impatiently at his eyes before turning back to the bed. "William, we need to intubate Gwynn, get some blood into her body and Charlotte will treat her wounds whilst I'm doing that," he raised his head, looking around the room. "Epi?" he called when he located the warlock standing at Lucas's bed. "Do you have a bathtub? Gwynn would like to get cleaned up, but she's not strong enough to shower."

Epi shook his head but started moving towards the back of the room. "I will arrange one." On his way past Gwynn's bed, he haphazardly waved his hand towards us and curtains appeared, seemingly hanging from fresh air as there were no fixtures. They drew themselves around the bed, which would have amused me endlessly in a normal situation, but nothing was humorous in our current circumstances. "I believe the little one needs some privacy," he announced gruffly.

Nonny kissed my cheek and hurried to follow him. "I'll make sure everything is prepared," she called over her shoulder.

"I'll go and do a blood round," Phelan announced, turning on his heel to slip through the curtains but I grasped his arm and he looked at me in surprise. I reached up to kiss his cheek gently.

"You're a good man, Phelan," I whispered against his ear.

I could swear he blushed before he slipped through the curtain and I turned back to our patients. Gwynn was calmer now with William by her side, lying passively as I approached. "We're organizing a bath, Gwynn, but I really want to heal your injuries first... is that okay?"

She nodded her assent, closing her eyes with a sigh and nestling on William's chest.

"Charlotte... I need blood while you do this," William said gruffly, "the scent of your blood too close..." he faltered, shutting his eyes. "My self-control is shot to hell."

I took the full bottle from beside the bed and unscrewed the top, handing it to him. "You're self-control is just fine, William," I announced as I began to work on Gwynn's injuries. "Your *self-confidence* about your self-control is the problem."

He considered my words for a minute, sipping from the bottle as his dull grey eyes followed my movements. "You may be right," he admitted quietly.

I continued to work silently until I'd healed all of Gwynn's injuries and then straightened up, groaning inwardly at the ache in my back and shoulders. "I am right, William. You haven't attacked a human in more than forty years," I smiled at him. "I think it's time you cut yourself some slack. I'm going to go and work on Rowena." I pulled open the curtain surrounding the bed and spied Nonny, requesting her help to get Gwynn into a bath. The sooner she had the opportunity to wash the memories from her skin, the better it would be for her, though I had to wonder how she was going to cope with the memories imprinted in her mind. They would be much harder to fix and it couldn't be done with soap and hot water.

Shaking off the thought, I strode towards Rowena's bed, feeling like I'd been on this ride for far too long already.

Rowena greeted me with unconcealed delight, holding me close for a very long time. "We have missed you so much, Charlotte," she whispered, clenching my hands in her own injured ones. Of the four women, she seemed to be coping best and had managed to drink two bottles of blood. Her skin was still too white, she looked utterly exhausted, but her eyes were beginning to return to a more natural hazel. "You look so different."

I caught her wrist in my hand and created a sigil, watching the skin heal over. "A lot of things have changed since I saw you last," I murmured.

"I can see that. You look wonderful, despite having given us blood," Rowena agreed softly. She took a deep breath, clenching her fists tightly. "I want to thank you, so much, for coming to our rescue." A fine trembling set up through her limbs and a shadow passed over her delicate features. "I was certain we were all going to die." Her attention flickered across to where Phelan was carefully carrying Gwynn towards the bathroom, Nonny hovering behind carrying the bag of blood which was now feeding Gwynn through a tube in her nose. "What they did to us..." she broke off and the trembling increasing exponentially as her slim shoulders shook with emotion.

I was grateful when Jerome appeared and he spoke soothingly to Rowena while I worked in silence. The numbness was wearing off, leaving the anger and rage and helplessness in its wake and I knew it wasn't a good thing. I still had six people to heal, still had to face Lucas. Still had so many things to deal with. I wished the numbness would come back and forced myself to focus on the present, to take one step at a time. I needed to stop feeling sorry for myself and move on.

Conal reappeared from the bathroom. "That feels *so* much better," he announced. "But I'm going to have a shitload of bruises again." His hair was still damp and he'd dressed in jeans and a black American Choppers t-shirt. He stopped beside me, where I was working on Ripley.

"And thankfully, you don't stink like rotting carcasses," I agreed with a sly grin. "What took you so long?"

"Epi provided plenty of showers, but not nearly enough hot water. I was just gonna give up when he appeared, muttering something about the need for a bathtub."

"Thank goodness for that. You stunk."

He grinned. "Just because you got to the shower first, Sugar."

"Haven't you heard, it's always ladies first?" I replied easily.

"There aren't too many ladies I know who'll take on a demon, a transformed Angel and a pack of vampires," he said with a wink. "And what was it you called the Drâghici leaders? The Three Stooges? Way to go to piss them off, Charlotte."

I shrugged. "What can I say? I call it as I see it. And you know as well as I do, the plan *was* to annoy them."

"Well, you certainly did that. Which reminds me, I must have a word to Epi about that fearless sigil. Not such a good idea..." He laughed as I aimed a quick punch at his shoulder and he sidestepped it easily. "Agility has worn off too,

Heartache is hard, Numbness is easy...

Sugar. I'll rustle up coffee." He studied my face for a couple of seconds, his brow furrowed. "You're still looking mighty pale. How's the head?"

"Throbbing," I admitted.

"I'll get you some painkillers," he offered.

"Thanks."

Ripley watched this exchange silently, and he abstained from making any comment when Conal walked away, although his eyes revealed his curiosity. He motioned to the healing sigil I'd placed against the cross the Drâghici had branded on his thigh. "How does that work?"

I shrugged a little, unsure how to explain something of which I had little understanding. "To be honest? I haven't got a clue. Suffice to say, it works effectively." I motioned towards the bottle he held clasped between his fingers. "Drink some more, Ripley. It'll help you feel better."

Taking a steadying breath, I made my way next to the one person I was most dreading talking to. Lucas. I could have avoided him and treated one of the other men, but I needed to get this over and done with.

My heartbeat accelerated as I approached him and I struggled to control it, hyperaware that he would hear the tempo change. It was a strain to produce an unconvincing smile, which faded as hastily as it had appeared. "Hi," I said warily.

"Charlotte," Lucas responded, blue eyes gazing at me intently. "Wait a moment, please." He raised the bottle he'd been holding to his lips, drinking until he'd drained the contents. When he lowered the bottle, he smiled sheepishly. "I'm struggling with your scent."

"It's been a while," I agreed quietly. I eyed the bottle cautiously. "Okay now?"

He attempted a shrug and winced. "I believe so."

I settled down at his side, keeping my movements slow and cautious.

"It seems there were a lot of things about you we hadn't discovered." His gaze grazed across my arms, where some of the sigils remained strong and blue against my skin. "Phelan says those markings give you special abilities?"

"Yeah," I felt painfully self-conscious as I reached for his wrist, marking his skin and while the wound was healing I pointed to some of the sigils on my own arms. "Agility... Endurance... Strength... Courage... Stamina."

"And fearlessness?"

I looked up sharply, but he was lying back against the pillows, his expression enigmatic.

"Yeah. It's my personal favorite. Without it, I'm not sure I could have worked up the courage to face the Drâghici."

"I thought you were remarkable," Lucas responded. "Seeing you walk into the Consiliului stronghold - you were incredibly confident."

"It was mainly due to the fearless sigil," I admitted. "When I walked in there - I really didn't have a care in the world. No fear whatsoever." The liberating effect of the sigil had astounded me. "But Conal seems to think it wasn't such a good idea."

"You and Conal," he paused, visibly swallowed. "Are you a couple now?"

I met his eyes, stunned by the abrupt question. "Um... no...well..." I muttered lamely. With a heavy sigh, I shook my head. "It's complicated."

"I'm good at complicated," he replied evenly.

For a moment I stared at him, thinking of a dozen different ways to continue this discussion and discarding every single option as being too complicated. "Can we talk about this later? When we can have some privacy?" I glanced around, aware of everyone else in the room. Having this discussion with Lucas was going to be difficult enough, without having an audience.

"If you wish," Lucas agreed. His gaze held mine for a few seconds more, then he directed his attention to the Hjördis in my hand. "When I first saw you in Sfantu Drâghici and you removed your jacket, the marks were all brilliantly blue and covered every inch of skin." He studied my bare arm, his eyes tracing the marks. "Some of them have disappeared."

I returned to my first aid efforts, forcing my attention to the burns on his chest and swallowed deeply, trying not to gag as I healed the deep slashes where a silver knife had gouged his skin open. "They're indigo when I first mark them. As the power of the sigil is used up in combat, they fade and then disappear. These were drawn early this morning, they'll fade away to nothing in the next day or two."

"Do they hurt you?" He studied his own arm, where I'd hastily drawn the invisibility sigil above his wrist, but it had vanished. "When you drew the mark on me, it felt as if it burned."

"They hurt you more. When I mark my skin, it's like being scratched with a needle." I reached forward, bringing my face closer to his as I worked to heal the gash on his cheek. His aroma wafted towards me and I pushed down the crazy urge to hold my breath, to avoid his scent overwhelming me and making me do something crazy. Like throw myself into his arms and kissing him. The mere touch of his skin against mine was already causing electrical energy to spark through my fingers.

"Because you're an Angel," Lucas responded huskily. "I can hardly believe it."

I slipped further down the bed, continuing to work. "It takes a bit of getting used to," I muttered.

Holden was lying beside us and he entered the conversation. "When did you discover all this?" Like Lucas, he held a bottle of blood balanced on his thigh and I realized he bore a remarkable resemblance to his brother. Holden kept his hair much shorter, but it was the same shade of blonde and his sky blue eyes watched me with interest.

"About three months ago. Conal took me to a cookout at his parents' home and I met Nonny. She's the Tremaine pack's secret keeper. When she began to understand what I could do, she brought me here to meet Epi and he confirmed what I was after a lot of tests and discussion."

Conal appeared, brandishing a mug of coffee. He handed me a couple of painkillers and I swigged them down with the coffee, savoring the wonderful aroma of the brown liquid beneath my noise.

"Nonny's finishing up with Gwynn, once she's settled back into bed she's gonna get some food cooking. No doubt you're starving, Sugar."

"Absolutely," I agreed with a little smile.

Conal lifted his gaze to Lucas. "How're you feeling?" His voice was impassive, the look on his face carefully neutral.

Lucas's return gaze was equally blank when he responded. "Better, thank you."

The tension between the two men could have been cut with a knife and I squirmed uncomfortably between them. I would have willingly faced off against another demon, rather than be sitting here with the two men I'd fallen in love with.

It was a mess, and it was all my own fault.

Chapter 4

Explanations

"Food's up!" Nonny announced from the kitchen doorway.

There was a noisy stampede as the Lingard men raced towards the kitchen and Nonny grumbled at them good-naturedly. "Charlotte, you stay there, honey. I'll bring yours out."

I sank gratefully onto the floor, content to sit and relax after treating everyone's injuries. Nick, Rafe and Ralph had returned about half an hour ago, loaded down with bag upon bag of blood. Despite Conal's ministration of Tylenol, my head was still pounding and I was nauseated.

Nonny appeared with a tray and Striker whistled. "Lottie - you gonna eat all of that? Seriously?"

There was no comparison between the pile of food on my plate and what the men were eating - mine was at least double the quantity. Nonny had outdone herself with three large steaks, a couple of baked potatoes slathered in sour cream, collard greens and two cobs of corn, smothered in butter. "Absolutely," I confirmed, licking my lips and tucking in.

Conal slipped down onto the floor beside me and grinned at Striker. "Charlotte has the metabolism of a hummingbird. We have to keep stuffing her with food, otherwise she starts dropping weight rapidly," he explained. "With all the training, we discovered very quickly that you have to keep feeding her. Constantly."

"She eats like a world championship wrestler," Phelan agreed, his voice filled with admiration. "I've never seen anyone who can consume as much food as Lottie can."

"She ate well enough at our house," Striker said, eyeing my plate doubtfully. "But nothing like that."

Jerome was chatting to Nonny, who'd joined us for dinner. "You're doing the right thing with the steak, Nonny, she'll benefit from anything with a lot of protein to help her body recover from the blood loss."

Nonny nodded her understanding. "We've got protein shakes in the refrigerator."

"Excellent," Jerome smiled. "She should have one now, two more each day and she'll need iron rich foods for the next week or two. Plenty of leafy green vegetables, lots of red meat."

I smiled at Jerome. "Back to being my Doctor?"

He grinned and winked. "Someone has to keep an eye on you, young woman. You have a penchant for getting yourself into trouble astonishingly quickly."

"I'm not doing it on purpose," I grumbled good-naturedly. The food was improving how I felt; despite Nonny's ministrations I hadn't eaten since before we left early this morning and it was apparent hunger hadn't helped my mood or the queasiness.

"Nah, trouble finds her naturally," Nick remarked. He was sitting at the foot of Lucas's bed, plowing through his own dinner. "Though I gotta admit, she's a damn good fighter... for a human girl."

"Thanks for the rousing endorsement," I laughed and the sound surprised me. It felt like I hadn't laughed in forever. Glancing around at my friends, for the first time since this horror began I was both thankful and grateful for the blessings I'd received. The Tines were weak and had suffered enormous tribulations, but I'd healed their external injuries and they would regain the strength they'd once had in time. Already some of them were looking much better, despite still being covered in dirt and grime, their irises were gradually returning to normal and the blood intake had been put to work inside their bodies, their lips no longer blistered and cracked. Lucas and Striker had already discussed showering after dinner and Ben had requested his bed be raised as he was more comfortable sitting up now the wounds were healed over.

"You did good, kid," Phelan agreed on his way back from the kitchen. He had a six pack of beers and handed them out to the werewolves and shifters before settling on a wooden chair. "Although I have to agree with Conal - that fearless rune makes you crazy reckless."

I poked my tongue out at him and devoured some more food, taking the protein shake Nonny proffered. "I don't know about me being crazy - but I'm fairly certain the Consiliului are *all* nuts."

"Why would the Consiliului attack a werewolf pack?" Ben questioned aloud, his forehead creased into a worried frown. "What possible reason would they have for doing that?"

"For the same reasons they're attacking other supe's - to start a war," Conal stated soberly. "From what Charlotte's figured out, they want control of all the supernatural groups around the world. They're intending to kill anyone who isn't a pureblood."

"They've attacked other packs? How do you know this?" Lucas asked.

As succinctly as possible, Conal explained the entire situation. How I received information from the spirits and the nightmares I regularly endured.

Epi joined in the discussion, explaining my role as Nememiah's Child and the history of the Angel children, their role on earth and my responsibility to create peace amongst the supernatural groups. He discussed his vast knowledge of Nememiah's Children, how they'd died out over a thousand years ago and how his study of them had become his life's work.

Conal took over again and I was happy to sit back and let them deal with it. I wasn't entirely certain the Tines were up to this discussion so soon, but looking at their shocked and worried faces, I knew it wouldn't make a difference whether they were told later rather than sooner - they were going to be distressed either way. "We discovered there was another Angel child - Archangelo. The Consiliului have created him and he's a hybrid vampire and angel. They wanted Charlotte to complete the set - they were planning to create Charlotte and then have Archangelo and Charlotte create a race of demon/angel hybrids." The dark look in his black eyes showed exactly what he thought of that idea.

"Charlotte, you know that's an impossibility," Lucas remarked.

"No it isn't, apparently." I grimaced, laying my knife and fork on the now-empty plate. "Epi believes my blood is a genetic characteristic which can't be overridden. If I have a child - with anyone - whether they're human or supernatural, the child retains the angel blood. If the Drâghici had succeeded, the process would have created me, but Epi believes Archangelo and I retain the ability to reproduce and the children would be a hybrid mixture of both demon and angel blood."

"That's entirely correct," Epi agreed sharply. "I am rarely wrong."

"Speaking of Archangelo, Lott, that was an outstanding throw. Never thought you'd be capable of something like that," Striker announced proudly.

"I've had plenty of practice," I said. "For the past three months, it's all we've done. Epi's teaching me everything he knows about Nememiah's Children, he and Conal have been training me to fight." I glanced at Lucas and saw jealousy simmering in his expression, before he quickly swallowed it down.

"I thought you'd killed him," Phelan remarked. He crossed his ankle over one knee, looking thoughtful. "You're positive it was him you saw?"

I nodded. "It was definitely him, standing at the gates in a bloodstained shirt. He watched as I entered the portal, not moving, just... staring." I shrugged. "At least I gave the Drâghici something else to think about - I doubt they were thrilled that the tourists got an eyeful of Archangelo like that. Hard to explain away the blood."

"If he really is vampire, he'll be difficult to kill," Holden said. "A chest wound would never do it, Charlotte. You shouldn't have been able to pierce his chest with that weapon the way you did." Holden sipped from his bottle, looking thoughtful. "Are you sure he's vampire at all?"

"You saw him yourself, Holden. He is vampire, undoubtedly. He smells like vampire," Ripley announced. "But definitely something more."

"We don't take a hit like that to the chest," Striker argued. "A knife, a throwing star, whatever the hell that thing is that Charlotte threw - wouldn't have any impact on vampire flesh."

"A silver knife did," Lucas responded quietly. "You bear scars as proof. Perhaps the weapon Charlotte wielded has that same capability."

A shocked silence descended in the room and Striker's eyes flashed with fury and blatant frustration.

"Charlotte's weapons aren't silver, that much we do know. Frankly, we don't know enough about Archangelo to ascertain what he's capable of, or how to kill him. There have been no Angel children for over a thousand years and never one that's been created as vampire. Obviously he bleeds and his skin seems as fragile as Charlotte's," Conal said, his composure diminishing the tension which had permeated the church. "But I guess we don't know whether the usual ways of killing a vampire will work either, until we try it."

"Killed many vampires?" Striker asked coldly.

"No, but I'd be a fool if I didn't know how it was done," Conal retorted.

"Striker. Enough." Lucas's voice was coldly authoritative. "These people have provided us rescue and shelter. You will give them respect."

The battle Striker fought to still his tongue was in evidence, from the clenched fists to the sharp line of his compressed lips. He focused on his hands, until he inhaled visibly and the muscles in his shoulders loosened. "My apologies," he muttered.

"I assume Archangelo must be killed," Jerome questioned.

"There's no choice," I announced. "The Consiliului are killing indiscriminately in their quest for power. They've already murdered dozens that we know of, maybe more and they're using Archangelo to help them do it. Archangelo's a dangerous weapon at their disposal. If it's a choice between killing him or allowing the Consiliului to proceed with their plans and attempt to capture me to... mate with him, I'll choose killing him."

They all lapsed into thoughtful silence and I waited, wondering what they were thinking. Were they shocked? Were they repulsed that I would consider killing someone without a second thought? A quick peek at Lucas from beneath lowered lashes confirmed he was watching me, but his face was mask-like, with no emotion detectable.

"Come along, Katie. Time for a bath. And guess what? Uncle Epi has got a real bath for you now. No more showers."

Nonny captured the little girls hand and led her towards the back of the church. I kept forgetting we had a small child amongst us and should all be careful about what we discussed in her presence. Would she have nightmares tonight? With everything she'd seen and heard today, it wouldn't be surprising. I knew I would probably dream about what I'd seen and done - and the dreams wouldn't be pleasant.

"How many of the vampires were at Sfantu Drâghici?" Epi questioned, after assisting Jerome to exchange empty blood bags for fresh ones on the women.

"Three," Conal answered. "One of them was the blonde guy with the curls." He glanced at me for confirmation.

"His name is Arawn. We met two others, Odin and Hyperion, but we didn't have photos of them."

"So that makes six?" Epi confirmed.

"Seven," Lucas said. "There are seven members of the Consiliului. The three you mentioned, plus Bellona, Qadesh, Bendis and Enlil." He glanced pointedly towards the beds where the women lay, before his gaze returned to me. It was apparent he wanted this subject deferred and I nodded my acknowledgement.

"And there was one kickass demon," Marco added with a grin. "That one was a monster."

Epi abruptly sank down onto the edge of Holden's bed. "A demon? What did it look like?"

I shrugged, sipping my drink. "Big. Black. Ugly. Sharp pointy teeth, big snappy claws. The usual."

"As I regularly tell you, young lady, sarcasm is the lowest form of wit," Epi chided.

"Well on a humor scale of one to ten, sarcasm is the best I've got right now," I replied. Epi's beady eyes studied me, pointedly waiting for an answer. I huffed out a heavy sigh. "About fifteen feet tall, two mouths, double rows of teeth, tentacle things all over its head, stood upright, big claws. How's that?"

Epi's brow puckered. "Who called this demon from the Otherworld?"

We all heard the change in Epi's voice. There was a tension, an edge which hadn't been there until Marco mentioned the demon we faced. "Archangelo. He created the pentagram."

"You're certain of that?" He glanced from me to Nick for confirmation, his stare piercing.

Nick pursed his lips, raising one eyebrow. "Don't ask me, I was still a rock when this was happening."

"Why, old man? What's so important?" Conal questioned.

"It means there is someone else involved in this plot and Archangelo is far more dangerous than I'd ever imagined."

Nick straightened up, grey eyes narrowing. "What does that mean, exactly?"

Epi stood up and paced back and forth between the beds, deep in thought. "Archangelo is part angel, part vampire. He should not have the ability to call demons."

"Well, he did," I insisted. A glance at Conal confirmed his confusion mirrored mine. "Odin ordered Archangelo into the room when I called them on his existence. He told Archangelo to show me something to prove his power. He drew a pentagram and out popped an ugly big demon."

"Who should have the ability to summon demons?" Conal asked.

"Warlocks, of course, as you have observed in the past few months, I can summon them. Some witches, although they tend to frown upon the practice.

And wizards, although there are very few of them alive now." He continued to pace up and down, while we silently watched.

"So you're saying?" Rafe pressed, losing patience with the protracted silence.

"I'm saying that the Consiliului have a warlock, a witch or possibly a wizard in their service. And whomever that is, *they're* teaching Archangelo the capacity to summon demons," Epi explained impatiently, adjusting his glasses. "Of course I assumed with demon blood in his body, he would have extraordinary powers, beyond the normal abilities of an Angel child. But I'm stunned that he would be able to summon a demon. He should not have the magical talent to manage such a feat."

"So... if you didn't expect them to be using demons, *why*, exactly, have we been fighting them for the past three months?" Conal asked dryly.

"Because I suspected we would come across them during this battle. It was the original role of Nememiah's Children to rid the world of demons. When I first met Charlotte, I thought that was why she'd presented herself now, because we faced a threat from the Otherworld. Now though, it appears we face a bigger threat than I first suspected. The demons aren't going to come from the Otherworld of their own volition. They're being summoned."

Phelan caught my eye and lifted his eyebrows in question, and I shrugged blankly, shaking my head. I had absolutely no idea what Epi was getting at, why this was so important. "Okay, Epi. Spit it out. What the hell's wrong with this scenario that's got you so bothered?"

Epi stopped pacing and stared down at me, his eyes shadowed with exasperation. "I keep forgetting how little you know, child. One thousand years ago, Nememiah's Children were placed on this earth and part of their role was to rid the world of demons."

"Yeah, we know that," I interrupted, impatient to get to the point, whatever it might be.

Epi glared and continued. "Those demons found their own way here. There were many of them, but they came through from the Otherworld of their own free will - finding a way to portal to our world to create mischief and mayhem. Very few were actually summoned to our world from this end." He shook his head, slipping his glasses off and wiping them on his tunic. "This is bad, very bad. If Archangelo has the ability to bring demons from the Otherworld..." he paused, placing his glasses carefully onto the bridge of his nose before he met my eyes. "Your description of the demon you faced today. It sounds like an

Omias. Nasty things." He shuddered a little. "You did remarkably well to battle it and survive. Which reminds me, you will require a poison sigil if it's fangs broke your skin. It carries a slow-reacting poison which will ultimately destroy your vital organs."

"Gee, thanks for the heads up, Epi." I drew the Hjördis from my pocket and marked a poison sigil hurriedly against my arm.

"Which, may I point out, is why I ask for an accurate description of these demons. Big, black and ugly does not suffice," Epi retorted.

"Can we get back to the point of the matter?" Conal said impatiently. "What does it mean if Archangelo can call these demons?"

"I originally surmised that Charlotte and Archangelo made their appearance now because we faced a future threat. Something that had not yet presented itself. Then when the Consiliului plan became apparent, I thought she'd been placed here in the present to ensure future harmony between supernaturals, assuming the threat was a war between the various supernatural groups. The Children of Nememiah had also undertaken that role. But now, to find out Archangelo is transformed and has the capability to summon demons..."

"The point, Epi," I interrupted loudly. "Get to the damn point."

He turned to stare at me, his blue eyes magnified behind his glasses. "Archangelo called one Omias from the Otherworld today. If he can call one, he can easily call one hundred. Or one thousand."

"Can't we fight them?" Striker asked. Characteristically, Striker was delighted at the thought of a brawl, weak or not. His earlier anger had been washed away, replaced by cold enthusiasm for tackling the enemy.

"We can fight them. But we can't kill them," Nick explained heavily.

Lucas frowned. "Why?"

I closed my eyes, understanding exactly what Epi's point was and my heart sank. "They can only be killed with the weapons, the Katchet and Philaris I used today. Those weapons can only be used by Nememiah's Children." I sighed. "Which means I'm the only one who has the ability to send them back to the Otherworld."

There was silence for a minute, while everyone digested Epi's words. Now that Epi had finally gotten to the point, I could see why he was so concerned. If Archangelo could summons hundreds, perhaps thousands of demons from the Otherworld... how could one person defeat them all? I studied my arms, determining which sigils still had an effect. It seemed courage was operational, because I was positive I should be feeling a lot more panic than I was.

"You're sure they can't be killed by us?" Striker said. "I know you guys are strong, granted, but what about a vampire? Could we kill them?"

Conal shook his head. "We've tried everything. Even with six of us against one demon, we can cause a huge amount of injuries, but it's the weapons Charlotte uses which return them to the Otherworld."

"I should have made sure he was *definitely* dead," I muttered.

"We certainly need to find out more about him, Charlotte. You will need to contact your spirit friends, see what advice they give you," Epi ordered. "In the meantime," he glanced at the large, old-fashioned wristwatch he wore. "I suggest you and Conal head back to the apartment, get some rest and meet us back here in the morning."

If the ground had opened up and swallowed me - right at that minute I would have been grateful. Hell, if a demon had erupted from the ground and swallowed me, it would have been an improvement.

The silence was absolute, you could have heard a pin drop inside the church. Keeping my head low, I tried to ignore the uncomfortable sensation of staring eyes, everyone contemplating Epi's casual inference to Conal and I living together. Not that it wasn't true - we *did* live together.

Technically.

I hadn't considered what would happen after the Tines were rescued. There was no room here for us - the church was packed to the rafters with bodies. Between Nick and his men, Epi, Nonny and Katie, plus ten vampires, there was no room for anyone else and it made sense that those of us who lived in the area would return to our own homes. It was something I should have thought through - and while I was at it, much more thoroughly. The heat of a blush travelled across my chest, racing up my neck to fill my cheeks with color.

"We should stay here," I mumbled self-consciously. "You'll need help..."

"Nonsense. There are plenty of us here to keep an eye on our charges," Epi announced, completely oblivious to my distress. "You have had an eventful day, child. You need to rest, particularly after giving blood to your friends."

Conal drew himself to his feet and held his hand out. "Sugar?" He made it a question, waiting for me to make up my mind.

I couldn't go. Could I? How would that look to my friends... to Lucas? On the other hand, it would hurt Conal's feelings if I abandoned him like yesterday's newspaper because Lucas was here... oh *hell*. I didn't know what to do. I let Conal pull me to my feet but kept my eyes downcast, not willing to face anyone.

Conal leaned forward to whisper against my ear. "Stay or go, Charlotte?"

An interminable period of time passed as I wavered in indecision. "I'll stay," I finally whispered.

He straightened up, his back stiffening. A quick peek confirmed he was angry and hurting, the tension apparent in his stubbled jaw line. "Fine." That one word confirmed everything was far from fine.

"Conal..."

He'd already dragged his car keys out of his pocket and turned on his heel to head towards the door.

"I'll see you in the morning," Conal announced. He didn't turn back, refusing to look at me or anyone else.

I searched the room and found Ralph sitting by Ripley's bed, sending him a frantic message with my eyes. I was enormously relieved when he understood what I was trying to convey and stood up. "Conal, hang on. Phelan and I will come with you. I need another beer or two before I'll sleep, after the day we've had."

Phelan whispered against my cheek as he left. "We'll keep an eye on him, don't worry." With a gentle squeeze of my arm, he followed Conal and Ralph out and Epi locked the door behind them.

I wish I could say I held my head high and didn't allow the events of the past few minutes to affect me, focusing instead on caring for the Tines. I wish I could say I walked across to Lucas and sat down to have an open and honest discussion regarding my relationship with Conal.

I did neither one of those things. Instead, I kept my head lowered and walked away from them, skulking out to the small room Epi had created for Katie. Nonny had bathed the little girl and settled her to sleep, sitting on a stool beside the bed she was brushing her fingertips through Katie's dark hair. When she saw the stricken look on my face, she slipped from the room and returned a few minutes later with a pillow and blankets, creating a makeshift bed in the corner. I slumped down onto the blankets and Nonny settled cross-legged beside me, proving once again she was far more supple and active than most elderly people.

She brushed her fingers through my curls when I turned onto my side and stared at the wall. Despite feeling wretched, my eyes stubbornly remained dry and the lump in my throat was painful to swallow past. Nonny continued to gently finger brush my hair and it was only as I drifted off into a fitful sleep that I heard her speak, her voice low and tinged with sadness. "We can't help who we love, mi pequeño ángel."

Chapter 5

Awkward

The following morning I woke early, blinking rapidly in the dusky light which filtered into the room. There'd been no nightmares, a welcome surprise when undisturbed sleep happened so rarely. Cautiously stretching my limbs, I discovered I was sore, but not unduly so. The bruise on my arm was enormous and nearly black in the early light.

My mood was tranquil this morning, resigned to the situation I found myself in. Hiding out wasn't going to resolve anything and my friends needed help. Whatever the situation between Conal, Lucas and I would lead to, for now I intended to get my mind back in the game and behave like an adult.

Within half an hour I'd showered and changed into fresh jeans and a t-shirt. Refusing to skulk for a minute longer, I headed out into the main part of the church, glancing around in stunned silence at the scene before me.

The vampires were asleep.

Not all of them, certainly, but there was no doubt the women were all sleeping, as were Ripley and Ben. They were tucked up in the beds, curled in various states of repose and quite definitely in the relaxed state of slumber.

William was still lying beside Gwynn and he smiled, offering a little wave. Further down the room, Striker and Holden were laying on top of the sheets, looking much improved on the previous day. Both men's hair had been washed and brushed, the filth and dirt gone. They were dressed in borrowed clothes and talking quietly together, drinking from bottles of blood. A fleeting glance at Lucas's bed confirmed he was absent.

"Lucas is showering," Nonny announced, handing me a mug of coffee. "Rafe is keeping an eye on him, they're still a bit shaky this morning."

I sipped the too-hot coffee, inhaling the wonderfully bitter aroma of Nonny's special blend. "They're… asleep?"

Nonny nodded, glancing around at her charges. "Lucas says it's part of some regenerative process, they'd suffered so much damage over an extended period of time, he believes their bodies have shut down to allow the blood to heal damaged tissue more rapidly."

"Did Lucas sleep?"

Nonny shook her head. "No. Neither did Holden or Striker. Jerome believes it might be because they were more physically powerful to begin with, consequently they will recover more rapidly." She raised an eyebrow, glancing across at William. "Your young friend there, William, he slept for a little while. He seemed brighter when he woke again, so perhaps Lucas and Jerome are correct."

It was utterly astounding. For long months I'd lived with the Tines and never once had they appeared tired. I'd never seen so much as a yawn from any of them. To watch them sleeping peacefully… it was surreal. Studying the dark rings beneath Nonny's eyes, I squeezed her shoulder. "Have you slept?"

She nodded. "Yes, I had a few hours, then took over from Jerome and allowed him to get some sleep. We are all fine."

"Thank you, Nonny. You've been a trooper."

Nonny grinned. "They are good people, Charlotte. It's been an honor to help you and your friends." She crossed her arms and surveyed the room, carefully checking her charges. "I'll get you some breakfast," she announced a moment later. "Conal telephoned ten minutes ago, he's on his way."

"Is he…okay?"

"He's fine, Charlotte. He knows how difficult this is for you. For both of you *and* Lucas." She shook her head. "To have the love of one good man is a great thing. To have the love of two good men is indeed a wondrous thing."

"It's a painful thing," I muttered, the words slipping out before I'd had a chance to regroup.

Nonny offered a solemn nod. "Indeed it is, but you must choose what is best for you, mi pequeño ángel. Conal is my grandson and I love him dearly, but you can't choose what is best for either him, or your friend Lucas. You must choose for yourself and yourself alone." She uncrossed her arms and turned away. "I'll get you some breakfast."

I wandered across and stopped by William's bedside, calling out a hello to Holden and Striker. The two men grinned and waved their bottles in salute before I turned back to William. "How is she?"

William glanced down at his precious wife, curled against his side. "She's a little better today, but she's been restless," he admitted. "Her sleep, if that's what this is, has been affected by her memory of our captivity."

"I wish I could have come sooner, William. Epi was insistent we had to wait until as close as possible to my birthday to retrieve you."

"Why?" William asked. There was no condemnation in his question as he gazed at me calmly. I wasn't sure I would feel the same way in his situation.

I sighed, slumping onto a chair beside the bed. "My abilities have increased swiftly in the past few months. According to Epi, Nememiah's Children reach their peak at the age of twenty one." I glanced at my watch. "Which is today."

William smiled warmly. "It's your birthday today?"

I nodded, not worried in the slightest about missing the occasion. "We suspect the Drâghici discovered the same information and learned they'd made a mistake in creating Archangelo too early. By creating him when they did, his abilities were inhibited from increasing further. Which is why they kidnapped you," I admitted sorrowfully. "They needed something to draw me in, force me to come to Sfantu Drâghici."

"What happened wasn't your fault."

I jumped at the sound of Lucas's deep voice. He was standing at the end of Gwynn's bed, Rafe hovering beside him. Lucas offered Rafe a tense smile. "Might I have a chair?"

I watched Rafe grab a chair and place it beside mine. Lucas lowered himself onto it, the fine lines around his eyes conveying how much energy taking a shower had cost him. Despite the evident strain, he looked magnificent. Damp hair hung darkly against his pale skin. His eyes were midnight blue, the silver swirling slowly around his irises. He'd dressed in a pair of dark grey pants and a sage green t-shirt which spanned the expanse of his chest snugly and a flare of desire erupted low in my body.

"What happened wasn't your fault," Lucas repeated patiently, as though he wasn't certain I'd heard him the first time. "The Consiliului are nothing if not determined. Odin has delusions of crazed grandeur, which we became... painfully aware of, during our enforced confinement."

"I should have warned you," I protested, "but I honestly didn't think they'd come to Montana, when they already knew where I was."

"The Drâghici have always used whatever means they had at their disposal to obtain objectives," William spat angrily.

"I'm so sorry, William," I whispered, deeply guilty about what they'd suffered.

"I don't blame you, Charlotte," William assured me hurriedly. "The Consiliului are owed the entire culpability." He looked tenderly at his beautiful young wife and his eyes hardened. "Arawn will pay for what he did. I intend to kill him myself."

"For now, our concern needs to be for our Kiss, William," Lucas reminded him gently. "Revenge can be withheld for now."

William's jaw clenched tightly as he drew his anger back inside and I watched the coldness visibly recede from his eyes. When he spoke again, he sounded calmer. "What happens now you are twenty one? Why does it make a difference?"

"It's a genetic thing. When I'm twenty one, I reach some sort of maturity level. I can't be created, nor turned into a werewolf."

"So you can't be bitten?" Striker asked. He and Holden strolled over and joined the group around Gwynn's bed.

"Oh, I can still be bitten by just about anyone," I explained with a wry smile. "The difference is, I'm now immune to becoming vampire or werewolf."

"Are you immortal?" Holden asked curiously.

"No, not at all. I can be killed by virtually any means. It was why timing was so important in coming to Sfantu Drâghici - if we'd attempted a rescue too early and things went wrong, they would have created me. If we left it too late, waited past my twenty first birthday, they would have murdered you all." I rubbed a hand across my cheek, recalling the anguish I'd endured over past weeks.

"Good morning, child. I trust you slept well?" Epi strode across the room, his tunic today a bright red and matched with dark grey pants. "Any nightmares?"

"Nope," I announced, offering Nonny a grateful smile as she handed me a plate filled with crispy bacon, scrambled eggs and fried tomatoes. "Not a thing."

Remarkably, Epi took this lack of news better than I'd expected. "No matter, you were extremely fatigued. The rest will have done you good." He studied my face for a moment. "Although you don't look well-rested child, your skin is far too pale." He studied the bruising on my arm. "Did you treat that with a sigil?"

"Yeah," I said, around a mouthful of egg. "A couple of times."

Epi shook his head, muttering under his breath. "Not good, child, not good at all. Might I suggest you refrain from feeding your friends again, we can't afford for you to be ill."

"Wasn't planning on it," I agreed easily.

He wandered off towards the kitchen, still muttering beneath his breath and William smiled. "He's an interesting... man."

I wasn't entirely certain it was the first word William thought of to describe Epi and giggled. "Interesting is one word for Epi."

"He's right, however," Lucas said quietly. "You took an incredible risk yesterday, in feeding us."

"It had to be done," I muttered. "You weren't getting out of there without help."

"Still, you were incredibly courageous, Charlotte. To allow us to drink your blood when our thirst was so dire - it could have ended very badly," William added in a low voice.

I looked into his eyes and he returned my gaze somberly. "I had faith in you, William. In all of you. Maybe your ability to control your thirst is stronger than you imagined."

"I, for one, will not take the risk again," Holden said. "You tasted delightful, of course, but William is right. It was a terrible danger to you."

I grinned at Holden, liking the big vampire more each time we spoke. "Don't worry, I won't be offering a second time."

Holden grinned back, sipping from his bottle. "We certainly have had a baptism of fire since our first meeting, Charlotte."

I picked at a piece of bacon on my plate. "How did two brothers both become vampire, by the way?"

"Mom didn't tell you?" Striker questioned.

I shook my head. "Never asked."

"You know Charlotte respects our privacy, Striker," Lucas reminded him. He offered me a gentle smile and I warmed under his intense gaze.

"Yeah. Probably a good thing she's the angel and not me. I'd be poking my nose in everywhere and getting into a heap of trouble," Striker admitted proudly.

"So..." I pressed. I had wondered how unusual it was to have two men from the same family become vampires. Had it happened simultaneously, or on separate occasions?

Striker leaned back in his chair, settling in to tell the story. "I was born in 1906, in Norway. Mom and Pop migrated to America from Norway when I was three and we settled in Arkansas. Pop had a small farm, but we never had two cents to rub together. With twelve sisters and brothers, we pretty much led a hand to mouth existence."

Holden took up the tale. "I'm twelve months younger than Striker. When he was twenty, Striker took off, determined to make his fortune somewhere other than Jacksonport, Arkansas. We'd both grown sick of the poverty, trying to make ends meet and Mom was so worn out, dealing with thirteen kids. Our Pop was a bast..." Holden caught himself and modified his words, "bit of a drunkard, half the time he couldn't work in the fields 'cos he couldn't get out of bed. Striker was sick of it, and decided to leave and find work somewhere, so he could send money back for Mom to help feed us kids."

"Mainly, I just wanted to get the hell out of Jacksonport and away from Pop," Striker admitted.

"Striker was a heck of a fighter, used to always head into town when the carnival rolled through. They had bare fist boxing competitions and Striker would scrape up the entry fee, then fight the biggest, toughest motherf... ah, bad guys they could put him up against."

The guy had layers of muscle tightly wrapped over more muscles, it was little wonder he'd be able to hold his own in a fistfight. "I assume you won?"

Striker shrugged. "Not every time, but enough that I made a bit of cash to help Mom. When I decided to leave for good, I figured fighting would be the easiest way to make my fortune. It was the one thing I was really good at."

"Which turned out to be not the only thing you were good at," Holden laughed.

"You'll embarrass Lottie," Striker grumbled. "She blushes like a tomato."

I glanced from Holden to Striker, a tiny frown creasing my forehead.

"She doesn't embarrass nearly as easily as she used to," Rafe said, ruffling my hair affectionately.

"Really? Where's the fun in that?" With a smile, Striker continued. "I was a popular guy. I joined a travelling carnival, appeared as the strong man in sideshow alley, which is when my hair got to be so long. They wanted me to look like a Viking." He smirked at the memory. "Playing a strong man didn't pay much, the real money was in the fist fights which occurred after the show closed at night."

Holden took up the story again. "Striker had quite a way with the..." he glanced across to confirm Marianne was still sleeping soundly, "... ladies. One of the perks of being part of the sideshow, was the women who threw themselves at him. In copious amounts and with alarming regularity."

"Yeah, yeah. Don't let my wife hear you saying that," Striker growled. "She doesn't like the reminder of my past."

"Anyway," Holden continued with a delighted grin, "one of the ladies who showered my brother with attention happened to be a..."

"...vampire." Striker finished the sentence. He sipped from his bottle, and his demeanor darkened. "Didn't even see it coming when she bit me. All I remember was the excruciating pain as she drank my blood and wondering why I couldn't fight her off, when I was so big and she was this itty bitty little thing. It was only later that I learned what she was, and that she had enough strength to do whatever the hell she wanted. By then, it was too late. I was vampire, she was my maker and she had plans to have me fighting in her own little sideshow alley." His face hardened. "The bitch used me to fight other vampires, but it wasn't a matter of betting a couple of bucks this time. Nah, she intended for it to be a battle for existence or final death and the stakes were much higher. She used me as a way of building up her own resources, to increase her power base."

"Which is where I come in," Holden said. "Striker had been missing for four years and I'd been searching for about three and a half of those years, trying to find out what happened. It was the darndest thing - for six months, he'd written regularly, sending a few bucks to help Mom out and then, suddenly, there was nothing. Mom was so worried, wondering if something had happened, so I decided to search. Tracked down the carnival he'd been working with and they told me he'd taken off one night with a woman and they'd never heard from him again."

"How did you find him?" Rafe questioned.

"They gave me a little information about the woman he'd been seen with, told me she turned up every now again, did some betting on the fights and then disappeared, often with one of the men in tow. It took a long time, but with some investigative work and a hell of a lot of stowing away on trains all over the country, I caught up with her at another carnival in Texas. They'd given me a fairly good description and it helped that she was a real stunner - you couldn't have mistaken her for anyone other than who they'd described."

"Qadesh." Lucas's cold voice made me jump, I'd gotten engrossed in Striker and Holden's story and almost forgotten he sat with us. "The Goddess of Love and Sexuality."

The name rang a bell and I stared at Lucas in growing horror. "Qadesh?" I remembered her from the photos Nick had provided when we'd planned our raid on the council. Petite and beautiful, Qadesh had hazel eyes and hair so blonde, it looked white. Sexy, buxom - everything a man could be attracted to. I turned to Striker and saw the shame in his eyes. "Qadesh created you?"

"And Holden," Striker agreed quietly.

Lucas's words rang in my mind. "Wait - Goddess of Love and Sexuality? What does that mean?"

The three men were silent, all lost in their thoughts until Lucas spoke, finally answering the question. "Qadesh took her name from an ancient Egyptian Goddess. All the Council chose their names in the same way. Qadesh is the Goddess of Love and Sexuality because her ability is to create lust and craving in others around her. She can make you do anything she desires, and it can drive a man to the edge of insanity."

"What sort of things?"

Rafe put a hand on my shoulder, meeting Lucas's eyes. "Lott, I'm not sure you really want to hear the answer to that question."

"You mean...?" Seeing the hard stare in Rafe's eyes, the discomfort in the faces of Holden, Striker and Lucas, what Rafe was alluding to blossomed. It seemed it wasn't only the Tine women who'd been sexually assaulted during their captivity.

"So... she created you?" I asked Holden, deferring any further questions regarding Qadesh and her role in the council.

Holden nodded. "I was besotted from the second I first saw her. She fawned over me, pretending to be concerned about Striker. She told me she couldn't imagine what had happened to him." He lowered his gaze, embarrassed. "I fell for it - fell for her, to be honest. Didn't take long before one thing led to another, and we ended up having sex in some barn just outside of Austin, near where the carnival was camped." He shrugged awkwardly. "Next thing I knew, I woke three days later and my whole world had changed. I was vampire."

"What happened?"

"She took me to her Kiss - at that stage she wasn't with the Council, ran a Kiss of about seventy vampires. Let me see Striker, then told me we were both hers to do with as she pleased. We ended up fighting for her, doing... other stuff, for... I guess, twenty years or so." He shuddered, rubbing a hand across the back of his neck. "We both thought we loved her, both fought for her attention. She was like a drug you couldn't resist, no matter how damn hard you tried. She set us up to fight one another, to hate one another and it took nearly all that time for us both to see what she was doing."

"Seeing her again in Sfantu Drâghici - it was like a nightmare," Striker said abruptly. "Having her..." He broke off and clenched his fist around the empty bottle abruptly, pulverizing it into tiny slivers of crushed glass.

The sharp sound of breaking glass brought Nonny and Epi running from the kitchen and they arrived to find Striker holding his head in his hands, rocking back and forth on the chair. I dropped onto my knees in front of him, avoiding the broken glass to kneel at his side. Gently, carefully, I wrapped my arms around the big man and rubbed his back soothingly as he trembled.

"Do you believe the Consiliului will continue with this plan for a war?" William asked quietly, his gaze fixed on Striker's blonde head. "If they've lost the opportunity to create you, is there any point? Surely they'll back off and stop this atrocity."

"I know they will. There isn't a doubt in my mind." Rubbing my hand in reassuring circles on Striker's back, I could feel his body trembling under my fingers.

"How can you be so sure?" Lucas asked. He'd placed a reassuring hand on Holden's shoulder, giving him comfort as Holden stared at his brother in dismay.

"The nightmares Epi was talking about - I see things, learn things from them. The Drâghici intend on taking over the supernatural world. Losing out on me was just a blip on their radar, it won't stop them."

"Can Odin really be this presumptuous?" Holden asked Lucas. "Will they all follow him into such an obscene undertaking?"

Lucas considered the question carefully before he answered. "You know as well as I do, they will. Odin and his Kiss have always considered themselves superior. As the years have passed, they've become more and more fanatical in their hold over the vampire world." He paused briefly, accepting a fresh bottle of blood from Nonny with a nod of acknowledgement. "I'm afraid what Charlotte says could be true."

"And Charlotte? You will fight against them?" William questioned softly.

I sighed gloomily. "I have no choice in the matter. Whether I like it or not, this is apparently my destiny."

"Then I will join you in the fight," William announced determinedly.

My eyebrows rose. "You will?"

"Of course we will," Lucas agreed. "We'll fight this battle with you."

"We all will," Striker lifted his head, staring down at me with an icy blue coldness in his eyes. "If the Consiliului wants to start a war, we'll give them a fucking war." His gaze flickered across to where Marianne lay curled on her side, her hands tucked under her cheek. "It'll be my pleasure to send every single one of them to hell. Starting with that bitch, Qadesh."

Chapter 6

Confrontation

As the day wore on, my nerves began to disperse and I relaxed. Striker bounced back swiftly from his despair, before long he was laughing and smiling again and I marveled at his ability to recover so rapidly. As Holden pointed out in a quiet moment - vampires were resilient. Given what they were subjected to during their long existence and the violence which surrounded them almost constantly, they had to be tough.

When Conal arrived with Ralph and Phelan in tow, he greeted me with a warm smile. There was no sign of last night's tension and he seemed relaxed, which in turn had me loosening up and worrying less.

Lucas was treating me with cordial politeness and he and Conal managed to be in the same room without glaring daggers at one another. I wondered if things were looking up - although I still had no idea how to fix the problem.

By lunchtime, the male vampires were up and dressed, each and every one looking much better with every passing hour.

By late afternoon, Nonny and I had gotten Rowena, Marianne and Acenith into a hot bath as each had awoken and we'd carefully washed their hair and removed all traces of their incarceration. It was a startling repeat of what Marianne and Rowena had done for me, so many months ago when I'd been hurt and helpless. I tried to pay no attention to the signs of what they'd endured and carefully washed away the evidence. When we'd finished our task and gotten them dressed, Rafe or Conal would meet us at the bathroom door and lift the women easily into their arms, gently depositing them with their respective partners to be held and comforted. I smiled when I saw Acenith curled up in Ripley's lap like a tiny kitten, snuggled against his chest. Warmth flooded my chest to see how solicitous Ripley was towards her, how he gazed down at her face as though she was the only woman in the world and gently caressed her face, pressing tender kisses against her skin.

While we were busy in the bathroom, Lucas borrowed Phelan's cell phone and got in contact with Thut's Kiss in Egypt and the Fitzgerald Kiss in New York. It was a relief to discover they'd been untouched by the initial machinations of the Drâghici Kiss and Lucas cautioned them to go into hiding. He'd made other phone calls which confirmed what we'd said - the Drâghici had attacked groups around the world. It was a sobering reminder of how accurate our information had been to date.

After dinner, the Tines, the Lingard and Tremaine men, Jerome, Nonny and Epi sat together talking. It was pleasing to see them manage to get along. I'd been worried the different factions would find it difficult to co-operate, but a common enemy had united them as nothing else could. They discussed the Consiliului's plans at length and argued pros and cons of how to approach the problems we faced.

I sat apart from the group, half-listening to their conversation but also taking time to speak with the spirits, whose discussion revolved around the exact same crisis. The spirits were less forthcoming with solutions to our problems, but I really hadn't expected otherwise. As with everything in this new life I was forging, I'd long ago accepted I wouldn't get answers handed over on a platter. I concentrated on their murmured conversations as they spoke at length about Archangelo, gleaning what insights they would give me. I'd learned Archangelo had less spiritual powers than I, but he'd always be stronger due to being created. No great surprise there. There was one thing the spirits and my friends agreed on - he had to be killed. The million dollar question, was how?

I slipped away and headed towards the kitchen, desperate for more coffee. The more time I'd spent with Conal and Lucas, the more my nerves had begun to amplify again. It wasn't only caffeine I sought - I needed space to try and pull my thoughts together. Whether I looked at Lucas or my gaze came to rest on Conal, similar emotions tumbled through my heart. How could I love both of them? It wasn't acceptable to love two men at once. What could I do to fix the problem? What should I say? I had to explain my actions to Lucas, if there was any chance of our pursuing our relationship. But how could I do that to Conal, betray the love he'd offered me? How could I just abandon him, as if nothing had happened between us in the past five months? The same questions had been swirling endlessly through my head in the past twenty four hours and I was no closer to a solution.

"Charlotte?"

I spun around from the bench, to discover Lucas standing in the doorway, his arms crossed over his chest. He was recovering rapidly and other than a scar where Arawn had cut open his cheek, there was little evidence visible. He was utterly, magnificently handsome as he gazed at me from across the room.

"Um, hi."

For a long moment he was silent, his eyes focused on mine before he spoke. "I think you're avoiding me."

I sighed, biting my lip anxiously. "You're right, I probably am," I admitted. "But there isn't a lot of privacy around here to talk."

"And I can't leave the building, so there are few choices available to us." The church sat in consecrated ground and even though Epi had placed some sort of enchantment over the building itself to keep them protected, the grounds were out of bounds to the vampires. Whilst Lucas didn't believe anything untoward would happen, it was a risk they weren't willing to take. In the past few weeks, the knowledge Lucas and his Kiss had taken as gospel regarding their kind had been tipped on its head.

He strode across the room and captured my hands, brushing his thumbs across my knuckles. "All I want is the truth, Charlotte."

The silver was swirling in his eyes and I focused on that when I spoke. "I love you, Lucas. I've always loved you. I've never stopped loving you, not for a minute in the five months since I left."

His gaze turned towards the doorway. "And Conal? I've seen the way he touches you, the way he looks at you."

"I love him, too," I confessed and saw a shadow of pain pass across his handsome features. For a moment I longed to be wearing a courage sigil, because I was feeling like a coward. Inhaling deeply, I tried to explain. "The past few months, I've spent a lot of time with Conal. He's been there, through all the craziness of learning about Nememiah's Children."

Hurt darkened his eyes, but he remained composed. "I would have been there for you, Charlotte. If you hadn't insisted on staying away from me."

I sighed heavily, trying to figure out how to explain. "I thought I was doing the right thing. I didn't know how I managed to hurt you that afternoon in Puckhaber."

"But once you knew, you could have come back," Lucas pointed out, his voice incredibly calm.

"It wasn't that simple, Lucas. I needed to be here, to learn about Nememiah's Children and to work with Epi. I honestly thought I was keeping you safer by not telling you what was happening. I thought being away from you was the best way to keep all of you safe from harm."

Lucas laughed, the sound echoing harshly around the kitchen. "That worked out well, didn't it?" He sobered. "You could have picked up the phone and explained."

"I thought I was doing the right thing."

"And in the meantime, you were falling in love with Conal," he stated icily.

"You don't understand." I looked up at him, sick at heart from my mistakes. "It took time to understand what this all meant. I couldn't contact you until I understood how I managed to hurt you, how to prevent it from happening again. When I left Puckhaber, I was so frightened and confused. Acenith contacted Conal and he... he came and rescued me. Brought me back to Jackson and looked after me when I was so depressed, I could barely bother to get up in the morning."

"Looked after you?" His blue eyes were burning with fury as he stared down at me. "What does that mean, exactly?"

I squeezed my eyes shut, desperate to compose the right way to answer his question. "I don't want to hurt you," I pleaded softly.

"You've already done that," he stated, his voice colder again. "I want the truth, Charlotte." He squeezed my hands painfully and I flinched. "Tell me the truth about your relationship with Conal. I think I deserve that much and it was glaringly apparent last night that you're living with him."

I couldn't deny him what he'd demanded. He deserved to know exactly what the situation had been for the past few months and if we were to have any chance of sorting through this mess, of moving forward, I owed him the truth. "I've been living at Conal's apartment since I moved down here."

"You're sleeping with him?" The question was asked through gritted teeth.

"Yes," I whispered. "But it's not what you think," I continued hurriedly. "When I first arrived, he had one bedroom and I had the other." I stole a look at

Lucas's face, saw the clenched muscle in his jaw as he squeezed his eyes shut, as though the act would block out my words. "For the past three months, he and I have shared a bed. He comforts me when I have the nightmares."

"No doubt he was very good at giving you *comfort*," Lucas spat.

It was my turn to squeeze his hands. "We shared a bed, he held me while I screamed. But we've never had sex."

"You've never had sex," he echoed, his eyes frigid with resentment. "What have you done, pray tell?"

Tears welled against my eyelashes. "We've kissed and he holds me in his arms. That's all. I swear that's all."

The betrayal was written plainly in his striking features. A dozen different emotions flickered across his face, like thunderclouds before an approaching storm. Finally he spoke. "I don't know you anymore. You act differently, you speak differently. Damn it, you even look different!" His voice rose as he lost control of his temper, the anger cutting through me like a knife. "You tell me now that you've been sleeping with Conal, but it's okay because you didn't have sex! Did you honestly believe I would just accept this and we could move on as though nothing happened?" He ran his fingers through his hair in frustration. "Five months ago, the woman I knew would have blushed at the mention of sex. Now you tell me you've been sleeping with *another man* and you're asking me to believe you still love me?"

"Lucas, I'm..."

He cut me off with a fierce shake of his head. "I've spent the past five months - *existing* - because you made me promise I would! Hoping you would come back to me. *Shit*, I even decided my Kiss would remain in Puckhaber, when we should have been moving on, because of you! And all the time, you were sleeping with Conal! How the hell did you think that would make me feel?" He stalked away, leaning against the bench wearily. "You should have left me in Sfantu Drâghici - they would have killed me and you would have been free to continue your relationship with that fucking *dog* without complications!"

The verbal attack hurt no less than if it had been a physical assault. I knew everyone in the other room must be listening, they'd heard every word of our argument. Crossing my arms against my chest, I struggled to keep the tears from falling, but failed miserably. "I told Conal you would be mature about this. Clearly I was very wrong."

I stalked away, pushing past him and out of the kitchen. Conal met me at the doorway, his expression grim. "Please leave me alone," I begged quietly. Ignoring the silent stares of everyone in the room, I wrenched open the door and strode out into the steamy Mississippi heat, slamming it shut behind me.

Chapter 7

Choices

I stumbled through the darkness, stomping across the uneven ground until I came to a grave and I slumped onto the edge of the concrete tomb. Furious tears splashed down my cheeks and I scrubbed my hands across my face.

My arm was stinging and the Omias wound was seeping blood again. "*Crap.*" Retrieving the Hjördis from my pocket, I created yet another healing sigil. The skin healed over, taking longer than usual and it didn't seem to be holding together well.

"I imagine the sigil struggles because of the amount of blood you lost," Epi suggested quietly, lowering himself onto the tomb beside me. "Ben told me what you did to ensure their safety. Whilst I commend your bravery, I wouldn't recommend a repeat performance. You are one of a kind, child. There is no replacement for your blood."

I focused on the Hjördis, twisting it over and over against my fingers. "I'm not one of a kind, Epi. Archangelo is still alive."

"Ben, Ripley and I have been discussing that topic," Epi remarked. "I had wondered what might happen in the process of creation. Normally a vampire becomes stone-like - their skin is impervious to most weapons and it takes incredible strength to behead one."

"They're not as impervious as they thought," I muttered mutinously.

"No. Much to their horror, we have discovered some of the myths from the past have elements of truth in them. As so many do."

"Will they go back to how they were? Or will they be affected by silver and holy water from now on?"

"We have no way of knowing. Only time will tell."

"So what's the deal with Archangelo?" I asked curiously. "The Philaris tore into his chest, straight into his heart. He bled like a human."

Epi sighed, tugging at his tunic. "Yes, he bled like a human, but he is not human. He is a curious mixture of angel and vampire. I believe he is, on some levels, as fragile as you are. But the vampire venom in his system allows him to regenerate."

I lifted my chin and stared at him. "So he's what? Immortal? He can't be killed?"

"Oh, I'm sure there's a way," Epi retorted lightly. "We have only to find it." He patted my knee. "*You* have to find it."

"Great." I stretched my legs out, rotating my ankles to ease the stiffness. "I can't even sort out my own love life, Epi. I wouldn't put too much faith in my abilities right now."

"Ah, yes," he said, shifting his weight so he faced me. "Surely you could foresee that your feelings for Conal and Lucas were going to cause some difficulties?"

I twirled the Hjördis between my fingers. "I can't help how I feel."

"And neither can they." He sighed, gazing across the moonlit churchyard for a long moment before he spoke again. "The angel blood which runs through your veins is strong and pure, Charlotte. It's that purity which draws everyone to you. It is what draws those two men, vampire and werewolf, to you."

"Fabulous," I retorted irritably. I inclined my head towards the church. "Are they killing each other in there?"

Epi allowed himself a brief smile. "I think that was their initial plan. Right now though, they're talking."

"Talking?" I repeated blankly. I wasn't sure I liked that any idea any more than them coming to blows.

"They are both adults, Charlotte. As much as they share a love for you, they also know they must find a way to work through this. The situation we find ourselves in; the likelihood of war with the Consiliului means both Lucas and Conal have to work together for the greater good. If they talk through this situation like grown men, it must surely be better than fighting one another."

"I'm not sure I like that idea," I muttered mutinously. "Couldn't you just do some spell on them both, make them forget any of this ever happened?"

"As I may, or may not have told you recently, I am not some two bit magician," Epi grumbled. "I most certainly do not use magic on people to adjust their feelings."

I drew my hair to one side, tying it in a loose knot. "I've made a mess of things," I admitted sheepishly. "I don't understand how I got into such a disastrous situation."

Epi watched me, blue eyes scrutinizing me carefully. "You are young, child." He made it sound as if that explained everything and I thought he'd stopped, but he continued a moment later. "Remember when we talked about love a few weeks ago? When I said there were all types of love?"

I nodded morosely.

"You produce that love, through the purity running through your veins."

"So this is all my fault." I kicked at the dirt, stubbing my toe in the process.

"To an extent. It would certainly have been helpful if you had managed to fall in love with only one man," Epi offered sagely and I scowled at him. "Charlotte, each and every person in there loves you. Even Phelan who struggled with his suspicions. He now loves you, too."

"You don't think I've got enough problems? He's married, for God's sake!"

Epi sighed. "You think like a recalcitrant teenager. Different types of love, child. All strong, all having a profound effect on those feeling it. Ben and Rowena love you as they would their own child. Striker, Ripley; the Tines as a whole, love you as a sibling. The Tremaine pack, the Lingards' - all have differing but valid reasons. Phelan sees you as a daughter, as does Ralph. Marco regards you as a very cool big sister." He tapped his fingers against the edge of the tomb. "I feel my own love for you, equivalent, I would suggest, to a grandfather's fondness for his granddaughter. Of course, you can be a painfully infuriating granddaughter - but a beloved one just the same. This is the effect your blood has on the people around you."

I rubbed my toes through the dirt as I considered his explanation. "So Conal and Lucas - they're both in love with me and there's nothing I can do to fix this? Is that what you're saying?"

"No. You are always looking at things as if there is only one perspective. There is always darkness and light, fire and ice and the spectrum in between. The blood that runs within you, in turn confuses you. It allows you to see things only in the opposing sides of the spectrum, nothing in between. You love strongly; you are capable of hating just as strongly. It's the line in between which blurred for you, purely because of the angel blood."

I forced myself to look at the wizened old man. "I'm sorry, Epi. I'm not following you."

"Charlotte, your life has been unusual to say the least. As you admitted to me, you grew up an only child before your mother remarried. You had siblings, who were tragically lost before you could develop a true relationship with them. This was followed by a number of years you spent on your own, before you came into contact with the Tine Kiss."

I twirled the Hjördis between my fingers thoughtfully. "So - are you trying to tell me I'm emotionally stunted?"

He eyed me patiently. "I'm telling you that you find it difficult to see the trueness of your relationship with these two men. You love them both, it's obvious to us all. But one of them - and I don't know which one - holds something more for you."

"How do I know? And they both love me - how do I sort this out without hurting them?" Tears brimmed against my lashes. "How do I fix this without losing either of them? I need them both in my life, Epi."

Epi pulled himself to his feet, smoothing down the front of his tunic. "The answer is within you, Charlotte. I've seen you in the past few months with Conal and now I've seen the way you look at Lucas. The love you feel is evident for both of them. But you need to consider your emotional and psychological relationship with them. They both offer you something you need. Only you can work out which need is the most important."

He strolled towards the church and I stared after him, dumbfounded by his abrupt departure. "Well, thanks Epi. That's cleared everything up perfectly," I yelled at his departing back. He waved his arm in response and continued towards the church without pause.

For a long time I sat in the churchyard, immersed in thought and wondering if there was a way of fixing things. I wanted both Lucas and Conal in my life. Despite knowing how selfish it sounded, I couldn't imagine being without either one of them.

The weather was cooling, although humid and sultry, a hint of a slight breeze rose in the night air, relieving the oppressiveness. There were no other sounds, no cars driving by, none of the hustle and bustle that being in the suburbs should produce. I could only assume it was because of the other supernatural creatures who dwelled around here.

I dropped the Hjördis back into my pocket and pulled the Katchet out, twirling it between my fingers. The long thin blade glowed softly in the darkness and I ran my fingers over the sigils marking the golden handle. I ran the tip of the blade lightly across my right hand, studying the vivid red mark where Archangelo's Philaris had sliced into the palm.

I couldn't choose between Conal and Lucas and didn't want to live without either one of them in my life. I was terrified of the possibility that if I chose one over the other, I would lose the one I rejected, that he would disappear and never be seen again. The thought was intolerable. I lay back on the tomb, morosely staring up at the stars glimmering in the moonlit sky above. It was a clear night, the moon creating ambient light over the church yard and highlighting the gravestones which stood tall and silent over their dead charges.

The sensible thing, would be to go inside and speak to Conal and Lucas - that would be the *adult* thing to do. Right at the moment, however, I didn't much feel like being an adult. In fact, I wanted to kick my feet like a child and throw a temper tantrum. Fatigue would eventually force me inside though, I could hardly sleep on top of someone's grave - it was bad enough that I was lying on it. I hauled myself into a sitting position and stared in bewilderment at the sight before me.

A door had materialized next to the tomb. A white wooden door, which, to all intents and purposes, appeared to be supporting itself - standing with no surrounding frames or features. Slipping the Katchet into my back pocket, I approached it curiously, wondering if sheer exhaustion was causing me to hallucinate.

Touching the door tentatively, I discovered it wasn't an illusion and the wood was cool and smooth beneath my fingertips. I turned the handle and opened the door, taking a cautious step inside.

It was apparent this was Epi's doing when I found myself inside a small bedroom. It was compact, with walls painted ivory and dark wooden floors. There was a bed against the centre of one wall, with a mahogany headboard and matching drawers. The bed had an elaborately embroidered quilt in shades of brown and gold, with several comfortable-looking pillows propped against the headboard. The room was pleasantly cool after the sultry heat outside and I brushed my fingers across the quilt. Epi had apparently decided I wasn't returning inside any time soon, so he'd created this little oasis in the churchyard. With no further deliberation, I stripped down to my bra and panties and slipped beneath the covers, relishing the clean cotton sheets against my overheated skin.

I expected to have trouble sleeping, but almost as soon as my head hit the pillows I dropped into a deep sleep. Despite the emotional turmoil, my sleep was free from nightmares and I slept soundly throughout the night.

I was refreshed when I woke and the nausea and overwhelming exhaustion had dissipated to a more tolerable level. It was a novelty to find soft light filling the room, despite the lack of windows and I marveled at Epi's abilities. A glance at my watch confirmed it was a little after ten in the morning and birds twittered and called to one another outside.

Rolling over onto my back, I stretched and luxuriated in the comfortable bed. Epi definitely needed a hug. I contemplated getting up, or if I should wallow for a little while longer. My belly made the decision, rumbling ominously as a reminder that it was well past breakfast.

My thought processes were less snarly this morning and I knew what my decision had to be. It seemed obvious in the clear light of a new day, there was only one decision I *could* make. The only way forward was to ensure both men remained in my life and only one option would work. With a smile, I pulled the covers back and slipped out of bed, dressing quickly.

I traipsed across the rough ground and pushed open the door, stepping into the cool interior of the church. The mouth-watering aroma of pancakes assaulted my senses and I scouted the room, identifying the source.

The majority of the beds had disappeared, leaving only the ones where Marianne and Gwynn still lay. Epi's bookshelves were back in position around the walls and a long scarred table sat in the centre of the room with my friends gathered around it.

"Morning, everyone," I called out. I spied Nonny, serving pancakes to Rafe from a large platter. I snatched one, ripping it apart and popping a piece into my mouth. "Nonny, I think I love you."

Lucas was at the far end of the table and uneasiness grew when I noticed Conal was sitting beside him. I walked around the crowded table to them. "Can I speak to both of you, please? In the kitchen?" Without waiting for a response, I turned and strode through to the kitchen, devouring the pancake as I walked.

Choices

Conal appeared first, then Lucas and they stood silently, waiting for me to speak. I took my time, pouring coffee into a mug, adding sugar and cream. Stirring it briskly, I sipped the hot liquid before I turned to face them.

"Okay," I began with a deep sigh. "I've really made a mess of things with the two of you."

They remained silent, watching warily.

I didn't know where the unexpected burst of courage was coming from, but I intended to exploit it while I could. "I can't stop the way I feel. I love both of you, and that complicates things."

"You think?" Conal snorted. "You're doing my head in, Sugar. I thought you were going back to Lucas, that's what you told me you planned to do."

"And you made it clear how much that was going to piss you off when I didn't come back to the apartment the other night."

He crossed his arms over his broad chest, his eyes narrowing. "I'll deal with it."

I shook my head, sipping the coffee. "I don't want you to deal with it." I turned to Lucas. "I'm not even sure you want me back."

"I love you, Charlotte, nothing has changed the way I feel," he responded quietly.

"Thank you," I breathed softly. "I love you, too." The contrast between their reactions was startling. While Lucas's eyes warmed, Conal's grew icy and I gazed up at him until he met my eyes, anger simmering in his. "I love you, Conal. I love both of you and I've realized how impossible this is. I can't have both of you. So, for better or worse, I've made a decision."

"What's that?" Conal questioned. He watched me intently, his black eyes somber.

"I can't be with either of you," I announced decisively.

Both men stared in disbelief and I continued hastily, trying to explain. "Lucas, you said yourself, I'm not the same girl you knew in Puckhaber."

"That's true, Lucas conceded."But it doesn't make any difference to how I feel."

"Conal, we've spent the past five months together and even you admit I'm not the girl you first knew." I tapped my fingers nervously against the coffee mug. "I guess I'm a work in progress and we have no way of knowing if either of you will like the finished product. I don't know what's going to happen in the future." I smiled cynically, rolling my eyes. "Chances are, I'll be dead in the future, if the Consiliului get their own way. All I know for certain is that I'm Nememiah's Child and I have a responsibility to follow this through. It makes more sense to avoid being in a relationship, until I see if I survive this thing with the Drâghici."

Lucas took a step forward, but I held out my hand.

"I mean it. When all's said and done, I'm twenty one years old and the first time I've gotten involved with a man… two men, I've screwed it up. Right now, I need you both in my life and the only way that will work is for us to be friends. I don't want you to be jealous of one another and I'm not planning on giving you anything to be envious about. But what I'm facing - I'll need all the help I can get. If you both decide to blow me off, I'll understand and if you decide to seek a new relationship with someone else, well, I'll just have to accept it. It's exactly what I'd deserve." I stopped abruptly, the courage quickly ebbing away as I studied their faces anxiously. "But I'd appreciate it, if you were to support me through this."

I didn't have any idea how they would react. Was I asking too much? It would be understandable if they both walked away and I never saw them again.

Their eyes met for a long moment, before Lucas spoke. "I will support you, Charlotte. I don't like your decision, but I love you. I'll help in any way I can."

Conal rubbed his fingers through his hair, and huffed out a frustrated breath. "You know I'll support you, Sugar. The Tremaines' stand behind you. We'll be there, every step of the way."

The breath I'd been holding whooshed quietly past my lips as I smiled at them. "Thank you." Clutching my coffee mug, I stepped past them both. "If you'll excuse me, there are pancakes out there with my name on them."

I slipped out through the open doorway, leaving the two men standing dumbstruck behind me.

Chapter 8

Transfusion

I snatched another pancake from the stack Nonny was distributing and walked over to Epi, who stood with Ben and Jerome. I leaned over to kiss Epi on the top of his bald forehead, delighted when a flush spread across his wrinkled cheeks. "Thanks, Epi."

"I assume you've sorted out your complicated love life?" Epi questioned, his voice as dry as the grass outside.

"Yeah, I have," I agreed quietly. "I'm staying single."

Epi narrowed his eyes. "Is that what you really want, child?"

I shrugged, the gesture non-committal. "It's the choice I have to make. I screwed this up and it's the best decision out of a host of bad ones. Besides, I'm Nememiah's Child. I need to concentrate on that for now."

"If that's what you think best, child. Can we get back to dealing with more serious concerns now?"

"Sure," I responded easily, popping another small piece of pancake into my mouth. "Can I finish breakfast first?"

"You can, as soon as you inform me of your nightmares," Epi retorted.

"Not a thing. Slept soundly all night."

Epi looked perturbed. "That's disappointing. I was hoping for some useful information."

I rolled my eyes at his nonchalance. "Geez, Epi. How about 'that's wonderful, Charlotte! Great to hear you had another good night's sleep for a change.'?"

Ben eyed me with barely concealed amusement. "I see what you mean, Epimetheus."

I glanced from one man to the other, eyes narrowed suspiciously. "What now?"

"I was telling Ben that as you have accepted your role as Nememiah's Child, you have grown very determined - and remarkably cheeky - for someone so young."

"You wouldn't have it any other way, old man." I glanced at Marianne and Gwynn, who still lay in the beds, listless and pale. "Is everyone improving?"

"They're doing much better with the help of your sigils," Jerome said. "You'll put me out of a job."

"Marianne and Gwynn will be fine. We're recuperating slowly," Ben agreed. "The blood is aiding our recovery, but we'll need to hunt before we'll regain anything near full strength."

"Cow blood's not doing it for you, huh?"

"It's helping to regenerate us, but not as fast as fresh blood would," Lucas said, appearing at my side. He smiled, but it didn't reach his eyes. "The strength we gain from blood directly relates to the battled required to obtain it. Bear and mountain lions would heal us faster than bovine."

"So everyone will get better, right?"

There was a long pause and Lucas and Ben exchanged a cautious look. "We're not entirely certain what will happen," Ben admitted, glancing at the other vampires seated around the table.

"We have lost most of our abilities, Charlotte. For those of us with enhanced talents; telepathy, thought reading, empathy… they've been wiped out as though they never existed," Lucas added. "There's no guarantee they will return."

"And to discover we could be affected by the very things we'd disregarded as myth," Ben continued. "Lucas and I have spoken with Jerome and Epimetheus regarding the possible repercussions, whether we will remain susceptible to silver and holy water…" He broke off, a haunted shadow in his brown eyes. It took him a few seconds to regain his composure, then he shrugged. "We don't know whether we'll recover completely."

"I'm so sorry," I murmured. "If I'd gotten there sooner…"

"You couldn't do that, Charlotte and we understand why," Lucas said. "For now, we'll need to continue regaining our strength and hope for the best possible outcome."

"And in the meantime," Striker announced, draping an arm around my shoulder, "we need to forget our sorrows and celebrate your birthday." He handed me a cupcake with a candle buried in the icing and kissed my cheek affectionately. "Happy Birthday, Lott."

"Thanks, Striker. Did you bake it yourself?"

He snorted. "Yeah, right."

Rowena hugged me affectionately and I was thrilled to see the improvement in her health. "I'm sorry we don't have a gift for you."

"Are you kidding? Having you here is the best birthday present I could receive."

Striker slumped back down into his chair and sipped from the bottle he was holding, shuddering his aversion. "No offence, Lott, but cow blood tastes awful."

"You should be grateful," I announced indignantly. "Do you know how many cows we had to transfuse to get that blood? Dozens!"

Lucas choked on the blood he'd been in the midst of swallowing. A smile lifted the edge of his lips. "Transfused?"

"Yeah, I've still got the hoof mark on my ass to prove it," Phelan chuckled. "Lottie wouldn't let us take the easy route and slaughter a couple of cows. We had to do it the hard way."

There was an astounded silence, before everyone burst into laughter simultaneously.

"Don't look at me like that!" I protested. "I can't help it! Cows are kind of sweet. I didn't want to kill them."

"Let me get this straight," Ripley said slowly. "You did a transfusion. On a cow?" His eyes twinkled with unconcealed mirth.

"Yep, that's our Charlotte," Conal agreed, leaning on the back of Phelan's chair. "In fact, I think we did thirty five transfusions, on some thirty five separate cows. Right now, some poor sap's trying to figure out why his whole herd is anemic."

"Not to mention the other forty odd cows we hit yesterday," Nick smirked.

Raucous laughter accompanied this statement and I laughed with them. My desire to keep the cows alive had caused nothing but trouble a few nights ago when I'd realized we needed a blood supply for the Tines.

Ben, Epi and Jerome joined us around the table and William watched me in amusement. "Charlotte, you are unbelievable. You would take on that thing Archangelo produced and kill it, but you hesitate to kill a cow?"

"There's a difference," I pointed out. "The cow wasn't trying to kill me. The demon was."

The atmosphere rapidly shifted, smiles and laughter replaced by a deathly silence.

"In over nine hundred years, I've never seen a demon," Ben murmured. "I had thought they were a legend."

"They have always existed in the Otherworld," Epi responded briskly. "They were eradicated from Earth by the original Nememiah's Children before your birth. But now, if Archangelo is capable of bringing them to our world, it's a situation fraught with peril."

"If Charlotte's an angel, couldn't she learn the same ability?" Ripley asked. "Couldn't she summon demons and have them attack the Drâghici?"

"Charlotte is untainted by demon blood. The very reason Archangelo can summon demons must be attributed to his curious mixture of angel and demon blood," Epi explained. "Charlotte's power lies in her ability to harness and direct the power of the spirits. I assume you saw her rather satisfactory use of spirit energy to create orbs during your recovery in Sfantu Drâghici?"

"Very impressive," Holden agreed, throwing an encouraging smile in my direction. "How are they created?"

"Charlotte calls the spirits to her aid, both individually and in groups. In recent weeks we've worked on using the kinetic power of the spirits as a weapon. Those orbs she produces are the spirits' energy, which she can form into a ball of thermodynamic power.

"I imagine that's what happened in Puckhaber Falls," Lucas suggested.

"From what Charlotte explained, I believe that was a thermodynamic wave, rather than an orb," Epi corrected. "A complete fluke on her part. I was amazed she managed to produce it at all, given her lack of knowledge at the time."

"I owe you guys an apology for that," I stated, clasping my fingers together.

"I believe it is I who owes you the apology, Charlotte," Holden responded. "You thought I was attacking you and I'm so very sorry for that."

"Holden thought *I* was attacking you," William added. "He didn't realize we were trying to increase your ability to protect yourself."

There'd been more than enough apologies in the past twenty four hours and I diverted the conversation. "So Epi - you think there's someone else involved. Got any ideas who?"

Epi shook his head, brushing away imaginary crumbs from his tunic. "Vampires do not have the magical skills, so it's not a member of the Drâghici Kiss. It will be a warlock, witch or wizard. As to whom, I cannot be certain. We must trust you will receive information from the spirits or your nightmares."

"The spirits are a bust," I reported. "I spoke to them last night."

"Well, a nightmare then," Epi insisted. "Hopefully you will have one soon."

Conal rolled his eyes at Epi's complete disregard of the emotional toll of the nightmares and we shared a smile.

Epi was scrutinizing my arm when I turned back. The injury continued to cause trouble, refusing to knit together and the massive bruise on my forearm was no better. "Charlotte, you must mark further healing sigils," he ordered. "I will prepare a potion, attempt to counteract the lack of blood running in your veins."

Conal settled in a chair, scanning the wounds. "You still look pale, Sugar."

Jerome caught Epi's attention. "I've prescribed iron supplements in the past. It helped and has a similar effect on her blood as it would on human blood." He rolled his eyes. "Seems bizarre to suggest you aren't human."

"Yes, yes, that would help. However I believe in this case, she has lost more than iron supplements can overcome. Jerome, I'm sure you would like to see my preparation, it will be of interest to you, I believe..." Jerome and Epi disappeared into a room behind the altar, with Epi still waxing lyrical about his potion. Reaching into my pocket to retrieve the Hjördis, I remembered I was still carrying the Katchet.

I strode up to the altar, concentrating on the wall until the stone block shimmered. I plunged my hand into the stone, watching it vanish to leave the hollow space behind. I drew out the leather satchel and unrolled it, placing Archangelo's Katchet with my own. Tying the leather strap securely, I pushed it back into the cavity and brushed my hand across the opening to return the stone to its position.

When I turned back Lucas and the Tines were open-mouthed and it took me a second to realize why. I slipped into my chair and calmly drew the Hjördis from my pocket.

"How did you *do* that?" Acenith asked, looking bewildered.

"Epi taught me," I said casually. "He can do it, and the angel blood lets me do it as well." I held the Hjördis to my arm, marking more healing sigils. Epi was right, nothing was mending as it should. "I should probably warn you all, nobody can touch the weapons or the Hjördis." I shared an ironic smile with Conal. "They have a pretty violent effect on anyone who doesn't have angel blood."

"What sort of violent effect?" Holden queried, interest sparking in his blue eyes.

"Enough violence to blow me fifteen feet across the room," Conal admitted, rubbing the back of his head at the recollection. "Not enjoyable, I can assure you."

"What about humans?" William questioned, glancing at Katie who was busy drawing pictures by the fireplace, her face a picture of deep concentration.

"It wouldn't affect her because she's human, but we've been keeping her away from all the weapons and the Hjördis," Conal confirmed.

"How much does she know?" Holden asked in a low voice and he went up in my estimations for the obvious concern he held for little Katie and her safety.

"Not a lot," Nonny announced, dropping onto the chair beside Conal with a fresh cup of coffee, which she pushed across the table to me. "We've kept her insulated from as much as possible. She knows the Katchet and Philaris are weapons and the Hjördis draws 'pictures' on Charlotte and Conal's skin, but knows she can't have pictures on her skin."

"Although I did catch her out, drawing sigils on her arm with a magic marker last week. Katie say she wants to be an angel like Charlotte," Conal smirked at the memory.

William turned to Conal, sincerity shining in his eyes. "I want to thank you for keeping Katie safe. You've done us a great service, one which will not be forgotten."

"You can thank Nick - he agreed to bring her down here. After the Drâghici took you, we weren't certain what else they had planned and it seemed smart to bring Katie here," I said. "Epi has enchantments over the church and Conal's apartment, so she was safer here than anywhere else."

Lucas raised an eyebrow. "Enchantments?"

I grinned, much more comfortable now my decision had been made. "This is weird, you know - it wasn't long ago you were explaining everything to me. Now the situation is reversed."

"All you had to learn about was vampires," Lucas retorted with a wry grin. "It seems we have a lot more to learn."

I explained the intricacies of Epi's enchantments to them. "When he eventually got around to telling us about them, we asked Nick to bring Katie to Mississippi."

"Epi has a remarkably bad habit of forgetting to pass on vital information," Conal added with a touch of sarcasm. "The old bastard usually tells us what we need to know - about ten minutes after we needed to know it." He pushed back from the table and stood up, cracking his knuckles ominously. "We're heading down to Natchez. I've got some pack business to deal with."

"Does Quinn know we found out about him?" I asked quietly.

"Yeah." Conal was abruptly business-like, his black eyes narrowing with anger. "Ralph's brother and Kenyon detained him when we headed to Sfantu Drâghici. We're going to ask him some questions and I'm going to use my *own* special talent to find out what's going on." His expression softened when he leaned over to kiss my forehead. "I'll be back tonight, Sugar. Get some rest, I've got a feeling the old man's got something miserable planned for us in the next few days."

"It's bound to involve smelling like dead stuff," I agreed easily.

Phelan chuckled. "*Everything* Epi makes us do involves smelling like dead stuff." He pressed a kiss against my cheek. "See you later, Lottie. Bye guys." With a wave, they strode out and there was silence for a few seconds.

"Who *are* you, and what the hell did you do with the real Charlotte Duncan?" Striker demanded with a broad grin.

Chapter 9

Pick-me-Up

Epi returned a few minutes later, carrying a metal pitcher filled with steaming liquid. Jerome followed, watching my reaction with a mischievous gleam in his eyes. Epi dropped the pitcher onto the table in front of me and a tumbler shimmered into being beside it.

I peered in the top of the pitcher and wrinkled my nose in disgust. "What on earth is that?"

It smelled strongly of rotting garbage and when I poured a measure into the tumbler, it was a peculiar shade of brown. I picked up the tumbler, eyeing it with no small amount of apprehension. There was smoke wafting from the top of it, a fact which I found more than a little disturbing. "I thought you needed me, Epi? This crap looks like it's going to kill me!"

"Just drink it, and don't be such a baby," Epi grumbled. "It's an ancient remedy, extremely effective. You'll improve swiftly."

"Ancient's right," I agreed, holding the glass at eye level to study it suspiciously. "It looks like primordial ooze."

"I can assure you, Charlotte, it's harmless. I watched him make it," Jerome struggled to keep his face neutral and his eyes twinkled with mirth.

"Better you than me, Lott." Marco eyed the tumbler doubtfully. "Think I'd rather swallow demon blood."

"You *gag* on demon blood, Marco. I've seen you." Taking a small sip, I screwed up my face and swallowed it hastily. "Oh, *GOD*! What did I do to deserve this?"

Striker and Holden chuckled, clinking their bottles together. "Maybe cow blood isn't so bad after all."

"Get on with it, Charlotte," Epi ordered in a stern voice. "I want you to drink the whole pitcher. And try to refrain from using the Lord's name in vain. You are in church, child."

"Remember how I told you I liked you?" I glared at Epi, my eyes frosty. "Guess what? I've changed my mind. Can I have something to eat to help get rid of the taste?"

"You've just eaten breakfast," Epi sounded exasperated.

"I had two pancakes, that doesn't constitute a meal."

Epi waved his hand and a plate of sandwiches appeared. "Now drink," he demanded.

"Can I have a sandwich?" Marco asked, eyeing the plate eagerly.

"Get your own, Marco. Those are mine," I warned.

"Oh, for goodness sake! Life was much more peaceful without a bunch of teenagers around here," Epi spluttered. He waved his hand again and a larger platter of sandwiches appeared. The Lingard men were grouped together at one corner of the table and they launched a voracious attack on the food. "All they ever want to do is eat and sleep."

Nick selected a sandwich. "I'm way beyond a teenager, Epi."

"Not on my scale of age, young man," Epi sniffed.

I lifted the tumbler and shuddered as I swallowed it down hurriedly. I drained the contents and dropped the tumbler onto the table, barely controlling the desire to spit the liquid back out again. Picking up a sandwich, I tossed it into my mouth to try and get rid of the taste, before snatching up another one and eating that, too. Ripley helpfully poured another tumbler full of the revolting liquid and I eyed it in disgust.

"I've changed my mind," I announced. "I don't just not like you, I think I *hate* you." I tossed back the second drink, screwing up my face as I struggled to swallow it.

"Love me, hate me, I don't care. Just drink the damn tonic," Epi muttered. "I want you ready to train first thing tomorrow morning."

I glanced up in surprise. "You mean I get today off? And now who's saying naughty words in a church?"

"You gave half your blood supply to your friends. It doesn't leave me with much of a choice, does it?" Epi sniffed. "And it's my church, I get to do as I damn well please."

Striker was holding his fist against his mouth, trying in vain to suppress the laughter which was making his shoulders shake. "I really like the new Charlotte. And Epi's growing on me at a rapid rate."

Ripley smiled, his eyes filled with admiration. "You certainly have plenty of spirit now, Charlotte." He shared an affectionate smile with Acenith, holding her close against him.

"Oh, Lott's just chock full of spirits," Marco teased. "Dozens of them."

"You know what, Marco? Next demon we take on, I'm leaving you to finish off. Then you'll get a face full of demon blood and we'll see who's cracking jokes then."

"Now you know that's impossible, Lottie," Rafe responded.

"We really can't kill the demons?" Holden asked. He sounded disappointed and it reminded me again of how similar he and Striker were, both in looks and personality.

"Demons can be damaged by supernaturals, but they can't be killed. The weapons are the only thing which sends them back to the Otherworld. It's one of our current issues," I responded. "I'm the only one who can do the job." I picked up the tumbler, wondering if holding my nose would make this any better. As much as I didn't want to admit it, I felt better already. How that was possible when the liquid muck was so vile, I didn't know, but I figured it wasn't going to kill me.

"Surely that will be a huge issue?" Ben asked. "What happens if more than one demon is sent at a time as Epimetheus suggested?"

I shrugged with a nonchalance I wasn't feeling. "Guess I'll just have to fight harder. Epi's working on a solution." I slugged back another glassful and filled the tumbler one last time, delighted to discover I'd reached the end of the pitcher. I ate another couple of sandwiches in preparation. "You might make a lousy tonic, Epi, but you are pretty good at magicking sandwiches."

"I've told you before, young lady, 'magicking' is a ridiculous word and diminishes the magnitude of my abilities."

I ignored him, grasping the tumbler and chugging down the last of the tonic, wiping my hand across my mouth when I'd finished.

Everyone burst into a round of spontaneous applause and I smiled, mimicking a little bow as I stood up. "I'm going to brush my teeth," I stated, heading towards the bathroom. "Before they rot and fall out."

Pick-me-Up

≈†◊◊†◊◊†◊◊†≈

When I returned to the main room, it was to discover the men had gone missing. Acenith waved me over to where she was settled beside Marianne, with Nonny and Rowena. Gwynn was sitting up and she smiled weakly as I approached.

"Where is everyone?" I knew they couldn't leave the church, but for the life of me I couldn't figure out where they'd all gone. While the church had undergone some rapid transformation and expansion, it wasn't that big.

"Lucas suggested you might like some girl time and we agreed it was a wonderful idea," Acenith said. She was wearing a pretty floral skirt and a white t-shirt, her hair braided and laying across her shoulder. Her skin was almost flawless again, with only the tiniest trace of scarring on her cheek. Her emerald green eyes were bright, shimmering with bronze when she smiled.

Nonny grinned happily. "You have lovely friends, mi pequeño ángel." She was sitting cross-legged on an armchair between the two beds, her flowing skirt pooling around her legs. "Are you hungry?"

Shaking my head, I stood at the base of Gwynn's bed. "Between the pancakes and Epi's sandwiches, I probably don't need to eat until dinner time."

"But you will eat before then," Nonny chuckled. "You will be hungry again, long before dinner."

Gwynn patted the bed and offered me a wan smile. "Would you like to sit down?"

"Sure." I settled beside her and studied her face discreetly. She looked better, but still so very pale. "How are you feeling?"

Gwynn shrugged, a shadow passing across her features. "Improving." Seeing doubt in my eyes, she captured my fingers and squeezed. "Truly, I'm much better. It will take a little time."

"Where are the men?" I questioned again.

"Rafe and Marco are outside, playing with Katie. I believe they mentioned a game of ball. Everyone else is discussing the current situation in some room through there." Rowena motioned towards the back of the altar and I smirked. Epi seemed to keep magicking new areas as he needed them.

"They haven't had enough information already?" It seemed like all we'd done for the past two days was share intelligence.

"Lucas is reporting what we know about the Drâghici," Marianne explained. She pulled at the sleeve of her hospital gown, the small action telling. Marianne never fidgeted, hadn't show nerves or anxiety in all the time I'd known her. None of the vampires did. Yet here she was, fidgeting with her clothing anxiously.

"That will be helpful," I responded. "We didn't have a lot of information to go on."

"Enough of this," Nonny announced abruptly, her tone brooking no argument. "There has been enough sorrow in the past few days. Let us talk of happier things. Such as... how you lucky ladies managed to catch such handsome men."

Rowena chuckled. "In my case, I was pursued by my very handsome man, over a period of many years."

"And what about you, Gwynn? William is, how do you young people say? Hot?"

Gwynn giggled and then she put her hand to her mouth, stifling the happy sound. I wondered how she was going to react, but she surprised me. "Nonny, I'm as old as you are."

"Ah, but you're travelling much better, little one. You look, not a day over twenty one."

"Which is a relief, given that I was twenty one when I was created," Gwynn said agreeably. "If I looked older, there's something wrong."

Nonny hooted with delight. "So how did you meet William? Was it terribly romantic?"

Gwynn smiled tenderly, brushing her fingers though her hair as she contemplated her answer. "We met in Budapest, in 1999. William was backpacking around Europe, I was visiting my friend Eugene who had moved there perhaps a decade earlier. Eugene introduced us, assured me that William was a lost soul in need of a friend." She smiled shyly, glancing up from beneath lowered lashes. "He was very handsome and so shy, he could hardly speak when we first met."

"How did you draw him out of his shell?" Nonny asked. She was leaning forward, listening to Gwynn's tale with interest.

"I took him to the museums," Gwynn smiled. "William has a love of history and Budapest has many beautiful museums."

"I remember visiting the National Museum in 1965," Marianne said. "They have some magnificent exhibits. Did you visit the Museum of Fine Arts?"

Pick-me-Up

"I took William to every museum in Budapest," Gwynn laughed. "I think I wore him down with culture! You would love to visit Budapest, Charlotte, so many magnificent paintings - Ruben's Mucius Scaevola Before Porsenna, works by Titian, Gentile Bellini. It's a wonderful museum for an artist."

I smiled wistfully. "Perhaps one day."

"William was a perfect gentleman, every morning he met me at my hotel and we'd visit a new museum. He was incredibly polite, but kept himself aloof. Every attempt I made to draw him out of his shell was gently rebuked," Gwynn continued. She smiled, her pretty face glowing with a happiness which had been missing in the past few days.

"He's always been reticent," Rowena agreed.

"What did you do?" I asked. They obviously adored one another and I was curious to learn how she'd broken through William's barriers.

Gwynn looked sheepish. "I knew from spending so much time with William, he had deeply entrenched issues regarding being vampire. He truly believed his wife and child died because of his creation and blamed himself." She glanced at me, raising an eyebrow. "Did you know about that?"

I nodded. "Lucas told me, when he explained Katie's presence in Puckhaber."

Gwynn seemed taken aback. "You haven't spoken to William's ancestors?"

I shook my head and a smile curved my lips. "Not about William. He was so adamant about not having contact with them, I've avoided the subject."

"You are a good girl, mi ángel," Nonny announced, nodding in approval. She returned her attention to Gwynn, coaxing her to continue.

Gwynn smiled agreeably. "I saw William on my last night in Budapest, we were both invited to Eugene's for a party. I admitted I'd developed feelings for him, and asked him to return with me to America, but he refused. He was polite, but determined, insisting he couldn't be involved with someone else after the loss of his wife and son. He told me he wasn't sure he could love anyone again."

"What did you say?"

Gwynn chuckled. "I told him he was being an ass and if he wanted to remain alone for all eternity, that was completely up to him."

"What did he do?" Nonny clasped her hands together, enthralled with the story.

"Nothing. He watched me walk away. I was madly in love with him and thought I'd lost my chance. I returned to the hotel, collected my luggage and took a cab to the airport, refusing to stay another minute. After all, he'd never so much as kissed me. I'd made such a fool of myself."

"Not even once?" I asked.

Gwynn shook her head, waves of glossy copper hair falling across her shoulder. "Not a kiss, a hug; we'd barely touched hands."

"He let you leave? He didn't try and stop you?" I persisted.

"No. He watched me walk out the door, with that strong, emotionless expression he does so very well. I honestly believed I'd misread his attentions and he wasn't interested in anything but a brief holiday friendship."

"So what happened?" Nonny pressed impatiently.

"I caught my flight. I was staring out the window, utterly miserable at the thought of never seeing William again. I didn't want to speak to anyone, didn't want to see anyone. I'd deliberately chosen a seat which didn't have another passenger booked beside me." Her eyes twinkled with unconcealed delight. "Just as the plane was about to taxi to the runway, there was a ruckus at the door. When I glanced up, William was there, his backpack slung over his shoulder and a bouquet of red roses in his hand. He located where I was sitting and dropped down to one knee beside me. In front of everyone, he announced he'd been an idiot, he was in love with me, wanted us to marry and spend eternity together." She giggled again. "Of course, the rest of the flight had no idea of how factual he was being with the eternity part." She sighed dreamily. "And then he kissed me, for the very first time, in front of all those passengers. They broke into spontaneous applause, I got horribly embarrassed and we've been together ever since."

"That's so romantic," I said. It was hard to believe William would be capable of such a grand and public gesture, when he was always so quiet and introverted. It shed new light on the man and made me like him all the more for his loving gesture.

"William is a very romantic man," Gwynn agreed. "And I'm so grateful for him, even more so after what happened in Sfântu Drâghici." Her calm demeanor crumpled and she dropped her head into her hands.

We lulled into a painful silence as I wrapped my arms around Gwynn, holding her as she trembled uncontrollably. The other women gravitated closer, until we were touching and comforting one another. In that moment, surrounded by shell-shocked and traumatized friends, I silently promised myself

Pick-me-Up

the Drâghici would pay for what they'd done. They'd forfeited any chance of mercy when they tortured the Tines.

Within seconds the men joined us, having heard the ruckus from wherever they'd disappeared to. They formed a barrier around us and one by one, the men drew their women into their arms. When Lucas held his arms out to me, I didn't hesitate, willingly allowing him to draw me into his strength and hold me tight. Even Epi wrapped an arm around Nonny, as she and I sobbed, the only two with the ability to cry. It was a cathartic release for us and I wondered how the women would find their own release. They were unable to cry, unable to sob away their frustration and pain. It was a relief to see them held in the arms of their men and in turn, the men whispering soothingly to them. I hoped their support would get the women through this.

I slipped away as soon as I could, joining Nonny and Epi in the kitchen. I didn't belong out there with my friends, not when they were sharing a common horror which I'd had no part in. But I was determined they would never be in that position again.

Epi patted my shoulder awkwardly. "I think you should go back to bed for the day, child. There is too much emotional turmoil for you to deal with right now."

My eyes narrowed suspiciously. "Are you kidding me? You're really giving me the whole day off? For real?"

"You need to regain your strength. The tonic is helping, but you will need more sleep than you've had recently. With Conal back in Natchez, there's no point in training today. Besides, we hardly have the room right now."

Nonny handed me a mug of hot coffee. "I agree with Epimetheus, mi ángel. You have had a traumatic time of late, you should rest... right now."

It wasn't the way she'd intended to finish the sentence, but I could guess what she'd originally planned to say – *while I still had the chance*. The Drâghici would be furious – not only had I escaped their clutches, but I'd stolen the Tines from right under their noses. Now that I was twenty one, I was of no further use to them. I'd gone from being a potential kidnapping victim to a potential murder victim in the space of twenty four hours. I smiled tiredly. "Cool. I'm not going to argue with you."

"Go back outside, child. The room is still waiting there for you."

Chapter 10

Enchantments Broken

It took a long time to settle after I walked back out to the room Epi created. While I was worried about my friends, I couldn't help them the way they could by rallying around each other. After five months apart, it would take more than a few days to regain the relationship I'd had with them. The break-up of my relationship with Lucas and subsequent relationship with Conal would no doubt further complicate matters.

Lying back on the bed, I spent some time speaking to the spirits, then listened to their gentle murmurs as they soothed me into a deep sleep.

Standing on the plush red carpet of the Drâghici throne room, I faced the dais where the seven elaborate thrones had stood. They'd been destroyed when the wall and door were demolished behind them, fractured pieces scattered over the dais. An army of vampires were cleaning up after the mini earthquake which battered their stronghold as we escaped. Some were dragging their dead across the floor, the bodies limp, dragging flaccidly across the marble.

A narrow wooden table had been placed near the dais and Archangelo was lying on it, arms hanging limply at his sides. I walked towards the table cautiously, wondering if they could see me. I knew this was a nightmare, but it was so realistic I suspected one of the vampires would look up at any second and confront me. My heart hammered as I stared down at Archangelo. His dark curls glistened under the lights, his features relaxed and peaceful. His eyes were closed and he seemed to be... asleep. I couldn't understand why he would be sleeping – he was vampire. Was he regenerating from the wound I'd inflicted?

"It has taken effort, but I've discovered a draught which will put him into a sleep-like state. I don't recommend excessive use – it's a powerful potion and might kill him if administered too often."

The speaker was a tall man who stood beside Odin, Arawn and a woman I recognized from our photos as Bellona, head of Drâghici Security. He was painfully thin, wearing a floor length cloak of pale grey which shimmered under the lights. He drew the hood back from his head, revealing a skeletal face. He appeared to be human, his skin marked with the wrinkles of an endless life. Clean shaven, a long jagged scar marred one cheek and his brown eyes were shadowed by dark circles.

"It's about time you overcame this problem. Perhaps now he'll give us useful information," Odin announced, watching Archangelo expectantly. "How long will he remain in the sleep?"

"It is difficult to say." Bran paused solicitously, peering at Odin discreetly. "If he'd been given longer to mature before he was turned..."

"Yes, yes. You've made your opinion clear time and again, Bran. If he'd been created later, he may have developed the ability to see events during his sleep. As I have told you repeatedly, he had to be created before he developed a full comprehension of his ability and became worthless to us. Whilst he remained human, there was a possibility of him developing the same ridiculous sense of morality that the girl has," Odin sneered.

"I'm certain you're decision was the right one," the grey clocked man agreed, bowing solemnly towards Odin. "I never meant to suggest otherwise. Forgive me."

"Of course, my friend. My temper is short after what that bitch did to our stronghold." Odin glanced around the room angrily. "She will pay for her treachery and she is useless to us now." He shook his head, then returned his attention to Archangelo. "You believe this sleep-like state will give him the ability to observe her?"

"Yes, Odin. He will dream as she does, see her actions and be able to pinpoint her location. Then you will be able to proceed with your plan."

"Wonderful." Odin turned his attention to Arawn and Bellona. "You see? Our plan is not in disarray, it merely requires some fine tuning. We will discover where the girl is and she will be eliminated."

"If you had allowed me to attend the meeting with the girl, she would already be eliminated," Bellona retorted snidely.

Odin narrowed his eyes at the dark skinned woman, but didn't respond to her taunt. Bellona's eyes widened, her gaze fixed on Odin and she shivered delicately.

"Odin, do not use your mind tricks on me," she demanded from between gritted teeth.

"Do not propose to tell me what I should and shouldn't do," Odin retorted angrily. "You will recall who is in charge here." For a moment he continued to glare at the woman and then blinked slowly.

Bellona wavered on her feet for a second or two before drawing herself back under control. There was a sheen of perspiration on her dark brow when she lowered her gaze. "Yes, Odin." Her clenched fists suggested it was difficult for her to remain silent.

"We will discover where the girl is and eliminate her." Odin glanced at Archangelo and patted his head as though he were a beloved pet. "She was eminently unsuitable for Archangelo, would never have agreed to mate with him to create the hybrids. We will continue to search for another."

The gray-cloaked man cleared his throat. "Odin, there is no indication of another Angel. My studies suggest there are only two, one man and one woman."

"As you've told me before, my friend – your research has not left you with perfect knowledge of the mythology. There are any number of areas where the records of Nememiah's Children have been lost to history, so there is no reason to believe your knowledge is complete."

"But Odin..."

Odin shook his head stubbornly, adjusting the cravat at his neck. "There will be another female. It is a requirement for our plan and I will not hear further nonsense regarding there only being two. Your knowledge is undoubtedly flawed."

The grey-cloaked man opened his mouth to respond, but then paused, smoothing all traces of annoyance from his wizened face. "My knowledge would have been far more complete if not for the Warlock Vander," he announced. "If he had shared the information he'd collected in its entirety..."

"No matter." Odin waved his hand languidly, cutting off further discussion. "Our plans will continue regardless. I will not have all our carefully laid strategies waylaid by one stupid girl and her friends. Look! He stirs!"

They leaned forward expectantly, watching as Archangelo slowly opened his eyes. He was still wearing the shirt he'd worn during the attack, stained with blood from the Philaris slashing into his chest.

Archangelo drew himself into a sitting position, swinging his muscular legs off the table.

"What have you learned?" the gray-cloaked man questioned impatiently.

"She's hiding in an old church in Jackson, Mississippi. I have the location. The vampires she stole are with her. The church is warded, but the protections can be easily removed." He rubbed his knuckles over his eyes, a human trait which seemed at odds with what I knew him to be.

"Excellent news, Archangelo! Excellent news!" Odin announced triumphantly. He turned towards the grey-cloaked man. "You and Archangelo will direct the attack on the church. Get rid of the enchantments and kill them all." Turning to Bellona he smiled viciously. "Bellona, you will have your opportunity. Archangelo will assist you in sending younglings to attack the Lingard and Tremaine packs. We have your excellent tactical skills to thank for the locations of their encampments. Kill them all. No survivors. The bitch and her friends cannot live."

"You told me I would get the girl," Archangelo muttered mutinously.

"My dear boy, you can have any girl you want. But not this one." He waved a dismissive hand. "Now go, and do my bidding."

"There are purebloods in the werewolf encampment," Arawn mentioned quietly.

Odin tossed him a contemptuous look. "They are aligned with the bitch. They won't conform to our new system of governing." He shook his head determinedly. "No, Arawn. I will not allow this. You will have plenty of other flesh to torture before we complete our goal. Besides, what is the loss of a few more dogs?"

Arawn grinned, bright blue eyes crazed. "No loss at all. But I will mourn the loss of a chance to tap that green-eyed bitch."

Odin chuckled mirthlessly. "You did more than enough with her friends, Arawn."

"But I didn't get to kill them," Arawn pouted.

"There will be other opportunities for you to kill and maim in the upcoming months, Arawn. You're desires for torture will be sated, I assure you..."

With a shriek, I snapped open my eyes, clutching my hands to my temples, trying to quell the acute pain as dozens of voices screamed warnings. I was drenched in sweat, my body trembling from head to toe. Curling into a fetal position, I battled to regain control over the spirits, fighting down panic. What had I just witnessed? Was it real? Or had it been a particularly realistic nightmare? The ear-piercing babble of the spirits convinced me it was real and I slipped from the bed, scrambling to find my clothes and slipping them on hurriedly.

An immense clap of thunder reverberated overhead, the sound rolling and echoing through the room. The ground vibrated beneath my feet, as if the earth was shifting and rippling. I crept across the darkened room, opening the door an inch to peek outside. The sky was sooty black, as if every star in the heavens had been abruptly snuffed out. There was no moonlight visible and despite knowing the church was directly in front of me, I couldn't see a thing in the impenetrable darkness. Reaching for the Hjördis, I cursed when I remembered I'd left it inside. *Stupid, Charlotte, really stupid.*

I risked a second peek through the door and saw a red glow overhead, which cast eerie shadows across the church grounds, but at least it provided a little light. A little light to make out the numerous bodies creeping around beyond the gates. My heart plunged. They were attempting to leap the fence, but I assumed Epi's enchantments were holding them back. It was hard to believe what I was seeing, I'd been so convinced Epi's magic would keep us safe here – now we were under attack.

The ground rumbled ominously beneath my feet and a patch of dirt erupted near the gate, soil exploding upwards. A distinct smell of sulfur wafted across the cemetery, which from experience could only mean one thing. Standing frozen in the doorway, I watched in disbelief as a demon formed in the church grounds, followed by a second and then a third. They pointed in unison towards the reddened sky and I made the split-second decision to make a run for the church. It was now or never.

Wrenching open the door, I didn't bother trying to be stealthy. I had to get back to the church as rapidly as possible, before the demons cut off access to the building. My bare feet crunched over the dry grass as I sprinted towards the front doors, my mouth dry and heart pounding with terror.

Another thunderous roar erupted, loud enough that I stopped in my tracks, covering my ears to protect them. The sound converged with a tumultuous crash of shattering glass and I clapped a hand over my mouth to stop a scream which threatened to erupt. The sky appeared to be crumpling and falling to the ground. Massive pieces struck the ground and showered over my head and I realized it *was* glass – shards the size of windows descending like deadly missiles.

And I had another massive problem - besides the vampires outside the gate and demons in the churchyard – I wasn't wearing shoes.

The vampires were streaming across the fence, vaulting it easily, their eyes crazed beneath the muted red light. It took a few valuable seconds to understand what was happening – Epi's enchantments had been destroyed and were collapsing all around me. We were in serious trouble. The first three demons had been joined by two others and they were shuffling enmasse towards the church. I had about thirty feet to cover - thirty feet covered with splinters of broken glass. Taking a steadying breath, I called on the spirits for assistance, pitching waves of energy towards the vampires in an attempt to keep them back. I dashed towards the church with a mix of satisfaction when the first group of vampires were flung back towards the gates - and agony as broken glass sliced into the soles of my bare feet.

I wrenched open the heavy door, nearly colliding with Nick and Rafe on the other side. I slammed the door shut and twisted the heavy locks with trembling fingers.

"What the hell's going on?" Nick demanded.

I shoved by him, skidding as blood poured from my gashed feet. "Big trouble. *Really* big trouble." My feet were throbbing, my head pounding from the roar of voices in my mind. I longed to take a few seconds to inform the spirits that I knew we had a damn problem, but merely shook my head to try and clear a cohesive thought pattern through the cacophony of sound. "Get something to put across the door," I yelled back to Nick.

"What's wrong, child?" Epi studied me calmly, while Lucas and the Tines gathered around, their expressions anxious.

"Like they say in the movies, our shields are down. We're being attacked," I announced grimly. I glanced towards the Tines and grimaced. "You might want to start holding your breath – I'm bleeding all over the floor." I rushed past them, snatching up the Hjördis from the table and heading towards the altar. "And help Nick reinforce the door!"

"No matter, I can deal with that," Epi responded brightly. He waved his hand towards the doors and they wavered, morphing into a wall of solid rock.

"Nice one, Epi, but it won't keep them out for long."

I concentrated on the wall and waited impatiently for the stone block to fade away. Reaching inside the opening, I snatched up the satchel of weapons and wrenched it open, slipping the belt around my waist. Loading Katchet and Philaris onto the belt, I tried in vain to ignore the throbbing in my feet.

"What's out there?" Lucas demanded quietly.

"At least three dozen younglings and five demons – at last count." I ran my fingers over my left foot, gingerly pulling pieces of glass from the wounds. Lucas's nostrils flared and he shuddered, closing his eyes tightly. "Didn't I tell you not to breathe?" I demanded.

"I can't speak if I don't breathe," he reminded me gruffly. He straightened up, gritting his teeth.

"Good point." Turning my attention to my right foot, I repeated the same procedure.

"Charlotte, what can we do to help?" Ben asked. His concern was etched in his face as he glanced at Rowena. "None of us are strong enough to fight yet."

Rubbing cautiously across my feet, I confirmed they were glass free before drawing healing sigils on each foot in turn. The skin knitted together instantaneously and I breathed a silent thanks to Epi for the vile concoction he'd made me drink. Standing up cautiously, I was happy to discover my feet felt okay. "We can't fight, there are too many of them. We've got to get out of here."

Nick reached my side, eyes narrowed. "Do you want us to transform?"

"No, Nick. These things are big."

"Hey, we took on the Omias and won," Marco grumbled, a slight teenage whine detectable in his voice.

I tucked the Hjördis into a pocket. "Trust me, Marco. These things make the Omias look like a midget arm wrestler from Hoboken."

"Really?" Epi's eyebrows rose in interest. "What did they look like?"

I was growing increasingly jumpy as the seconds passed and pushed past the old man, searching for my cell phone. "They were big, black and ugly. With really sharp teeth, really big claws." I gritted my teeth. "Epi, as much as I love these in-depth demon discussions, I don't think this is the time."

"Of course, yes. You're right," Epi responded tartly. "But Charlotte..."

"Enough, old man," Nick growled. "Save it for later."

I shot Nick a grateful smile and glanced around the sea of faces before me. "Nonny, get Katie, bring her stuff with you." Locating my cell phone, I snatched it up. "Nick, get onto your pack. Tell them to move and do it quickly. They've got trouble headed their way. We'll meet them at the rendezvous point."

"Gotcha," Nick nodded his agreement, setting off at a run towards the room where he had been sleeping with Rafe and Marco.

I punched the shortcut button for Conal and waited impatiently as it rang. With a frown, I flicked it shut, worrying about why Conal didn't answer. Epi's shelves of books caught my eye and I motioned to him. "You need to pack up anything you need that's vitally important. The Monster book of Demons might be a great place to start." I closed my eyes, reaching out to the spirits. *Shut Up! I know they're out there and I promise I'll get everyone to safety. But stop yelling at me!* I sighed with heartfelt relief when they quieted, although it had the unpleasant side-effect of making the sound outside increase tenfold.

Striker was back to his usual enthusiastic self and bounced eagerly on the balls of his feet. His blue eyes were excited, ready for some action. William had scooped Gwynn into his arms and held her petite body close to his chest. From the corner of my eye I spied Epi holding a large rucksack and wave his arm in a wide arc. Every book from the shelves disappeared simultaneously. When I glanced at the rucksack, it was bulging at the seams, but Epi swung it nimbly onto his shoulder as if it weighed nothing. "Remind me to get you to pack if I ever go on holidays, Epi."

Nonny reappeared with Katie and the tiny girl ran across to where William stood with Gwynn. Ripley scooped the little girl into his arms and he pressed a kiss against Katie's cheek. Nick strode back through the room and nodded curtly. "My people are on the move. Did you get Conal?"

I shook my head, throwing my phone to him. "Keep trying." Behind us, the steady pounding on the stone walls made the overhead lights swing with the force being exerted on the building. "If you get him, they need to move out and get to safety. They've got younglings on the way to their caves."

"How do you know all this?" Jerome demanded. He'd been standing quietly to one side, with Marianne and Rowena.

"I had a nightmare," I explained brusquely. "Epi, I need some floor space."

Epi waved his hand again and the long table vanished. I knelt down, marking a pentagram on the stone floor with the Hjördis, placing sigils in four of the five corners. Envisioning our destination, a sigil appeared in my mind's eye and I drew it in the fifth corner. The ground beneath the pentagram began to glow, erupting into a circle of shimmering golden light. "William, you and Gwynn first, then Ripley and Acenith. I'll give you 30 seconds, then I'm sending Nonny through with Katie. You'll need to give them a hand when they come through, we don't want them to fall and get hurt."

William nodded tersely and stepped through the portal without question. Ripley dropped Katie down onto my lap and grasped Acenith's hand, dragging her quickly through the portal after William and Gwynn.

"Okay, Katie. This is really cool, isn't it?" I gave the little girl a bright smile and squeezed her in a brief hug, trying to reassure her.

"Will it hurt?" She stared at the portal with round eyes.

"No, honey. It's more like a fairground ride. This is how angels travel all the time. You want to be an Angel, don't you?" She nodded and I helped her up onto her feet.

"Is Nonny coming?" she demanded in a high voice.

"Yep, Nonny's coming with you. She's going to hold your hand."

Nonny crossed herself and uttered a few words in a language I didn't understand. She clasped Katie's hand and stepped up to the portal, eyeing it with unease. Straightening her shoulders resolutely, she stepped through without a backward glance, gently guiding Katie.

The pounding against the walls was increasing steadily and I worried about how much time we had to escape. "Striker, you and Marianne. Go."

"This thing makes me nauseous," Marianne admitted with a weak smile.

"Me too. See you soon." They stepped through. "Rowena, you and Ben next."

Ben rubbed his hand across the top of my head and smiled gratefully. "I owe you our thanks again." He and Rowena stepped through, disappearing from sight.

"Jerome, you and Epi, then Nick and Rafe, Marco and Holden. Get through as quick as you can."

Holden strode forward on his turn and winked at me. "That thing outside makes the Omias look like a midget arm wrestler from Hoboken? Nice one, Charlotte, I like your sense of humor."

There was an ominous rumble from outside and I flinched as the solid rock wall started to crumble. "Charlotte, let's go!" Lucas urged, reaching for my hand.

"Two seconds." I drew a sigil on the ground beside the portal, the Hjordis burning it into the stone in vivid blue lines. "Okay."

Lucas wrenched me to my feet and a massive blast detonated behind us. The church wall collapsed in a cloud of choking dust as we ran and I saw the demons leaping over the shattered stone before I was drawn into the swirling maelstrom of the portal.

Chapter 11

Rendezvous

I wasn't ever going to get used to this and I certainly wouldn't like it. Lucas and I hurtled through the portal and when we reached solid ground again I was nauseated and dizzy. I would have fallen but Lucas caught me, holding me tight against him. "Easy, Charlotte."

"Jeez, I hate that thing." I peered around in the darkness to find Epi kneeling, blocking the portal after our appearance. "Epi, any chance of some light?"

I expected some objection about using his powers for such a menial task, but he surprised me by agreeing to the request immediately. Epi gestured towards the ground and a tiny flame materialized on the soil, rapidly growing into a healthy blaze. The fire cast a flickering glow over the immediate area and I inhaled deeply, relieved we'd gotten out unharmed. "We're safe. They can't follow us here."

"You drew a mark on the floor before we left the church. What was that?" Lucas asked.

"An explosion sigil. We needed to slow them down, stop them following us into the portal. It might have killed a few of the vamps, if we're lucky, but I doubt it did anything to the demons besides annoy the heck out of them."

"Will the demons attack others around the church?" Ben asked.

"No, they're essentially stupid things. They will have been programmed with a simple instruction. 'Kill Charlotte', I imagine," I responded drily. "They'll return to the Otherworld now their orders have been thwarted."

"Where are we?" Striker questioned. He was eyeing the surrounding area with interest.

"A couple of miles out of Crater Lake National Park in Oregon. I'm new to this portalling thing, can only go to places I can visualize. We used to camp here, when I was a kid." Nick was attempting to contact Conal again on my cell phone and he disconnected the call, shaking his head. "Nick, give the phone to Nonny, see if she can get anyone from the pack."

"How did you manage to portal into Sfantu Drâghici?" Lucas asked.

"Epi did it. He can't use a Hjördis, but he has the ability to create portals with magic. I got us back to the church, because it was a fixed location in my mind."

Epi was speaking to Ben and Jerome. "... don't know how they located us. It was impossible with my enchantments."

"That would be my fault," I admitted guiltily.

Epi stared, his eyes wide. "How can that be?" He dropped the backpack and scrutinized me through his thick glasses.

"The nightmares." I met Ben's eyes as I explained. "The nightmares give me information and I see current events, even when they're far away. I could see you in Sfantu Drâghici and knew what was happening to you." Ben flinched and I lowered my gaze. "Archangelo was created before he developed the ability. But now Archangelo can find me in his dreams."

"That's not possible." Epi shook his head firmly in denial.

"Charlotte, he's vampire. He doesn't sleep," Lucas said gently.

"He does sleep, they've developed some sort of potion to make him sleep." I explained all the facets of the dream and told them about the gray-cloaked man and his role in the Consiliului's plans.

Epi cackled with delight when I concluded, looking positively gleeful. "I knew it! I knew who it would be!"

"How about you let us in on the secret?" Nick grumbled.

"Alberich Bran," Epi announced triumphantly. His toothless smile dimmed a little when he realized we were staring at him blankly. "Alberich Bran was my apprentice. I trained him and he assisted my search for Nememiah's Children."

"So he knows what you do?" The implications were alarming, it meant the Drâghici knew far more than we'd allowed for.

Epi peered over the top of his glasses, eyeing me coldly. "Of course he doesn't, child. He was a pitiful apprentice, he wanted to harness the power of Nememiah's Children for all the wrong reasons. He was interested in exploiting for his own gain, not the quest for peace upon this earth." He smiled smugly. "I kicked him out."

"Kicked him out?" I repeated blankly.

"This was many centuries ago, before I moved to America. Long before most of you were born. I lived in medieval Europe and was studying Nememiah's Children when Alberich Bran was indentured to serve an apprenticeship. He worked with me for a little over a year, but I discovered his interest was disreputable and requested he leave my employ." Epi crossed his arms over his narrow chest, nodding firmly. "Although he knows much about Nememiah, there is a great deal more he doesn't know. Concerned about his nefarious purposes, I withheld much information from him."

Nonny was talking on the cell phone and gesticulating wildly at me. She handed me the phone with a delighted grin.

"Conal?"

"Hey, Sugar." Relief coursed through my veins when I heard his husky voice.

"Where are you?" I demanded. "Why didn't you answer your phone?"

"We've been a little busy here, Sugar. We were attacked by younglings."

"Is everyone okay?"

"Fine. We got away safely, don't worry." His deep voice was calm and soothing and a little bubble of happiness grew in my chest, knowing he was out of harm's way. Glancing across to discover Lucas watching me, I turned away uncomfortably.

"How did you know they were coming?"

"I've had the pack running routine patrols since the last attack. One of the sentry's picked up vamp scents and warned us. We got out of the caves and collected our cars. We're on our way to you now," he paused. "Nonny says you got attacked."

"Yeah, five demons and about thirty five younglings. We portalled out and we're at the rendezvous point now."

"What about Nick's pack? They okay?"

"Yeah, they had vampire's heading their way too. Nick warned them and they're on their way." I paced back and forth across the ground, pungent pine needles beneath my toes. "But we've got a problem – I'm the one they're tracking."

"What?"

I explained the events of the night again. "It might not be safe for any of you to be near me. This Alberich Bran told them they couldn't use the potion very often, but it means they'll be able to locate me every time they do."

"We're still coming to you, Charlotte. There's safety in numbers," Conal insisted. He lowered his voice an octave, letting it become a sexy rumble. "Perhaps you should still be sleeping with me, Sugar. I could keep the nightmares away from you." The humor was clear in his voice and I knew he would be smiling at the other end of the line, even as butterflies stirred low in my abdomen.

"Shut up."

"See you in a couple of days." Conal disconnected the call and I slipped the phone into my pocket, relieved now everyone was safe.

Epi was examining me suspiciously. "What is all this about a rendezvous point? How come I didn't know about this?"

"Half the time, you forget to tell us what's going on. Guess this time, we forgot to tell you old man. Sucks to be you." He grumbled under his breath and I grinned. "While we're on the subject of not telling me stuff, who the hell makes defensive shields out of *glass*?" Epi stared at me for a minute, then stalked away in a huff, dragging his rucksack behind him.

I turned back to the Tines, who were huddled together in a group. "Well, this is home for a few days at least and I'm guessing you could all do with some fresh, non-bovine blood. How about you head off and hunt while Nick and I get things sorted out here?"

Striker whooped with delight and he and Marianne ran off into the woods immediately. Ripley and Acenith quickly followed them.

"Since when did you manage to discuss our thirst without so much as blinking an eye?" Lucas demanded quietly. He sidled up beside me, one eyebrow raised in question. "Five months ago, you couldn't bear the thought."

"Five months ago I hadn't discovered all the other things which happen in this world. You needing to drink blood seems pretty minor in the whole scheme of things."

"I'll stay and help," he suggested.

I gave him a gentle shove. "Go. We're safe here for now." From the corner of my eye I saw Epi producing a large tent out of nowhere and he headed inside, followed by William who still carried Gwynn. "I think I need to go and smooth Epi's ruffled feathers. Go and find something nice for dinner." I watched as he and Holden disappeared into the darkness.

"Are you sure you don't need help?" Ben offered.

"Nah, we'll be fine." Their eyes were still shadowed by purplish-black bruising, despite the amount of cow blood they'd fed on. "Go and hunt. You both should go."

Rowena reached out and pulled me into an affectionate hug. "We'll be back soon, Charlotte. We missed you so much, whilst you were gone."

"I missed you too," I responded honestly. "Now go. I'm certain there must be something out there you'll like." Ben caught Rowena's hand in his and they ran off into the darkness, Rowena's skirt flowing around her legs.

"So, Lottie. What do you want us to do?" Rafe and Nick sidled up beside me and Rafe draped an arm across my shoulders.

I sighed. "Before anything else, I'd better go and eat humble pie with the old man..."

Chapter 12

Nightmares

I threw myself onto the ground in the small clearing I'd come across, breathing heavily after running through the forest for more than twenty minutes. I had a stitch in my side and folded over on myself, trying to relieve the ache with my arms wrapped around my legs.

For long minutes I lay on the ground panting, adjusting my breathing to take short, shallow mouthfuls of oxygen – any more tore at the pain in my side and made it feel like a knife being dug into the skin around my ribs. The pain gradually dissipated and feeling better, I sat upright and viewed my surroundings.

The forest encircled the clearing, tall pine trees on all sides. There was the perfume of summer in the air, the soaring trees filled with the sounds of local wildlife; honeyeaters, woodpeckers, sparrows and the like. Squirrels were frolicking in the long grass, scooting up and down the tree trunks as they foraged in the vegetation before returning to the protection of the trees.

Certain the stitch had dissipated, I flopped down in the grass, feeling it scratch against my bare arms as I settled comfortably on the ground. I rested my forearms across my eyes to block the small amount of sunlight which penetrated into the tiny clearing.

Four weeks had passed since the escape from Jackson and the suspicions I'd had regarding Archangelo had been unerringly accurate. The Consiliu-lui could only use the sleeping potion roughly once every seven days, but it was enough to cause us endless problems. Every time Archangelo entered the potion-induced sleep, he was able to trace us and we were forced to move locality, fleeing from both demons and vampires with negligible amounts of warning. It had been difficult enough the first time, when we'd fled the church – now we had a bigger group with the merging of Conal's and Nick's packs. We'd also been joined by the Bustani Kiss, who'd fled Egypt after an unsuccessful attack by the Drâghici and flown to the states to join us. Thut had been incensed by the Council's decision to attack his small Kiss, when he was one of the oldest and most respected vampires in existence and swore he would help defeat them. Harley Fitzgerald and his small group had also decided to join us. Whilst they hadn't yet been attacked, Harley decided against taking any chances and joined his group with ours. During the past two evacuations, we'd lost fifteen people when they didn't make it through the portal in time. I took each and every death personally – these people had put their faith in me and the very act of staying with us was putting them in even greater peril.

Morale in the encampment was at an all-time low. In the first few days after escaping Jackson, the werewolves and shifters who'd joined us viewed me as a savior. With each new attack, their faith was being eroded. They were losing confidence in my capacity to help them and they were all aware the Drâghici were locating us with Archangelo's induced sleeps.

To make things worse, we were receiving sketchy reports of other attacks. A shape shifter pack in New York had been slaughtered. A werewolf pack in Norway were decimated by an attack which killed every man, woman and child. All over the world, the Consiliului were continuing their campaign to eliminate anyone they deemed unsuitable. And we were hiding, running from one place to the next, descending into anarchy through a lack of cohesive organization. Other groups had begged to amalgamate with us and I was denying them the opportunity – I couldn't keep the numbers I had safe, more would only increase the catastrophic death toll.

And everyone was terrified. Including me.

Even worse was the reality that despite every effort, we were no closer to a solutions for killing the demons. The newcomers had commenced training and whilst they could successfully kill the younglings, demons were another matter entirely. The angel weapons alone had the power to eradicate them. Nobody – neither werewolf, shape shifter nor vampire was powerful enough to send a demon back to the Otherworld. It wasn't for a lack of trying. Day after day Conal and Lucas were out in the field, urging Epi to create demons to practice on but despite them both being amongst the strongest of the group, they couldn't get rid of them.

And a myriad of other troubling issues continued to plague us. We were headed into October and winter was fast approaching. We needed somewhere to live, where we could settle. We'd been making do by camping since leaving Jackson, with Epi producing tents enough for everyone to share. But winter would see the need for something solid, when the weather would make it much too cold to camp. But if we could only manage a week in any one location, how the hell would we organize a more permanent living arrangement for the group?

We desperately needed structure. Whilst the supernatural could survive by hunting for sustenance, we had a contingent of humans who didn't share the same ability and needed both nourishment and protection. We had children in need of education, people in need of medical treatment and only this morning Jerome had warned us one of the shape shifters and a werewolf were nearing the end of their pregnancies and would require somewhere safe to deliver their babies.

I sighed heavily, wanting to switch off to the problems I was dealing with on a minute by minute basis. I'd come up here to escape, if only for an hour. The issues were beginning to overwhelm every waking moment and I dreaded getting up each day. Despite the desire to switch off, multiple worries continued to filter through my mind as I agonized over what we should do. Everyone looked to me for answers and I had nothing.

Rolling onto my stomach, I rested my head against my crossed arms. The sun overhead warmed my skin, made me sleepy. I'd never felt more like running away than I did right now. Maybe it would be better for all of them if I did. It was what I'd been trying to explain to everyone this morning – if I was away from them, they'd be safer. The Drâghici were intent on locating and killing me and would murder every person surrounding me without blinking an eyelid.

Conal argued passionately against the proposal, refusing to consider breaking up the group. Some of his argument made sense - he insisted everyone was in danger whether we were together or not. And as he'd pointed out, while they were with me, at least they would receive advance warnings of imminent attacks. But the guilt was crushing every time I thought about it. The Drâghici were hell bent on destruction and they'd continue to pinpoint my position while Archangelo kept drinking the potion. Risking everyone I loved, people I couldn't bear to think about losing.

Lucas wouldn't consider being separated from me. Neither would the Tines. Epi was staunchly determined to remain at my side, insisting he could teach me more than anyone else. But I thought Conal and Nick's people should separate away and seek somewhere to hide. To my intense frustration, Conal and Nick refused to consider it as an option. Thut had further infuriated me by calmly announcing he was here to stay, his dark eyes determined.

The meeting had concluded abruptly when I lost my temper. Lucas, Conal and Nick had collectively sided against me and I'd stormed out in a rage, wanting to escape from everyone and avoid the recriminating looks from people wondering if I could help them at all.

To top it off, the continuous apprehension was destroying the one thing we needed the most – collaboration between the factions. The panic which was threatening to overwhelm everyone was creating mistrust. In the past few days, there'd been a number of skirmishes amongst the groups. If it wasn't nipped in the bud, any hope of winning this conflict would be destroyed before we even began to fight.

"A penny for them."

I rolled over to discover Marianne, casual in a white tank top and her favorite tattered jeans with the safety pin decorations. Her blue-streaked hair was slicked back, framing her delicate features and revealing the earrings dangling from her earlobes. A second glance confirmed the earrings were shaped like miniature Elmo's from Sesame Street and I managed a tiny smile. She sat down gracefully, cross-legged in the grass as I hauled myself up to sit opposite her.

"Trust me, Marianne. My thoughts aren't worth a penny." I yanked a long blade of grass from the ground, savagely tearing it into small pieces. "How did you find me?"

Marianne gazed at me for a moment, arching one perfectly shaped eyebrow. "Charlotte, remember me? The vampire? I followed your scent. Which, I might add, is rather aromatic and very delicious." She grinned wickedly and I was delighted to see her looking so much healthier. It had been a long battle for the vampires and it wasn't over. The starvation and torture meted out by the Drâghici was still affecting the Tines. Their special abilities were functioning in fits and starts – only Rowena had completely recovered her empathic ability. Ripley was occasionally getting access to people's thoughts but Striker and Acenith were frustrated by the continuing absence of their ability to calm moods. While they had regained full physical strength, they were still enduring psychological problems related to the kidnapping and Lucas believed the loss of their 'special' abilities was a direct effect of the damage to their psyches.

"Lucas told me what happened this morning," she announced.

I groaned aloud. "These people are relying on me and I don't have any way of helping them." I yanked another stalk of grass from the ground to destroy.

"You've done so much, Charlotte. It's your ability to foresee the attacks which is keeping so many people alive."

"They all hate me, they think I'm not doing enough." I plucked at the grass, tearing pieces off and flicking them away. "And they're right - I'm not. We've moved five times in four weeks and every time we get settled, we have to make a run for it. People have been killed. There are only so many places in my mind to portal to. And this thing with the demons – Marianne, how do we overcome that?"

"I don't know." She reached across and caught my hands in her own, halting my destructive assault on the clearing. "I assume everyone's already suggested the obvious - asking the spirits for advice?"

"Yeah," I muttered. "Lucas and Conal are both frustrated with me, they're under the illusion it's like asking for subway directions. But it's not, the spirits never give a straight answer. I get snippets of images, advice about good and evil, right and wrong and then nine times out of ten they announce the answer is inside me." I couldn't keep the frustration out of my voice. "And Epi's no better, he keeps assuring me I'll find the answers if I search for them." I inhaled sharply, drawing my emotions back in under a tight reign. "Being an angel *sucks*, quite frankly. It's like being in a pitch-black room, trying to find your way out with no candle, no torch."

Marianne studied me for a minute, her head tilted to one side. "Lucas and Conal are both frustrated because of the decision you made in Jackson," she pointed out evenly.

"Marianne, what else could I do? I love them both – I don't want to hurt either one of them!"

Marianne sighed heavily, her eyes filled with sympathy. "You're hurting both of them. And yourself." She leaned forward to capture my cheek against her cool fingers. "My poor Charlotte. You must be so lonely on your own."

I shook my head, resolute in the belief that the decision had been the only one I could make. "It's better this way."

Marianne dropped her hand from my cheek and enclosed my hand in hers. "For whom?"

I snatched my hand away and rubbed my temples. "For them. I don't know if I'm going to survive this, Marianne. Odin and his goons are hell bent on killing me and most likely will. I don't want Conal and Lucas to grieve like I did, when I lost my family."

Marianne frowned a little, clasping her hands together in her lap. "I understand your concern, I really do. But don't you understand? They would both mourn your loss whether you are involved with them or not. They love you, Charlotte. Closing yourself off from them is not going to change how they would feel if the worst happened."

I couldn't stop my unhappy scowl. "I guess it's not only them I'm trying to protect. Marianne... if either of them die, I'll never forgive myself. Knowing how they feel about me, how can I make a choice? How could I choose Lucas, if there's a chance Conal could die? How can I choose Conal, knowing the same thing? How can I live with myself if the one I didn't choose died, knowing how they felt about me? Whatever choice I made, someone would get hurt."

"What's your heart telling you?" Marianne asked gently.

I shrugged and decided to be honest. There was no point in hiding my emotions from Marianne, we spent so much time together and she knew me well. "My heart tells me I belong with Lucas. It's always told me I belong with Lucas."

Chapter 13

Speak the Truth

Even as I spoke the words, I was tormented by the thought of spending my life without him.

"You should tell him," she urged.

"I can't, Marianne! I thought I could, but I *can't*. Conal knew I intended going back to Lucas – up until we rescued you that was always my intention! But I felt so guilty about what I'd be doing to Conal by dumping him so coldly and then I felt so uncomfortable when I first saw Lucas again and it all got so *complicated*."

"Charlotte, the way you've chosen to deal with this isn't working. Neither of them will move on while they think they have a chance with you. You owe it to them to clear this up. Make your decision and tell them," Marianne announced determinedly.

"I *did* make my decision. I told them I wouldn't pursue a relationship with either one of them."

"Which neither of them believe," Marianne pressed. "They both imagine you'll eventually choose one of them. Neither Lucas, nor Conal are going to attempt a relationship with anyone else while you're undecided. They won't risk doing something to hurt their chances with you." The hurt must have shown on my face because she continued, her voice softer. "You deserve happiness, Charlotte. You deserve to love Lucas and spend as much time with him as you can. Conal deserves the opportunity to meet someone else, to pursue a relationship where he won't be second choice."

I cringed, knowing she was right. "I'll think about it," I agreed quietly.

"That's all I'm asking, Charlotte."

"You just want me to get back together with Lucas," I pointed out.

"That's not true. I want... we *all* want you to be happy. Whether that is with Conal, or Lucas is completely your choice."

"But you'd prefer it to be Lucas."

Marianne shook her head firmly, her lips creasing into a smile. "I'm not getting involved in a debate over this. You have to choose who will make you happy and I like both men." She scrutinized me carefully. "Now let's move on to another subject. What are the spirits saying that you're having trouble understanding? Maybe I can help."

I screwed up my nose. "Half of it doesn't make an ounce of sense. It's like when I knew you were in Sfantu Drâghici and we had to get you out. I had parts of the puzzle, but not all of it and it took weeks to figure out what all the signs and clues meant. Right now, it feels like I have half the information I need and I'm stumbling around in the dark. Like a jigsaw with half the pieces missing."

"I love jigsaw puzzles," she responded with a bright smile. "Tell me what you do know and let's see if we can't figure it out."

"Marianne, I've never seen you do a jigsaw puzzle."

She shrugged delicately. "Work with me here, will you? I'm offering to help, the least you could do is accept the offer."

I huffed out a sigh. There wasn't any point to hashing this out all over again, nothing was making sense and I was in a bitch of a mood. Glancing at Marianne, I saw her narrow her eyes and cross her arms, clearly determined. "Fine. I keep getting a vision in my dreams, it's a city surrounded by a big wall. I don't recognize it as somewhere I've been before. It's surrounded by open land and in the distance, there's a forest. There's a big archway, with a heavy wooden gate and sigils are marked on the walls on either side of the gates, ones I haven't used and don't recognize."

"What else? What do the spirits say?"

"They keep telling me I need to go home. Initially I thought they meant Puckhaber, because that's the only place I've considered home in recent years. Then I wondered if they meant where I lived in Georgia with my family. Neither answer is the right one though, because the spirits keep telling me I'm wrong." I thought silently for a few minutes, frustrated about the lack of concise information I was receiving and sick of the worry which gnawed continually in the pit of my stomach. "The spirits keep showing me a wing, like the birthmark

I have on my neck. Then they talk about completing the circle, whatever the hell that means."

Marianne considered what I'd said for a few minutes, her ocean blue eyes taking on a faraway look as she stared into the distance, her expression thoughtful. "This place you're seeing – how do you feel when you think about it?"

"What do you mean?" The question startled me out of my own musings.

She huffed out an impatient breath. "Does it feel dangerous? Safe? Give you warm and fuzzy thoughts?"

I narrowed my eyes, but contemplated the question. "It makes me feel... calm. Peaceful. When I'm seeing it, I can smell the sweetness of the earth surrounding the city, the scent of wild flowers floating on the breeze. The trees have the rich smell of pine and I can hear the wind rustling through the leaves. It gives me a sense of deep contentment, as though I would be safe there. But I don't know it, Marianne. I don't know where it is... whether it's even a real place. I'm not certain if it's a place to provide a haven for our group, or if it has something to do with the fight with the Drâghici? It doesn't matter, either way, because I don't know where it is, or how to find it."

We both lapsed into silence and while Marianne pondered thoughtfully, I called to the spirits. Mom appeared, calm and serene.

"Mom, you've got to give me more information – please?"

Her green eyes were tranquil and she offered an apologetic smile. *"I can't, Charlotte. Only you can do this."*

"I don't know what to do! I'm frightened that I'll get it wrong! And more of these people – my friends are going to die if I can't help them."

"Charlotte. You have the answer..."

I interrupted hurriedly, struggling with my temper. "Mom! Don't tell me I have the answer inside of me, because if I do, it's not making any sense. And what's with this..."

Marianne gripped my arm and shook it urgently. "Charlotte!"

"What?" Mom dissipated, carried away on the breeze when my attention was diverted to Marianne.

"Think like an angel!"

Staring at the excited woman before me, I wondered if she'd gone nuts. "Marianne, I don't..."

She jumped up, dancing around excitedly. "You're thinking like a *human*! The place you're seeing in your vision – what if it's a haven for Nememiah's

Children? What if the place you're seeing *isn't* somewhere you've been before? What if it's somewhere only Nememiah's Children would regard as a safe refuge and you can only envision it because you know what you are now?"

My mind raced as I considered the possibility. Perhaps I'd been looking at this from the wrong angles? I'd been considering our options from a human point of view. It never occurred to me that the haven we were looking for, the safety would come in the form of a sanctuary known only to Nememiah's Children. Closing my eyes, I probed the visions I'd seen, searching for guidance. With sudden clarity, I decided Marianne might just be right. I jumped to my feet and stared at her, eyes wide with excitement. "We need to talk to Epi."

"It'll be faster if I piggyback you."

Eyeing her warily, I considered the option and dismissed it. Despite her height, Marianne was incredibly slender. "Marianne, I don't think..."

"Vampire – remember?" She stepped forward and turned her back to me. "Jump on."

I stepped awkwardly behind her and made an inelegant and halfhearted leap onto her back. Marianne snorted her amusement and used her arms to hitch me up effortlessly, so my thighs were braced around her waist. And then she ran effortlessly, her movements swift and fluid. Within minutes, we'd reached the ramshackle tent city we were calling home and Marianne dropped me lightly to my feet. Holding hands, we walked past the many occupied tents and I saw surprise registering on the faces of those around me. I realized they were reacting to an emotion in my expression which hadn't been visible for weeks.

Hope.

Chapter 14

A Safe Harbor

We burst through the entrance to Epi's tent, where he was sitting with Conal, Lucas and Ben. They were congregated around a wooden table and turned in unison as Marianne and I hurried in through the open tent flap.

"Got over your temper tantrum, young lady?" Epi scolded, glaring over the top of his glasses.

"Epi..."

"The next time you call me names like you did this morning, I'm going to turn you into a pile of frog spawn..."

"Epi, I'm sorry..." I stopped abruptly, narrowing my eyes when I caught the trace of a smile curving Ben's lips. "Wait a minute – turn me into *frog spawn?*" Marianne saw my green eyes beginning to flash with anger and nudged my elbow swiftly. I inhaled sharply, making a conscious decision to remain composed and ignore Epi's goading. "Epi, Marianne and I have been discussing..."

"With any luck she has talked to you about controlling that terrible temper of yours..."

"Epi, will you *listen* to me for a minute!"

All four men stared at me. Lucas raised an eyebrow but remained silent, whilst Ben and Conal both frowned. Epi just continued to glare.

Taking another deep breath, I struggled to control the frustration I was experiencing. The old wizard had that effect, particularly when he was threatening me with being turned into frog spawn. "Nememiah's Children – where did they live in the past?" I waited, holding my breath, knowing everything hinged on his verification of what I believed.

A Safe Harbor

Epi's brow furrowed and he adjusted his glasses. "Well, let me think." He stood up hurriedly, with flexibility which belied his age. He plunged one hand into his rucksack, rummaging around for what seemed like an eternity. At last, he produced another of his old leather-bound books, flicking through pages while I edged towards him expectantly.

"What's this all about, Sugar?" Conal's long legs were stretched out, his booted feet resting on the table.

"I've been going about this the wrong way," I muttered, watching Epi calmly turning pages in the book. "The vision I've had about somewhere safe for us to go – I didn't recognize it for what it truly was."

"Huh?" Conal lowered his legs and turned to stare at us.

"Charlotte couldn't recognize the place she's been seeing," Marianne explained, "because she's never been there. We think it might be a place the original Nememiah's Children used as a safe haven."

"Over a thousand years ago?" Lucas questioned. "Would it even exist now?"

"Here!" Epi announced triumphantly, pointing to a page. "Nememiah's Children resided in a place called Zaen, where they lived and trained, a city provided for them by Nememiah. It was, as Marianne suggested, a safe haven for the Angel children, protected by powerful enchantments rendering it impervious to attacks."

"That's where we need to go," I announced.

"Wait a minute," Ben cautioned. "Whilst I appreciate your enthusiasm - and we're all aware of your desire to get everyone to safety - I have to agree with Lucas. We're talking about a city which existed more than a thousand years ago. It may well have been destroyed during the final battle which decimated the Angel children. We don't even know where it was."

"Ben's right, Sugar." Conal sounded sympathetic, his dark eyes guarded. "Surely if this place existed, someone would have discovered it before now?"

"Not necessarily," Epi muttered, continuing his study of the book. "Enchantments powerful enough would render it indiscernible to human eyes. It may have continued to exist throughout the ages and no-one would ever locate it because it's unmappable and unplottable."

"But after a thousand years?" Ben sounded doubtful. "Surely after a thousand years, it will have deteriorated and collapsed. Disappeared from existence. If it is unmappable, who would know how to find it?"

"I do," I announced confidently. "Epi, the portals work using sigils?"

"That's correct, child." Epi lifted his gaze from the book to watch me inquisitively.

"And I portal to places I know, places I can see in my head and the spirits give me the correct sigils?"

"Yes."

"Then I can get us there," I declared emphatically. "I can see Zaen, it's in here." I tapped my forehead with my finger. "I didn't recognize it for what it was, but now I'm certain. Zaen exists and the spirits will provide the sigils so we can get there."

"Whoa, Sugar. I don't think creating a portal and waltzing through is such a good idea." Conal stood up and put his hands on my shoulders, his expression sincere. "I know how much you want to get everyone to safety, but we don't know what we'll find on the other side of the portal. You can't be certain that what you're seeing is this Zaen."

"I know it in *here*, Conal." I pressed my fist against my chest. "Sitting around waiting for the Drâghici to locate us again isn't solving anything. Neither is moving from place to place with five minutes warning." Tears formed in my eyes, blurring my vision. "Every time I sleep, I witness what the Consiliului are doing to anyone who won't agree to their enforced rule. I see people being killed and tortured... babies and children being murdered because they're not pure bred." I took a trembling breath, trying hard not to break down completely. "I'm not sitting around here any longer. This is a chance for us to find some safety and security." I shrugged his hands from my shoulders impatiently and turned to Lucas. "Please, Lucas. You know me... you trust me. We need to try this," I pleaded.

Lucas returned my gaze, blue eyes regarding me seriously before he stood up. "Charlotte's right. We can't keep moving week after week, we need somewhere secure to live, somewhere other groups can join us. If this place exists, it would give us a place to train and try to overcome the problems we have defeating the demons."

"But if we go through the portal and there's nothing there?" Conal asked quietly.

"Then we come back and think of another plan. But if we don't try, we won't know."

"Lucas is correct," Epi agreed. "We must try this. Our current situation is tenuous and the attacks will continue, of that I have no doubt."

Conal's gaze flickered to Ben and he nodded. "Okay, Sugar. We'll try to find this Zaen." He glanced at his watch. "It's too late to set out now. How about first thing in the morning?"

With a bright smile, I threw myself into his arms and hugged him. "But Epi will need to move our group to a new location before we go, somewhere I don't know about. That way, if they put Archangelo into another induced sleep they'll be safe."

"Agreed," Epi said. "That seems wise. It also means we can concentrate on our attempt to locate Zaen without worrying about what's happening back here."

My eyes widened as I stared at Epi in astonishment. "You're coming with us?"

"Of course, child. I know more about Nememiah's Children than any of you. You will need me."

"Conal, Nick, Epi and I will accompany you, Charlotte. Conal, will you go and find Nick, bring him up to speed?" Lucas requested. "And let everyone know they'll be on the move in the morning."

"Are we telling them about this Zaen?" Conal asked quietly.

"We'll investigate first. Tell them we might have a place and are checking it out, but they're being moved for their own safety in the meantime."

Conal nodded and slipped through the tent opening. The squaring of his broad shoulders suggested that despite his doubts, he felt good about having a plan.

Epi was rummaging through his rucksack, shoveling things from side to side and extracting books, arranging them on the table in preparation for our journey. Marianne hugged me tightly, offering me a sweet grin. "I love you."

"And I love you." She kissed my cheek and danced from the tent, happier than I'd seen her in days. Conal was right – it felt good to be doing something constructive and for the first time in ages, it felt like we might have something to look forward to.

I sensed Ben move to stand beside me and looked up into his calm face. "Charlotte, Jerome can give you something to help you sleep. It might stop the nightmares," he suggested, examining the dark circles rimming my eyes.

I huffed out an impatient sigh. "Ben, we've been over this. The nightmares give us an indication of what the Drâghici are doing. Although the spirits warn of impending attacks, they don't tell me what's going on in other places. The nightmares, visions - whatever you want to call them, they do. I think it's more important to know what's going on, more vital than worrying about a peaceful night of sleep."

"One night won't do any harm," Ben countered. "And I'd feel better knowing you were heading off on this reconnaissance with a good night of rest." He rested his hand against my shoulder, his eyes betraying his concern. "You may need a clear mind to deal with what you find."

"Ben's right," Lucas coaxed huskily. "You must sleep."

It seemed easier to acquiesce to their quiet determination and I nodded tiredly. I was exhausted, it was true. Ben hurried off to find Jerome and extract some sleeping pills from him. I glanced up at Lucas and he smiled warmly, pressing a brief kiss against my cheek. It reminded me of the conversation with Marianne and I lowered my gaze, a flush of desire warming my body. "Thank you for believing in me."

"I have always believed in you, Charlotte," he murmured. "Go back to your tent, I'll bring the medication to you in a few minutes."

Leaving the tent, I caught sight of Conal calling his pack together for their meeting. Turning in the opposite direction, I headed towards the small tent I called home. Kneeling down, I crawled inside and fell tiredly onto the sleeping bag. I wanted to resolve this situation with Conal and Lucas and knew Marianne was right. The heated glances, the desire which hooded their eyes when they looked at me – I wasn't being fair to either of them, or myself.

Lucas appeared a few minutes later, carrying a small packet of tablets and a glass of milk. He knelt in the tent beside me, passing me two of the tablets and then the milk, watching as I swallowed the tablets down. "I'll leave you to sleep," he announced and turned to go.

"Lucas, wait." I levered up onto one elbow, supporting my face against the palm of my hand. Biting my lip, I tried to compose what I needed to say in my head. "I'm... I'm sorry about everything," I admitted quietly. "I wasn't being fair to you or Conal by refusing to be involved with either one of you."

His expression hardened visibly and when he spoke, his voice was cool, which sent a tingle of anxiety straight up my spine. I'd expected him to smile and draw me into his arms, then kiss me until I was breathless. The tone of his voice warned of a vastly different scenario. "Charlotte, you've made your choice and you were right. I am vampire. You're not. A relationship between us was doomed from the start. You made the right decision – for both of us. I belong with another vampire, someone of my own kind. I would be... happier with my own kind."

I stared at him in disbelief, my heart hammering wildly in my chest. "You... what are you saying? I've seen the way you look at me! Now you're suggesting you... you don't love me anymore?"

"I'm afraid so. I'm not certain I truly loved you in the first place. I shouldn't have allowed this to continue for so long. The desire you see," he glanced away for a second, then back, "is my normal desire for blood, nothing more. I can see now I was infatuated, the scent of your blood overwhelmed me with desire which I mistook for something else. Now that I've tasted you, controlled the thirst, I can see it would never work between you and I. It's only the scent of your blood which affects me, and I can control it now. You'd be much happier with Conal, he's a better choice for you." He paused, eyes cold and his jaw set in determination. "Go to sleep, Charlotte. You have a big day tomorrow."

Chapter 15

Shock

Lying flat on my back, I stared at the canvas overhead, my mind in turmoil. What had just happened? Over and over I repeated the conversation I'd had with Lucas, trying to figure out where it had gone so wrong. I'd seen the way he looked at me – had I really mistaken love for blood thirst? I cursed Marianne silently, she'd pushed me to make a decision and what had it gotten me? Certainly not what I'd expected. I'd gone from the comfort of knowing Lucas loved me, to having him assure me he didn't. I was better off before I'd opened my big fat mouth, when I'd at least had the illusion of there being a chance to resolve this. His words echoed over and over in my mind. He didn't love me, wasn't sure he ever had. He'd only wanted my blood, from the very beginning. Was he telling the truth?

There was only one person to blame for this disaster and that was myself. I'd made so many mistakes, errors of judgment I couldn't take back, couldn't erase. The responsibility rested squarely at my own two feet. If I hadn't left Puckhaber when I did, if I'd stayed in Montana – maybe we'd still be together. Or would Lucas have come to this decision regardless of the decision I'd made? Had he really only been with me because of my blood? It had the taste of truth, I knew how he'd struggled with bloodlust around me. Maybe tasting my blood had been enough to clear his mind of any lingering doubts. He'd even seemed relieved to admit how he felt. Ambrose's words came back to me – *'I thought he'd tired of his little pet'*. Was that all I'd ever been?

The sky was darkening outside, the light dimming as the sun lowered overhead. I had no idea how much time had passed and was ignoring the sounds of movement outside the tent, until Conal popped his head through the small flap. "Sugar, are you asleep?"

"No." I sat up in the sleeping bag, pushing my hair back from my face. "What's up?"

Conal slipped inside the tent and sat cross-legged on the floor. "I was going to ask you the same question. What's up between you and Lucas? Why the decision for Ben to go on the search for Zaen tomorrow? Lucas says he's not going, says Ben's taking his place."

I sighed. "I tried to talk to Lucas earlier. It didn't go well and I guess] he's decided against being around me for now."

Conal gazed at me, his expression thoughtful. "May I ask what you talked about?"

"Nothing that was helpful," I responded morosely. Inhaling sharply, I let the air exhale through my nose. "Marianne spoke to me earlier, made me see I wasn't being fair to you or Lucas. I guess she made me admit to myself that even though I love you, my emotions for Lucas are stronger." I peeked up at him anxiously, worried about his reaction. "I love him, Conal. I belong with him, but when I tried to tell him that," I choked back a sob. "He told me he doesn't want me."

"What did you say to him?"

"I told him I was sorry and that I'd been unfair to him and you."

Conal gazed at me for a long while, black eyes solemn. "Sugar, you know he's only saying that because he wants to make this easier for you, right?"

My breath caught in my throat. "What?"

"I'm betting he lied to you," Conal stated evenly.

I shook my head. "I don't understand."

Conal sighed, brushing his fingers through his hair. "Charlotte, you've made this much more complicated than it needed to be. Before Lucas got back, you'd made up your mind what you were going to do. I accepted that – I told you I accepted you were going back to him." He smiled, his eyes filled with warmth. "I love you, Charlotte, but I've always known you love him more. I think Lucas heard you say you hadn't been fair to either him or me, and he decided to let you off the hook. He told me a couple of weeks ago that he would do whatever it took to make you happy. He said if he thought I was the better choice for you, he would give you up. I'm guessing he thought you were trying to make a decision, and by telling you he didn't want you – it was his way of stepping out of the picture."

"I didn't want to ever hurt either one of you." Tears welled against my eyelashes.

Conal caught my hand in his. "Charlotte, this was inevitable. You will go back to him, you were always going back to him. I knew that. You and him, the relationship you have is almost symbiotic. He can't live without you and you can't live without him." He brushed his thumb across my cheek, rubbing the tears away. "I told you before, I will always be here for you. Always. You're my best friend." He leaned forward, pressing a tender kiss against my lips. "You need him, Sugar, you always have. He completes you." He got to his knees and crawled towards the tent flap. "Go and find him, Charlotte. When I saw him an hour ago, he was devastated. Talk to him and get this sorted out, so we can get on with doing what we need to do." He slipped out through the flap and left me alone with my thoughts.

I stared after him, long after he'd disappeared, thinking through what he'd said. In a sudden burst of frenetic energy, I slipped on my boots and crawled out of the tent. I walked through the camp, trying to see Lucas amongst the crowds of people who were sharing this area of the forest. I stopped at Epi's tent and found the old man, Ben and Rowena sitting around the table. "Do you know where Lucas is?"

"I believe he's going for a walk, he head out towards the south an hour or so ago," Rowena explained. "But Charlotte…"

"I'll be back later, we'll talk then," I promised, hurriedly turning and heading off at a jog towards the south. Leaving behind the tents and detritus of our encampment, I entered the forest, finding the tranquility a sharp contrast to the hustle and bustle of our tent city. Slowing down to walking pace, I inhaled the scent of the trees overhead, listened to the rustle of the leaves beneath my feet as I wandered. This would be easier if I had vampire abilities but I was confident I'd run across him eventually.

Lucas. With that one word, my stress fell away. Conal was right, I belonged with Lucas and always had. He was the one I wanted to be with. Conal had promised I wouldn't lose him and I had to believe that. He would always be my friend and a surge of hope rose in my chest. This had always been the way it should be, it had just taken a while for me to figure it out.

Shock

I walked further into the dense woodland, so deep that no sound penetrated, the only noise coming from the soft whisper of leaves rustling overhead. I stopped walking, listening for any sound in the forest with me. Closing my eyes, I processed the miniscule sounds that reached my ears, until I picked up the softest murmur of a voice. I listened carefully until I could be confident of the direction, then set off, my feet muffled by the heavy growth of moss underfoot. I walked for maybe another ten minutes and the closer I got, the more clear the murmur of two distinct voices became. Lucas must have brought someone with him, I thought, as I twisted and turned on the makeshift path. It didn't matter who it was - I'd ask them to give Lucas and I some privacy so we could discuss our relationship and sort out the confusion between us.

Stepping out from behind a cluster of thick-trunked trees, I came to an abrupt halt, the breath leaving my lungs in a sudden, shocked exhale.

Lucas was standing beside a huge tree, his shirt casually discarded on the mossy ground. Bare-chested, he had Jennifer from Thut's Kiss wrapped tightly in his arms. He was kissing her and she was returning the kiss just as passionately, with her arms draped around his neck. I watched in fascinated horror as Jennifer's fingers entwined in his hair and Lucas traced his fingers down her back until he caught her lush backside in his hands and pulled her hard against his body.

I squeezed my eyes shut, fighting a rush of queasiness which threatened to have me gagging. This was the last thing I'd anticipated and I froze, hoping when I opened my eyes again, it would all be a really, *really* bad dream.

Regrettably, nothing had improved when I did force my eyes open and I stumbled backwards, desperate to escape. My foot caught a branch lying on the ground and it snapped loudly beneath my boot. Lucas and Jennifer instantly turned as one to where I stood, their eyes wide at my unexpected appearance.

Lucas extricated himself from Jennifer's arms and she smiled easily, not the slightest bit embarrassed. "Forgive us, Charlotte. We thought we were alone out here."

I watched as she did up the buttons on her shirt, casually concealing the lacy black bra which had been exposed. Lucas's focus remained on me, his blue eyes filled with anger, but his face remained expressionless. He turned to Jennifer, murmuring something against her ear and she raised her hand to his cheek. Pressing a gentle kiss against his lips, she offered him a warm smile.

It was more than I could endure and I turned away. With an embarrassed flush creeping over my skin, I lurched through the trees and began to run, ignoring the pain of branches slapping across my skin as I trampled blindly through the forest. My only need was to get as far away from Lucas and Jennifer as possible and to nurse my badly broken heart.

Chapter 16

Distress and Desire

Dashing through the woods, I didn't consider where I was going or what to do next. My breathing was ragged, my lungs laboring painfully as I struggled through the darkening woods, oblivious to everything but the need to escape what I'd witnessed. Hot tears ran down my cheeks and I stumbled against a gnarled tree root, crashing heavily onto the mossy ground. Wrenching angrily to my feet, I was intent on putting more space between myself and Lucas when I felt his cool hand grab my arm and he spun me roughly around to face him.

"Charlotte, stop!" He gripped both my arms with his hands and I moaned, pummeling my fists against his chest.

"Let me go, *let me go*!" I shrieked, fragile emotions rapidly escalating into cold-blooded fury. The vision of him kissing Jennifer flew across my thoughts again and I struggled harder to escape his clutches.

"No. I will not let you go until you calm down and talk to me," he responded, gripping my arms more firmly. "Stop this, Charlotte."

I continued to beat against him, hurting my fists as I struck futilely against his solid chest. "*No!* I don't want to talk to you. Go back to *Jennifer*!"

"Charlotte – what the hell are you doing out here?" His voice was icy, his anger making the silver in his eyes flash like lightning strikes.

"I came to find you. Conal said you lied about not loving me, says you were trying to make this easier for me and pushed me away so I could choose him." I glared at him, my eyes every bit as icy as his voice had been. "Apparently, he got it all wrong. You looked like you were doing just fine with *Jennifer*." I spat her name out furiously, the rage and resentment flowing through my veins like a fast-acting poison.

For a minute, Lucas continued to grip my arms and his eyes burnt into mine, but I held my head high, staring back angrily. "Charlotte, the whole world doesn't revolve around you, for Christ's sake!" My eyes widened at the harshness of his tone as he continued. "What did you expect me to do? I thought I was doing the right thing by telling you I didn't want you. You were so damned confused about how you felt, I thought it would be easier for you if I took myself out of the equation. So that you could be with Conal if that's what you wanted!"

"I don't want Conal! I came out here to tell you I wanted *you*! That's what I was trying to tell you back at the tent. But I never dreamed you would move on quite so *rapidly*!"

Lucas suddenly released my arms and turned away, rubbing his hands roughly across his face. "It didn't take *you* long to move on! Why should the rules be any different for me? He turned back to face me, the muscle in his jaw trembling beneath the skin in his rage. "Charlotte, you started this! *You* were the one who moved on first. You left *me*, remember? And you've admitted yourself, you've been sleeping with Conal for the past three months!" His eyes were a maelstrom of silver lightning strikes and I could see my tear-ravaged face reflected in them as he continued to yell. "Do you think that makes me feel any different than you do now, when you've caught me kissing Jennifer?"

"At least you didn't see me kissing Conal!" I yelled.

"I didn't need to! *Christ*, Charlotte! You honestly think I haven't thought about him kissing you for the past four weeks? I can't get it out of my mind! I've wanted to kill him, knowing he's been in your bed, held you against his body, as I've wanted to do all this time!"

I watched him warily, my breath coming in short, sharp bursts. "Were you going to have sex with her?" I demanded suddenly.

His eyes narrowed and he frowned down at me. "What if I was, Charlotte? You left *me*! You have no right, *no right at all* to judge me on what I was or wasn't going to do with Jennifer! We're two consenting adults. It's none of your business, who I decide to have sex with!"

I bit my lip, teeth pressing hard against my skin. "Why?" I moaned. "Why would you hold back from me for so long and yet you'd give yourself to her without a second thought?"

Distress and Desire

His shoulders slumped dejectedly. "You know why. She's vampire, as I am. I don't have to be careful with Jennifer, like I did with you."

Against my will, I recollected him kissing Jennifer and knew without doubt that if I hadn't turned up, he would have been having sex with her now. The image of her full breasts revealed in the lacy black bra was seared into my memory. "This is exactly why I was so confused about my feelings for you and Conal!" I spluttered furiously.

"*What?*" He stared down at me incredulously.

"I *love* you! I love you with all my heart, but I need the passion, not just the strength and decency! That's what Conal gives me, what I wasn't getting from you! Anger and arguments, passion and lust – he kissed me as though..." I stopped abruptly, horrified by my admission and the anger seeped from my body like water draining from a bathtub.

"He kissed you as though he'd never stop," Lucas finished the sentence, his voice lifeless. "He can do that, Charlotte, because he poses no danger to you."

"Don't you get it, Lucas? When you kissed me, you were always holding something back, always thinking about what you were doing. You don't touch me and kiss me as though it's the only thing in the world that matters. You're always so... *restrained!*"

"Because I *have* to be!" Abruptly he was livid, his eyes flashing under the moonlight. "Yes, I lied earlier! I lied about everything! Because I desire you more than you can possibly imagine! You think I don't want to hold you so tightly against me that I can feel every facet of your skin against mine? You think I don't want to kiss you deeply, as I know you've kissed him? To have my mouth and body invade yours, to run my lips over your skin, to feel the absolute exquisiteness of plunging myself inside you, making love to you over and over again?" He watched me ruefully. "Charlotte, I want everything, I want to make love to you and I think about it every minute of every single damn day. God knows I would like to lose control and do everything I've dreamed of with you. I hate the fact he's been in your bed, he's touched you and held your body against his. It kills me to know he's had what I've always wanted. But I *have* to keep control, you know that!"

We stood for a minute, both breathing heavily and watching one another. "I want you to lose control," I announced quietly.

"Don't you think I want to?" he yelled. "I *can't*, Charlotte! I drank your blood in Sfantu Drâghici and it was the most exquisite thing I've ever tasted! The scent of you as we stand here, *everything* about it makes me want to pull you into my arms, to put my fangs against your perfect neck and bite, to have your blood fill my mouth and my senses..." He looked aghast by what he'd admitted, his eyes filling with horror.

"But you stopped! When I asked you to – *you stopped.* You can control this, Lucas, you did that day, when your thirst was as extreme as it could ever be! With my blood already in your body, it will protect me. You won't bite me. It will stop you from biting me." Frustration filled my voice as I told him what he needed to hear. "If you really love me, you'll do this. Don't hold back. Kiss me and make me forget about him. Prove to me that you want me, as much as I've always wanted you!"

He stared at me, blue eyes flashing dangerously and I thought for a moment he would back off and refuse. It took my breath away when he grabbed me, roughly pulling me into his arms and kissed me instead. His lips were cold and hard against mine and he pulled at the bottom of my tank top, yanking it up and ripping it from my body before he continued the kiss. He ran his tongue across my lips, forcing his way into my mouth while his fingers felt their own way, undoing the satin bra I wore. He released the clasp and tore the slip of material from my chest, rubbing his cool thumbs across my nipples, making them swell with need. My knees gave way and Lucas caught me up in his arms, dropping to his knees on the ground and laying me back against the cool moss. He raked his eyes over my naked chest before he tore his own shirt from his back and dropped over the top of me, his hands on either side of my body to hold him up.

"You can't possibly believe this isn't what I've wanted to do since the day I met you," he muttered hoarsely against my throat, before trailing kisses down my neck and chest. His lips closed around one nipple and I arched upward as he suckled against me, pulling on an invisible cord which tightened parts further down my body. "This is all I've thought of, I want to feel you, touch you. All I've thought about is you. How incredibly beautiful you are, and that I've wanted you," his eyes trailed a burning path across my skin, from my face down to my breasts, "as only a man can want a woman." In a brief instant he dropped gently on top of me, his hard chest pressed against my breasts, his mouth invading mine and I gave in to the feel of his skin against me, rubbing across the tensed muscles in his back and relishing the hardness between his legs which pressed against my groin. Lucas rained kisses against my skin. "I *love* you, Charlotte," he groaned against my mouth. "I have always loved you and I will *always* love you."

I drew a ragged breath and held him tightly. "I love you too," I whispered softly. "But I don't want to do this."

He drew away until he lay at my side, gazing down upon me. "What's wrong?"

I sat up, covering my breasts with my arms. "I love you, Lucas, I love you with all my heart, but I'm not ready to do this. Not here and not now." I reached for the bra, slipping it on and doing up the clasp, then wrenched the tank top back over my head.

He was frowning when I looked up, his dark eyebrows closing in on one another and I reached out to touch his cheek, watching him as he closed his eyes and breathed deeply against my wrist. "Are you punishing me for what happened with Jennifer?"

I shook my head and smiled weakly. "No, not at all. But I've dreamed about being with you for so long and," I glanced around the rapidly darkening forest, "this is not how I imagined it."

Lucas pulled himself upright and sat opposite me, his glorious physique making me sigh inwardly for what I was missing out on. "I see. How exactly did you imagine it?" he asked huskily. He caught me in his arms and drew me towards him, nestling me against his chest as he encircled me within his arms.

"I never imagined making love with you straight after seeing you kissing another woman," I admitted quietly.

He played with the curls against my neck, trailing his fingers across my shoulder. "It was an experiment," he admitted in a low voice. "Jennifer knows how I feel about you, knew how destroyed I was, thinking I'd lost you forever. You know how much she loves men and she wanted to help, to see if she could make me forget about you." He leaned forward, kissing my neck softly and I shivered in the cool evening air.

"Have you slept with her before?"

Lucas looked startled, a frown creasing his forehead. He considered the question for a long moment, before answering truthfully. "Yes. Jennifer and I have come together at times in the past. We've never had a truly romantic relationship, I guess you could call what we had, 'friends with benefits'."

"Oh." We lapsed into silence and Lucas toyed with my hair, waiting patiently for me to consider his answer.

"Was it working?"

"What?" Again he looked startled and he stared down at me seriously, one eyebrow raised in question.

"Forgetting about me."

Lucas turned my chin so he could look into my eyes. "Not in the slightest. All I could think about was the fact that it *wasn't* you." He sighed heavily. "I was trying hard to convince myself I could be with another woman, but all its proven is that you are the only woman I will ever want." He kissed me, biting my lower lip gently. "You are everything I have ever wanted."

"I promise you," I smiled softly, wrapping my fingers around his strong jaw, "we will make love. Just not right here and right now."

Lucas lifted me away from him and stood in one graceful movement. Reaching for his shirt he slipped it on, before pulling me up into his arms. "I will hold you to that, my love."

Chapter 17

The Hunt for Zaen

I was sitting high on the hill overlooking the encampment when Lucas located me the following morning. From this vantage point I'd been able to observe the camp being dismantled and Epi creating the portal to take our people to safety. I'd chosen this spot specifically, knowing it was far enough away to prevent accidentally overhearing their destination. I'd walked up just before dawn and settled on a low smooth rock to watch the sun rise.

Arriving back at camp last night, the Tines had been absolutely delighted when they realized Lucas and I were reunited. Rowena had alternated between the horror of knowing Jennifer and Lucas had gone out into the woods together and being unable to stop me from following them, to absolute joy in knowing we'd sorted out our differences. There had been hugs and handshakes all around. Even Epi grinned with delight, although he'd taken the opportunity to grumble about how I was supposed to be sleeping, not roaming through the surrounding forest looking for Lucas.

Conal approached after we'd talked to the Tines, kissing my cheek tenderly and shaking Lucas's hand. "Look after her," he'd warned Lucas. "If you hurt her, I swear I'll kill you."

"Duly noted," Lucas responded.

It had been awkward when Thut and Jennifer approached. "You are a very lucky woman, Charlotte," Jennifer had said. "He loves you as he will never love anyone else." She'd turned her attention to Lucas, smiling warmly at him. "I'm so very happy you've found one another again." And then she'd whirled away with Thut, offering us a last, stunning smile before she left.

Lucas joined me when I finally returned to the tent to get some much-needed sleep. We lay together in the small space, rediscovering one another and talking more naturally than at any time in the past few weeks. The combination of the sleeping tablets and being in Lucas's arms ensured the first solid night's sleep I'd enjoyed in weeks.

For the past half hour or so, I'd been marking my arms in preparation for our journey to locate Zaen. I was completing the last of them as Lucas strode up the hill toward me.

"I will never get used to that," he remarked quietly as he watched me creating the intricate pattern of the agility sigil on my left shoulder. "To think they appear on your skin so boldly and then disappear is truly extraordinary."

I slipped the Hjördis in my pocket and stood up. "As extraordinary as me being an angel?"

"I knew from the minute I met you that you were extraordinary, Charlotte. Being an angel has absolutely nothing to do with it." He wrapped his arms around my waist and drew me against him, kissing me while his hands roamed lightly across my back.

When he released me, Lucas caught my hand in his and we walked back to the abandoned camp, where the others were waiting for us. It had been agreed when we returned last night that Ben would still accompany us on the trip this morning, despite Lucas rejoining the group.

Epi had erased the pentagram by the time we approached and had his backpack slung across his shoulders. "Ah, you are already prepared, child," he said, eyeing the indigo sigils which emblazoned both my arms, shoulders and upper chest. "Very good, very good indeed."

I stared at Epi, subduing the desire to laugh. He'd discarded his standard attire of tunic and trousers for camouflage pants, black lace-up boots and a black t-shirt, the same uniform all the men had adopted for reconnaissance and training. On the other men, it looked both sexy and kind of militarist. Against Epi's bald head, wizened face and large glasses, it looked completely bizarre. "Now you need to mark the sigils on us," he stated.

Conal groaned and tore his t-shirt over his head. "Crap. I hate this bit."

"Not as much as I do," I muttered as I retrieved the Hjördis and began marking sigils on Conal's tanned arm.

"Come on, Sugar, you love it. All women like making men suffer." Conal's voice was teasing, but the agony was clear in his eyes as the Hjördis burnt the sigils onto his skin. I worked as quickly as I could, wanting it to be over.

"Lott should get a job in a tattoo shop after we defeat the Consiliului," Nick suggested as I marked his skin. "You'd get a job easy."

"Yeah, right," I muttered, completing the agility sigil and starting on stamina. "I'm sure everyone would want a set of bright blue sigils."

Epi held out his arms when I'd finished with Nick and I grimaced. "Epi, do you really think you need sigils?" I questioned gently, not wanting to hurt his feelings. "You've never had them before."

"I have indeed, Charlotte." He pointed to the wing on his shoulder, so similar to my own birthmark, but defiantly black even after centuries. "Now get on with it, child. We're burning daylight."

"Excuse me?" The old man never spoke in modernisms and I stared at him in astonishment.

"It's one of Conal's expressions," Nick explained with a grin. "Epi likes to think he's cool."

I drew the sigils for agility, endurance and strength on Epi's arm and he admired the marks cheerfully. "I really don't understand why you young bucks complain so much," he goaded the others. "It doesn't hurt that much."

"Only because you're so old," Conal grumbled sourly. "Half your body died years ago and you just haven't noticed." His mood was erratic this morning, which I put down to Lucas and I being back together. It hurt my heart to know he was unhappy, but I hoped with time he would come to terms with the changes in our relationship.

Ben stood before me, his t-shirt discarded in readiness and I worked on his muscled bicep, biting my lip when I saw him wince more than once. "I'm so sorry, Ben."

"Don't apologize, Charlotte. You're only doing what you need to do," Ben reassured me, pulling his shirt back on when I'd finished.

Lucas obligingly pulled his t-shirt off, gripping it one hand and holding his other arm out towards me. I shook my head minutely, remembering his kisses last night and a flutter of desire tingled low in my body as I gazed at his naked chest. I caught his wrist in my hand and began to draw an agility sigil high on his shoulder, concentrating hard on his arm so I wouldn't see the pain in his eyes.

"Why do you always do that, my love?" he whispered against my ear.

"What?"

"When you see my chest – you always suck in a little breath," he murmured. "It's very endearing."

I met his eyes and saw the desire I felt mirrored. "Could it be because you're absolutely perfect in every way," I whispered back. "And I think you're incredibly, gloriously sexy."

"Nearly finished?" Conal growled.

Lucas allowed himself a tiny smug smile and I turned back to his arm, working swiftly to complete the sigils. I hated doing this to them, loathed the acrid smell of burning flesh when the Hjördis burnt the sigils onto their skin. Lucas stood patiently as I completed the marks, muscles clenching tightly in his arm. When I finished he flexed his arm before slipping his t-shirt on.

"Okay, let's do this," Lucas announced.

I knelt to create a pentagram on the flattened grass, calling on the spirits for assistance. I recalled the image of our destination from my memory and waited patiently whilst the sigils appeared in my mind, one after the other. As I'd suspected, not one of them were ones I'd used before and I turned back to the pentagram, marking the five corners. When I'd completed the fifth sigil, I got to my feet and watched as it glowed and brilliant shafts of pure white light erupted from the circular centre.

"Well, that's different," Nick remarked quietly. "What happened to the gold light?"

"It doesn't matter," Epi rebuked. "What matters is whether it takes us to Zaen."

I tucked the Hjördis into my pocket and was about to step through the portal when Lucas caught my arm in a vice-like grip. "Conal and I will go first, Charlotte. We don't know what's through there and the differences in the portal are enough to concern me."

The two men stepped through the portal together and disappeared. Nick followed a second later, throwing me a wink before Ben strode through after him.

"Ready to go, child?' Epi asked, picking up his rucksack and throwing it onto his stooped shoulder.

The old man and I walked into the shimmering white light together. This portal was different, the shimmering patterns of light surrounding us during the journey brighter, more psychedelic in their nature and the intensity was blinding. As we stepped out at the other end I was violently ill and fell to

The Hunt for Zaen

the ground, retching onto the dirt. Lucas held my hair back from my face and rubbed my back tenderly as I emptied my stomach. Wiping my hand over my mouth shakily, I was grateful when Conal handed me a water bottle. "Portal travel isn't good for you, Sugar."

"I definitely prefer cars," I agreed mildly. Wiping a clammy hand over my face, I sat on the ground and sipped the water until the nausea subsided. When I felt a little better, Lucas helped me onto my feet.

"Looks like we're out of luck, Sugar," Conal remarked.

I blinked and shook my head, unable to understand why he was suggesting we were out of luck when just fifteen feet away was the massive wall of Zaen? It was shining in the early morning sunlight, sheer granite walls more than thirty feet tall circled off into the distance. Gold and green grasses swayed gently and grew to the very edges of the wall, providing a bright color contrast against the glistening white stone. To our right, a colossal wooden gate was inset into the rock, bound together with thick bands of iron, it curved upwards into an arched point. Over the top of the doorway, writing was carved into the granite and sigils appeared in neat rows down either side of the gate.

"We might as well portal back," Nick announced in disgust.

"Charlotte?" Ben placed a hand on my shoulder, the gesture meant to be soothing. "I know you must be disappointed."

I shrugged his hand away and took a few steps towards Zaen, turning back to look at them in frustration. I knew my eyes were filled with a combination of excitement and confusion. "It's here!" I waved my hand towards the massive structure. What I'd seen in my visions - it was *exactly* what I could see only feet away from where we currently stood. There was a stone pathway leading from the gates and it disappeared in the far distance. On either side of the path, a flat plain of land spread for miles, covered in the green and gold grass which swayed in the gentle breeze. I could see the path led to a thicket of ancient forest, spreading across the horizon, a dark green blur of trees which rose towards the blue sky overhead.

"Sugar, there's nothing here," Conal insisted. His dark eyes filled with concern, as if he truly believed I was hallucinating.

"Lucas, surely you can see this," I pleaded. "Zaen – it's right there!"

Lucas focused where I was pointing, but it was clear from the look on his face that he couldn't see a thing. It was the same with Epi, Nick and Ben – they were all staring at me as if I was mad. I inhaled deeply, aggravated that we'd reached what I was certain would be a safe haven – but only I could see it. In frustration I picked up a stone, took aim and threw it towards the sparkling white granite.

The rock spun towards the wall and a curious thing happened. In the split second when it hit the granite, a flash of white light erupted from the wall, brighter than a stroke of lightning.

The rock ricocheted back towards our group, Nick ducking for cover as it sped past him, narrowly missing his head.

"Okay. That was kind of weird," Conal remarked slowly. Rubbing the back of his neck, he stared at where the stone had hit the wall.

"It appears Charlotte is correct," Epi announced. "Zaen is there. However, only she can see it."

"Gee, thanks for the rousing endorsement," I responded in tone leaning heavily towards sarcasm.

"Angel blood," Ben announced. "She can see it because of her blood."

"And we cannot, because we have demon blood within us," Epi added. "Yes, that must be it!" He turned to Nick. "Shape shifters are an anomaly, contrary to the normal workings of the supernatural. You cannot see it?"

"An anomaly, huh?" Nick turned in the direction the rock had bounced from and stared intensely for a minute. "Nope, can't see a thing."

"Concentrate, Nick," I urged. "Try and think beyond what you believe to be true and try and visualize what you think should be there. Look for a wall."

Nick stared at the space again, narrowing his eyes. "Okay. I can see… sort of… glimpses of something. Like it's appearing and disappearing behind a thick fog." He turned to Conal and Lucas. "It's there. Lott's right."

"Of course I'm right," I grumbled, walking towards the gate with the intention of trying to get in. Running my fingers across the white stone, it was almost perfectly smooth with no signs of visible tool marks. Each massive block met the next in near-perfect accuracy. There was nothing to suggest the wall wasn't created from one immense piece of solid stone and I ran my fingertips across the sigils, trying to discover a way inside.

"It's not going to be much use if we can't see it," Conal said, watching as I ran my fingers across the invisible-to-him wall. "And it's certainly useless if we can't get in."

"Shut up," I grumbled.

"Describe what you can see, Charlotte," Lucas urged.

I told them about the walls, how tall they were and the heavy wooden gates which stood to my right as I continued to study the sigils. "There's writing over the top of the gates. I think it's foreign, I can't understand it."

"Try to pronounce it and I might be able to translate," Epi suggested. He'd sat cross-legged on the ground a few feet from the gate and was digging through the rucksack, pulling out books and laying them in a neat semi-circle around his legs.

"*Permissum totus question templum ostendo suum famulatus ut Nememiah pro ingressus*," I stumbled over the words, struggling with the pronunciation.

"You won't need the books, Epi," Lucas announced with certainty. "It's Latin. It says 'Let all seeking sanctuary show their allegiance to Nememiah before entering.' "

I stared at him, one eyebrow arched questioningly. "You understand Latin?"

Lucas glanced down at me and smiled. "You can learn a lot of languages in one hundred and fifty years."

"Looks like we've come to the right place, Lott," Nick agreed. He was hovering beside Epi, his lean body a bundle of nervous energy. "How're we going to get inside?"

I frowned, running my hands over the sigils on either side of the wall again. I stepped backwards to study both sides of the gate, trying to find something – anything which would give me a clue. With a little distance, I realized one sigil was missing on the right side of the gate. I stepped forward, studying the blank stone carefully, searching for any kind of clue as to why this one part of the stone was devoid of a marking. I placed my palm flat against the stone where I thought the sigil should have been. A flash of light traced around my outstretched hand and the stone trembled beneath my skin before white light blinded me.

Chapter 18

Nememiah Revealed

Opening my eyes, I blinked uncertainly in the stark whiteness surrounding me. The ground was cold and hard and I struggled upright, perturbed to discover I'd been lying on a stone floor. Where was I? My head was throbbing and nausea churned in my stomach. One second I'd been standing outside the gates of Zaen but when I'd put my hand against the stone wall... well, whatever had happened it seemed I'd been transported here. Wherever *here* might be. I contemplated the surroundings cautiously but there was nothing to see, no deviation from white. Overhead, all around was the same monotonous whiteness. There was no sound, only the noise of my erratic breathing to alleviate the profound and disorientating nothingness.

"Why do you seek entrance to Zaen?"

My breath caught in my throat and I jerked onto my feet, instinctively reaching for the Katchet.

"You do not need weapons here, child." The voice echoed around the expanse and was serene. The timbre of the decidedly male tone was soothing to my ears and I relaxed incrementally until I realized what was happening and tensed up again, wary of the voice's owner despite how nonviolent he might sound.

I rotated in a slow circle, searching the horizon until I saw him. Or perhaps *it*? I blinked, trying to comprehend what was gliding towards me and fighting the urge to flee. As it came closer the shape became distinguishable, with the body and form of a man, draped in luminous white robes. Much taller than any human man I'd ever met. Feathered wings protruded from his shoulder blades and his face was perfectly formed with pale skin, brilliant green eyes and long blonde hair, so fair it blended in with the surroundings. As he gazed down upon me, I came to the staggering realization that this was an honest-to-God angel. Was he Nememiah?

"Yes, child, I am Nememiah. Maker and protector of Nememiah's Children. They begat from me and carry my blood." He glided slowly, coming to a halt opposite me. He had to be fifteen feet tall and as he stared, a sensation of immense peace trickled through my limbs, as if my bloodstream was filled with a calming analgesic. An overwhelming urge to touch the magnificent arc of feathered wing overcame me, but I tamped it down, clenching my hands into fists. "You carry the weapons of Nememiah's Children and I see the mark upon you, distinguishing you as my child. Yet, you are but a child yourself. Why do you seek entrance to Zaen?"

Opening my mouth to respond, I saw him lift a finger to his lips, silencing me. "There is no need to use voice here, child. I can hear you without spoken words, using only your mind." I realized his mouth wasn't moving when he spoke, yet his voice was somehow being projected into my head. He extended one arm, touching his index finger to my forehead. The touch was warm against my skin, but not unpleasantly so – then realized that he was drawing everything he wanted from my mind, as if we were watching a movie together. He began in my childhood, watching me and Mom, what happened when Mom met Pete, the violence and the murders. I cringed when he watched me murder Pete, aware that he was seeing exactly what had happened. Would he strike me down because of what I'd done? He remained impassive as he watched two years of endless travels before I met Lucas and his friends. He saw the kidnapping by Armstrong and my time with Conal, kissing him as he licked my wounds. We flashed forward to Lucas and I at the top of the mountain, Lucas's kisses and holding me against him as though he would never willingly let go. Then Holden running towards me, Striker, William and Lucas converging in an attempt to stop the catastrophe which was imminent and the wave of power I'd thrown out towards the vampires. I watched myself sobbing incessantly when I'd left Puckhaber and lying on a bed in a hotel room, having fallen into an exhausted sleep. He continued to fast forward through my life, every single second of my existence in the past twelve months rushing through my mind at a dizzying pace. When we reached the point where I'd touch the wall of Zaen, he removed his finger from my forehead and I slumped to the floor, devoid of energy.

Nememiah glided away, moving smoothly across the floor as though he didn't rely on feet to transport himself. He turned back, green eyes speculative. "You are indeed my child. But you bring with you to Zaen others of the supernatural world. They cannot seek sanctuary in my city, it is only for children of my blood to take refuge. They must leave."

"*No!*" The word erupted from my lips before I could think and Nememiah stared at me, eyes narrowed. I attempted to explain the situation. "You've seen what we're facing. You've seen what the Drâghici Consiliului intend to do. My friends must be able to enter Zaen with me, I need their help to defeat this threat and they need somewhere safe to live."

Nememiah was thoughtful for a long time and I watched him anxiously. "It is true, this is a most unusual situation," he finally admitted. "The Children of Nememiah were put on this earth by my hand a millennia ago to provide guidance and leadership to the very creatures you now align yourself with. And yet, my Children fought amongst themselves in their fervent desire, their very human yearning, for power and control. Perhaps it was erroneous to give my blood to create a new generation." He turned and glided across the floor, moving back and forth as I watched. He appeared to be pacing, without his feet ever touching the floor. Of course, in the long white robe, I couldn't see his feet, so I wasn't even certain he had any. When he finally stopped, he directed his intense gaze back at me. "The placing of you and the other one was an error on my part. I can foretell of future events and could see a time when my Children would be needed to keep the Earth at peace. It was not forecast for me upon the stars that the very reason I created you would become a motive for others to seek your power."

It was like he was talking in riddles and I found the courage to say so. "Please explain what you mean. I don't understand."

"There are events which will come to pass in the future – for which Nememiah's Children will be needed. You and the other one were pre-destined to join with each other and copulate, to create a new generation of my Children. The events I prepare for are centuries into the future." He brushed his fingers across his jaw thoughtfully. "Your power and abilities have matured far earlier than I had envisaged, purely through the choices you have made and the desires of other supernaturals who seek power for their advantage."

Digesting his words for a few minutes, I tried to analyze the meaning. Was he saying I wasn't meant to use my powers? Perhaps I'd only ever been meant to have mild psychic ability but what I'd gotten involved in, who I'd gotten involved *with* had changed all that. It was utterly creepy to think I was supposed to meet Archangelo and have children who would be pure angels. Now Nememiah's plan had been blown out of the water with Archangelo on the dark side and myself on the light.

"That is correct, child," Archangelo announced. "This was indeed an error and I must now repair the damage I have created." He lifted his right arm and I cowered, frightened of his intentions.

"*Wait!*" He lowered his arm slowly and I spoke hastily, certain he was going to kill me if I couldn't convince him there was another way. "Epi says you created Nememiah's Children from your blood and their purpose was to keep the Earth free of demons and keep order amongst the supernatural."

He remained silent, hovering impassively, his entire face so expressionless it might have been carved from marble.

"It went wrong though – Nememiah's Children fought amongst themselves and it became a battle for supremacy and control over the supernaturals. They killed the demons, but they considered themselves superior beings to the other supernatural creatures, didn't they? And they fought over the amount of control to administer over those they were meant to protect. Not unlike what the Consiliului are doing now. It's all about control."

"What is your point, child?"

"I'm the only pure Nememiah's child now. Archangelo has been created as vampire and he's tainted with demon blood." It was my turn to pace, pondering what I was trying to explain, trying to ignore the trickle of fear in my chest as I imagined what he'd do if I didn't convince him. "What if... what if your plan was flawed from the beginning?"

Yikes, that was probably a really, *really* bad thing to say to an angel. You probably weren't meant tell an angel his plan was flawed... ever. I expected a bolt of lightning to strike me dead any second now. I chewed my lip anxiously, wiping my clammy hands on my pants.

"Go ahead, child. I do not dispense death with bolts of lightning. I am still listening."

"What if... What if Nememiah's Children shouldn't be leading everyone? What if this should have been a democracy from the beginning? You said yourself, Nememiah's Children were tainted because they considered themselves superior. Shouldn't the supernaturals be treated as equals to Nememiah's Children? They should be allowed to unite together to create harmony and understanding amongst one another. That's what I've been doing with my friends; we work together for the greater good of everyone and to fight against others who would threaten those they consider inferior to themselves."

"And yet you have seen for yourself the suspicion and hatred amongst them. They need leadership."

"They need guidance, not leadership. They need a path to follow." My eyes brightened with sudden understanding. "Let me try this. Allow my friends permission to enter Zaen and give us safe haven. Give us the opportunity to try and fix this problem."

I lapsed into a wary silence, not certain he would agree to the request. Unexpectedly, he nodded his head. "I will give you what you ask for, child. You may attempt to bring these creatures together in harmony, but be warned. If I do not 'fix this' myself, by removing you and the other one, I will not become involved in how the situation resolves itself. I will caution you; the other one being created to vampire makes him stronger, more physically powerful than you can ever hope to be. Whilst you have the power of Angels behind you, he has the power of demons and vampire. Only one of you will survive in the end. Are you willing to take that chance? Are you willing to assume responsibility for future events?"

"Yes," I whispered fervently. "Thank you." He began to drift slowly away and I spoke rapidly. "Wait! How do I get my friends inside Zaen?"

He turned back and I could almost swear there was a smile quirking his lips. "Nothing worthwhile is ever easy, child. There are things you must deduce for yourself. I have given permission for the supernatural to enter Zaen – how to do so remains your task to discover. The Warlock Vander has the answer."

Chapter 19

Nememjah's Mark

The ground was hard beneath my back and warm lips were pressed to mine, blowing air into my open mouth when I came around for a second time. It took a couple of confused seconds to comprehend what was going on. One – I was back with my friends and two – it was Conal who was pressing his lips against mine.

Instinct kicked in and I curled my hand into a fist, slamming it into his jaw as I twisted away from him. "*What* are you doing!"

"Charlotte! Thank, God! We thought you were dead." Lucas drew me into his arms and onto his lap, his voice tense and I clung to him, trying to clear the confusion in my head. As he stroked my hair, I could feel a tremor in his hand.

Ben knelt beside us and ran his fingers across my forehead. "She seems fine," he reassured Lucas.

"*Shit*." Conal appeared, rubbing his jaw gingerly. "I was giving you CPR for Christ's sake! I wasn't kissing you." He grinned suddenly. "Admittedly, it was bringing back some really pleasant memories."

Lucas's low warning growl rumbled through his chest and I rubbed his cheek. "It's okay, Lucas. I'm all right now."

Epi was standing a few feet away, his eyes anxious and rubbing his hands together nervously. Behind him, Nick stood stock still, his arms wrapped around himself as though he was cold.

"What happened?" Lucas asked quietly. "You put your hand against the wall and then you collapsed. You weren't breathing, you didn't breathe for more than twenty minutes. You scared me to death."

"And that isn't easy, considering he's dead already," Conal agreed sarcastically.

I ignored Conal and explained my meeting with Nememiah to them, how I'd convinced him I could fix the mess we found ourselves in. I carefully left out the part where he'd said only Archangelo or myself could survive. It was information I need to think about and absorb for myself before I divulged it to anyone else. "He's given us permission to enter Zaen. Now all we have to do is figure out how."

"Well, on the bright side, we can all see Zaen now," Nick announced thoughtfully. "When you placed your hand on the wall, it appeared to all of us."

I extricated myself from Lucas's arms and stood up, surveying the heavy oak gates. "Well, I suppose it's a start. I'm guessing it's got something to do with keeping demon blood outside the walls, that's what will stop you from going in," I announced after some consideration. "I imagine I can walk straight in now, by placing my hand back on the wall again."

"Which you are most certainly *not* going to do," Lucas announced firmly. "Not until we can go in there with you. We still don't know what we'll find behind the gates." He grasped my hand in his, as if he half expected me to stroll over to the gates and march in immediately.

"Lucas, translate the message from the top of the gate again, please," Epi said.

"Let all seeking sanctuary show their allegiance to Nememiah before entering," Lucas read.

Epi settled himself cross-legged on the ground amongst his piles of books and began to search through them. Ben and Conal stood together studying the gate. "Charlotte, showing your allegiance is all fine and good, but are the gates meant to open on their own?" Conal questioned.

I sighed heavily. "Do I *look* like I have any idea?" Conal was already in my bad books for the kissing remark.

"Alright, while Epi is trawling through his books, let's try something," Conal announced abruptly. He strolled over to the gates and stood directly before them. "I hereby swear my allegiance to Nememiah." He touched the rough oak gate and instantly he was flung backwards through the air, landing heavily on the dirt some fifteen feet away.

"Conal!" I shrieked and sprinted towards him, Ben and Lucas right behind me. I dropped to the ground beside his collapsed form, rolling him over carefully. "Conal! *Conal!*" Ben pressed his fingers against Conal's neck, searching for a pulse and nodded, obviously relieved to locate it. Conal groaned and reached up to rub the back of his head gingerly with his fingers. "See, I knew you still cared about me, Sugar."

"Of course I care about you. Shut up, you idiot." I stood up hastily and stalked back towards the gate. I stared at the smooth blank spot in the row of sigils, quite positive this was part of the way to enter. The first time I'd been transported to wherever Nememiah called home, but I wanted to know what would happen if I pressed my palm against it a second time. Cautiously, I did just that.

The gates shimmered and vanished, leaving a tall arched opening. Stepping back, I peered through the darkened opening and saw it was a vaulted tunnel, running roughly fifteen feet long with the white granite on either side and overhead. It seemed that the length of the tunnel must directly relate to the thickness of the granite walls and they would provide a great amount of security for our people. Walls that thick would be difficult to breech. At the other end of the tunnel, I could glimpse a cobblestoned street and part of what looked like a small house.

"Why is it that you got all the cool powers?" Nick asked with a grin.

"Yeah, that's right, Nick. Because transforming into a wolf just isn't cool at all," I retorted, giving him a friendly shove. "Epi, I've got the gates open."

"So can we just walk in now?" Conal had limped back to where I stood, with Lucas and Ben beside him. "Or is this just Nememiah's way of teasing us?"

"Oh, I should imagine there's more to it," Epi agreed enthusiastically. "Nememiah's Children considered this a sanctuary. If anyone could break the gates down, presuming they could get past the initial enchantments, there must be more to keep them out."

Lucas was examining the words above the open gate. "I don't believe this relates to a verbal command," he said, pointing to the words. "*Permissum totus questio templum ostendo suum famulatus ut Nememiah pro ingressus* – it says *show* your allegiance. Not speak of allegiance."

Nick stepped towards the opening. "Well, you guys reckon I don't have any demon blood in me. Why don't I see if I can walk through? Then we'll know if it's the demon blood, or something else."

"Nick, I don't believe that's a good idea," Ben cautioned.

"What, don't think I'm as tough as the werewolf?" Nick challenged with a smirk. He took a step, his foot breaching the threshold of the gates and he too, was blasted backwards.

Nick was sitting up when I reached his side, inspecting his leg. His pants were torn and he'd grazed most of the skin off his calf and knee from sliding across the gravel. Lucas stood a discreet distance away, far enough to keep the scent of blood from reaching his nostrils. "Okay, so much for that idea. It isn't the demon blood," Nick announced with certainty.

"Ben did try to warn you," I retorted lightly, grabbing the Hjördis from my pocket to create a blood sigil. I stopped abruptly, staring at the Hjördis.

"Lott? What's up?" Nick asked curiously.

"I think I've got an idea." I hurriedly completed a sigil on his leg and Lucas helped him to his feet while I ran back to Epi, who was still immersed in his books. "Epi – the wing sigil you have on your shoulder. Who gave it to you?"

Impatience crossed his features as he glared at me for interrupting him. "I told you, child. It was marked upon me by the last of Nememiah's Children before the final battle we fought against the breakaway group."

"*Why* did he give it to you?"

"It marked me as a comrade to the Children of Nememiah, provided everyone with proof of my allegiance..." He stopped suddenly, his eyes drawn to the words over the gateway. "Of course! Of course! Well done, Charlotte, I believe you may have worked out the puzzle!" He leaped up and stared at the gateway, his fingers interlinked behind his head as he studied it. "That's it," he muttered to himself.

And he stepped through the gateway.

I held my breath, worried that if I was wrong, Epi was about to blasted from the doorway as Conal and Nick had been. But nothing happened. He stood inside the tunnel itself, grinning jubilantly.

Lucas and Nick reached my side and Lucas slipped his arm around my waist. "You've figured it out, then?" His voice was filled with amusement as he watched Epi performing a crazy little dance on the cobblestones lining the tunnel floor.

"It's the sigil on Epi's shoulder, it was marked by the Leader of Nememiah's Children during their final battle. It gives proof of his allegiance to Nememiah's Children," I explained, giggling at Epi's antics. Epi stepped back out through the open gateway and the giant gate re-materialized, cutting of access to Zaen.

"Oops," Epi said, staring despondently at the gates.

"It's okay, Epi. I think that's meant to happen," I called out. "Try opening it yourself. Place your hand on the blank spot in that row of sigils." Epi did as I suggested and sure enough the heavy gates shimmered and disappeared again. I was amused when Epi joyfully danced again, leaping around like a person... well... a person much younger than fifteen hundred years old.

Nick pulled off his t-shirt and turned so his back was towards me. "I'm guessing we're about to get another sigil."

"Nick, I'm pretty certain this one is permanent. Are you sure about this?" I warned him in a low voice.

"Of course it's permanent," Epi shouted gleefully. "It must be! The mark is designed for those who pledge their undying commitment to Nememiah's Children. It marks those of us willing to die for such a noble cause!"

"So if I mark this on him – will it work?"

"I believe so, but I must warn you, young man. You find the sigils being marked on your skin painful. They are nothing, nothing at all compared to the agony this one will cause. You must be very certain before you agree," Epi said, his manner abruptly becoming serious.

Nick met my eyes and smiled his encouragement, knowing how much I hated hurting any of them. "Don't listen to the old man, Lott. We know how he tends to exaggerate." He knelt on the ground, making it easier to reach his shoulder and I started to mark his skin with the sign of the wing. It was apparent that this mark was different to all the others when he cursed beneath his breath and the muscle in his back tensed as he clenched his hands into tight fists. By the time I'd completed the intricate wing, Nick was literally shaking with pain and my tears were dripping down his shoulder where I'd worked.

"I'm sorry, I'm so sorry!" I moaned when I'd finished.

Nick pulled me into his arms for a comforting hug, a surprise in itself because he wasn't usually demonstrative. While he and I had shared a rocky relationship to date, we'd settled into a polite affiliation since rescuing Lucas. He was so controlled, kept his emotions tightly in check under a cool veneer. Now though, he was hugging me gently and I wrapped my arms around his waist. "It's okay, Lott. You had to do it." He released his grip and pushed me away with a tender smile.

Conal approached, his shirt already removed and grasped in one hand. He turned his back to me and knelt down and I shook my head. "I can't," I whispered. "I can't do this to you." The scent of burnt flesh was still hanging in the air and I couldn't escape it.

"You can, Sugar. You have to," Conal announced firmly. "Besides, this'll give us an indication of whether we have traitors in our midst. If they won't take the mark, they aren't dedicated to the cause."

"Exactly!" Epi agreed cheerfully. He was in the process of collecting his copious books and shoving them back into the rucksack, oblivious to the trauma this was putting me through.

I wavered uncertainly, worrying about doing this to Conal, who I loved so much despite choosing Lucas. I'd made my decision, but it hadn't changed my feelings for Conal and I didn't want to physically hurt him, on top of the emotional pain I'd created yesterday.

"Hey, guess what? This thing actually works." Nick was standing inside the gates of Zaen, having opened the gate himself and stepped through without injury. He winked at me from inside the tunnel. "Looks like we're on a winner."

"Crap. Looks like we're committed now, Sugar," Conal said. "Let's get this over with."

Taking a deep breath, I started to draw the same mark on his left shoulder, cringing inwardly when I saw him shudder. "I'm so sorry."

"Stop apologizing and just draw the damn thing, will you? The faster you do it, the faster it's over," Conal urged, gritting his teeth. I worked hurriedly, trying to breathe through my mouth so I wouldn't inhale the pungent scent of burning flesh. Conal glanced back over his shoulder when I'd finished and managed a grim smile. "Always thought about getting a tatt. Looks like I got myself a free one." He stood up and brushed his lips across my cheek. "I love you, Sugar. I know you had to do it."

Ben took Conal's place, kneeling so I could begin to work on his mark. I gritted my teeth determinedly, wishing I was anywhere but here, doing this. Ben kept his eyes shut and was holding his back stiffly by the time I'd finished. He stood up and slipped on his shirt, then held me in his arms as I sobbed uncontrollably against his chest. "Shhh, Charlotte, it's all right," he murmured against my ear. "You are only doing what is required for us to have safety."

When he released me, Lucas took his place, taking the position Ben had vacated. For once, seeing his bare chest didn't elicit a reaction as I stepped towards him, my hand trembling as I lifted the Hjördis to begin the mark. I hesitated and Lucas caught my gaze, his eyes filled with sympathy. "Charlotte, you have to do this. Please."

When I began to draw the mark, I heard him inhale sharply as his skin began to burn. He gritted his teeth and shut his eyes as my tears fell against his skin. By the time it was finished, Lucas's muscled arms were flexed in agony, his hands fisted tightly. He stood up and drew me into his arms as I cried. "My love, it's over now. You've done all you needed to do. I love you." He lowered his mouth to mine, kissing me tenderly and I returned the kiss, wrapping my arms around his waist and holding him tightly.

"Alright you two, enough already," Conal growled roughly. "Now we've got these things, let's see if this Zaen is all it's cracked up to be."

Chapter 20

Sanctuary

Conal and Nick led the way through the long tunnel, their bodies tensed as they strode warily through the darkened expanse. It was much cooler here than outside and their boots clicked loudly against the cobblestones, echoing back from the stone walls.

"Who built this?" Nick questioned.

"Nememiah himself," Epi supplied, trotting along behind them and looking exceptionally tiny beside Ben.

Lucas and I held hands, walking behind Epi and Ben and I squeezed Lucas's fingers apprehensively. He glanced down and offered me a comforting smile. "I don't think there's anything to worry about, Charlotte. It's taken us five hours to figure out how to get in here, so I'm not expecting anything remotely demon-like inside the walls."

We reached the end of the long tunnel and I blinked when brilliant sunlight swept over us. Then I came to a standstill, open-mouthed at the sight before us. I'd seen this in my visions, memorized everything I'd observed and yet the reality was so much more overwhelming than the vision had ever been. A row of houses stood before us, spreading out in both directions and neatly following the curves of the great wall. They could be described as cottages, more than houses – quaint and Tudor in design, two stories high with whitewashed walls and visible beams. They resembled a picture I'd seen of Shakespeare's cottage in England. Each building had a thatched roof and tiny, mullioned windows and they were arranged in terraces of six, with an alleyway breaking up the row before they repeated again in another terrace of six.

"I don't understand," Lucas said. "Zaen hasn't been inhabited for more than a thousand years, yet these buildings look... perfect."

I let go of Lucas's hand and walked towards the nearest cottage, stepping cautiously up the whitewashed steps to the rough hewn wooden door. I touched the door tentatively, thinking it might all be a bizarre illusion, but the wood was solid beneath my fingertips. I couldn't even begin to imagine how these houses could still be standing, perfect after more than one thousand years. Reaching for the quaint iron door handle, I turned it and stepped inside.

The cottage was neat and tidy, with simple timber furniture. I wandered from room to room with the men following behind, all of us stunned into silence. The rooms were small but functional, clean and spotless. Conal caught up with me in the little kitchen and drew my attention upwards towards a light fitting. "Electricity. There must be a generator within the walls of the city."

Lucas turned on the faucet and clean fresh water poured out, as though it had been turned on only recently. "Running water," he commented softly. "The cottages appear to have been built in the Tudor period, but they've been thoroughly modernized."

Nick came clattering down the stairs from the second floor. "There's two bedrooms and a bathroom up there."

We left the cottage and stepped into the sunshine, wandering along the cobblestoned street we turned up through one of the narrow alleyways, which led to a further thoroughfare, curving in the shape of the outside wall. This street had cottages on either side, facing one another across the narrow street.

"How big is this place?" Ben wondered out loud as we turned down yet another narrow alleyway and entered a further row of cottages.

"Big enough for all who seek sanctuary," Epi answered with delight.

Dusk was falling rapidly when we met in the central courtyard we'd discovered earlier in the day. After extensive exploration, we'd confirmed the immense granite walls were completely spherical, as had been suggested from outside. Inside were row upon row of cottages, following the curve of the outside walls with each row of cottages becoming progressively smaller in number as they reached the centre of the city. The final, inner circle held a spherical lawn of perfectly manicured green grass. In the centre of the grass stood a large glass building, which Epi thought might be a meeting hall. With turrets and towers, it looked like a crystal palace and was beautiful with the sunshine casting a rainbow effect over the glass panes.

A narrow moat surrounded the grass, intricate ironwork bridges spaced at precise intervals to provide access.

Lucas, Ben and I were sitting on the grass when the other three men arrived back from their reconnaissance. Ben was sitting cross-legged on the grass whilst Lucas sat up, arms extended behind his back to support himself. I lay on the grass with my head resting on Lucas's thigh, watching the color of the sky deepen from palest blue into the mauves and purples which announced the day's end.

"Well, you three look nice and relaxed," Epi announced. He mounted one of the bridges and walked across the grass. "What did you discover?"

We'd decided to split into two groups once the vast size of Zaen was established, so we could cover as much ground as possible. Ben, Lucas and I had taken the area to the east, while Conal, Epi and Nick took the western half.

"The majority of the eastern side is housing, all pretty much identical. We did discover the energy source," Lucas explained. "There's a bank of four generators on the eastern perimeter, built into the wall. Can't for the life of me figure out what's powering them – it's technology I've never seen before."

"I'll take a look in the morning," Conal responded. "I've had some experience with generators, might be able to figure it out."

I waved a hand lazily towards the row of buildings which encircled the eastern side of the grass. "These all look like shops and those over there are houses, bigger than the cottages, more ornately furnished. Lucas thinks they might have originally housed the leaders of Nememiah's Children but Ben and I think we should convert one into a hospital, one into a school for the children and maybe we can create a communal Mess in the third one." I glanced at Epi and flashed him a hopeful smile. "Speaking of eating, Epi – I'm starved. Did we pack any food?"

Epi dropped his rucksack onto the grass and sat down beside me. "What? Now I'm a caterer?" he grumbled. "As I keep telling you, child, I am..."

"I know, I know. Not some two-bit magician." I pulled myself into a sitting position, crossing my legs. "But I'm starving and I haven't eaten since breakfast."

"And she threw that up when we got here," Conal agreed. "Come to think of it, I'm pretty hungry myself."

"And I'm with Charlotte," Nick announced. "Starving."

"Fine," Epi grumbled. He waved a hand across the grass in front of me and a platter of barbeque chicken appeared, steaming hot and smelling utterly delicious. Alongside it, plates, cutlery and two bowls of salad appeared and I snatched up a plate, piling it high with food.

"What did you find on the western side?" Ben asked Conal as I dived voraciously into a chicken drumstick.

"More housing, a few areas of parkland which should be excellent for the kids to play or for training, and an armory."

"Weapons?" Lucas questioned.

"Not much good to us. Angel weapons. Row upon row of Hjördis, Katchet and Philaris," Conal responded. He met my eyes. "Don't suppose Nememiah gave you any clues in that regard?"

I shook my head in the negative. "As I keep telling you, I don't ask questions and get straight answers. Everything I learn has to be earned somehow." I scooped up some potato salad, popping it into my mouth and chewing thoughtfully. "So what do you think? Can we offer our group safety here?"

Lucas shrugged. "It has everything we need. Battlements, areas for training, shelter now that winter is coming on. We need to investigate the woods in the morning." I knew he was considering a food supply for the vampires and a place for the werewolves to roam at full moon.

Conal nodded in agreement. "That wall is fifteen feet thick. It's going to keep just about everything out. And the blast it gives off should hold most things back."

"I think it's perfect," Nick agreed.

"Where do you think we are, exactly?" I asked curiously. "There's no reception on my cell phone."

Conal flipped his own phone open and shut it again, frowning. "Mine's not working, either."

"Does it really matter?" Epi queried. "It's probably the safest place we are going to find."

I had to agree with him. Running, changing locations week by week was not doing our small group any good. Having somewhere relatively safe with the bonus of shelter from the incoming winter seemed to make this our best option.

"Alright. Why don't we complete the reconnaissance in the morning and head back, start moving people through the portal as soon as possible," Lucas suggested.

"Wait a minute," I piped up, realizing the repercussions of the decision. "Archangelo is being put into a sleep cycle about once every six to eight days."

Lucas nodded, an eyebrow raised in question.

"We moved three days ago and we've moved the group to another location this morning. That's four days used. He doesn't know where they are, but as soon as he's put into another sleep cycle – he's going to locate me."

"Which means he'll know the location of Zaen," Conal said, obviously picking up on the predicament. "How many people are in our group now?"

"One hundred and thirty three adults, forty children and infants," Epi announced immediately. He saw my surprised look and continued. "Ben thought it was important that we keep track of numbers, so we know how many we need to feed and support."

"Which means we've got two days to get everyone into Zaen safely," I said, doing some swift mental calculations. "It's not going to be possible."

"Why not?" Nick frowned.

"Because," Lucas said slowly, "they all need the mark before they can enter the gates. Only Charlotte can mark them."

My eyes filled with tears, the dinner I'd been enjoying quickly forgotten. "I can't do it! I might be able to put the mark on the adults, but the kids? The babies? No, I *won't* do it."

"Charlotte, the mark will save them," Epi responded, sounding entirely reasonable.

Nick spoke. "Couldn't you talk to Nememiah again? Maybe you could ask him for another option. Won't his spirit be inside your head now?"

"No, Nick, it won't," I stated coldly. "We didn't exactly shake hands and I need physical contact to pick up on the voices. This was an Angel, not some guy I met on the street."

Nick scowled. "Alright, you've made your point. It was a stupid suggestion."

"Sugar, it's our only option." Conal was watching me, his eyes filled with sympathy for what I would have to do. "Think of it as... an immunization."

I stared at him for a long moment, filled with disbelief at what he was suggesting. "Can you honestly tell me that having that mark burned onto your skin *wasn't* the most painful thing you've ever endured?" I'd observed all of them during our foray through Zaen, seen all four rubbing their shoulders as though the mark was still incredibly painful, even after it was completed. Conal returned my gaze, his charcoal eyes confirming everything I needed to know.

I stood up, noticing they'd all lowered their gaze and wouldn't look at me. "There has to be another way," I announced angrily. "I will not burn that mark onto the skin of children, innocent kids who've gotten mixed up in this disaster through no damn fault of their own." I turned and stalked away, wanting to be anywhere but here right now.

Chapter 21

Negotiations

I paced dejectedly through the narrow streets, my mind a maelstrom of swirling images, my heart aching at the thought of burning that mark on children and babies. The thought of doing it to Katie – who looked at me with complete trust and implicitly believed in me, was more than I could possibly bear.

Unfortunately, without the mark they would be stuck out there, on their own without protection from the Consiliului. It was an impossible situation, one I could see no way of overcoming. Everything we'd tried to get into Zaen had failed – except that mark. The majority who would be entering through the gates had a percentage of demon blood and had no way of gaining access without the mark. There were a percentage of our group who were human and I guessed they would meet no obstacle in entering the city. But the children – *all* the children would have a percentage of demon blood in their bodies.

Frustration and anger welled up again. The others saw everything so calmly – it wasn't them who had to do this. Even without the obstacle of marking the children, how could we get everyone marked and inside the gates before Archangelo had a vision and located us? It was going to take time. Marking the wing on each man had taken about fifteen minutes apiece. That added up to an hour for every four people in our group and the statistics were one obstacle I couldn't overcome. Archangelo would be able to locate me wherever I was and I doubted that would change because we were in Zaen. He had the blood of angels running in his veins and would be able to locate Zaen exactly as I'd done.

Slumping onto the stairs outside one of the cottages, I abruptly felt exhausted and much older than twenty one. My thoughts turned to Lonnie, my friend

Negotiations

whose only major ordeals in life were what to wear on a date and getting to college classes on times. Her world and my world, which had once been on a parallel path had veered wildly from one another. I envied the normality she had and questioned again why I'd been chosen for this task.

Even if I managed to get these people to safety, what then? Would the Consiliului continue to come after us, or would we have to go to them? What about the predicament with the demons? If it came down to a war, how could we possibly hope to win when I was the only one who could use the weapons? The hopelessness of the situation was overwhelming. My head ached with the number of unanswered questions swirling around.

The sky had darkened swiftly and the moon appeared over Zaen's high walls, bright and luminous against the blackening skies. It looked like Earth's moon and I was convinced Zaen was somewhere on our own planet. As to exactly where, I couldn't be certain, but it certainly appeared it wasn't known to anyone but us. Nothing this vast, so immense could exist without someone finding it before now and I wondered how it could have remained hidden over hundreds of years. A sudden glow of light caught my attention and I watched as the street lights turned on at spaced intervals, bathing the cobblestones in a soft golden glow.

Without conscious thought, I shifted into my usual meditative posture with my legs crossed and hands resting lightly on my knees, trying to quell my anxieties. I wondered if I should speak with the spirits, if they would have any answers or would just confuse me more. Epi had explained why they were reticent in providing answers, remarking that Nememiah's Children had been guided by their own integrity and sense of justice. They had used the spirits to guide them and provide support, but ultimately had made all their major decisions for themselves. Which was easy for them – there were dozens of them. Only one of me. One frightened, confused twenty one year old woman. I focused on my breathing, deliberately clearing my mind of the tortuous thoughts which overwhelmed me, willing myself into calm. I longed for some way to speak to Nememiah, but I'd been too nervous to ask him if I could contact him again, too overwhelmed to consider I might need his guidance. Would he even give me guidance if I asked? Our conversation had only succeeded in creating more questions than answers. By receiving Nememiah's permission to bring supernatural beings into Zaen, I'd already broken away from the very core of why his Children were first created.

Nememiah's Children had ultimately destroyed themselves. Nememiah's vision of his children keeping peace amongst the supernaturals had failed because ultimately they'd fought amongst themselves, in a quest for superiority they shouldn't have had. Were they any different to the Consiliului? They'd taken a position of authority, viewing themselves not as equals, but superior to the other supernatural groups. They'd kept the supernatural groups subservient by becoming a ruling power. And in turn, Nememiah's Children had fought amongst themselves, in a battle over their very existence. Some decided they'd taken their control too far, others felt it hadn't gone far enough. It was becoming apparent Nememiah's Children had other internal issues to deal with, evident from the luxurious houses around the central circle, which were far more opulent than the numerous cottages. Not only had they believed themselves superior, ultimately in-house disparity had destroyed them. I felt at least part of the solution to our problems was to ensure we provided equality for everyone. No one group could be considered superior or inferior to another in our dynamic.

My thoughts turned to the rest of the puzzle my spiritual guides had left me with. We'd discovered the meaning of the wing, it would allow people into Zaen. But complete the circle? What did that mean? I wondered if it had anything to do with Zaen itself and the circular structure of the city. Or did it mean something else entirely? I didn't have a clue.

I had to bring equality to these groups, that much I was certain about. Within my own close group of friends, Conal was werewolf, Lucas vampire, Nick a shape shifter. Although it had been rocky, the longer they worked together, the more they were coming to rely on one another. Could I manage that with everyone?

"I am here, child. Ask your questions."

My eyes opened wide, shocked by the sound of the familiar voice. There was no-one to be seen in the narrow street.

"I am here in your mind, child. You may not call to me as you do the others, but I will give you guidance if I see fit."

Nememiah's voice echoed in my mind as the spirits did. I closed my eyes, trying to locate him, searching for his image.

"There is no need for us to meet again. I will be a voice calling to you, nothing more. Ask your questions."

I took a minute to consider what I thought was the most urgent of the multitude of questions I had. *"The mark of Nememiah – the wing I have to mark on my friends to allow them into Zaen – do I have to do that to everyone who seeks sanctuary with us?"*

"It is necessary for the protection of Zaen itself. I granted you permission to bring others to this city, but they must pledge themselves to me before they gain entry. The mark is their word of honor."

Tears filled my eyes. "But we have children in our group, little babies. I don't want to cause them pain."

"All of life contains pain."

I thought about his response for a minute, turning it over in my mind before I chose how to respond. *"Children are innocent. They have no choice in what we've become involved in, but they need somewhere safe to live. They have taken no decisions to join this fight. It doesn't seem fair that they must be marked."*

There was a long silence and I was beginning to wonder if he'd abandoned me, if I'd said something which displeased him. At last, he spoke. "The children may enter the walls without the mark. You are correct, they are innocents and cannot be obligated to take sides until they have the maturity to do so. All those who have reached the age of sixteen must, however, bear the mark if they seek shelter."

"Thank you." My relief was a tangible feeling in my soul.

A long pause and then, *"Is there anything else?"*

"We must fight demons and I'm the only one who can utilize the weapons. The others need the ability to use them. How can I make that happen?"

He was silent for a long time again, pondering the question and I waited patiently. "There is a way, child. But the use of the angel weapons must be earned. My weapons, which were created for my Children alone, are extraordinarily powerful. You must find a way to discover who amongst you have the strength to use them. Be warned, not all will use them for the purest intentions. Not everyone surrounding you can be trusted, child. Fear, suspicion, anger, distrust and bigotry are all strong emotions and can be as destructive as the foe against whom you align yourself. Give only to those you trust the power of the weapons themselves. The answer is within you."

I frowned, wondering if I had the courage to ask my next question, the temptation to do so almost overwhelming.

"You have another question, child," Nememiah stated calmly.

"Can we win?" I said it aloud and the words echoed down the empty street, bouncing off the buildings.

"You are young. You think in terms of light and dark, fire and ice. I cannot give you the answer you seek. It depends on the courage within yourself. I told you that only one of you, one of my children can survive this war. Can you willingly accept death, if that is your destiny? Can you readily accept the deaths of those around you, in this fight you are destined to battle? The answer is cast in a future that even I cannot readily interpret."

"I kind of expected that," I agreed dryly.

"I have faith in you, child. You have already come far and in you there is the gift to love deeply, to care for others as equals. It is this ability which convinced me to give you some of the answers you sought. But I can only guide you, as can the spirits you harness. Ultimately the decisions must be yours. You will lead your people, you will fight the battles. You will make the sacrifices which will either achieve your goals, or see you fail. I am merely a spectator. I will be watching."

I knew he was gone instinctively and wouldn't answer any more questions. Slowly gaining an awareness of my surroundings, I opened my eyes. It wasn't surprising to find Lucas sitting on the step, watching me in silence.

"Hi," I breathed softly.

"Hi yourself." He slid across the stone step, wrapping his arms around my waist. "We were worried about you."

I sighed. "I'm okay. I needed to clear my head, think things through." I straightened out my legs and leaned against him, drawing from his strength. "I had another conversation with Nememiah."

"I figured that was who you were talking to. You can locate him?"

"No, but apparently *he* can contact me if he feels the urge," I answered ruefully. "I had some questions and he agreed to answer them."

"Anything helpful?"

I repeated the discussion I'd had with Nememiah. "So he's given me permission to bring the children in without them needing the mark."

Lucas was silent for a few seconds, digesting this news. "Well, I guess it's better than nothing." He kissed the top of my head. "I know how difficult this is for you, Charlotte, don't think we're dismissing your feelings. We all know how much you hate what we're asking you to do."

"Now all we have to do is figure out how to allow others to use the weapons and guess what 'complete the circle' might possibly mean," I said. "That should give us plenty to think about."

"Oh, I think there are some other things to think about," Lucas remarked, his voice deepening. He tilted my chin and kissed me, his lips forceful against mine as he molded me against his body. I was immediately overwhelmed by the potent desire he ignited and a soft moan escaped my lips. Lucas pulled away a little, his lips resting against my cheek. "For instance, now you've come back to me, I have to deal with the overwhelming force of my desire for you. All I can think about is making love to you. When I look at you, I envisage you as you were last night, lying on the ground, my body pressed over yours..." His voice had dropped to a husky whisper as his mouth found mine again and I clung to him, dissolving into a puddle of rampaging hormones.

He released my lips and traced his fingertips across my back. "You know, there are a multitude of houses around us, all unlocked and every single one of them appears to have a perfectly serviceable bed," he suggested throatily, before adding, "and I keep imagining plunging into your sweet body and making love till the sun rises. And beyond."

I giggled softly, dragging myself up onto my feet grudgingly. "Come on. We'd better go and tell the others what's happening. And we need a plan to get everyone through the portal to Zaen."

"I'm willing to make do with a couple of hours," Lucas suggested hopefully.

"While that's an admirable offer," I agreed with a smile, "I'm voting for the all-night-long-until-the-sun-rises theory."

"I'll hold you to that, my love," Lucas growled. "And I hope to God it will be sooner, rather than later."

Chapter 22

Disbelievers

Stepping out of the portal, I wavered on my feet for a couple of seconds, the familiar wave of queasiness washing over me. Conal gripped my elbow to keep me from keeling over. "Not getting any better?"

"Nope." I breathed deeply for a minute or two, waiting for the nausea to subside. "How are we doing here?"

Conal led me through the camp and I was conscious of the murmurs and stares as I walked alongside him. "Good. We've talked to everyone and the majority have decided to join us in Zaen. Any trouble at your end?"

"No. Archangelo was put into the induced sleep about an hour ago. As soon as the spirits warned me, I took off. Didn't even glimpse a demon."

"So we've got what? Five days to get everyone through?"

I nodded my agreement. After much discussion we'd agreed we needed the biggest window of opportunity to get the group marked and transported through to Zaen. The men had portalled back to camp after our reconnaissance to prepare everyone and explain the plan. I'd taken off on my own, travelling to another area and hunkering down to wait for Archangelo's potion-induced sleep. Once he had my location and the spirits warned of the imminent arrival of demons, I'd portalled back to our previous campsite, contacted Lucas via cell phone and Epi had provided the instructions to allow me to return to the group.

"Where's Lucas?"

"He and Ripley are interviewing another group of weres who turned up this morning, wanting to join us. They took a hammering a couple of nights ago, lost fifteen members," Conal explained. "Ripley's proving handy at gaining information from the groups, vetting them and making sure they're okay before we agree to them joining us."

I looked at him sharply. "Has his mind-reading ability come back?"

Conal shook his head. "No luck yet. He's just damn good at getting them to open up to him."

I shrugged, disappointed with this news. "Having him talk to the new people sounds like a good plan anyway." I glanced up into his handsome face, ignoring the increased pace of my heartbeat. "Any problems with cooperation? How are these people getting along with one another?"

"Not much trouble between our original groups. There's a certain level of trust developing between the blood su..." He saw my eyes narrow and corrected himself with a twinkle in his own eyes. "...*vampires*, my pack and Nick's, but some of the new ones are still wary."

"They need to get over it." I announced, flicking my hair back from my shoulders. "There's no room for fighting amongst ourselves if we're going to survive this." We reached Epi's tent and Conal stepped back, allowing me to go through the doorway first.

"Ah, Charlotte! Good to have you back with us, child." Epi's step was sprightly as he marched across the room to hug me. "No trouble?"

"No." I turned from him to greet Rowena and she held me tightly for a long time.

"You look so tired," she fretted, studying my shadowed eyes with concern.

"I think it comes with the territory," I responded quietly. "Sleeping isn't my favorite activity these days."

"Are you aware of any further attacks?" Ben greeted me with another affectionate hug and I relished being back in their protective embrace. Ben and Rowena had taken it upon themselves to act as my surrogate parents and it was deeply comforting.

Nodding glumly, I passed on my news. "A group of shape shifters somewhere in Portugal – the majority of them appeared to escape. And a werewolf pack in China were slaughtered outright when they fought back," I confirmed heavily. "About forty five men, women and children. The Consiliului appear to be upping the ante."

Rowena's dismay was apparent, her smooth forehead creasing into a worried frown. "Charlotte, I'm so sorry you're witnessing this through the visions. It's little wonder you're so exhausted."

"There's nothing we can do about it now," I responded. "Our biggest prerogative has to be getting the group through to Zaen."

"Epi and I have prepared a list of everyone who needs the mark and transport," Ben announced. "We've agreed on groups of ten, starting with the women and children."

I dipped my head in acknowledgement, grateful for Ben's outstanding organizational skills. "Sounds good. Let's get to work."

Epi eyed me suspiciously, one hand perched on his narrow hip. "Wait a minute. What happened to 'let's eat first'?" There's always a 'let's eat first'."

"Beat you to it, Epi." I turned to leave the tent. "I grabbed breakfast at Burger King before I portalled."

Conal grinned and followed me back outside, with Ben. Looking around the crowd of people in front of Epi's tent, it was obvious word of my arrival had travelled swiftly.

"They don't look like they trust me," I stated to Conal in an undertone.

"They're scared, Sugar. They hardly know you, and we've told them what this entails. It's bound to make them anxious."

"You've shown them the mark?" I eyed the crowds cautiously.

"Yes, we've explained everything. We have about twenty people who are refusing to go," Ben answered, pointing to a cluster of people in the throes of packing their belongings. "And perhaps fifteen others who have elected to go, but don't want the mark. They intend to camp in the forest outside Zaen."

"We can't protect them out there," I protested. "They'll be at the mercy of whatever the Consiliului throw our way if they aren't inside the gates."

Conal squeezed my shoulder, his hand warm. "We can't force them, Sugar. We can only offer them the option. After that they have to make up their own minds."

I knew he was right, but it bothered me to think they would be out there, unprotected by Zaen's heavily fortressed walls.

Conal cursed, his heated words startling me and I glimpsed a posse of men striding towards us, people I didn't recognize. "Some of our rabble-rousers," he muttered under his breath. He addressed one man who stepped forward from the group. He was of medium height with a stocky build and dark wavy hair. "Marrok, what are you doing here?"

"Ensuring you're doing the right thing for the pack." The man stared at Conal sullenly, his grey eyes cold. I didn't recall meeting him, but obviously he was a member of Conal's pack and none too happy about the decision Conal had made on behalf of their group.

"You've had everything explained to you." Conal's anger was substantial and his energy washed over me in uncomfortable waves. "The pack elders agreed to this decision."

"And as a pack elder I want further explanation from the one ordering this evacuation." Marrok's tone was insolent and a brush of energy from him raised goose bumps on my skin. "Surely you have no objections?"

I touched Conal's arm, ignoring the static it created against my fingertips. He glanced at me and took a deep breath. "No objection, Marrok."

Marrok stepped back into line with his compatriots. The emotions seething from the five men was palpable. They were big, strong men and the shortest of the five, apparently the elected spokesperson, abruptly stepped closer, no doubt an attempt to intimidate me. His ruddy features were filled with anger and frustration.

"You're the angel?" he stated without preamble.

"Yes." I stood my ground, a warning hand on Conal's arm, aware he'd attack this man if he said anything Conal considered inappropriate. "I'm Charlotte Duncan."

"These people tell us the only way to get sanctuary in this Zaen is by having that mark burnt onto our skin. Why can't we get in without taking this mark?"

"We've already explained why, Reynolds," Conal growled. "Without the mark, Zaen itself will prevent you from entering. It's protected from anyone who carries demon blood in their bodies."

"Shut up, Tremaine. I'm speaking to *her*, not you." Reynolds response was belligerent as he eyed me with contempt.

I caught hold of the back of Conal's shirt, hoping to stop him from reacting to Reynolds. "Conal's right. You can't enter Zaen without the mark of the wing," I answered patiently. "It's the recompense you must make for the sanctuary Zaen will provide."

The crowd was increasing, no doubt drawn by the tense atmosphere and most likely wanting answers to the same questions Reynolds was asking. "If you're an angel, why can't you just let us enter without the mark?"

"I'm following the rules given to me by Nememiah," I explained calmly. A reassuring hand clasped my shoulder and Lucas stepped up beside me, his eyes blazing with fury. Ripley stood beside him, jaw tensed as he watched Reynolds warily.

"Did you have the mark burned onto your skin?" This question came from a short, dark woman who'd stepped up to join the men.

I shook my head. "The mark was already on my skin, like a birthmark."

"You see?" Reynolds turned his attention to the crowd, his dark eyes scanning them to ensure he had their attention. "We all have to be tattooed, but she doesn't have to suffer at all! *She* doesn't have to endure the burning of a mark onto *her* skin to give her entrance to this magical Zaen!"

"You're being unreasonable, Reynolds," Ben responded, his voice calm and his tone measured. "Charlotte has suffered more than enough since this began. More than you could ever imagine."

"She looks fine to me, bloodsucker!" Reynolds yelled. "Where was she when my pack were attacked? Where has she been while we've been hiding out here?"

"She was providing you with safety," Lucas snarled. "By staying away, she ensured your sorry ass was out of harm's way while she was being chased by demons."

"*Safety*? We've been hiding here like a bunch of scared rabbits! This is *safety*?" He shook his head, laughing mirthlessly. "And what if we don't want to fight? What if we want to live our lives as they were before?"

Reynolds' rounded face was flushed with antagonism. I was struggling to decide whether he was blustering because he was frightened, or aggressively angry about being marked. Or perhaps a combination of both. Either way, I was sure I didn't like the man. "That's up to you," I responded quietly. "You said your pack were attacked. How do you expect to go back to living your life as it was before? Do you think that the Consiliului will forget about your existence? Do you imagine they'll leave you alone?" I shifted my gaze from Reynolds to the other men around him, saw them shuffling uncomfortably. I prayed they were taking into consideration the uncertainty of their future and realizing there would be no hiding from the Drâghici. "If you join with us and accept the mark, you'll be given sanctuary in Zaen. I won't force anyone to fight, but you'll be expected to cooperate with one another."

It was immediately evident that they weren't thinking about what I'd said as carefully as I hoped. "That's easy for you to say, you consort with the bloodsuckers and shape shifters! They've been our enemies for thousands of years," one of the men sneered, his hands clenched. "And you want us to believe that you're going to be our savior? That you'll lead us in this fight? You're a woman!"

The first wave of anger swamped any well-meaning intentions I'd had of keeping my cool. The past few days hadn't been easy, I was tired and in desperate need of a long, hot shower. Frustration welled up as I considered the stupidity and discrimination of these men and their petty arguments. "You all have a choice," I announced grimly. "I don't. My intention is to provide you with equality, safety and the opportunity to live in a world where you have the freedom of choice to make your own decisions. I won't compel any of you to come with us to Zaen. I won't coerce you to have the mark of Nememiah's wing. You can all make your own decision. But let me warn you – nearly all of you have lost someone, watched them murdered by the vampires and demons. The Drâghici Consiliului intend to take control of your world. They are creating a colossal army of vampire – at least two thousand that I'm aware of. On top of that, they have the power to summon demons from the Otherworld, to reinforce those younglings. If you think you can fight against that on your own, protect your families and packs – go ahead. I'm not going to stop you."

"So this is the leeches against the rest of us!" Reynolds shouted, completely bypassing the point I was trying to make.

"That's not true," Lucas pointed out. "We stand at Charlotte's side. You know we're vampires who don't hunt humans. The Drâghici consider us an aberration and intend to kill us as surely as they'll kill you." His energy was washing over me as much as Conal's was, and I resisted the urge to rub my hands over my arms.

"You need to make this choice," I said loudly, determined to end this conversation one way or the other. "Nobody will force you to go. You're all free to go to your homes and wait for the Consiliului, the youngling vampires, the demons. You can decide to work with us, to fight with us, or you can choose to take your own path. To be honest," I announced in a cool voice, "I don't really care what you decide to do. If you can't work with us, then we're better off without you. For now, I have more important things to do – getting the people who *want* to help themselves transported to Zaen."

I spun on my heels, striding away as tears welled in my eyes. Conal and Lucas wrapped their arms around my waist as we talked back towards where the portal had been earlier.

"I'm proud of you, Charlotte," Lucas reassured me with a gentle kiss on my forehead. "That was very courageous."

Conal smiled. "Lucas is right, Sugar. You gave them something to think about." He kissed my cheek, his black eyes twinkling with delight. "But I would have happily decked Reynolds for you."

"What's the deal with that Marrok guy?" I questioned curiously.

"He's a bastard," Conal responded bluntly. "He's always been a troublemaker."

"How'd he get to be a pack elder?"

Conal grimaced. "He's smart and he's tough and if he wasn't such a bastard, he'd be useful to have around." Seeing my startled look, he continued. "Marrok has been on the council for years, even before my father became Alpha. He's got his eye on the prize."

"The prize?" I repeated blankly.

Conal shrugged. "Don't worry about it, Sugar. It's pack business."

Ben squeezed my shoulder gently, capturing my attention. "Two thousand younglings?" Concern was etched in his usually passive face. "That's an unbelievable army for the Consiliului to amass."

"I heard Odin talking about it in one of my visions. They have a group of vampires constantly creating new ones."

"Younglings are unstable, difficult to control," Lucas added grimly. "They suffer a bloodlust which is overpowering."

I straightened my shoulders, tensing myself to deal with the day ahead, and pushing the thought of a hot shower to the back of my mind. "While I'm not happy with the vampire development, we've got other problems to deal with. For now, we've got to get these people moving." I pulled the Hjördis from my pocket and sighed. "Let's get on with it."

Phelan was the last to be marked, having remained behind as I'd worked my way through the dozens of people needing the wing. Our efforts were prolonged as more people arrived, seeking refuge. Word of mouth was spreading about our claim of safety and groups of people had arrived in the past days, requesting sanctuary.

Reynolds and his group, along with the other men who'd joined his mini uprising had, surprisingly, agreed to having the mark. I wasn't sure why, and Reynolds had been remarkably sullen when I'd met him again, but at least he'd been silently sullen. I'd take what I could get at this stage.

The sun was setting on the seventh day when I completed the mark on Phelan's shoulder. It had been risky to remain in one place for so long, knowing Archangelo could be placed into a potion-induced sleep at any moment, but there'd been little choice with so many people needing help.

Phelan shrugged on his shirt, doing up the buttons as I slumped in an exhausted heap on the ground. All around us the grass and vegetation had been trampled as dozens of people portalled to Zaen.

Lucas, Epi and the Tines had already gone through – they'd been needed to organize the massive task of housing, food and supplies for the nearly three hundred people under our care. Lucas and I had barely seen one another since I'd portalled back seven days ago – he'd been on one of the first trips out. We'd been separated for days and I missed him. It seemed since we'd reunited, circumstances kept us constantly apart.

Nick and Rafe were waiting patiently, remaining after the last group went through. Nick announced they were here to keep me company, but I knew it was extra protection. Everyone was edgy, knowing Archangelo could send demons at any given minute.

"Ready to go, Lott?" Phelan queried with a warm smile. He rubbed his hand across his shoulder, grimacing a little. "You look like you could do with a stiff drink, and after that little adventure, so could I."

I got to my feet slowly. Every muscle was aching after seven days of constant work with the Hjördis. Having spent hour after hour bent over people's shoulders, my shoulders and neck throbbed and my hand was cramping.

"I'm not heading through yet," I answered, glancing away evasively.

Nick's head rose sharply and he narrowed his eyes. "What the hell are you talking about?"

"You need time to get settled. At most we've got twenty four hours till Archangelo locates me again. It's better for everyone if I'm not there, it buys another week of peace to get settled."

"Lucas is going to be seriously pissed," Phelan stated uncertainly. "He got me to promise I'd bring you with us on this last trip."

I smiled, aware that Lucas knew me too well. He'd clearly guessed in advance that I would think of this, make this decision. "Tell him I'll be there in a couple of days. I swear."

"Lott, this is crazy – sooner or later the Council are going to know about Zaen. Another week won't make much difference," Rafe argued.

I shook my head, determined to follow through with the decision. "Another week makes a lot of difference. We still don't know how to kill the demons. Another week might give us the answer, before we have to face them."

"Charlotte, I'm not letting you stay," Nick growled, hands resting on his hips.

"You don't have a choice. I've made up my mind," I announced, glaring at him.

"I'll pick you up and carry your ass through the portal," he retorted.

"That'll be difficult," I said lightly. "I'm the one who has to create the portal."

"Won't stop me from picking up your ass as soon as it opens," he snapped.

"I'm not going, Nick," I responded quietly. "I have to do what's best for the group. You have to admit, the best thing for everyone is to buy them that extra week, give them time to settle in and get organized. I'm not being unreasonable, it's the sensible option."

I knew he couldn't find a reasonable way of disagreeing. "All right," he finally announced grudgingly. "But you better promise me you'll stay safe. Marianne and Rowena, shit, *all* the women will kill me if anything happens to you and I let you stay behind."

"You're not *letting* me stay behind," I responded, annoyed with his domineering tactics. "I'm choosing to stay." I knelt and created a pentagram, marking sigils which had become second nature in the past week. The portal opened and I stepped back, feeling indescribably lonely. But it was the right thing to do. "See you on the other side."

"You get through that portal the minute Archangelo comes out of the sleep," Nick ordered firmly. With one last, frustrated look, he stepped through the portal.

Phelan hugged me warmly. "See you soon, Lott." He too, stepped through the portal and I was left with Rafe.

"He worries about you, you know," Rafe said quietly.

"Who? Nick?" I was surprised by his suggestion that Nick actually thought about me, let alone worried about me. We'd had a rocky relationship from the beginning and seemed remarkably good at getting on each other's nerves.

Rafe grinned. "Yeah, Nick. He's got that whole gruff exterior going on, but he cares about you, Lott. He's worried about you being on your own."

"I'll be fine," I responded quietly and stepped forward to offer him a hug. He wrapped his long arms around me and squeezed me tightly for a second, before stepping through the portal.

For a couple of minutes I stood and watched as the portal flickered and closed. I was emotionally and physically worn out. I longed to recreate the connection, join Lucas in Zaen – I missed him so much, but common sense told me I'd made the right decision.

I scrubbed away the pentagram, locking it off before I created a new one. Envisaging where I wanted to go, the spirits provided the sigils and I waited as the portal opened, shimmering with a golden glow.

Dusk was falling in Puckhaber when I arrived, taking a moment to gaze at Lucas's house in the semi-darkness. Even in the fading light, the damage done by the Consiliului was apparent. Windows smashed, glass lying everywhere and the front door was ripped from its hinges. I trudged slowly across the patio and entered the foyer, stepping cautiously into the darkened living room. Flicking the light switch, I blinked rapidly when the room was abruptly bathed in bright light.

The house was in ruins, furniture overturned, glass showered everywhere. The piano was on its side, the lid torn away. Memories of Lucas and the others playing seemed like they'd happened an eternity ago. I walked slowly through the room, sad to discover the house – my home for so many months - had been trashed so badly. I wandered into the kitchen, my stomach rumbling. The refrigerator was operational, but the food had perished over the past few months. The freezer was more rewarding, Rowena had purchased frozen meals when I was living here and they were still stacked in neat rows. I chose one at random, popping it into the microwave which had escaped destruction.

While the food defrosted, I headed upstairs to the room which had once been mine. I peeked into each room I passed, finding each one ransacked. Rowena would be appalled to see the house desecrated by the Consiliului, when she'd always kept it so picture perfect.

The bed was overturned and Lucas's belongings were strewn everywhere. I sorted through the rucksack I carried, finding fresh underwear and clothes then headed down the hall for a lengthy hot shower. It had been weeks since I'd enjoyed this kind of luxury and I relished the opportunity to stand under steaming hot water with no time limit.

Heading back downstairs, I heated the now-defrosted meal and dropped it onto the table, tipping a chair upright to sit and eat. There was damage surrounding me, the remnants of life before I'd discovered my responsibilities as Nememiah's Child. It seemed like a million years ago and I wondered if life would ever revert back to normality. *Of course,* I mused, *had it ever truly been average?*

Would I live through this? Nememiah's prophecy continued to haunt me. Archangelo and I couldn't both survive – one would die before this ended. I hadn't spoken to anyone about Nememiah's prediction. With a pensive sigh I threw the empty meal container into the sink and went upstairs, intent on getting some much-needed sleep.

Shunting the mattress, I finally got it to lay flat on the carpet and located a blanket to throw over myself. It only took minutes to collapse into a deep and exhausted sleep.

I was standing in the marble room at Sfantu Drâghici. There were no vampires in attendance, only Alberich Bran and Archangelo stood together and Archangelo was clearly angry. His green eyes flashed as he gesticulated at the older man. Bran wore the same grey cloak but the hood was drawn back, allowing me to see his face clearly.

"I want the girl! She's destined to be mine! It was written in our futures, we were to marry and create a race of angel children!"

"Calm yourself, Archangelo." The older man's voice was a deep baritone, his pitch sharply moderated. "The Drâghici need the girl dead. We must complete this task. Without the girl, the supernatural creatures will have no leader. This has gone on for far too long, she has escaped every time."

"That's not my fault!" There was an obvious whine to Archangelo's voice, like a child who was being denied what he wanted. "I've done everything asked of me!"

"Without the girl, we will have everything we've ever wanted! Riches, and the supernatural at our feet. The control of the demons is ours and ours alone. The Consiliului have only the ability to create younglings. Ours is the true power in this union."

"The girl should be mine. She's my destiny! I want her!" Archangelo repeated. "The Drâghici are just a bunch of old vampires, who've been around too long."

The older man sighed, clasping his hands together as if in prayer. "Silence, Archangelo," he warned in a low voice. "Those are dangerous words in this place. Odin and his Kiss control what we do - for now. We need their assistance, their ruthless tactics, to round up and control the supernaturals. They have the numbers to bring them to heel. But, when the time is right, we will take control. For now, however, we must allow Odin to believe they have complete power and that we are merely pawns in a game they run." Bran paused, choosing his next words carefully. "But the girl must die, Archangelo. She is too powerful, as you've see in your visions. She is becoming the natural leader of the very creatures we wish to control. This has gone on for far too long."

"I want her. Her scent, the perfume of her is an addiction I will not give up! I must have her."

"You cannot have her. It is an impossibility. But I promise you, I will find you another. Perhaps someone who bears a resemblance to her," Bran promised.

"I don't want another! I want her, you old fool!" Archangelo yelled. "She should be mine!"

Waking with a jolt, I launched up onto my elbows, my mind swimming with the vision. My hair was damp and stuck to my neck, skin drenched in perspiration. Taking a couple of steadying breaths, I slumped back against the mattress, pulling the blanked up over my chest. Visions like this were commonplace, they happened so regularly that I expected them every time I went to sleep. But the thought of Archangelo's... *obsession*... that was seriously creepy.

Thinking carefully over the vision, it was discomforting to realize Archangelo and Bran weren't aligned with the Drâghici as we'd believed. From the information I'd overheard, they considered Odin and his cronies as a tool at their disposal, doing the groundwork before they took over as leaders of the supernatural. It was a worrying development in an already unsettling state of affairs. I wished it was possible to bring the others up to speed with this latest development but with no cell phone reception, they would remain in the dark until I returned to Zaen.

The rapid pace of my heartbeat slowly decreased and I curled up under the blanket, wanting to go back to sleep for a while. The visions disrupted my rest, leaving me relentlessly tired and I wondered if I could get another couple of hours of uninterrupted sleep. With little to do whilst waiting for Archangelo's next induced sleep, I might as well make the most of the opportunity to rest and recharge my batteries.

Pushing the thought of Archangelo firmly from my mind, I concentrated on something far more exhilarating – my relationship with Lucas. I hoped he wasn't too angry with my decision to stay away from Zaen, but even if he was, making up would be fun. Since we'd overcome our issues and returned to one another, we'd barely had any time together, but the kisses we'd shared were wonderful. Slipping into a delightful daydream, I wondered when we would make love for the first time. I was certain it would be soon, Lucas was making it abundantly clear that he wanted me as badly as I wanted him and the look in his eyes left no doubt about his intentions, his blue eyes filled with obvious lust. The daydream chased the last thoughts of Bran and Archangelo from my mind and I drifted back into a settled sleep.

When I woke for a second time, it was to the sound of my own screams, the pulsating throb in my head beyond description. It was beyond pain, the voices of hundreds of souls, shrieking at me in dire warning...

Chapter 23

Attack

Scrambling to my feet, I was grateful I hadn't bothered to undress last night. Snatching up the belt of weapons, I squinted against the sunshine filtering into the room. Waking so abruptly from a deep sleep, I was disorientated, fumbling to hook the belt at my waist and hastily dragging on my boots. It was a struggle to get a single coherent thought through the cacophony of voices in my head.

A noise downstairs had me lifting my head in dread. It might already be too late. Cursing inwardly, I tightened the bootlaces and crept out of the bedroom, listening for sounds from downstairs. Archangelo and Bran were growing progressively more expeditious in sending demons. They seemed to be concentrating on sending demons when I was alone, saving the younglings for attacking the groups. Whilst Archangelo's angelic abilities had reached their upper limit, the curious mix of demon blood meant he was improving the speed with which he located me. Worse, he seemed to be gaining a tolerance for the potion Bran plied him with, falling into a light doze and waking swiftly. My window of opportunity to escape was reducing with every passing day.

Moving down the hallway, I took the stairs slowly, cautiously laying weight on them to keep noise to a minimum. I slunk across the landing, before creeping down the next stairway. My skin was clammy, my heart in my throat as I slowly made my way, quelling the urge to sprint out of the house.

Reaching the last step, an unearthly howl erupted and a demon rushed straight at me. It was seven feet long, scorpion-like, with eight pincers, four down each side of its body and an elongated tail which tapered to a razor sharp barb. I stumbled backwards, tripping on debris and fell heavily to the floor.

Before I had a chance to recover, the demon was standing over me, its jaws snapping as I struggled to hold it back. With my left hand clutching its throat, I groped for the Katchet, catching it in my fingertips and settling it into my hand to stab at the creature. I managed a couple of good blows, but not enough to create any damage. Behind the demon, I detected a scrabbling sound, as though a giant centipede was running over the wooden floor. Twisting to see what made the sound, I knew I was in a whole stack of trouble. I regretted not taking the time to mark my skin before coming downstairs, I was completely unprepared and had no additional abilities available.

The demon towering over me swung its elongated tail, slashing down below my left shoulder with the barbed tip. The spike pierced deeply into the soft skin beneath my collarbone and I screamed, my eyesight blurring as pain seared in the muscle. Its wide jaws inched increasingly closer to my face and saliva trickled down my neck, burning my skin. I slashed clumsily with the Katchet, but it was having little effect.

Growling and snarling, the demon inched closer, its putrid breath hot on my skin. I dropped the Katchet and thrust against its neck, desperately trying to keep it away. In the background, the second demon scuffled noisily across the floor. Although outside my field of vision, terror had me believing it was nearby and ready to join the attack.

A sudden burst of gunfire exploded and the demon retreated abruptly, hissing its fury. I scuttled backwards, conscious of searing pain in my chest. I heard the shotgun being reloaded before another two shots were fired and the demon retreated further into the kitchen.

Gasping for breath, I was reaching for the Katchet when I heard a familiar voice. "*Charlotte*? What the hell was *that*?"

The pain amplified when I turned to the man behind me. "Sherriff Davis?" I was nauseous and I realized the demon's spiked tail was likely poisonous. The toxin was entering my bloodstream and starting to affect my muscle control.

Sherriff Davis aimed the shotgun at my chest and I was under no illusions – he *would* shoot if he felt threatened. "Where the hell have you been? You've broken your probation, kid. I've got a warrant for your arrest." His eyes narrowed suspiciously. "Where's Lucas and the others? What happened to them?"

I groped in my pocket for the Hjördis and he tightened his hold on the shotgun, aiming at my head. "Look, I need to do something about this... wound or I'm going to be dead... in about twenty minutes. Maybe... less," I gasped breathlessly. Any oxygen in my body felt like it was swimming through molasses and my motions were becoming shakier as the seconds passed.

He considered my words and lowered the gun. Scrambling sounds came from the far end of the living room and I twisted frantically, afraid the demons were about to attack.

"What the hell are they?" He watched as I tugged the Hjördis from my pocket and held it up to my chest. My hand shook and sweat poured from my skin.

"Demons," I gritted my teeth as I marked a poison sigil against the wound, followed by a blood sigil.

His eyes widened as he saw the indigo markings appearing on my chest. "What's that – *thing* you're using?"

"Look, as much... as I'd like to... answer all your questions... you've only... frightened those things... off for a... minute. Maybe two," I answered, stumbling over the words. "They're... here... to... kill me."

"Kill you? What the hell's going on? Where's Lucas and the others? They've been missing for weeks."

"They're... safe." I gasped as my lungs tightened spasmodically. The poison must be travelling through my bloodstream swiftly, and agonizing pain was spreading throughout my limbs.

The demon growled and scuttled across the room, clearly over the shock of the gunshots and intent on its target. I pulled a Philaris from my belt and threw it, hoping the delirium wouldn't affect my aim. The Philaris hit the demon and it dropped to the ground, pincers wriggling frenetically as it folded in on itself and disappeared.

"Jesus, Mary and Joseph." Sherriff Davis's eyes widened.

The second demon scrambled through the room. I tried hauling myself onto my feet, but had lost the ability to control my legs. The Sherriff crouched beside me, glancing from the gaping wound in my chest to the demon blood which covered my skin and mingled with mine.

"We need... to get out... of here," I moaned. "Right... now. Will... you help...me?"

He hesitated, brown eyes wide beneath eyebrows knitted together in alarm. "Okay." Tucking the shotgun over his arm, he hauled me up onto my feet.

"We... need to... get... outside," I muttered and he dragged me towards the door. Behind us, the second demon scuttled, multiple legs slipping on polished wooden floors.

"I have to take you in, Charlotte," Sheriff Davis grunted as he helped me down the steps. "You're under arrest for violating probation."

"You... can... try. But that... thing won't stop... till it... kills me," I panted.

"Well... *shit.*"

"Put... me... down here," I whimpered. The pain defied description, a burning sensation which was spreading through my arms and down into my torso. I wasn't confident that the poison sigil could stop the toxin and a brief glance confirmed the blood sigil wasn't coping either. Blood poured from the gaping hole, soaking my shirt.

He lowered me carefully onto the ground near the steps of the house. "We... are in... a whole lot of... trouble. That... demon is... not going to... be stopped... by your gun. Will you... trust me?"

He scrutinized me warily. "Do I get a choice?"

"Not... if you... want... to live." Archangelo might see this man the next time he was put into a sleep and the Drâghici would find out who he was, might come back here to kill him. He'd seen the demons, they couldn't let that knowledge loose without resorting to damage control. "Undo... your shirt."

"Excuse me?"

"For God's... sake! If I don't...do...this, I can't..." Articulate thought was beginning to elude me. "Just do it... will you... please?"

He astounded me by doing exactly as I'd requested, yanking off his heavy blue jacket and hurriedly undoing the buttons on his police shirt. With a trembling hand, I reached toward him. "This... will... hurt." Drawing the wing on his arm, I struggled to remain conscious and hoped I'd actually gotten it right. It had to be the swiftest mark I'd ever drawn.

"You weren't kidding," he growled, dragging his shirt over his shoulders and watching as I drew a pentagram. I envisioned where we needed to go and completed the sigils a moment before the centipede-shaped demon burst through one of the windows, got its bearings and scrambled towards us. The Sherriff raised his rifle and aimed, shooting at the demon, but barely slowing its forward momentum. I hooked another Philaris from my belt and threw it, catching the creatures head. It screeched when I hurled a spirit orb towards it. The orb was weak, but retained enough power to knock the demon onto its back, its legs waving frenetically as it tried to right itself.

The complete pentagram shone with dazzling white light and Davis stared at it incredulously. "*Shit*. What the hell is that?"

"Our... ride. Help... me... please?"

He hooked the rifle over his forearm and pulled me up. "What do I do?"

"Just step... forward..."

Hauling my limp form along beside him, he hesitated for a split-second, staring at the portal in disbelief. Seemingly resigned to the situation, he stepped into the circle of light resolutely.

We stumbled out of the portal into the central circle of Zaen. Barely conscious, I heard the screams of those witnessing our arrival before I slumped to the ground and succumbed to blessed darkness.

Consciousness returned in small increments, as I became aware of the crisp scent of freshly laundered sheets. The cool cotton stuck to my overheated skin. The next thing was pain. My chest burned, an ache deep within the flesh which pounded unmercifully and echoed throughout my body.

Somewhere nearby, a door opened and footsteps approached. I heard the creak of someone settling heavily in a chair.

"How is she?" Conal's voice reached me, anxiety apparent in his husky voice.

"No change," Lucas responded quietly. The direction his voice came from the opposite side of the bed and I pictured them in my mind. *"And I've told you before, I will happily update you. You don't need to be in here with us."*

"In your bedroom? Why? Are you frightened I might launch myself in there with her?"

"The thought has crossed my mind," Lucas answered ruefully. *"I don't trust you with her."*

"Why? Because she's in love with me, too?"

A heavy sigh. *"Yes, because she loves you, too."* I heard sounds, footsteps, then Lucas spoke from somewhere else in the room, further away from where I lay. *"Are we making any progress down there?"*

"Not really. Charlotte's plan isn't as successful as she would have hoped. We have vampires, werewolves and shape shifters mixed together in the housing. The werewolves are keeping to their own kind, as are the shape shifters."

"And they're all avoiding the vampires," Lucas agreed. *"Jerome is running the medical clinic and has no patients. The werewolves refuse to be treated by a shape shifter."*

"She's fighting suspicion and hatred that reaches back over thousands of years. They're hard habits to break, for everyone. The only ones getting along are the kids and the teenagers. Everyone else distrusts each other."

"And yet you and I can get along?" Lucas pointed out.

"Is that what we're doing?" Conal chuckled softly.

"You and I share a unique set of circumstances – we have a commonality the others don't have. We are both in love with this woman."

They lapsed into silence for a long time, before Conal spoke again. "Isn't there anything else we can do for her?"

"Jerome, Epi, Nonny – they've done everything they can. The poison from the Naberius is acutely venomous. We're fortunate she brought Clint back with her, otherwise we wouldn't have a clue what we're dealing with. The fever seems to be dissipating, but the healing sigils have struggled because she received such a massive dose of toxin." Lucas sounded frustrated. "And nobody can mark her with more sigils."

"You know," Conal began cautiously, "I could lick the wound. It might help dilute the poison."

"Believe it or not, I would actually let you do that if I thought it would do any good," Lucas responded quietly. "Despite my intense jealousy, I would do anything if I thought it would help her."

"You're jealous?" Conal sounded incredulous. "You're the one who has her – what the hell have you got to be jealous about?"

"Because as much as she loves me, I share her love with you. And... I'm aware that in many ways, you would have been the better choice for her."

"In many ways?" Conal spat scornfully. "I would have thought in all ways I was the better choice for her. For starters, I'm alive."

"That's true, dog. But she makes me feel as if I am alive, in every way possible. If I truly believed you were the better person for her, I would walk away. Permanently."

"Really?" Suspicion colored Conal's reply. "You would do that?"

"I would. I love her too much to do anything else. But for right now, I need her and she needs me. And unfortunately, she needs you too. She's tied to both of us, her need is an emotional bond which cannot be broken."

Conal shifted in his chair and wrapped a warm hand around my clammy arm. "I hope she recovers soon. Her absence is creating bigger issues than we started with. Rumors are swirling down there – that she's dead, that we can't win this war and today I heard something which was totally bizarre."

"What?"

"Someone said Charlotte was a murderer. That she killed her father."

"Step-father," Lucas corrected quietly.

"It's true?" Conal's shock reverberated around the room. I'd never told him my background and I'd only enlightened Epi because he'd insisted on knowing my past when he investigated my role as Nememiah's Child.

"That's Charlotte's business and no-one else's. She has the right to decide whom she tells about her past," Lucas replied firmly. "And I can't see why it's a problem. You've killed. I've killed. We're supernatural beings. No doubt the majority of those in the group have killed."

"They see her as human," Conal responded. "They don't expect humans to kill like we do."

"It's none of their business," Lucas growled. "And for the record, humans mastered the art of killing one another long ago."

Another long silence. "Is Clinton settling in okay? This must be a hell of a shock for him."

There was a smile in Lucas's voice when he spoke. "Sherriff Davis is tough, it's a requirement for a Police Chief. It's quite the learning curve for him to accept all this at once, but he's coping well and he has a soft spot for Rowena. She's helping to acclimatize him to our world. He seems to be happy enough joining us, insists he wants to stay, in fact."

"How are you going to explain that back in Puckhaber Falls?" Conal inquired. "Won't they notice their Sherriff is missing?"

"Epi is a creator of miracles," Lucas said. "As far as the good people of Puckhaber Falls are concerned, Clinton has retired and gone travelling. They're none the wiser."

"That old bastard is pretty clever," Conal agreed. He traced his fingers down my arm, catching my hand in his.

"Must you do that?" Lucas asked. "I will endure you being in here with us, but you're pushing the boundaries by holding her hand as though she is yours."

"You know, if you hadn't gotten yourself kidnapped by Odin and his band of merry vampires, chances are she would have still been mine," Conal retorted.

"She would never have stayed with you. Sooner or later, she was coming back to me," Lucas responded coolly.

"Oh, I think she could have forgotten about you eventually," Conal snapped. "She wasn't thinking about you very much when she was in my bed."

"Do you have to remind me of that? It fills me with..."

"Fills you with what? Anger, jealousy?" Conal responded helpfully.

"The desire to kill you," Lucas stated icily.

"Well, that makes two of us. It's crossed my mind once or twice that if you were dead, she'd come to me," Conal pointed out. "Oh wait, technically you can't get killed. You're already dead."

I decided enough was enough. I forced my eyes open, blinking rapidly before I spoke, voice scratchy from lack of use. "If you two don't stop arguing, I swear I'll kill both of you."

"Charlotte!" The relief in Lucas's voice was tangible and he appeared in my field of vision, blue eyes anxious. I blinked some more, adjusting to the light in the room. Lucas captured my fingers in his and for a split-second I considered the oddness of the situation, lying here with a vampire holding one hand and a werewolf holding the other.

I licked my dry lips and endeavored to focus my thoughts. "What day is it?"

"Monday. You came through the portal Saturday morning," Lucas said. "That was quite an entrance."

"Thanks." Struggling to sit up, searing pain exploded through my chest and I sank back on the pillows. "Why do I feel like an elephant sat on me?"

"You got a huge dose of poison from what Epi tells us was a Naberius," Conal responded. "It made a hell of a mess of your chest, but you're healing now. Epi came up with something to counteract the poison because the sigil you'd marked couldn't cope with the amount of toxin injected into your bloodstream."

"No doubt whatever Epi concocted tasted like crap," I muttered.

"Whatever possessed you to go back to my house?" Lucas questioned.

I attempted a shrug and rejected it as a terrible idea. "Guess I wanted somewhere that I would feel secure."

"It was fortunate you made that choice. If you'd encountered those demons and Clint didn't turn up when he did, you'd be dead by now."

"He wanted to arrest me."

"We've resolved that issue, my love."

Conal and Lucas exchanged a look, but didn't say anything more on the subject. I was grateful, I didn't want my reticence to tell Conal about the past to create another point of contention between the two men. They already had plenty to bug each other about. "Is Sherriff Davis okay? I marked him with the sigil so we could portal into Zaen. I wasn't certain I got it right."

"It was perfect and he's fine. Possibly somewhat mystified about everything but he's settled in okay." Lucas brushed his fingers across my forehead, a question in his eyes. "Why did you mark him? He's human."

"Nobody gets in without the mark. That's the rule." I cleared my throat, licking my lips. "Besides, I didn't want to take any chances and find out he's got some supernatural blood hidden away. Can I have a drink?"

"Of course. I'll get you some water," Lucas disappeared from the room and I turned to Conal, saw the concern in his face.

Squeezing his fingers gently, I spoke in a hushed voice. "Conal, you need to move on. I'm not leaving Lucas, I love him."

"And you love me," he responded, his voice equally quiet.

I sighed, my heart filled with sorrow. 'Yes, I do. But I'm not leaving him for you. You know that."

"I know," he stated. "But I'm in love with you, Sugar. For better or worse, that's how it is. There is nobody else I want. Maybe in time there will be, but I'm okay with it for now."

Watching him, I wondered if there was anything I could say, something I could do, to make him move on. It was frustrating to accept I couldn't. I sighed again and rubbed the back of his hand. "I wish I could fix this."

"It's right enough for now. You need me and you need Lucas." He ran his fingers tenderly across my cheek. "Charlotte, I can accept this as long as I can spend time with you. Call me delusional, tell me I'm crazy – but this is enough for now. Knowing you love me even a little bit, I'll accept that and someday I'll meet someone else. Give me time."

Lucas appeared with a glass of water and if he'd overheard our conversation, he gave no indication. He handed me the glass and I sipped the water gratefully, the cool liquid dousing the fire in my throat.

"So things aren't going too well, I assume?" Lowering the glass, I leaned it on my thigh. It was disturbing to discover the weight of a full glass was a struggle to hold in my current condition. I was even weaker than I thought. "I leave you guys in charge and you can't manage the simple task of making people get along?" There was teasing in my voice, an attempt to keep the mood light.

"Charlotte, it isn't an easy thing to do," Lucas said. "They don't like one another, there are centuries of hatred and mistrust working against us."

"We've got to find a way of overcoming it," I retorted determinedly, despite how awful I felt. "The only way we have of fighting the Consiliului is with a unified force."

"*I* know that. *He* knows that," Conal agreed. "But the rest of the group aren't getting the message."

Jerome knocked at the open doorway, limping in to the room with Rowena close behind. "Ah, you're awake," Jerome announced in his booming voice.

Rowena leaned over to hug me, pressing an anxious kiss against my cheek. "You frightened us terribly, Charlotte. You should have come back with Nick and the others!"

My lips hovered in a tiny smile. "Duly noted. I thought I was doing the right thing."

"Well, don't do it again," Jerome ordered. "You seem to have a unique knack for getting injured when you're alone, young lady." He checked my temperature and pulse, frowning heavily. "Better than it was, I'll admit, but I want more healing sigils on that injury as soon as possible."

Conal lifted the weapons belt from the top of the oak dresser and handed it to me cautiously, taking care not to touch the weapons.

The injury was covered in thick white gauze, taped down around the edges. Jerome pulled the gauze away and I stared at the damage in dismay. The centre of the gaping hole was still a shocking mass of torn flesh, only the edges were knitting together with the aid of the sigil. The skin around the wound was tinged black where poison was still seeping into my bloodstream. Raising the Hjördis, I marked both a blood and poison sigil. The skin began to bind together, leaving a glossy pink circle. The blackish tinge grew fainter and the veins near the surface of my skin reduced in size as the poison sigil worked on the toxins in my bloodstream.

"That's an impressive damn trick."

Sherriff Davis was standing in the doorway of what was becoming a rapidly filling bedroom, along with Nick and I smiled at them both. "Sherriff; Nick."

"I'm supposed to be arresting you," Sherriff Davis announced with a smirk. He was out of uniform, wearing an olive green t-shirt which stretched across his broad chest, and tailored black pants. "But given what I've seen the past few days, I'm gonna give you a reprieve."

"I'm not," Nick growled. "Charlotte, I told you I'd kick your ass if you got into trouble out there."

"I believe you told me you were going to haul my ass through the portal. You didn't say anything about kicking my ass." It was difficult to tell whether Nick was truly angry, or if he was teasing and consequently I was anxious about his reaction. It seemed he and I were always at odds with one another.

To my surprise, Nick grinned. "Well, I got my ass kicked by Rowena, Marianne, Acenith *and* Gwynn when I got back here without you. Seems only fair that you get the same deal."

I grinned back. "Can it wait till I'm feeling better?"

Nick stepped across to the bed and pressed a quick kiss against my forehead, his expression filled with relief. "Yep. You get a reprieve for now. But if you ever..." He inhaled sharply, before continuing. "Don't put me in that position again, or you really will get an ass kicking."

"Deal."

Sherriff Davis crossed his arms over his broad chest. "How're you doing?"

I attempted another shrug, found it worked marginally better than the first time. "Okay, I guess. Thanks for your help."

The Sherriff pursed his lips. "Not sure I did all that much. Seemed you had it all under control. Kind of."

I smirked. "I'm pretty sure I was in a heck of a lot of trouble. You're pretty handy with a rifle."

"Wasn't doing much against those critters." He inclined his head towards the weapons belt in my lap. "Seems like you have much better ammunition."

Lucas interrupted to urge me to reapply the sigils. They'd faded swiftly, presumably due to the amount of damage I'd suffered.

"There's no options, you know," I murmured as I finished a second set of markings. "These people have to learn to cooperate with one another."

"I think it might be an impossibility, love," Lucas warned.

"There isn't a hope in hell," Conal added.

"I think they need a wake-up call," I declared.

Chapter 24

Rally

After tightening my boots, I stood up, glancing at the reflection in the mirror. Weakness still beset me from the attack and the receding poison was creating a light sheen of perspiration over my skin, but the sigils were doing their job. The newly-healed skin on my chest was shiny and pink, but it would fade in a few days. I was certain I would be left with a scar, the injury had been too extensive to disappear entirely.

Stepping from the bathroom, I picked up the weapons belt and slipped it around my waist. It hung low on my hips, the weapons in easy reach whenever I need them. Impulsively I reached for the Hjördis, marking one final sigil on my chest.

Lucas tapped at the door. "May I come in?"

"Sure."

He pushed open the door and stood in the doorway, wearing camouflage pants and a black t-shirt which hugged his chest. "Nick and Conal are waiting downstairs. Are you ready?"

"As ready as I'll ever be." Shoving the Hjördis into my pocket, I looked up at him with a shy smile. "Lucas - technically, I think we're living together now. I'm fairly certain that means you don't have to knock on our bedroom door."

"Old habits die hard, my Charlotte." He was gazing at me, his eyes drifting across my black tank top and camouflage pants. "And I'm hoping to make the 'technical' aspect of us living together a thing of the past. Soon." Longing was evident in his dark blue eyes, as he focused on my breasts and his gaze lingered. "Do we have to do this?" he inquired huskily. "I'd much rather stay here." He bridged the gap between us and drew me into his arms, his mouth finding mine for a long kiss. "These clothes – they say women like a man in uniform, but I find you're having a similar effect on me." He ran his fingertips along the ridges of my spine and I shuddered, goose bumps forming on my skin.

"Trust me," I whispered, lowering my hands to his backside. "I'd rather stay here, too. It's been a very long time since I've spent a night with you."

"Far too long," he agreed, kissing me again, biting my lower lip gently. He glanced down at my chest. "Is that a fearless sigil?"

"Yeah. I thought it might help."

"It's certainly helping in one area," Lucas nuzzled my neck, pressing his body against mine so I could feel him, hard and firm beneath his pants. "You do realize you're holding my ass, don't you?"

I laughed huskily. "Yeah, I do. I've never heard you say that word before."

"You're a bad influence on me," he smiled.

"Probably. But for now, we have other things we need to do."

Lucas emitted a heavy sigh, but allowed me to drag him downstairs to the tiny living room, where Conal and Nick were waiting for us, dressed in similar camouflage pants and t-shirts to Lucas.

Conal groaned aloud. "Damn it, Charlotte! I thought we'd decided the fearless sigil was a bad idea?"

"Stop looking at my chest. Then you wouldn't know it was there," I retorted mildly.

"Let's face it Sugar, in that top, it's pretty much... *out there.*"

Lucas snarled, the sound rumbling through his chest and I squeezed his hand forcefully.

"Down boys. Enough." Heading towards the front door, I stepped out into the rapidly descending dusk. "Besides, public speaking isn't my thing. I figure a little bit of fearlessness isn't going to go astray."

Our quartet strode through the silent streets of Zaen, the three men dwarfing me in size, but that wasn't the purpose of their attendance. I wanted the new residents of Zaen to observe that werewolves, vampires and shape shifters could be together, working as a united group and this little demonstration of unity might help.

As we drew nearer to the central courtyard, my nerves accelerated despite the fearless mark. A steady buzz of voices grew louder as we approached and I made a conscious effort to keep my pace steady and my shoulders firm.

The population had been summoned to the meeting, told only that it was compulsory to attend. As we approached the outskirts of the crowd, they began to notice our arrival and stepped back, creating an avenue to stride through. A hum of recognition broke out as I made my way into the centre of the circle and stopped, waiting while they settled. Nick, Lucas and Conal stood a few steps back, standing side-by-side.

Looking around the assembled crowd, I saw the Tines standing together with Nonny and Epi. With them was Sherriff Davis and he nodded in recognition. Nonny smiled brightly, holding her two thumbs up. I returned the smile before turning my attention back to the waiting populace.

"For those of you who have met me," I began, pacing around the circle, "and those of you have not – I'm Charlotte Duncan. The Angel Child of Nememiah." I paused for a moment, allowing this information to sink in. "There have been a number of rumors swirling around Zaen in recent days, including one which suggested I was dead." Shaking my head, I offered them a little smile. "As Mark Twain once famously said – rumors of my death have been greatly exaggerated."

"Yeah, but you got mighty close this time!" Striker yelled.

I grinned at him, before turning back to the sea of people, scanning the faces. "Another rumor you may have heard is that I'm a murderer." Some people glanced away uncomfortably, others stared defiantly. "It isn't a rumor. It's the truth." Hushed whispers rippled through the crowd and I waited for them to settle. "I killed my step-father three years ago. Was I right to do that? Was I wrong? Like everything in this world, it helps to have the full story before you make your decision." Raking my gaze across the solemn faces, I paused for a moment. "I made a decision between right and wrong. It was my decision to make."

The silence was absolute now, as they waited to hear more.

"The truth is, I killed my step-father. After *he'd* murdered my mother, my two sisters, my baby brother. How you feel about my actions is your choice. I believe justice was done. I don't regret the decision and feel no sympathy for the man I killed. I believed in the choice I made." I began walking again, holding each individual's gaze in turn as I passed.

"And now, you have to make a decision between right and wrong. As we speak, the Consiliului Suprem de Drâghici Vampiri are amassing a sizeable vampire army, all younglings who are less than a year old. Unstable, danger-

Rally

ous and volatile, there are more than two thousand of them. Nememiah created two Angel Children – the Consiliului have created the other one to vampire. In conjunction with a warlock named Alberich Bran, they have the ability to summon demons from the Otherworld." I paused, giving them plenty of time to absorb this statement. "All of this is because they believe they're going to right a wrong. Those amongst you with mixed blood are considered an abnormality – they've decided you're an abomination, that you need to be exterminated. They intend to make you into a supreme race of supernaturals, based on their vision of what's tolerable and what must be eradicated." I stopped in the centre of the crowd, my expression grim. "What the Consiliului are doing is not dissimilar to what the Germans did during World War Two by annihilating the Jews. What happened in Croatia in the nineties. The massacre in Rwanda. It's ethnic cleansing. Eradicating anyone they've deemed unsuitable. I've heard complaints regarding the mark, which was required so you could enter this city." I'd spied Reynolds in the crowd and stared at him, watching him lower his gaze. "Yes, the mark is permanent and yes, it's painful. I've heard some of you think it comparable to what the Germans did, tattooing the Jewish population with identification numbers." My voice grew more confident. "That's where the comparison ends. Whilst the Germans used their tattoos to mark their victims, the wing you now bear is what provides you with sanctuary within Zaen. It's part of our plan – to keep you alive and keep you safe. Here, you are protected from the mass murder being perpetrated against others like you. Be thankful for the mark, knowing it stands between yourselves and what awaits you out there." I waved my hand towards the massive walls. "The mark is providing safety for you, your families and your loved ones – surely it's a small price to pay for the security those walls now provide you with?"

I pointed to Conal when I continued. "The Drâghici's plan is straightforward. He will be given the right to live, because he's pure-blooded. But that right bears a heavy penalty. He must bow to their rules, conform to their laws." I pointed to Nick. "He will die. He's a shape shifter, an abnormality. There's no room in the Consiliului's plans for anyone they deem an aberration." I pointed now to Lucas and he watched me solemnly. "And he will die. They'll kill him, because he's an anomaly. He doesn't drink the blood of humans and chooses to survive on animal blood." I began to pace again. "Look amongst yourselves. Many of you are half-blooded. Some of you love someone who isn't supernatural. Purebloods amongst you will have friends, relatives who are human or carry mixed blood. All are wrong in the Drâghici eyes. All will be slaughtered."

Turning to face Nick, Lucas and Conal, I chewed my lip thoughtfully. "These three men have one thing in common. Yes, they're different because of their bloodlines; because of their species, if you will. But they fight together, work together and manage to overcome their suspicions of one another in a common goal. To stop the Consiliului – to protect all of you. And to win this battle."

I scanned the faces before me. "All I keep hearing is you can't trust one another. You can't work together. You've hated one another for thousands of years. The mistrust you show to one another makes this situation untenable. You *have* a common goal – survival. You all have the ability to right this wrong. A wrong which will be perpetrated against every single one of you."

Drawing a Katchet from my belt, I waved it in the air. "Twelve months ago, I believed I was human. Perfectly normal. I didn't believe in *any* of you. Werewolves; shape shifters; vampires." With a wry smile, I shook my head. "All stuff of fiction. Then I met a group of vampires, who took me in when I believed there was nothing left to live for. They cared for me, offered love and protection, both from themselves and others who already knew what I was. I met werewolves, who did exactly the same thing. Protected me, believed in what I was, nurtured my abilities. And shape shifters." I smiled at Nick and he winked. "They too have accepted me and given me support when I needed it most."

Confidence grew when I was sure the group around us were really listening, their silence encompassing. Whether they believed or not, I couldn't tell, but I had their complete attention. "I discovered I was a child of Nememiah. An Angel child. And I have a mission – to save you from annihilation by the Drâghici and their allies."

Flicking the Katchet between my fingers nervously, I contemplated how much of my own thoughts to admit. "Believe me, there have been times when I've thought it would be easier to run away, not face the battle I know is approaching. But I know it's not an option. Part of my power lies in my abilities with these weapons. Another part is in my mind, working with ancestral spirits and accessing their help to defeat our enemies. And part of my powers lie here…" I pointed to my heart. "In my love and friendship with vampires, werewolves and shape shifters. Running away is not an option because I'm prepared to lay down my life to protect you. But you must offer allegiance to one another for us to succeed."

Striding closer to the people in the circle, my voice rose. "In my world – the human world – it's not so different from yours. Racism, intolerance – both a normal part of life. Asians, Caucasians, Europeans, African Americans and American Indians – there's a mountain of intolerance to overcome." I raised my eyebrows scathingly. "So when I hear you don't get along – it's nothing new. Black skin, brown skin, white skin – there's racism and intolerance between them all. There are two things that draw all together, two commonalities, for both humans and yourselves." Stopping in front of one of the Lingard pack, I twirled the knife between my fingers. "If I cut you, shape shifter, what color is your blood?"

He was solemn when he answered. "Red."

Next I headed towards Phelan. "And you, a werewolf. If you're cut, you bleed. What color is your blood?"

"Red." His response was loud and firm, filled with confidence.

"If I hold this dagger to my own skin and cut, the blood will be red. Something we all have in common."

"What about the vamps?" Someone called out. "The only blood in their bodies belongs to their victims!"

"Yes, that's true." I agreed quietly. "The creation process changes their bodies, removes their own blood, the need for human food. But they have something else in common with you. The second commonality I spoke about. They have love, affection, understanding. They care deeply about what is happening to all of us and they want to help."

"Vamps don't care about anything!" Another voice yelled.

"Yes, they do," I responded, looking across to my friends. "Ben Becket spends his time helping youth homeless who have been abused. He tries to make their lives better by helping them get an education, finding them housing, helping them escape from desperate circumstances. And he's loved me, as a father loves a daughter. He's here now, with you, willing to support you in this nightmare we now face."

Holden, Striker and William stood together, their expressions solemn. "Those three vampires will fight at your side against our common enemy. They're brave men, strong men – loyal and fearless. They're also vampires – but that has nothing – *nothing* to do with their ability to love, to protect and nurture those they care for. Striker and William are both married. I've seen how much they love and adore their partners. They're protective, caring, nurturing of the women in their lives. They've protected me, saved me in more ways than you can possibly imagine. All these vampires, every single one of them, made a choice between right and wrong. They've decided on your side in this war. *Our* side."

"They're vampires! They'll attack us!" One woman yelled anxiously.

"They won't. I'm well aware this small group of vampires are not the norm of what you've seen. I'm certainly aware, from my own bad experiences, of how brutal, how aggressive, how bloodthirsty and murderous vampires can be. I understand your fears, your concerns. I've had them myself. But I need you to trust me - have faith in this small group of vampires – accept them as part of our team, people who are on the same side. They will not attack you. Every single one of them has made the choice to feed only from animals and their commitment is indisputable."

"Everyone makes mistakes! What if they make a mistake?"

"They take precautions against that. They feed regularly and often." They were doubtful and it was difficult to decide how to convince them. It was probably only the passing of time which would provide them with enough evidence to start trusting, but time was one thing I didn't have. "Vampires were human once. With families, with children. Fathers, mothers, sisters, brothers. Daughters and sons. These vampires, the ones here with us now, they've made a choice – a decision to make the best of their existence and avoid human blood, avoid murdering humans for nourishment."

"Avoid it!" The same woman shrieked. "What if they're in a situation where they can't avoid it? Vampires suck their victims dry!"

"This vampire," I turned back to Lucas, offering him a grim smile, "and his Kiss, were kidnapped by the Drâghici. Tortured, nearly killed, they'd been denied nourishment for weeks. When we rescued him and his Kiss, the only way to help them escape was to allow them to drink my blood." The crowd hushed, as if they'd inhaled collectively and held it. "I chose to cut my own arm open, allow them a small amount of my blood."

"You'd be dead if that were true!" A man's voice shouted.

"It is true. They drank my blood. It helped to sustain them while we got them out of Sfantu Drâghici. They drank my blood and had the self-control, the willpower to stop themselves. Never before that day – not since that day – have they attempted to drink my blood again."

"It's a lie!"

Rally

I turned to the speaker and found myself facing Marrok. I was beginning to seriously dislike him. "Give me a reason?"

The older man stared at me in confusion. "Huh?"

I shrugged. "Give me a reason. What reason would I have to lie to you?"

He flushed red, shuffled on his feet uncomfortably. "It has to be a lie."

"Why?"

"I don't know why, but you're feeding us bullshit," he spat angrily, regaining some of his swagger.

A quick glance at Conal found him furious, his hands clenched into fists and his fiery stare burning holes into Marrok. "Again, I ask you why?" I responded calmly. "Were you there?"

"No."

"You've been with our group since the Drâghici attacked you. You've lived with the vampires since then. Have you been attacked?"

"No."

I smirked, deliberately trying to annoy him even more. "Noticed anyone dead? Any bloodless bodies? Somebody missing from your pack?"

A few people around him began to titter and chuckle and Marrok glared at them. "No."

"Found any fang marks on anyone? On yourself?"

"*No!*" He yelled angrily. "You're being ridiculous!"

I chuckled, pleased I'd gotten the reaction I'd wanted. "No, Marrok. You're being ridiculous. Worse still, you're small-minded and suffer from an inflated ego. You believe you're better than the vampires, probably the shape shifters and certainly better than me."

"That's bullshit," he huffed angrily.

"You're a racist, Marrok. You don't belong here. Pack up your belongings, your family and leave. There's no room here for your bad attitude." I turned away from him, as though he no longer existed.

Chapter 25

Understanding

Conal raised an eyebrow at me, but I ignored him and waited patiently for Marrok to speak. I had no doubt he was going to.

"You can't do that!" he finally spluttered and when I turned back, he'd lost some of the ruddy color from his face.

"Yes, I can." I waved my hand to encompass the wider group surrounding him. "We'll ask everyone's opinion, allow the group to make an informed decision about whether you stay, or if you leave."

"I want to stay!" The woman standing beside Marrok spoke up, her pale blue eyes wide as she glanced nervously at Marrok.

"Jenny?" he said quietly, staring down at her in disbelief. "If they kick me out, you'd come with me!"

She shook her head firmly. "I'm safer here, Marrok. I'm only half-blood. So are Gideon and Justin."

I assumed Jenny was his wife and Gideon and Justin, their sons. I made the decision to let this play out on its own, instinct suggesting this would work better than anything I could tell these people to convince them.

He puffed up his chest. "I would protect you."

She threw her hands up in the air. "How? How will you protect us from the Drâghici? You've seen what they did, you've watched them kill our friends!"

He motioned towards Lucas and the other vampires. "They're vampires, Jenny! They can't ever be trusted!"

She raised her chin defiantly. "I don't believe that. I've spoken with the one named Rowena. That girl, Acenith – she helped me when we were allocated a cottage. They're nice."

"Nice? *Nice!!*" he spluttered. "What about when they get thirsty? You won't think they're fucking nice then!"

For a long moment, there was silence and a lone tear trickled slowly down Jenny's cheek. "I'm not leaving, Marrok. I can't leave and take the risk of Gideon and Justin being killed. I can't... and I won't."

In many ways it was sad, watching this tableau being played out in front of so many strangers. It was unpleasant to watch Marrok slowly deflating, but it was encouraging to see the genuine love for his wife in his grey eyes as he wavered between his own fervent beliefs and the panic at being asked to leave without his wife and children by his side.

"Nobody will force you to leave," I offered quietly, watching Marrok wrap his wife in his arms, holding her close to his chest while she sobbed. "We're not your enemies, Marrok."

Lucas, Conal and Nick still stood together, their hands relaxed by their sides. "Vampires. Werewolves. Shape Shifters. You all see one, or two of their species as adversaries. I can assure you, these men, all the men in this city, are not your enemies. They're your allies. You can unite, if you choose to do so. And you have something else you must come together against. Demons."

I nodded curtly to Epi and he waved his hand, creating a replica of a Naberius, the scorpion-like demon I'd battled in Puckhaber only days before. People around us shouted and screamed, some backing away nervously and I held up my hand for silence. "*This* is what you're facing. Worry less about the vampires, more about these. This demon is a facsimile, a copy. Hence why it stands here indecisively. The mouth is full of teeth which drip pure acid – that's what gave me these burns across my neck." The marks were still vividly red, where the Naberius saliva had sizzled on my skin.

"The spike on the tail injects poison. That very same poison was coursing through my body when I portalled into Zaen with Sherriff Davis a few days ago. It stabbed me here," I showed them the massive shiny red scar, "and injected a massive dose of poison into my bloodstream. They're lethal, they're toxic and they will do anything to kill all of you when they've been programmed to do so. This is what the Consiliului will attack you with." The creature was motionless, watching as I walked around it warily. Psychologically I knew it wasn't real and wouldn't harm me, but the memory of the real Naberius made me uneasy. "The Drâghici are using Archangelo and the warlock to summons these creatures from the Otherworld. They're deadly, brutal and they each have their own lethal physical characteristics. They will be used in this war."

"But how can we fight... that?" The voice came from the crowd, someone calling out in disbelief.

"We can teach you. We can mark you with sigils, to protect you and help you in battle. But it will need all of us, every single person here and more, to overcome the obstacles we face." I nodded curtly at Epi and he waved his hand, making the Naberius shimmer and fade away. "They can be killed. They can be stopped." I pointed to the still-red scar on my chest, walking around to ensure everybody could see it clearly. "This is what a Naberius did to me four days ago. It had been ordered to kill me. The Drâghici will send demons who've been ordered to kill werewolves, shape shifters and vampires. Unlike you, they're not going to discriminate."

Inhaling sharply, I hardened my tone, wanting to make sure they understood exactly where they stood. "You all have a choice. Right or wrong. Fight or flee. I don't have those choices. I am the Angel child and my path is chosen. I fight on the side of right and I will fight no matter the odds. But if you can overcome your prejudice against one another, my chances of returning a peaceful world to you will increase. Now I ask you - who amongst you will overcome your petty differences and fight with me?"

Even with the effect of the fearless sigil, a trickle of panic rippled up my spine as I wondered if I'd convinced anyone with my speech. Lucas spoke up instantly. "The Tine Kiss fights with you." I threw him a grateful smile and he winked.

Thut stepped forward, regal and distinguished and he swept his gaze across the crowd. "The Bustani Kiss will fight."

Nick put his hand on my shoulder. "The Lingard Pack are joining the fight."

Conal added his commitment. "The Tremaine's will fight for the rights of everyone." His gaze was focused on Marrok, eyeing him coldly, waiting for his reaction. Marrok's eyes were intense, his forehead pulled down in a scowl, but he remained silent, only nodding his head in silent agreement.

Reynolds stepped forward, his expression a mask of grim determination. "The Reynolds Pack will join this battle."

One by one, the leaders of each group stepped forward and announced their intention to join us and the stress gradually receded from my shoulders. When the last of them had pledged their allegiance, I spoke again.

"Thank you for your commitment. We start training tomorrow." I smiled warmly, relief like a drug coursing through my body. "But tonight, we toast our allegiance to each other."Epi...?" Glancing across at the old man, I saw him rolling his eyes, but he did as I requested.

Vast tables appeared in front of us, laden down with food, alcohol, sodas and juice. The gathered crowds cheered noisily and swarmed towards the banquet.

Closing my eyes, I swayed a little as relief pounded through my veins. Despite the firm conviction that this gathering needed to occur, I hadn't convinced myself we'd get them to come together as a cohesive unit.

"I believe that was one of the best speeches I've heard," Ben announced, reaching my side. "And I've heard some excellent speeches in the past thousand years," he added with a wink. He hugged me for a long time, kissing my forehead. "I'm so very proud of you, Charlotte."

"Thanks. To be honest, I wasn't sure it was going to work."

"Of course it worked. That was amazing, Sugar." Conal wrapped me in a bear hug and kissed my forehead affectionately. "You were incredible."

"Yeah, it was pretty damned incredible." Sherriff Davis arrived with Acenith and Marianne, standing back as the two women hugged me.

"Thanks, Sherriff."

He smiled wryly. "Charlotte, I think you can start calling me Clint. I'm not the Sherriff of anything now."

"You're sure about staying?"

"Yep. Wouldn't miss it for the world." He smiled, his tall, heavyset body still holding the countenance of a Sherriff. "Nothing this exciting ever happened in Puckhaber."

"It's dangerous, Clinton," I warned.

"Hell, you're talking to a guy who go shot in the line of duty. The world's a dangerous place, Charlotte." He shrugged. "I've got no family, nobody who'll miss me. I like these folks," he said, waving his hand towards Acenith and Marianne, "even if they are vampires. And I figure if this group gets bigger, you'll be needing a Sherriff to keep the peace."

I was swamped by a wave of well-wishers during the next hour or so, as one after another, people approached to meet me or pass on their congratulations.

I kept trying to locate Lucas, craning my neck to search for him, but he was nowhere to be found.

Phelan appeared, handing me a glass with a devilish twinkle in his eye.

"What's this?" I asked, eyeing it warily.

"I've been trying to get you to have a drink since you turned twenty one," he announced with a cheeky grin. "This seems like the perfect time."

I sipped the drink cautiously, swirling the liquid around my mouth before swallowing it. "What is it?"

"Scotch and Coke. You don't really look like a beer drinking kind of gal," he chuckled.

I took another small sip. "It's okay."

"Great," Phelan winked. "Plenty more where that came from."

"Are you trying to lead my girlfriend astray?" Lucas stepped up behind me, wrapping his arms around my waist.

"Girlfriend. I like that," I announced happily

Lucas tilted my chin and kissed me hungrily, until I felt for a moment as though we were the only two people on the planet. When he released me, his eyes shone with warmth and desire. "Of course you're my girlfriend."

"I know. I've just never heard you call me that before. It makes me feel... special."

He kissed my nose. "You've always been special, Charlotte."

We were separated again as I circulated through the group, talking to the many people who wanted to discuss our situation. It was overwhelming, a frenzy of people and faces until I eventually located the Tines, who were sitting with Lucas, Epi and some of the Reynolds pack. By then, Phelan had given me a second whisky, followed by a third and all was right with my world. I slumped down on the bench beside Lucas and wriggled until I'd aligned myself against his thigh. Someone had brought a CD player to the circular grassland and Epi again performed his magic, removing the empty food tables and creating a wooden floor on the centre of the grass, where a few people were already dancing together.

Lucas kissed me lightly. "You taste of scotch," he announced, before deepening the kiss. "Mmmm, I remember that taste."

"Phelan keeps giving them to me, but he's complaining that I don't drink fast enough," I explained seriously.

"How many have you had?" Rowena asked.

"This is my third." I waved the glass in his general direction.

"That's not a bad average, Buffy," Striker said, grinning. "Don't think you're likely to get out of control with three scotches."

"I already feel out of control," I announced happily. "I never dreamed we could get everyone to consider becoming a cohesive unit and yet, look around..." I waved my arm expansively, before pointing my finger accusingly at Striker. "Will you *stop* calling me Buffy!"

"Hey, Lottie!" Marco ran up, his shirt hanging loose, eyes filled with delight. "I've found it!"

"Found what?"

"Every rebellion needs an anthem and I've found ours. Come dance with me." He yanked on my arm and I resisted.

"Marco, I've just sat down!"

"C'mon, this song is awesome. Exactly what we need to psych everyone up," he pleaded. "Please, Lott..."

"Go," Lucas whispered in my ear. "Once in your life you get to be twenty one. Go and dance with him."

I begrudgingly put down my glass and let Marco drag me onto the makeshift dance floor. The beat of an electro-pop song blared out through the speakers and Marco began to clap his hands, in time to the music. I followed his lead and when the vocalist sang, I understood why Marco said this was perfect for us. The words told of people being controlled, destroyed and continued with lyrics about fighting back, eventual victory. I swayed to the music, my inhibitions lost with the alcohol I'd consumed. Others joined us on the dance floor, dozens of people jumping to the beat, chanting the words. Marianne danced up beside me, then Striker and Holden, Conal, Sam and Phelan - dozens of others were on dance floor together. I glanced across the throng and found Lucas watching me, his eyes grazing across my body as I swayed and jumped to the music. He saw me watching him and slowly winked, making my pulse thump a little harder.

The song seemed to strike a chord with everyone, it spoke of our battle, described what we were up against. It was played repeatedly and I danced until my hair was soaked in perspiration and my feet ached. Working my way off the dance floor, I made a beeline for Lucas.

"Let's go home," I suggested, holding my hand out. He stood up, taking my hand in his before we meandered through the crowds, shouting goodbyes as we walked towards our cottage.

Lucas wrapped an arm around my shoulder and held me close. "Had a good time?"

"Wonderful," I agreed.

"I love you."

"And I love you." I stopped to kiss him and he wrapped his arms around my shoulders, holding me close. Someone wolf whistled and Lucas released me, grinning through the darkness towards where the shrill sound had come from.

"Striker?" I questioned.

"Holden." Lucas brushed his fingertips across my backside. "We'd get home faster if I carried you."

Nodding my agreement, he lifted me into his arms and ran swiftly through the rows of cottages until we reached our own. Dropping me gently onto the top step, he drew me inside. Pushing the door shut with his foot, he turned and watched me for a long moment.

"You have never been more beautiful than you are tonight," he said huskily. Before I could respond he pinned me against the wall, his hands cradling either side of my head as he kissed me. My heartbeat raced as his mouth invaded mine and I snaked my arms around his neck, pulling him against me. Lucas groaned and dragged his lips away from my mouth, his eyes dark as he gazed down at me. "Charlotte...?"

The unspoken question was visible in his eyes. I smiled, capturing his strong jaw against my fingers as I nodded tentatively, watching him close his eyes and breathe deeply against my wrist.

Lucas drew me into his arms again, his hands gentle against my back as he rained kisses over my skin and I inhaled the perfect aroma that emanated from his skin. "Go upstairs, love. I'll join you in a few minutes," he demanded huskily.

"What's wrong?"

Lucas's mouth lifted in a smile. "Nothing's wrong. Absolutely nothing. But I'd like to take a... precaution before we continue."

"You need to feed?" Having been out of the loop for a few days, I wasn't sure when he'd last visited the forest.

Lucas lowered his gaze, rubbing his hands across my waist. "I don't need to feed, love. But a male vampire can only maintain an erection while he has blood in his body from feeding." His lips brushed against my cheek, and he whispered against my ear. "I merely want to ensure our lovemaking can last for as long as we both want it to. I'll visit Striker, he has a blood supply available for just... such an emergency."

My face couldn't have been redder if I'd crash-landed on the sun. "Oh."

Lucas chuckled. "Don't worry, Charlotte. Striker and Marianne are still at the party, I'll slip in, grab what I need and be back within minutes. They won't know. Now go on, upstairs with you, my love."

I watched him slip through the door and then sprinted up the stairs, deciding a quick shower would be in order. I felt giddy, overwhelmed - knowing we'd finally reached the point I'd waited so long for was making me unexpectedly anxious.

I took a minute to stumble around the bedroom, pulling open a drawer to find the lacy negligees Marianne had bought. My heart was beating rapidly, nerves starting to become overwhelming. What if I disappointed him? What if, after all this time, it wasn't as satisfying for him as I hoped? He'd had countless decades of experience - on the other hand, I'd had no experience at all. I slipped into the bathroom, locking the door and rapidly stripping. Glancing in the mirror, I saw the flush of desire in my cheeks, the wild look in my eyes. The sigils I'd drawn hours ago had faded and I screwed up my nose at the large scar on my chest. It was healing, but still looked inflamed against my fair skin.

Leaning against the shower wall, I tried to quell my nerves before I faced Lucas. I wanted to be with him so badly, every inch of my body was on fire with desire, but I was terrified. I'd never been with a man - although I knew the mechanics of sex, I'd never put my knowledge into practice. Panic trickled into my mind - what if I wasn't any good at it?

There was a quiet tap at the door. "Charlotte?"

"I'll be there in a minute," I called out. He was probably wondering what the hell I was doing. Hiding out in the bathroom? Yep, that was exactly what I was doing. I turned off the faucets, drying quickly with a soft towel. Dropping it to the floor, I ran my fingers through my long hair, pushing it into some order before I slipped on the delicate lingerie I'd selected.

With one long glance in the mirror, I noted the terror in my green eyes and took a steadying breath, unlocking the door and pulling it open.

Lucas had turned off the lights and in their place, dozens of candles threw soft light across the room. The candles were everywhere, on every surface - the drawers, the bedside tables, even lined up along the windowsill. My mouth dropped open before Lucas himself captured my spellbound attention. He was sitting up against the headboard, his upper torso naked and lust snaked through my groin. For the first time ever, he was *in* the bed - the sheet covering his lower body. We'd slept together many times, but always before now, he'd lain on top of the covers, cocooning me from the coldness of his skin. To see him laying there - beneath the covers - left no doubt of his intentions. I inhaled a shuddering breath.

"There you go again. That endearing little gasp of breath," he said with a soft chuckle.

"I can't help it. You're so perfect." I willed my feet to move and walked slowly around the bed.

"You look as though you'd like to eat me," he commented mildly.

"I thought that was your job," I retorted with a nervous giggle.

A shadow crossed his handsome features. "Please, don't joke about it, Charlotte," he requested quietly. "Even now - I'm terrified of hurting you."

The doubt in his voice propelled me to the bed and I slipped between the covers beside him, wrapping my arms around his waist. "You won't. I know you won't."

He groaned as he pulled me close, holding me against him. "You must tell me, if anything I do causes you pain," he whispered huskily. "It will be difficult for me to control everything when there are other... factors involved."

I ran my fingertips across his chest, brushing the pad of my thumb against his nipple and watching it harden instantly. "I trust you, Lucas. I know you won't hurt me."

He captured my mouth against his own, kissing me deeply. "I have never wanted anything as much as I want you," he said huskily against my lips.

"I'm yours," I responded simply.

Chapter 26

Confessions

When I woke the following morning, I was encircled in Lucas's arms, my leg slung across his thigh, my head resting on his chest. I lifted my head to look at him, startled to discover his eyes were closed. He looked peaceful and relaxed, his chest rising and falling and I shook him a little. "You aren't actually *asleep*, are you?"

He opened his eyes and they twinkled in amusement. "No. A lot of things have changed, but I'm still vampire. I don't sleep." He smiled softly. "I was merely enjoying the memories of making love with you last night." He drew himself up in the bed, lifting me tenderly into his lap and drew the covers over both of us. "How do you feel?"

I smiled blissfully. "Quite glorious."

"I wasn't too strenuous for you?" he murmured worriedly against my shoulder as he trailed kisses across my collarbone.

"You might have been a little bit... strenuous. But I thought it went pretty well, considering everything."

"Pretty well, huh?" He rolled his eyes, offering me a lazy smile. "Sounds like you think there's room for improvement."

I laughed in delight. "Lucas, it was wonderful. The most amazing experience I've ever had. Ever."

He looked a little smug over my declaration and we shared an elated smile. Lucas drew me tightly against him, draping one hand possessively across my hip. "The first time for a woman can be painful. Are you alright?"

I blushed and Lucas smiled indulgently, kissing the tip of my nose. "I'm a little bit... tender," I admitted huskily.

His eyes were grazing a path across my arms, a small frown creasing his forehead. "I think I was far too strenuous," he growled, scanning the numerous purple bruises which had blossomed across my skin, darker than the bruises from the Naberius attack. Fingerprints were clearly visible on my upper arms.

"I don't care." I eyed him curiously. "When we were making love - you didn't have the urge to bite me?"

"It was there, but I controlled it," he admitted. "Of course," he smiled wryly, "my mind was busy with other things." He held me closer and caught my chin with his fingers, lifting my mouth to his. "The feel of you, holding you against me all night. It's been everything I hoped for, Charlotte. I love you."

"I love you, too." I pulled back from him, so I could see his face. "And, I have a confession to make."

He gazed at me, his face expressionless. "I imagine this relates to your claim that I wouldn't bite you, because I'd tasted your blood?"

For a long moment I stared at him, the blush creeping up over my skin. "You knew?"

He laughed, the sound abrupt in the silent room. "I'm over one hundred and fifty years old, Charlotte. I'm a long way past naïve."

"I only said it because I thought it would help," I admitted. "You didn't believe you could control your thirst. I can't be created now that I'm twenty one, but I didn't know if you would ever overcome your need to protect me from yourself. All I was trying to do was help you believe you could." I rubbed his arm and smiled. "And I have to say, you did a pretty magnificent job."

"I love you for what you did, Charlotte. Nevertheless, you've put an incredible amount of trust in my strength of will. I'm still dangerous to you," Lucas said huskily.

"I know you won't bite me," I responded confidently, snuggling against him.

He was frowning, his expression serious as he gazed down at me. "Charlotte, as much as I love you, we still need to exercise extreme caution. I will always need to ensure I've fed well before we make love. To do anything else would pose too great a risk." He paused, trailing his fingers down my arm. "And there is the possibility of you falling pregnant. We took no precautions last night."

The first thought that crossed my mind was the delighted thrill of having his baby. The idea of us creating a baby - *our* baby was something I'd thought we could never achieve. But I knew where his thought process was coming from, we were in the middle of a war and now would not be the time for me to fall pregnant. "What do you suggest?" I questioned.

Lucas inhaled sharply, considering the problem. "I'll talk to Jerome. Perhaps he can recommend a combination of precautions we can take, which may avert a pregnancy," he suggested.

"And in the meantime?" The thought of stopping what we'd only begun last night didn't thrill me.

"Some precautions can be used immediately," Lucas reassured me with an easy smile. "I'm sure Jerome can suggest something. We won't have any guarantees, I doubt a vampire and an angel have gotten together before, so we're in uncharted territory. But we'll do the best we can to avoid a pregnancy." He trailed his fingers down my chest, cupping my naked breast in his palm and I shivered. "And I have *no* intentions of abstaining," he growled softly.

"So," I confirmed slowly, "if we can come up with some precautions, there's no reason why you can't make love to me whenever you want to. Or whenever I want to?"

"Well admittedly, that could be a problem. I think I want to make love to you all the time. Every minute of the day," Lucas murmured against my shoulder. "There will never be time for anything else." He ran his fingers across my arms, tracing the bruises tenderly.

I sighed unhappily, throwing off the covers and crawling out of bed. "As much as I adore that thought, Epi won't agree." Bright sunshine filtered in the window and I knew it was later than I would normally rise. "He's going to be spitting mad because I haven't turned up yet." Retrieving fresh clothes from the dresser, I turned back to find Lucas gazing at me longingly. "What?"

"You're used to the changes which have happened to you," he stated softly. "I'm not. You look... amazing. Curves in exactly the right places and you have a confidence about you that's... exceedingly erotic."

I chuckled. "Get dressed. We have to go."

Lucas rose sinuously from the bed and stood in front of me in glorious nakedness. For a long, *long* moment I reconsidered my decision-making process. But I knew we had to make an appearance, there was much to talk about and plans to be made.

Dressing quickly, I pulled on underwear and then my standard uniform of camouflage pants and black tank top, flicking my hair into a ponytail. Pulling my boots on, I watched with regret as Lucas dressed, hiding his stunning body beneath clothes.

Lucas caught me when I stood up, kissing me longingly. Pushing away from him, I caught his hand in mine. "Let's go, I need something to eat."

"It's nice to find some things about you haven't changed," Lucas grinned.

I headed for the bedroom door but Lucas restrained me, drawing me back towards him. "Perhaps you should wear a shirt that covers more of your skin, love," he suggest quietly, his gaze running across the bruises which were appearing everywhere. "Conal has enough reasons to kill me, without discovering what I did to you last night."

Looking up into his troubled eyes, I offered him a reassuring smile. "Lucas, I'm not going to cover the bruises, they aren't that bad and I had bruises anyway. I'm not ashamed of them."

A scowl creased his forehead, but he didn't argue. "I must increase my control when we make love. I will not mark you like that again."

I shrugged. "They're only bruises, Lucas. No different to what Epi subjects me to every day." I glanced down at my watch and groaned. "He's going to subject me to a lecture when I see him this morning." It was already a little after nine, far later than I would normally appear.

Timed almost perfectly to my announcement, there was a knock at the front door and I ran downstairs to answer it, Lucas following closely behind.

Marianne stood on the tiny stoop, dressed in a lime green jacket, faded and torn black denims and matching lime green boots. Her blue streaked hair was pulled up into cornrows, framing her beautiful face. She smiled happily when I opened the door and slipped inside. "I've been sent on a mission to find you," she announced, dropping daintily onto one of the living room chairs. "Epi seems to believe Charlotte was stolen by a demon during the night."

Lucas slipped an arm around my waist. "I let Charlotte sleep in this morning. She was enjoying a nightmare-free sleep and it happens so rarely, it seemed a shame to wake her."

I flashed him a grateful smile, an excuse for our tardiness was completely beyond me and Lucas's ability to lie convincingly seemed like a blessing.

Marianne scrutinized the bruises on my arms and a broad smile spread across her face, her eyes bright. She looked absolutely delighted. "I think something else *entirely* was going on here. You both look far too pleased with yourselves."

I blushed to the tips of my toes and Lucas smiled wryly at Marianne as she leapt daintily from the chair and kissed my cheek. "I'm so happy for both of you!"

"Marianne..." I began, a warning in my voice.

She placed her hand over her heart. "You're secret is safe with me, I promise." Marianne hugged Lucas briefly, kissing his cheek. "Striker thought there was blood missing from our fridge last night! Now you really should get moving, Charlotte. Epi is grumbling about turning you into frog-spawn again..."

As predicted, Epi was utterly incensed by the time we made our way into the meeting hall, his eyes blazing with anger and his skin ruddy with annoyance. "Where have you been?" he demanded furiously. "We have a multitude of items to deal with and you sleep in! Whilst I appreciate how difficult the time constraints upon you can be, it's imperative that you step up and accept the responsibility that's been thrust upon you! And that means being here on time!"

Behind him I spied the Tines, Conal, Nick and other people from the new packs. All were trying to hide smirks at Epi's furious tirade. We'd stopped momentarily at the large house which served as the Mess Hall and I'd scooped up an apple and banana for breakfast. I bit into the apple and chewed slowly. "Epi, you're going to give yourself a heart attack," I mumbled casually. "I'm here now - don't have a cow. Besides, I had a good night's sleep. No nightmares. You should be happy that I'm refreshed and ready for whatever you're about to torment me with."

For a moment, there was a very real chance his eyes would explode from their sockets, but he took a deep gulp of air and glared at me, a vein throbbing in his forehead. "Don't... have... a *COW!*" He appeared ready to launch into another outburst but Conal intervened, patting the ancient warlock's stooped shoulder.

"Relax, old man. She's not that late, I only got here fifteen minutes ago." Conal met my eyes, his own twinkling with mischief. When his gaze shifted to the bruises on my arms his face hardened, his attention shifting from myself to Lucas. "We're all struggling this morning after last night's celebration," he concluded quietly.

Ben placed his hand against the small of my back. "Charlotte, I should properly introduce you to our new associates." He led me over to an older man who was grey-haired and stocky. He reminded me of Conal's father, dressed conservatively in black linen trousers and a pinstriped shirt. He watched me soberly as Ben made the introductions. "This is Bill Conroy, he's the leader of the Black Raven werewolf pack from North Carolina."

I offered him my hand. "Mr. Conroy, it's a pleasure to meet you."

He eyed me cautiously, for a split-second longer than was necessary. "You'll be able to read my ancestors from a touch?"

I nodded. "That's correct. If you don't intend me harm, I'll have contact with them."

He held out his hand confidently and I grasped it, the new spirits trickling into my mind like a gentle flow of water. "Thank you for joining us, Mr. Conroy."

"Call me Bill," he insisted.

I smiled cordially. "All right, Bill."

Ben directed me to a second man, short and lean with dark brown eyes and wiry red hair. He wore a brown checked shirt and faded blue jeans, a large silver Harley Davidson buckle on his belt. "This is Nat Finton, he's the head of his shape shifter pack from Nevada. They were attacked the same night as the Tremaines."

Nat Finton held his hand out with no hesitation and I grasped it in my own, a rush of spirits entering my head. "It's nice to meet you, Mr. Finton."

"Nat, please," he insisted congenially. "It's a pleasure to meet you."

I considered my next question carefully before speaking. I was aware that for some packs, questions about their ability was considered rude and I didn't want to create animosity, but my inquisitiveness was overwhelming. "Nat, forgive me if I don't ask this with the correct terminology. I'm very new to this world, but I'm also curious. What sort of animal do your pack shape shift into?" I flushed with embarrassment, hoping I hadn't committed some supernatural faux pas with this line of questioning. "Is that even the correct term?" I questioned.

Nat smiled warmly. "The correct term is 'what animal do you shift into?'," he advised easily. "And no, it's not offensive to my pack for you to ask. In fact, I'd have been concerned if you didn't want to know what ability we have to fight this war with you. Me and my pack, we shift into panthers." A dark shadow crossed his features. "At least, what's left of my pack."

I listened to the new voices filtering through my mind for a couple of seconds. "I'm so sorry about the attack. I understand you lost two thirds of your people."

His brown eyes narrowed suspiciously. "You heard that from…?"

"The spirits I hear now I've touched you. Whit is glad you've decided to ally with us. He's sorry he's not here to join in the battle."

He shook his head ruefully. "That's my brother. Whit never did like to miss out on a good fight."

Ben guided me towards another man, but before he could introduce him, Joe Reynolds stepped before us, holding his hand out. "Miss Duncan - I owe you a sincere apology. I see now how dedicated you are to this - *our* cause."

I took his hand, shaking it firmly. "Apology accepted, and call me Charlotte."

"Charlotte," he repeated with a grin. "Be assured, Charlotte. Me and my pack are committed to this fight. We won't let you down."

His earnest expression and the honesty in his eyes convinced me, along with the voices that joined the collective in my mind. "Thank you, Joe. I appreciate it."

Ben introduced the next man. He was a tall African-American, in his late twenties. His face was fascinating, chocolate brown eyes which slanted like Conal's and unusual markings across his cheeks. I couldn't figure out what they were, not a tattoo, more like tribal markings which had been cut into his skin. He wore a faded Bob Marley t-shirt with black cargo pants and his curly black hair reached his shoulders. "Charlotte, this is Ambrose Wilkes. He's pack leader of the Halifax shape shifters. They've come from Canada, heard about us through Nat Finton, who was friends with Ambrose's father.

Ambrose lifted his hand toward me, with a broad grin. "Sure is nice to meet you, Ma'am."

I smiled up at him. He was taller than Conal and Lucas, maybe six feet seven inches. "Shape shifters - what animal do you shift into?" I asked, remembering what Nat had explained about the correct terminology.

"Well, Ma'am, we transform into tigers," he responded with a confident grin.

I opened my mouth in surprise, shut it again hurriedly. "Wow," was all I managed.

"We are a force to be reckoned with, if I do say so myself," Ambrose said proudly.

Listening to the murmur of voices I located the strongest strand from my mind. "I'm sorry about your father's death. You must miss him a lot."

"Yes, Ma'am, I do," Ambrose agreed and there was sadness in his voice. "He was a real good man."

"He's very proud of you, Ambrose. He's pleased you've come to Zaen and you're keeping the pack safe."

"I'll do anything I can to help, Ma'am," Ambrose's sincerity was obvious.

I smiled and shook my head. "You can start by calling me Charlotte - I'm not sure I can cope with the whole 'Ma'am' thing. Makes me feel like an army sergeant."

"Yes, Ma'... Charlotte," he amended with a sheepish smile.

Ben turned to Epi. "I believe that's the introductions complete. Might I suggest we take our places around the table and get down to business?"

At Ben's suggestion, we'd decided on a quorum of representatives - each separate faction, whether vampire, werewolf or shape shifter would have one spokesperson on the quorum and all decisions required a majority vote. The spokesperson could ask others to attend meetings, however only the spokesperson received voting rights, making it equitable for every group regardless of their size.

My pledge to Nememiah weighed heavily on my mind. I felt it was imperative for every group to be aware of their equality in the merger. My personal wish was to be seen as an equal by them all. I didn't want to be their leader, although Epi insisted that was how I would seen.

Lucas and Ben had been magnificent and I relied constantly on their advice with regards to keeping the factions unified. A twenty one year old girl needed all the help she could get.

"... so it seems there's a division emerging between the Draghici, Alberich Bran and Archangelo." I'd spent the past twenty minutes detailing my last nightmare to the quorum. "From what Bran said, I'm convinced he's using the Drâghici to complete the cleansing and then he intends to take over."

There was a thoughtful silence around the table, then Nat spoke. "How accurate are these nightmares? I don't want to sound insulting or be unduly skeptical, but is there a possibility your information could be wrong?"

Lucas answered, rubbing his thumb against my thigh. "Charlotte's nightmares have a one hundred percent accuracy level."

Ben inclined his head in agreement. "What Charlotte refers to aren't nightmares in the normal sense of the word. They are moments during her sleep cycle in which she's transported spiritually to Sfantu Drâghici. What she sees and hears is a live-time window into what is occurring."

"How does that work?" Ambrose asked.

"The honest answer? We don't know," Conal responded.

"The biggest problem is only seeing brief moments during the nightmares," I admitted. "I have no control over what I see and hear, sometimes I'm only receiving half the information."

"Charlotte doesn't always see the inner workings at Sfantu Drâghici," Lucas continued. "Sometimes she's transported to the site of attacks they're perpetrating. There doesn't seem to be a pattern to where she'll be spiritually transported."

"And how much I see depends on how long it takes to wake from the nightmare."

"Whatever the case, it's a useful talent," Nat said, rubbing his chin thoughtfully.

"Charlotte, Ben says you receive warnings from the spirits? How do they work?" Joe Reynolds questioned.

"The spirits warn me of impending attacks, usually by screaming at me in unison." I shared a wry smile with Lucas. "It's useful, but the window of forewarning is small."

"How small?" Nat asked.

"Usually less than five minutes."

"Why such a small warning? Don't the spirits know what's happening all the time?" Ambrose asked.

"Charlotte's spirit friends are a tool at her disposal, not a solution," Epi clarified. "The spirits work with Charlotte to protect her as Nememiah's Child. What Charlotte has elected to do is a divergence from the natural role of Nememiah's Children. In past history, the spirits that Charlotte harnesses were designed to protect her from demon attacks. Charlotte has revolutionized the process, using the spirits to warn us as a group of imminent attack. The spirits warnings are acting like a perimeter barrier - if Charlotte is in immediate danger, the spirits tell her."

Joe Reynolds looked thoughtful. "Now I understand - the warnings are designed to protect Charlotte and she's using them to protect us."

"Exactly," Conal agreed. "It works in the same way as the Government's Star Wars program. No warning until an attack is imminent."

"Unfortunately, it's a double-edged sword," I explained, smirking at Conal's analogy. "You're receiving the warnings, but you're also in the line of fire by being with me. The Consiliului want my head on a platter."

Reynolds shook his head and he scowled. "Seems to me it's better than having no warning at all. We had no forewarning of the attack on my pack. At least here, we'll know it's coming."

"That's what we believe, also," Ben agreed, giving me an encouraging smile. "Charlotte tends to worry that she's putting us in danger by being here, however, we believe we're more secure with her than anywhere else." He steered the discussion smoothly back to my recent nightmare. "I think we should be concerned about this latest development with Alberich Bran. He and Archangelo are in control of the demons, ultimately they must be seen as the greater danger to us all," Ben said thoughtfully. He was holding a pencil between his fingers, flipping it over and over again with rapid movement - an unusual state for a vampire who was usually so motionless.

"I don't like the implications Archangelo is making," Conal announced darkly. "It seems he might have developed an unhealthy obsession with Charlotte."

Chapter 27

Trust

Startled by Conal's abrupt statement, I met his eyes and saw concern, knew he was worried about me. As much as I appreciated his anxiety, we needed to be looking at the bigger picture.

"Conal, I don't think Archangelo's our biggest problem. I agree that he seems to be somewhat... obsessed, but for the moment I'm safe here in Zaen," I said reassuringly, scratching my head thoughtfully. "I think the bigger crisis is the Consiliului and their ethnic cleansing. We have to find some way of getting other people into Zaen before they're attacked."

"Charlotte's right," Lucas squeezed my thigh. "Without communication to the outside world, we have no way of contacting others. We're already seriously outnumbered and the Drâghici are continuing to amass their army of younglings."

"Could we approach these vampires? Tell them the warlock's plan?" Bill Conroy asked. He was sitting opposite Lucas and I, his arms crossed on the table.

"The Drâghici will not believe it," Lucas explained gravely. "They believe they're the most powerful supernatural group on Earth." He glanced down at me, his blue eyes bleak. "I doubt they would consider talking to us, nor give us an opportunity to explain without killing us immediately. They will be enraged that Charlotte and her friends rescued us."

"Not to mention Charlotte seriously busted up their stronghold," Nick added with a malicious smirk.

"Nick is correct," Ben added heavily. "The Consiliului are amongst the oldest vampire on Earth. Their belief in their superiority is absolute."

"They won't be swayed?" Ambrose queried.

Lucas shook his head. "They tortured us, raped our women while they forced us to watch. They won't be swayed." His voice was filled with barely concealed rage, and I felt the wave of energy from him as he struggled to control his anger. It was my turn to squeeze his thigh gently, reminding him of where he was. He glanced down at me and I saw him swallow, visibly force himself into calm.

There was a deathly silence in the hall for a minute or two as the men struggled to come to terms with Lucas's disclosure. Finally, Epi broke the quiet. "We must allow the situation to continue unfolding, allow Charlotte to gather more information from her nightmares and the spirits. When we have additional details, we will formulate a plan in that regard. Until then, we can do nothing."

"Agreed," Joe Reynolds spoke up, casting an anxious glance at Lucas. "We must find a way for others to join us here in Zaen." He swept his gaze across the others around the table. "At best we have two hundred people who can fight. Charlotte says the Consiliului have over two thousand, without even considering the demons. We need more."

Nat Finton spoke up, clasping his hands together on the table. "We should do reconnaissance around Zaen. We know from the position of the moon overhead and the sun that we're somewhere on Earth, likely the northern hemisphere. If we send out some small groups to try and pinpoint where we are, it might assist us in finding a way to contact others, offer them the chance to join us before it's too late."

I was quickly warming to Nat Finton. He was quiet and unassuming, yet seemed to harbor a powerful resolve to assist us in any way he could.

"I can send some of my men out, head out in compass point directions, get them to give us an idea of our location. The surrounds of Zaen can't be that enormous that we wouldn't have an answer within a day or two," Ambrose Wilkes offered.

Lucas scanned the other men sitting around the table, gauging their agreement. "Thank you, Ambrose. We'll accept your offer."

Ambrose stood up, stretching his muscular body in a cat-like motion. Tendons and muscles rippled beneath his t-shirt. "I'll inform my best runners, send them out straight away." He strode away from the table, heading towards the exit.

"Let's take a ten minute break," Epi announced. He pushed his chair away from the table and strode to where Ben sat, bending his head to begin a conversation. Lucas lifted his hand from my thigh and smiled. "I'll be back in a minute, love. I'd like a word with Nick before we continue."

I leaned forward to kiss him, my lips brushing fleetingly against his and when we parted, Lucas's eyes smoldered as he gazed at me. "I'm going to make a coffee."

Nonny had thoughtfully provided coffee making facilities for our meeting. Since arriving in Zaen, the elderly lady had proven a force to be reckoned with, presiding over the newly established Mess Hall and providing meals for everyone, assisted by a team of women she'd commandeered. Nonny frequently astounded me with her enormous energy reserves, willingly participating in anything asked of her. Epi was using some magical means to procure food, I wasn't sure where it was all appearing from, but knew better than to ask.

The memory of last night was still graphically fresh in my mind and pouring coffee, I allowed myself a little fantasy about Lucas holding me, making love to me. To my mind, every second had been perfect and I was comfortable in the fact that I hadn't disappointed him. A tiny smiled flickered across my lips - on the contrary, Lucas had given me the impression he'd been very, very satisfied with our first sexual encounter.

"Charlotte." Conal appeared, his dark eyes thunderous and his jaw tight with tension.

"What's up?" I crossed my arms instinctively, attempting to cover the bruises.

"Don't bother hiding them," Conal hissed quietly. "What did he do to you?"

"Nothing, they're from the Naberius," I lied swiftly, hoping to avert disaster.

"Bullshit. What did he do?"

My lying still stank. "It's not what you think," I began, my voice hushed. "He didn't intentionally hurt me."

Conal stared into my eyes for a minute, emotion flitting across his expression before he groaned aloud. "You let him *screw* you?" he accused angrily.

I reached out to touch his arm, but he snatched it away, his body language confirming his rage. "Conal, you promised you were okay with this," I whispered.

For a minute he was silent, before he shook his head furiously. "I'm trying to be, Christ knows I'm trying, but you can't blame me for being angry. He *hurt* you, for Christ's sake!"

"He didn't mean to, Conal." I was dismayed, not only because I didn't want to hurt Conal's feelings, but because we were in so public a place to have this discussion. "It wasn't intentional."

"Charlotte, he's capable of *killing* you. You know that, don't you? You know vampires usually kill their prey during sex, they can't control their urges!"

"He won't," I muttered, the flush of embarrassment rising over my skin. Lucas and Ben were close by, their hearing so incredibly acute and this wasn't a conversation I wanted overheard. "*Please*, Conal. Be happy for me. At least, *try* and be happy for me. I love him."

Conal's eyes softened. "*Shit.*" He raked his fingers through his hair. "I'll try. But I can't say I like it. Regardless of my feelings - Charlotte, he's incredibly powerful. All of them are. He could kill you, without even meaning to. He could crush you beneath his hands without realizing he's doing it." He ran his fingers through his hair again, drawing it back from his face. "I wouldn't do that," he added huskily.

He didn't flinch when I touched his arm. "Conal. *Please.* You have to let this go, you have to move on. I'm with Lucas. You said so yourself - I belong with Lucas."

"Charlotte? What's wrong?" Lucas materialized behind us, his midnight blue eyes studying Conal's tensed features and my flustered ones.

"She's fine. Everything a-okay here." Without another word, Conal stalked back to the table and slumped down into his seat.

"What happened?" Lucas demanded in a low growl against my ear.

"It's nothing," I muttered, stirring my coffee morosely.

Lucas watched me for a minute, his eyes hardening. "I assume he figured out what happened last night?"

I nodded miserably.

Lucas glanced back towards Conal and sighed heavily. "This is why I wanted you to cover those bruises, my love."

"He's frightened you'll hurt me," I admitted.

Lucas squeezed his eyes shut, as though he suffered some intense pain. "He's right. It is *absolutely* possible."

Troubled, I glanced away from the coffee I'd been stirring, hitting the cup so coffee slopped onto the table. "I don't believe that, Lucas."

Lucas captured my hand in his and stared down at me, his eyes fierce. "You should believe it, Charlotte. I'm capable of killing you, without even thinking about it." The ferocity in his tone was alarming. "Last night, whilst exquisite in every possible way, was dangerous for you. I controlled my desire to feed from your blood, but it was... difficult. Orgasm and feeding are intertwined." He rubbed his fingers across my arm, his cool touch soothing. "Last night, it was only bruises. I'm afraid however, that it could be much worse." He gazed into my eyes, his own filled with anguish. "If I lose concentration, if I forget for only a split second your humanity, I could crush you beneath my hands. Or even worse." Despite the natural pallor of his skin, he became even paler and the muscle in his jaw ticked. "You must never, *ever*, forget what I am, Charlotte."

My eyes widened as I stared into his handsome features, instinctively reaching up to brush my fingertips across his strong jaw. "I love you, Lucas. I know you won't hurt me."

He laughed harshly, a sharp noise which echoed through the large hall and caused several people to glance in our direction. Lucas gazed into my eyes, his own hard and bleak. "I know you love me," he murmured softly, "but Conal knows the reality. I will always be dangerous for you."

I frowned, trying to understand the underlying message in his words. "So... what? What are you saying? You've decided now you won't sleep with me again?" I demanded heatedly, barely remembering to keep my own voice low.

His features softened and he looked bemused. "What? No, Charlotte, of course that's not what I'm saying," he whispered huskily, a small smile playing on his lips. "I'm merely trying to impress upon you that it's dangerous... for you to become too comfortable in my presence." He leaned forward, pressing his cool forehead against mine. "Don't. Trust. Me."

"How can I not trust you?" I whispered. "You've done everything in your power to keep me safe since we met."

He smiled weakly. "Until you thought I attacked you in Puckhaber." Seeing me poised to argue, he held his finger to my lips, silencing me. "Charlotte, I'm only telling you the truth. I am vampire, you are human. Alright, angel," he amended when I opened my mouth to protest. "Either way, a relationship between us will always be dangerous for you. As much as I love you, I have the capacity to kill you. You're blood, it's incredibly potent to me and I've *tasted* it. I crave it, more than anything I've experienced before. You lied to me about your blood being in my system and I love you for doing that - for attempting to ease my concerns. And I adored making love to you. I don't ever want to stop. All I'm asking is that you always, *always* keep in mind exactly what I'm capable of."

I nodded, despite feeling slightly off-balance and uneasy. Between the altercation with Conal and now having Lucas reiterate so carefully about the danger he posed, I wasn't happy. Before I could say anything more, Epi called us back to the meeting and further discussion was postponed.

Taking my seat, I was relieved when Lucas took up his seat beside me and lay his hand on my thigh again. I interweaved my fingers between his, drawing comfort from his touch. Epi launched into a lengthy dialogue regarding demons after our break, giving me an opportunity to compose myself. It seemed after my happiness last night, today was turning into a waking nightmare. Conal's reaction troubled me greatly, he'd encouraged my return to Lucas and I hadn't realized how badly he would react when our relationship became sexual. And much to my chagrin, Lucas had been right - I should have covered the bruises. Now Conal knew Lucas and I had slept together, which was knowledge I would have much preferred he didn't know. Despite my desire to not hurt Conal, I seemed to be stumbling through life doing exactly that. I cursed my own naiveté - I wasn't experienced enough with the male species to walk this tightrope between two different men.

And Lucas had made me uneasy. I trusted him implicitly and having him warning me not to was disquieting. Surely a relationship between us had to be based in mutual trust? Wasn't that how relationships were meant to work? *Normal relationships, you idiot. Not a relationship between a vampire and human... or angel.* With chagrin, I realized Lucas's words had frightened me, knew he was speaking the truth. Without a doubt, my day was going to hell in a hurry. Taking a steadying breath, I sipped my cooling coffee and returned my attention to Epi, shoving the worries about Conal and Lucas to the back of my mind.

The most knowledgeable of our group, Epi spent time explaining the intricacies of demons, how they were summoned and their capabilities. Finally he broached the subject of our biggest predicament - why they couldn't be killed by anyone but myself.

"How many demons can they call to attack us?" Bill Conroy asked, rubbing one hand thoughtfully across his neatly shaven chin.

"Dozens. Hundreds. Thousands," Epi answered. "They have the ability to call them from the Otherworld as many times as they wish. There are no limitations."

"Charlotte, you can kill these demons?" Bill continued.

I nodded. "With the use of the weapons and the spirits." I shifted nervously on my seat. "I think I'd struggle against a thousand of them."

"We haven't seen your abilities," Ambrose commented thoughtfully. "It would be helpful to see how you fight these demons. See how we'll fit in, where we'll be able to help."

It was comforting to realize these men didn't intend to run away from the problem, chose to immediately beginning considering strategies.

"I cannot create demons within the walls of Zaen," Epi explained, "but certainly we can demonstrate outside the walls."

"What sort of damage can we do to the demons?" Joe Reynolds questioned. He leaned forward in his chair, seemingly enthusiastic now to learn and do all he could to assist.

"Charlotte, Nick and I have worked together for four months now - Nick and I can damage them. They can be bitten and injured. It's sending them back to the Otherworld that we can't manage," Conal clarified. "Charlotte uses the angel weapons and the assistance of the spirits to finish them off."

"How will the vampires be involved in this fight?" Nat Finton asked. He looked at Lucas, his expression suddenly sheepish. "No offence, but what happens if we bleed? Would you turn around and attack us?"

"It's a valid question. Blood is an issue, it can't be denied," Lucas answered honestly. "We've fought alongside Nick and his pack in the past with no difficulty when their blood was spilt." He glanced around the table, his expression serious. "The scent of supernatural blood is not tempting to us. My Kiss are feeding every few days, to ensure we pose no risk to the human population."

"As are my people and Thut's," Harley Fitzgerald agreed. He was dressed in an elegant pinstripe suit, his red tie held in place with a gold stick pin. "There is ample food in the forest surrounding Zaen and feeding every three days will keep our desire for blood at bay."

"We have also taken the precaution of having emergency supplies of blood placed in each vampire's residence," Thut added. "There will always be issues where blood loss could cause a problem, but I can assure you, we are taking every available safeguard against finding ourselves in a situation where we would put anyone at risk. We have all made the choice to live on animal blood, and to my knowledge, none of us have tasted human blood in more than four decades." He grimaced and nodded towards me. "Except of course, for when Charlotte fed the Tine Kiss during their extraction from Sfantu Drâghici and in that situation, Charlotte offered up her blood to ensure the Tines would not be killed by their contact with sunlight in their weakened state."

"To be perfectly honest," Ben added, throwing me a tiny smile, "working alongside Charlotte is more of an issue for us. Human blood is clearly what vampires yearn for. Whilst we've lived with Charlotte for some time, any blood spilled from a human is logically a problem for us and Charlotte will be most at risk, because she will be fighting with us."

"Guess I'll have to try hard to not bleed," I quipped nervously.

"Yeah, that'll work, Sugar - I don't think a day goes by when you don't bleed," Conal smirked. He seemed to have recovered his composure and smiled faintly from across the table.

"How will you overcome that issue?" Joe asked.

"It's another of our problems," Lucas responded. "For myself, it's a particularly complex issue." I stole a glance at him and he returned my gaze, concern apparent in his.

"You and Charlotte - I take it your relationship is more than friendship alone?" Ambrose said. He leaned back in his seat, watching us with curiosity. From the corner of my eye, I saw Conal's shoulders stiffen.

Whilst we hadn't kept our relationship secret, we hadn't broadcast it either. "Yes, Lucas and I have a… relationship," I admitted, subconsciously squeezing his fingers, searching for comfort. He intertwined his fingers through mine and squeezed back.

"So he's developed… an immunity to you?" Joe Reynolds asked, in what I thought was a delicate manner for a man.

Lucas heaved a sigh. "Hardly. Her blood is as potent to me now as the day we first met. I'm learning to manage the desire, but I doubt I will overcome it."

Bill Conroy was watching us, scrutinizing our reactions and I fidgeted uncomfortably. "I've seen some things in my time, but never heard of a relationship between a vampire and a human. They usually… don't get that far, or the human gets created."

"That's not an option in these circumstances. Charlotte is incapable of being created," Epi announced.

It seemed that this conversation was rapidly approaching dangerous territory, allowing the newcomers to bring their fears about other supernatural beings back to the surface. "You've never heard of werewolves and vampires co-operating with one another either, Bill. We're in a fairly unique situation.

Just because you discover something you haven't seen before, doesn't mean it can't work," I stated coldly.

Bill continued to stare for a split second, before he chuckled. "That's certainly true. If you'd told me a couple of months ago I'd be sitting here at a table conversing with shifters and vampires, I would have laughed at you. My apologies for my rampant curiosity."

"What about the younglings, Charlotte?" Nat Finton spoke, taking the conversation in a welcome change of direction. "Are you capable of killing them?"

"Not with the weapons," I explained, "vampires are far too strong. Their skin is changed during creation." I smiled half-heartedly at Thut and he returned the smile. "It's the equivalent of trying to stab granite with a butter knife. I rely on the spirits for assistance with vampires."

"And the other Nememiah's Child... Archangelo? Can he be killed?" Nat continued. "I've heard he's different to other vampires?"

"There will be a way," I agreed quietly. "But I don't know what it is yet."

"Archangelo is a unique state of affairs. A Nememiah's Child who's been created as vampire. His skin is as fragile and penetrable as Charlotte's, by all accounts," Epi responded. He clasped his hands together, his elbows leaning on the table. "Unlike Charlotte, he's apparently capable of regeneration. Charlotte attacked him with the weapons and to all intents and purposes, he should have died."

"But he didn't," I added.

"There will be a way to kill him," Epi reassured them. "Charlotte still has much to do in increasing her powers. She will become capable of killing him, I'm certain of it."

"I thought you said her powers had reached maturity," Lucas questioned sharply. "You said once she'd reached twenty one, her abilities wouldn't increase."

"I said *she* reaches maturity at twenty one," Epi responded irritably. "She hasn't yet harnessed the full scope of her abilities."

Even Ben looked nonplussed, making it obvious Epi hadn't mentioned this snippet of information to him, either. "Do we know how these abilities will work?"

Epi shook his head. "It very much depends on Charlotte. All of the abilities she will have are now available. She needs to work on harnessing the power - gaining complete control over it. The spirits will do her bidding, that's without any doubt." He pulled his glasses off, casually cleaning them with his tunic. "We need to learn how powerful she truly is. And the best way to do that is to increase the levels of difficulty she faces."

"Excuse me?" I eyed him suspiciously. "What *exactly* does that mean?"

Epi continued cleaning his glasses, before slipping them back over his ears and staring directly at me. "Charlotte, you are the only person who can kill demons. We must increase your skills by escalating the difficulty you encounter. You must be taken out of your comfort zone, harness the spirits in new ways." His tone was matter-of-fact and alarmingly casual.

"I don't like the sound of that," Lucas stated coldly.

"I hate to say it, but I have to agree with you," Conal muttered to Lucas. "What are you suggesting, old man?"

Epi's shrug was infuriatingly non-committal. "Let's break for lunch - no doubt Charlotte is hungry, she always is. And then I will demonstrate."

Chapter 28

Demonstrations

Walking towards the gates, I caught up with Conal and Nick, slipping into step beside them. After breaking for lunch, I'd dropped by to visit Nonny and grab a bite to eat, then rushed back to our cottage to mark my skin and twist my hair into a tight braid.

"What do you think Epi's got planned?" Nick asked, matching his stride to my shorter one effortlessly.

I grimaced uneasily - the subject had been on my mind ever since Epi's announcement at the meeting this morning. "I honestly don't know, Nick. Epi never tells me anything until I need to know."

"And half the time he tells us *after* we need to know," Conal agreed cynically.

"Have you seen Marianne and the others?" Nick asked. "They disappeared as soon as the meeting finished."

I didn't answer. We'd reached the gates, which were open to allow people free access. I stopped abruptly as we left the tunnel, staring in dismay at the sheer number of people milling around outside.

"Seems we've got an audience, Sugar," Conal commented, glancing down to gauge my reaction.

Dozens of people had allowed curiosity to get the better of them and stood in the late autumn sunlight, waiting expectantly. I spied Epi with Joe Reynolds and Bill Conroy and stalked towards him determinedly, Conal and Nick following in my wake.

"Epi, what's going on?" I demanded, hyper-conscious of the inquisitive gazes we were attracting.

"Charlotte, they have agreed to join our cause," Epi remarked placidly. "Naturally, they're curious about what you can do." He studied my arms, examining the sigils I'd marked. "Are those bruises new?"

I blushed. "They're from fighting the Naberius," I muttered. Pulling the Hjördis from my pocket, I turned to Conal who fixed me with a dark scowl.

"Frightened to tell him the truth?" he asked inaudibly, as I marked an agility sigil on his left shoulder.

"Conal, please don't," I whispered.

"Sugar, I only want what's best for you. I don't think the leech is it," he stated in an undertone.

I stole a quick glimpse at him, saw the thunderous expression in his eyes as he stared at me. "Conal. *Leave it*. He didn't hurt me intentionally." I took a deep breath, worried about hurting him further. "I love him, you know that."

He turned away, cursing under his breath and I hurriedly marked him before turning to Nick. Biting my lip pensively, I repeated the process on Nick while he talked to Rafe, trying to keep his mind off the pain.

When I peeked up from my work, I was alarmed to discover the crowd had grown even larger. Epi was muttering under his breath, holding his outstretched arms before him. Before my disbelieving eyes, a large cage-like structure flickered into being. Forty feet square, it looked like an enormous jail cell. "What is *that*?"

Epi looked extremely pleased with himself. "I'll be summoning bigger demons as your abilities progress. If we intend to have an audience, it is too dangerous without some restraint. I'll portal the demons straight into the cage, where you'll fight them."

"If we *intend* to have an audience? What do you mean, if we intend having an audience? I don't intend to do anything with a crowd like this! You told us you wanted the new leaders to see us train. You never said anything about half the city watching!" My nerves were fragile - Conal's hostility, combined with facing whatever Epi intended to throw at us - and adding a crowd of people was more than I could cope with.

"Don't be ridiculous, child. It's time these people saw what you can do," Epi declared, looking determined.

"Charlotte." I sighed with relief when I heard his voice, turning to Lucas whose skin was flushed with the tinge of pink which resulted from a recent feeding. The Tines followed behind him and Marianne folded me into an anxious embrace.

"We went to feed, so we could support you during Epi's demonstration," Lucas explained, eyeing the massive cage. "It appears it wasn't necessary." Marianne released me and Lucas drew me against him, brushing a brief kiss against my mouth. "I don't like the look of this."

"That makes two of us," I agreed gloomily. My anxiety levels had decreased incrementally with Lucas's arrival, but I was still deeply uneasy.

"I'm three," Nick added, observing the cage with a worried scowl. "And we don't need all these people watching us get our asses kicked."

"Epi, what happens when Charlotte uses spirit energy?" Conal demanded. "We probably shouldn't kill our new allies."

"Don't be ridiculous," Epi replied crossly. "I've thought this through very carefully." He tapped his fingers against the bars. "The material I used to create the cage will absorb excess energy. Nobody will get hurt."

"Except the people who are inside the God-damn cage," Conal muttered. He gripped two of the bars, trying to force them apart, the muscles in his back straining with the effort.

"You cannot break them, Conal," Epi said. "They've been designed explicitly to ensure the safety of anyone outside."

Conal released his grip on the bars. "Charlotte, it's up to you. You say the word and we quit now."

"This is not an optional activity!" Epi spluttered impatiently. "You cannot choose how and when you will fight the enemy. Charlotte, you must do this!"

I glanced at the crowd, aware of the eyes watching me. As much as I was infuriated with Epi for placing us in this situation, refusing didn't seem like a viable alternative. How could I retain the confidence of these people if they thought I was too frightened to fight? I rubbed my hand across my face and swallowed nervously. "Let's do it." I brushed my fingers over the belt at my waist anxiously, mentally verifying the weapons locations. Excitement shone in Epi's eyes and I wondered yet again what this 'demonstration' was going to entail.

Conal slipped through the small opening into the cage, crouching low to get through. Nick followed suit and straightened up, studying the massive cage suspiciously.

"Charlotte, I don't want you to do this," Lucas said against my ear.

"I have to." I smiled weakly, foreboding creating a tension throughout my body. "I'm reasonably certain Epi won't kill me." I leaned against his chest. "I'm more concerned about you. Maybe you shouldn't watch."

Lucas lifted my chin, his expressions solemn. "I will not abandon you, my love."

Rowena embraced me. "Stay safe," she whispered. Acenith and Gwynn both hugged me in turn before I slipped through the small entrance into the cage.

Epi pulled the cage door shut and we heard the dismal sound of the lock engaging, before I turned to Conal and Nick. "Guess we know how the animals feel in the zoo."

Epi called to us. "We'll start with something reasonably easy, as a demonstration for our new allies."

I gestured to confirm we'd heard and watched Conal and Nick transform. They were as different in wolf form as they were when human - Conal was a head taller than Nick, his coat black and shaggy, whilst Nick's fur was sandy and his coat was smoother and shorter. Both wolves dwarfed me as we waited together. Conal glanced at me with his fangs exposed and howled mournfully.

Closing my eyes, I tried to centre myself in preparation for what Epi would summon, tuning out the discussions all around us. I felt like a performing seal and nervously fingered the Katchet, its carved handle bringing comfort beneath my fingers. I bounced a little from one foot to the other, tensing in preparation and then I heard it. The familiar sound of the ground erupting, swirling mists of red and black emerging into the air when I opened my eyes. From around the cage, screams pierced the air as the demons stepped from the portal. Epi had chosen a Valafar and it was joined by the centipede-like Astaroth which had attacked me in Puckhaber. From the corner of my eye, I spied two younglings coalescing and cursed sharply. My anger at Epi amplified, knowing he considered this a wonderful demonstration for our new allies and was giving little regard to our safety.

I adjusted my position to keep all four threats in sight, instinctively protecting my back. Conal snarled and launched at the Valafar, lunging towards its enormous body he latched his fangs into its shiny black abdomen. The Valafar screeched, an unearthly sound comparable to the dragging of fingernails across a blackboard and lashed razor-like claws at Conal. Nick was sprinting towards the Astaroth, throwing himself at it and snapping at the numerous legs. When he lifted his muzzle, he had a couple of severed limbs dangling from his jaw, the legs still kicking erratically.

The two vampires stalked toward me, attacking from different sides. I raised my hands, throwing orbs of spirit energy at them. The vampire on my right was hit in the chest, slamming backwards against the cage which elicited terrified screams from the observers outside. He hit the metal bars and slumped to the ground.

The second spirit orb missed its target, as the vampire leapt in the same instant. He struck me at speed, throwing me to the ground and I was shunted backwards, gravel scraping skin from my back and bringing tears to my eyes. He gripped my shoulders, eyes filled with bloodlust and fangs fully extended. My right arm was caught awkwardly beneath my body, leaving me no choice but to throw a second orb with my left. The energy blasted him backward and I used the respite to get to my feet, ignoring the painful throbbing in my scraped back. A glance revealed both vampires were on the move - it was time to call for assistance. With a thought, some of the spirits materialized, seizing the vampires and forcing them against the bars.

I turned my attention to Conal and Nick, who were battling valiantly against the demons. Nick had a nasty gash across his snout which poured blood and Conal was thrown by the Valafar as I sprinted towards them. Slipping a Philaris from the belt, I pitched it wildly at the Valafar. It struck wide, hitting the demon in the shoulder and succeeded only in centering its attention on me. I drew a second Philaris from the belt and aimed more carefully - this one hit the mark, slamming into the Valafar's rounded chest. It folded on itself and I turned to the Astaroth. Nick was still biting and growling at the demon and Conal had joined him, limping on one hind leg but fighting courageously. More than half the Astaroth's legs were missing, many of the amputated limbs twitching erratically in pools of black blood on the ground. Nick and Conal continued their unrelenting attack as I dived onto the Astaroth's undulating back. It was difficult to hold on to the long, narrow beast, its skin was slippery with blood and other fluids. It took three failed attempts before I managed to wrench its neck backwards and get to the soft underside of its body. Using one arm to grip it, I used the other hand to repeatedly plunge the Katchet into its body. Black blood sprayed across me until at last I hit the right spot and with one final unearthly shriek, it began to disintegrate. I rolled away, panting heavily and trying to catch my breath.

Wiping a blood smeared hand across my forehead, I turned to the vampires, still being restrained by the spirits. Growling their anger, the vampires were snapping at the invisible force holding them, trying desperately to escape. Conal attacked one, ripping its arm clean out of its socket. Conal dropped the severed limb to the ground, the fingers scraping uselessly at the dirt. Nick was attacking the second vampire, reinforcing the work being done by the spirits.

"Conal, Nick!" I lifted my hands and watched the werewolves break off their attack and run to join me. They watched as I launched two orbs towards the vampires. The spirits dissipated in a pallid mist as the orbs reached their targets. Both vampires slammed into the metal bars, a sickening crunch permeating the air as bones were crushed into dust. They slid to the ground, their eyes dulling as the life force motivating them was extinguished.

I held my hands on my knees, sucking much-needed oxygen into my lungs. Sound penetrated my weary senses and I realized the crowds surrounding the cage were applauding, yelling their approval. It was surreal and I slumped to my knees, suddenly aware of the stinging pain across my shoulders and back.

"That was a truly remarkable display of your abilities, Charlotte." Bill Conroy reached my side first after Epi unlocked the cage.

"Thanks." My response was curt and I stood up, reaching for the Hjördis to create a healing sigil.

Before I could start, Lucas caught me in his arms, crushing me against his chest. "I *hate* watching you do that," he breathed.

"I'm okay, Lucas. But my back, there's blood," I warned him.

"I don't care," Lucas said, his voice intense. "All I care about is that you're alive and safe. Nothing else matters."

I stretched on my toes to catch his lips against mine and he kissed me fiercely, oblivious to all around us.

Conal howled dolefully, reproach in his black eyes. Even in wolf form, he was capable of making me feel guilty and I pulled away from Lucas.

"As you see, Charlotte controls the spirits to both attack her enemies and provide defense from them," Epi was explaining to Nat and Bill.

"Epi - Conal and Nick need to transform," I announced. I was still breathing heavily, my heart pounding. "And they don't want to do it with an audience."

"Of course, of course." Epi waved his hand and a small tent appeared inside the cage. Conal and Nick padded towards it, disappearing through the flap.

"What was happening - when the vampires were against the bars?" Joe Reynolds questioned. He seemed impressed by Epi's display and I hoped it was an encouraging sign.

"I used the spirits to hold them, while I helped Nick and Conal with the demons." Someone handed me a damp towel and I wiped it across my face, pleased to remove the stench of demon blood from my skin. I could feel my own blood trickling down my back and I twisted to mark a healing sigil against my shoulder.

"Wait, Charlotte," Ben cautioned, "You've got dirt and gravel in the wound." Someone handed him a bottle of water and he stood behind me, trickling water across the grazes to dislodge the gravel. "That's better," he announced approvingly. "You can go ahead and use the sigil now."

"Those... younglings - they're real?" Ambrose Wilkes asked Epi.

"We are using a replica I've created," Epi clarified. "The vampires you see are every bit as physically powerful as younglings. They are programmed to act realistically, as a vampire would do when attacking," Epi explained. "However, they don't feed as true vampires would. It seemed prudent to remove that hazard during training."

"Those fangs still look damned realistic," Ambrose remarked.

Rowena and Acenith appeared, along with Ripley and Striker and they greeted me with relieved hugs. Rafe and Marco were guarding the gate, stopping any other spectators from coming inside the cage.

"What sort of injuries can you treat with the Hjördis?" Ambrose asked, watching as the sigil burnt into my shoulder.

"Blood, poison, broken bones." I felt the skin knitting together on my back and the pain easing. "I can't fix internal injuries or bruising."

"Obviously," Conal said, his eyes cold and hard. "Otherwise you would have hidden those bruises on your arms. What the hell did you do to her, leech?" He eyeballed Lucas angrily and Lucas stiffened, a low growl rumbling deep in his chest. Energy began to flow off them in waves and my skin prickled, the hairs on the back of my arms standing up.

"Conal, don't," I said anxiously. "It's none of your business."

"Like hell it isn't!" Conal yelled. "I warned you about him!"

"I don't think this is the time or the place," Lucas warned under his breath. He glanced at the people surrounding us, who were watching with no small amount of interest. "Conal, I'm happy to discuss this with you. But *not here*."

Conal glared at Lucas, the tension between the men palpable. It was like standing on a precipice, with Conal's hot power washing over me from one side, Lucas's cool energy swamping from the other. "This isn't over," he spat furiously.

"Yes, it is," I stated firmly. The last thing I needed was Conal and Lucas battling one another. Conal was being ridiculously over-protective -over something which had nothing to do with him. A day which had started out so perfectly was degenerating to the point where I wished it was over.

Lucas caught my hand in his. "Let's get out of here."

"Charlotte cannot leave!" Epi interrupted loudly. "There is more to be done."

I glared at the diminutive old man. "What now?"

"We need to expand your skills, child. I want you to fight a stronger demon."

"Can I have this fixed before we do that?" Nick requested. He was holding a towel to the gash on his cheek, stemming the blood flow.

"Of course." I placed the Hjördis against his cheek, creating the healing sigil close to the ugly gash torn by the demon.

"Hope it's not gonna leave another scar," Nick murmured, trying to defuse the tension surrounding us. "Don't need another one."

"I'm sure it won't," I promised.

"You will not be participating," Epi announced. "Charlotte must battle this demon alone."

"Epi, I think Charlotte's done enough..." Nat Finton began.

"We've seen all we need to see," Joe Reynolds agreed.

"What the hell?" Conal rounded on Epi, his black eyes incredulous. "What do you mean, she's going to fight by herself?"

"Charlotte must learn to improve her attacks with the assistance of the spirits. The best way to do that is alone, without others for support," Epi responded, his tone calm and matter-of-fact, but his eyes bright with excitement.

Rowena gripped Ben's arm. "I think Charlotte's had enough for today."

"Epi, she isn't ready for this," Ben announced, eyeing me with worry. "It was only five days ago that she was attacked by a demon."

"And we could be under attack at any time," Epi retorted. "It's essential she do this."

Lucas cursed loudly. "This is insane." He pulled me against him and it felt as if he was shielding me from the old wizard. "I won't allow it."

Epi rounded on Lucas, eyeing him with disgust. "You won't allow it? You have no say in this matter! It is Charlotte's decision and she knows she must do it!"

"Given how you're looking after her at the moment, bloodsucker," Conal announced, "you're hardly the one to say what Charlotte can and can't do."

"Keep out of it, dog," Lucas retorted coldly, tightening his grip on me. "I will not tolerate Charlotte being put in danger like this."

Conal's anger exploded. "You put her in danger when you had sex with her last night! Why is today any different?"

It was impossible to miss the startled look Rowena and Ben exchanged and my own temper flared. Both men were trying to protect me, but I didn't need this outrageous possessiveness from either one of them -not when I was already under intense pressure. "Shut up! *Both* of you!"

Lucas and Conal glowered at each other, lapsing into a tense silence. Bill Conroy was watching me, gaze steady and eyes cool. I looked away, wishing the ground would swallow me whole and let me escaped this entire debacle.

Ripley touched a hand to my shoulder and smiled, though he was clearly troubled. "Epi, I don't believe this is a good idea. Charlotte is already under immense pressure and I don't think she's emotionally prepared for this."

"Emotionally prepared, physically prepared - none of this matters. The fact remains - Charlotte is our only weapon against demons, now and for the foreseeable future. She *must* carry on." Epi's skin was ruddy with anger.

"I'd rather do it without all these people around."

"You are being ridiculous, child! Do you honestly expect that you will fight in battle on your own? Others will always be surrounding you! Sometimes, child, you try my patience immensely," Epi snapped.

Conal and Lucas both growled simultaneously and I raised my hand. "*Enough*!" I was terrified at the thought of attempting a demon by myself but frustration was building at the situation I found myself in. Rage unexpectedly overwhelmed the terror and for a full minute I glowered at Epi, choosing to blame him for everything which had gone wrong today. I *hated* him for forcing me into this situation. "Fine. I'll do it. One demon and I'm out of here."

"Well I'm sure as hell not hanging around to watch this! Charlotte, you are out of your goddamn mind! And Vander's no better!" Conal shouted furiously and stalked away. I watched him depart, bereft at being abandoned. The bruises he was blaming on Lucas had made him angry - this was the final straw. He shoved through the cage entrance and headed towards the gates, his shoulders stiff with tension. I caught Marianne's eye and pleaded silently, relieved when she nodded and ran in the direction Conal had disappeared.

"Charlotte, I don't want you to do this." Lucas grabbed my shoulders, turning me to face him. His face was etched with worry. "You aren't ready for this! *Christ*, it was only a few days ago that you were nearly killed by a demon!"

"Lucas, I know you love me and you're trying to protect me." I squared my shoulders and knew my green eyes flashed with anger. I'd been pushed past the point of no return. "But don't ever tell me what I can or can't do."

Epi began to herd people towards the opening and Lucas glared at me, his eyes darkening as he battled to control his temper. "I want to keep you safe."

"Lucas, I'm a big girl and I'm Nememiah's Child. I have no choice."

"You do have a choice!" he stated furiously. "Nobody can force you to take on this demon! I can stop them from making you do anything! You are *mine* and I won't allow anything to hurt you!" He ran his fingers through his hair in frustration.

I looked up into his incensed eyes, my own incredulous. "I most certainly am *not* yours," I hissed. "I'm not anybody's! You may have slept with me, Lucas Tine, but that *doesn't* make me one of your possessions! I make my own decisions, not *you*!"

His eyes swirled with lightning bolts of angry silver and I knew he was livid, but frankly, I no longer cared. My own temper had detonated and I would willingly fight this demon just to prove to everyone I could do it. Including myself.

Without another word, Lucas turned and slipped out through the cage door, clanging it shut behind him.

Chapter 29

Facing Demons

It took a few minutes to centre myself, trying to calm the swirling storm of emotions which flooded my psyche. I needed to concentrate on the task ahead and I didn't dare look to see if Lucas stood outside, or whether he had abandoned me, too. Either way, I didn't want to see him or the Tines - if I caught sight of them I might lose the courage to do this. And for the moment, I was as equally infuriated with Lucas and Conal as I was with Epi. Standing alone in the centre of the cage was nerve-wracking, the knowledge that Epi was about to unleash a demon against me terrifying. Memories of the attack in Puckhaber Falls were foremost in my mind, the excruciating pain still agonizingly fresh.

Epi called from outside the bars. "Charlotte, you must concentrate on using your abilities, not the weapons."

"That's easy for you to say!" I yelled back through gritted teeth. "You're outside the freaking cage!"

A ripple of amusement wafted through the crowd, before they settled back into a suspenseful silence. Epi knelt to create the pentagram and I speculated anxiously over what he would produce. As the ground erupted near my feet, dread pumped through my veins. Epi had summoned a Naberius, the exact same demon which almost killed me in Puckhaber.

The crowd shrieked when the demon coalesced, clawing its way awkwardly out of the portal. I edged backwards, focused on its movements. Inevitably, it spied me and dashed forward, a thunderous howl emanating from its fanged jaws.

"Use the spirits, Charlotte!" Epi urged. I dove awkwardly to one side then jumped into the air when the Naberius snapped its crab-like limbs at my midriff.

The enormous black demon scurried towards me and I cursed, throwing two orbs at its chest simultaneously. The orbs hardly slowed its forward momentum. This Naberius was fifteen feet long, bigger than the one I'd battled previously and completed focused on killing me. Notwithstanding the huge dimensions of the cage, the Naberius took up a full third of the space, leaving me little room to maneuver.

The crowd were silent now, only the occasional gasp or stifled scream breaching the quiet as the Naberius continued its full-on assault and repeatedly missed me by the narrowest of margins. It moved so swiftly, there was scarcely time to escape its approaches - trying to counter-attack seemed impossible without relying on the weapons.

"Charlotte, CONCENTRATE!" Epi roared when I stumbled, the Naberius changing its path at the last second to corner me against the cage. Leaping upwards, I bounced over the demon's head, narrowly avoiding the ferocious fangs which snapped at my boots.

Hitting the ground hard, I rolled, hurling a third orb towards the Naberius. "*EPI, SHUT THE HELL UP!*" The Naberius stumbled backwards when the orb hit it mid-body, then began its deadly approach again, running with phenomenal speed. I resisted the overwhelming urge to pull a Katchet from the belt, instead eyeing the cage bars overhead. Springing upwards, I caught hold of a bar with one hand, swinging my body side to side until I could clutch a second bar with my other hand. The crowd screamed as the Naberius stopped directly underneath where I hung, its incredible size meaning those vicious fangs were mere inches below my feet. It snapped relentlessly, as it attempted to catch my feet in its monstrous jaws.

Gripping the bars firmly, I swung back and forth until I'd gained some momentum. With one final swing, I released the bars, using the velocity I'd achieved to boot the Naberius hard in the head, throwing it off balance. I landed awkwardly and twirled in the same instant, intending to summon the spirits but the Naberius was over me before I could react. In a terrifying repeat performance of what happened in Puckhaber, I resorted to holding its neck, trying to keep it away from my face.

Intent on my predicament, I was barely aware of the horrified screams from outside the cage. The Naberius lashed its tail up and over itself, the poisonous spike rushing towards my head. I wrenched to one side, heard the dull thump of the spike slamming into the ground beside me. Seconds later, it attempted the same tactic and I jerked to the opposite side, the familiar burning sting of Naberius saliva dripping onto my throat.

With my hands otherwise occupied, I chose the only other option I had at my disposal. I kicked at the demon, shoving my knee into its soft underbelly as hard as I could.

The first attempt provided a diminutive outcome, so I kicked repeatedly, the strikes harder each time. Each and every wallop to its underbelly rippled pain through my knee, but the demon finally lost its balance and slithered onto its side, striking the ground hard. I scrambled backwards and staggered to my feet. My mind whipped through emotions at an astonishing rate; fury at Epi for placing me in this situation, annoyance at Lucas for his possessiveness, sadness at being abandoned by Conal. And mostly, frustration with myself for a lack of cohesive ability under extreme duress.

The demon flipped onto its legs, limping slightly, but the injury was nowhere near enough to slow it down and with another unearthly shriek it began its assault again, pounding across the ground toward me.

I closed my eyes, raising my arms and tuning out the combined screaming of the demon and those assembled around the cage. Envisioning the spirits, I concentrated hard and begged for help. I watched them unite together into one brilliantly silver orb. Focusing on the sphere, I blinked my eyes open and saw the orb I'd created in my mind was now very real, floating above the ground, illuminating the cage bars with its intensity.

The demon was enclosed within it.

Every nerve ending quivered with the strain of keeping the orb intact. My arms remained stretched out, my fingers spread wide apart. With the voices of the spirits whispering guidance in my ear, I gripped my fingers into tight fists.

The orb exploded with a rush of fetid air and warm demon blood. The Naberius imploded, torn apart by the blast. Eyes wide, I sank to my knees on the dirt.

Lucas dropped to his knees beside me, capturing my face between his hands. "Charlotte! Are you alright?"

I nodded, the after-effects of the event making me shaky. My head ached, my body was gripped with tremors and all I wanted to do was get away from everyone. I scrambled to my feet, dazed and besieged. The sound of the crowd reabsorbed into my senses, but I was spent, beyond caring about anything.

"You see child! I told you the ability is within you to defeat the demons," Epi announced gleefully. His gaze flicked over the copious amounts of demon blood which coated my clothes and skin. "Go and shower."

He turned towards the pack leaders who'd followed him into the cage, effectively dismissing me. "You see, gentlemen! The Nememiah's Child is capable of defeating the demons singlehandedly. Exactly as I promised she could!"

I was abruptly and irrevocably incensed. Stone-cold wrath filled me, resentment buzzing through my body at what I'd been subjected to. Snatching a Katchet from my belt I gripped it in my fist. Lucas reached for my hand but I snatched it away, the anger pulsing through my veins. "*Don't* touch me!"

Epi turned at the sound of my voice and his eyes widened when he caught sight of the knife. "Charlotte..."

"*The* Nememiah's Child? *The Nememiah's Child*? That's all I *am* to you?" I cursed loudly and furiously, using language the likes of which I'd never used before, bitterness completely overwhelming. "You treat me like some sort of science subject, keep pushing me and pushing me! I'm a human being, Epi! *I'm not your damn guinea pig! Don't* think you can keep using me to prove your theories about Nememiah's Children and *don't* treat me like a show pony! I will not be treated like an object!" Vaguely aware of the shocked faces around me, I didn't pause in my tirade. "From now on, I train with *no-one* watching me - do you hear me? *No-one!* If you ever, *ever* put me in a position like this again," I pressed the knife blade against his chest, the point hard against his tunic, "I swear to God I will kill you myself! I will slice this knife through your miserable hide, gut you like a fish, tear your heart out and burn it!" I hissed the last few words, my face inches from his.

I turned and stumbled away from him. I swung out through the opening to the cage and slipped the Katchet back onto my belt, shoving my way through the crowd which had fallen silent during my outburst. I set off at a run, away from Epi, away from Zaen. Away from everything.

Without a shadow of a doubt, this rated amongst the worst days of my life. I ignored the people milling around, only seeing Rowena's stricken face, but I didn't want her comfort. I didn't want anyone to console me, wanted to keep my anger and rage like a warm blanket. Nothing and nobody could make me feel better after what I'd been through today. Resentment still blazing in my heart, I was fed up with everything.

I sprinted away from Zaen, ignoring the sharp pain in my knee and the revolting stench of demon blood which covered my clothing and most of my skin.

"Charlotte, wait! *Charlotte!*" Lucas had taken only seconds to catch up with me, which shouldn't have come as a surprise. We came to a standstill in the middle of the gravel path and I waited sullenly for him to speak.

"I owe you an apology," he offered. "I had absolutely no right to make you feel I was treating you as a possession." He glanced towards the cage, a wry smile lifting the corners of his mouth. "If nothing else, that display with the demon has shown that you truly are capable of looking after yourself."

My anger with him evaporated. "Apology accepted."

He reached for me, cupping my face between his cool hands, one eyebrow raised as he studied me. "That was much easier than I expected," he admitted. "I imagined you would be furious with me."

I sighed heavily. "I'm angry with myself, for losing my temper. For making such a mess of things with you and Conal. And I'm furious with Epi. *Especially* with Epi, for putting me in a position where I felt I had no choice. You wanting to protect me doesn't seem so terrible in the scheme of things," I admitted slowly.

He gathered me against him, holding me close in spite of the demon blood covering my skin and clothes. "Would you like me to come with you?" he murmured against my cheek as he sought my lips with his. "You obviously intend on having some time to yourself." His lips brushed against mine, initially softly, then more insistently and his aroma assaulted me, filling my senses with happy memories of last night. I breathed in deeply, running my tongue across his lips and he groaned, opening his mouth to mine. His arms tightened around me and I held my hands against his hard chest, feeling the layers of firm muscle beneath his skin.

Begrudgingly, Lucas released his hold and smiled down at me, his eyes warm as he waited for my response.

"I need to be by myself," I admitted gently.

"Of course." Lucas glanced back towards the cage, where people were watching us curiously - I hadn't gotten far before he'd caught up. "Sure you don't want a shower before you go?"

I screwed up my nose. "To be honest, I'm getting used to the smell, hideous as it is. And I don't want to face anyone right now, especially Epi."

Lucas chuckled. "After what you said to him? I think he'll be avoiding *you*. You told him you were going to slit him open, gut him like a fish, rip his heart out and burn it. Even we vampires don't resort to such measures. And I don't think he, nor I for that matter, have ever heard language like that coming from someone who looks so... angelic."

I flushed, mortified by my behavior and Lucas laughed, kissing my forehead. "You'll be back before darkness falls?"

"I'll come back once I've cooled down." I heaved a sigh. "Then I'd better talk to Conal."

Lucas's jaw tensed when I mentioned the other man's name. "Perhaps I should talk to him."

"I don't think that's a good idea. You'll probably kill one another."

"I give you my word, I won't kill him." He glanced back at the walls of Zaen. "It's probably better if I'm the one to speak with him."

My eyes narrowed suspiciously. "Why?"

He sighed, brushing a tendril of hair away from my face tenderly. "Because I, more than anyone, know how he feels. I'm aware it could have been me in the position he finds himself in now. You could have chosen to remain with him and it would have been me dealing with the overwhelming frustration and jealousy he's feeling now. He's in love with someone he cannot have."

What he was saying was absolutely true and I wondered again, how I'd made such a mess of things. Although I was gloriously happy with Lucas, I'd hurt Conal with the choices I'd made. It didn't matter that he'd said he was happy to accept my decision. Everything he'd said had been designed to allow me to make up my own mind. Which proved just how much he loved me and how hard it had been for him to discover Lucas and I had slept together. In his position, I didn't think I would feel any different. But the hard facts remained - he loved me and I didn't love him enough. "I need to get out of here," I muttered unhappily.

"Please, come back before nightfall," Lucas requested. He pressed his lips against mine once more before releasing me.

I followed the path leading away from Zaen, a wide gravel trail which cut through the land towards the woods and disappeared over the horizon. This was the first time I'd come out this way; naturally the werewolves and vampires had already explored the woods which were filled with abundant wildlife.

The sounds of Zaen receded as I jogged steadily, the only sound breaking the silence was the muffled rattle of weapons on my belt and my soft footfalls against the gravel. The stillness was all-encompassing and peaceful. Conscious of the painful throbbing in my knee, I slowed to a steady walk.

The path divided in close proximity to the woods, the fork to the right leading directly into the trees - the fork to the left curving around through grassland and disappearing into the distance. I stopped briefly, considering my options and turned to the left. As far as the eye could see, there was no change to the vista - behind me, Zaen had disappeared beyond the horizon.

The trail was strewn with copses of shrubby trees, their leaves a bright shade of green against the brilliance of the clear azure sky. Small rabbits and squirrels flitted across the path, startled by my appearance in their quiet domain.

On the right of the path, I spied a glittering patch and as I drew closer, realized it was a lake. I altered my direction towards it impulsively, slowing down still further as the grassland morphed into a meadow of wildflowers. It was late in the year for such a burst of color and I wondered again where on Earth we could be. Hopefully Ambrose's men would return with a definitive answer soon.

The lake was large, a hundred feet wide and nearly twice as long, the surface shimmering and the reflection from the sky overhead turning the water to a deep cobalt blue. The gentle wind rustling overhead rippled the water so it sparkled like diamonds.

Reaching the edge of the lake, I gazed across the water for a long time, lost in thought. Did the city's water supply come from here? The water was crystal clear, the sandy bottom visible and tiny black fish darted about. Slender reeds and cats-tails lined areas of the shoreline and birds twittered and soared in the sky overhead. It was a beautifully picturesque scene, the sort of place one might choose for a picnic.

I slumped down onto the sandy foreshore, releasing my hair from the tight braid and slipping off my boots and socks. Dropping the heavy weapons belt onto the ground, I stood and waded out into the water. It was pleasantly cool against my warm skin and I walked further from the shore. The heavy odor of demon blood permeated my clothes and skin, and what better way to get rid of the smell than to take a soothing dip in the lake? Deeper and deeper I waded, the ground beneath my feet dipping away sharply until I dove into the water.

I swam below the waterline for a few seconds before swimming back to the surface. The water was refreshingly cool and invigorating against my sweaty skin. Even my knee, which would no doubt be swollen and bruised later felt improved in the weightlessness created by the water.

Floating on my back, the water lapped against my body and I shut my eyes, listening to the steady murmur of voices in my head. Months after I'd accepted the presence of the spirits, I'd grown used to the constant background noise. For the most part I'd learned to ignore them, aware the spirits talked amongst themselves, their discussions not necessarily directed to me. Each time I met new people and received access to their ancestors, the groundswell of voices increased. Occasionally I speculated about exactly how many people shared my mind with me - hundreds, or perhaps even a thousand by now. Always there was a soft hum, whisper quiet as they spoke amongst themselves. The spirits were always louder when they spoke to me directly, but for the most part they were willing to leave me alone unless I was in danger or needed assistance. They'd never been blocked since my kidnapping - and sometimes I wondered if they were aware of everything in my life. Did they hear me cursing at Epi earlier? Were they there when Lucas and I made love last night? Where they aware of my fight with Conal? In the past they'd been vocal with their opinions - now they seemed agreeable to leaving me to my own devices.

Which was more than I could say about Epi. Annoyance filled me again as I thought of the spectacle he'd arranged today and I took a steadying breath, feeling the exasperation dissipate rapidly. It was too nice a day to hold on to my anger and out here, away from the hustle and bustle, I felt a sense of peace as I floated in the water.

The expectations on me weighed heavily. It would be so easy to walk away, go back to Lucas and tell him we should leave. It would be easier for Conal if I wasn't around to remind him of what he'd lost and Lucas and I could go someplace, anywhere in the world, away from all this. Surely the Drâghici would lose interest in me eventually, if I posed no threat to their plans? I would even consider Lucas's offer of attending College, if it meant I could have my old life back. I craved the peace of Puckhaber Falls, sharing a house with the Tines. They had been some of the most wonderful months of my life. A smile briefly appeared on my lips at the memory of Striker chasing the Wii controller around the room when I'd enlisted Mom's spirit to beat him in a game. Since their rescue from Sfantu Drâghici, I'd barely had time to spend with my adopted vampire family. All my time seemed to be taken up with Epi's demands and dealing with the day to day threats we now faced.

My casual musings were interrupted by hundreds of voices clamoring for attention. With my concentration lost and head pounding, I sank below the waterline clutching my hands to my temples. Voices screamed warnings and I curled into a fetal position underneath the water, powerless to cope with the onslaught.

"Slow down! Mom, talk to me - what's wrong? Everyone else, stop yelling!" The throng of excited voices dulled down, not to normal levels, but at least tolerable and I kicked to the surface, coughing and spluttering on water.

Mom's explanation was rendered unnecessary when I glanced at the water's edge - a portal was opening on the shoreline, near where I'd left my weapons.

Chapter 30

Angel Battles

Treading water, I watched in mounting terror as the portal opened. It was pointless trying to swim for shore - I would never make it in time. Better to wait out here, see what I was facing. *"Mom, what is it?"* The throng of voices had been too much to make any sense, but the spirits had calmed enough to allow my mother to speak clearly above the others.

"Archangelo. He's coming for you."

My heart stuttered in my chest, dread spreading through my body when Archangelo stepped out from the portal. Dressed in a white chambray shirt hanging loosely over black jeans, he stood uncertainly for a minute, his eyes straying to my boots and weapons where they lay discarded on the ground.

While he was distracted, I inspected my arms and stifled a groan. The sigils had faded completely after the earlier battles, leaving me with no additional abilities to draw on. Worse still, I had an injury - even now my knee felt swollen and tight in the cool water. I was tired and emotionally exhausted. Could it get any worse? Of course it could. I had no weapons. Nothing to help me fight this vampire.

Ducking under the water, I hastily deliberated on options, searching for inspiration. I set in motion the only dismal hope I had, calling to the spirits for silence and waiting until they hushed. *"Ripley, I'm in trouble, Archangelo is here. I'm at the lake, head to the left at the fork in the path. Ripley, help me! If you can hear this, send help, please!"* It was next to useless, none of the Tines had completely recovered and as far as I knew, Ripley hadn't regained his ability to read thoughts. But I didn't have any other course of action, couldn't get a message to anyone who would help me.

Holding my breath, I lingered under the water, trying to figure out a plan. I needed to find a way of helping myself. A plan of action, an escape route - I'd settle for anything right about now. I drew the topography of the lake in my mind, looking for an escape, somewhere to hide. The reeds seemed the best option, but Archangelo had vampire senses - heightened smell, eyesight and hearing. How could I get to the reeds without him knowing, when my lungs were already screaming for air?

I cautiously began to surface, aware that I would need all the oxygen I could muster if Archangelo spotted me. Letting my body float slowly upwards, my face broke the surface of the water and I opened my mouth, gasping oxygen into my deprived lungs.

Raising my head a little, I moved as slowly as I could to see the edge of the lake and cursed inwardly. Despite my intense efforts to keep quiet and not draw attention, he'd located me. His eyes fixed on mine and he smiled, striding out into the water.

I twirled around and began to swim away from him, but I'd never been a strong swimmer. I swam as fast as I could, aware that he was behind me and catching up fast. I risked a quick glimpse backwards and panicked - Archangelo was less than fifteen feet behind me, splashing through the water with phenomenal speed.

"Ripley, help! Help me!" I shrieked when Archangelo gripped me firmly against his body. I wriggled and squirmed ineffectively in his arms, but I had no strength to draw on in the water and any energy I'd had was long gone. Archangelo grasped me firmly with one arm across my chest and swam towards shore.

Reaching the shoreline, he carried me bodily from the water, holding me across his shoulder like a sack of grain. I pummeled against his back, screaming at the top of my lungs until he caught me around the waist and dropped me down to the ground. I scrambled away, attempting to run but it was a futile effort, his strength and speed completely impossible to battle. "Let me go! Let me go!"

He gripped my throat, his green eyes ablaze. "You are mine! You should be mine. You are not that other vampire's!"

The pressure of his hand against my throat was brutal, with one small movement he would snap my neck like a twig. I ceased struggling, accepting it was useless and instead stared at him defiantly. He was a good five inches taller than me and frighteningly powerful. "What do you want," I gasped, my voice barely a whisper with the pressure on my neck.

He looked confused for a moment. "You. I want you," he responded simply. He had a trace of an accent, possibly French, but his English was impeccable. "I have always wanted you, Charlotte. The Drâghici promised you to me." His grip against my throat relaxed incrementally and I struggled not to flinch under his obsessive stare.

"I wasn't theirs to give you," I stated coldly. I realized at once the words had been a mistake, as anger flared anew in his face.

"It was my destiny to have you! We're meant to be together, you and I. You should be my wife!" he spat venomously. "And yet, in my sleep, I saw you with that vampire! Allowing him to make love to you, when you are mine!"

Eyeing him warily, the pressure against my neck increased as his temper blazed. Archangelo had obviously taken the sleeping potion earlier than expected and he'd had a vision when Lucas and I had been together last night. "Do the Drâghici know you're here?" It seemed pertinent to try and keep him talking, in the hope that help would arrive. I was still broadcasting to Ripley, praying he would hear me and I needed to buy any time I could.

"No, those idiots know nothing," he spat derisively. He raised his hand, brushing his fingers across my cheek and I shuddered under the touch. "They don't comprehend that *I* have all the power. I control everything. Even Bran doesn't realize the true power of my abilities." As he spoke, he edged closer, his eyes focused on my lips.

Despite my scattered thoughts and the panic which was rising steadily, a question occurred to me. "How did you know where to find me?" He'd admitted to being placed into the artificial sleep last night, how could he know I'd be at the lake now?

The subject threw him for a moment and he stopped moving, staring down at me with wide eyes. "I stole some of the sleep potion. If I swallow only a sip, I can sleep for a minute or two. I like to watch you," he explained with a trace of embarrassment in his voice. For a second, he sounded almost human, displaying emotions which related more to humans than vampires.

Taking a risk, I pleaded to the shred of humanity I thought I'd seen. "What you're doing, Archangelo - it's wrong. Innocent people are getting hurt."

He laughed, the sound without a trace of real humor, hollow and loud in the quiet meadow and my error was revealed. "Innocent people. You and I, we are the only innocents. The werewolves, shape shifters, the Fey - they're nothing." He leaned closer again, running a fingertip across my shoulder and down towards my breast. "You and I - we are the rulers of this world." He watched me silently for a moment, sadness in his expression. "We should have been together. You should have been mine. If you'd allowed me to transform you in Sfantu Drâghici, we could have ruled together over all the supernatural, including those morons in the Drâghici Kiss." His eyes hardened. "But you gave yourself willingly to another man and betrayed me. And now that you're twenty one, I can no longer transform you."

My mind was racing, trying to get a handle on what he was planning and desperately searching for an escape. I flickered my attention towards my weapons belt, lying perhaps ten feet away from where we stood.

Archangelo chuckled. "You won't get to the weapons. Remember you attempted killing me once and failed. Why waste your efforts? I'm immortal, nothing and no-one can kill me." He released my neck, yanking me hard against the line of his body and meshed his lips to mine. He forced his tongue into my mouth and his hard arousal pressed against my belly. Using every ounce of energy, I thrust my hands against him and shoved. He stumbled away and I spat at his face in temper.

Archangelo raised his hand, slapping my cheek brutally before I had a chance to run. The force of the blow hurled me into the air and I landed heavily. Curling up in the dirt, I clutched my hand to my face and whimpered.

"I love you, and you treat me like shit!" he snarled, dropping to his knees beside me. He gripped my jaw between his fingers, squeezing harshly. He stared into my eyes, his own filled with wrath. "I came here to bring you back to Sfantu Drâghici, to persuade you we're meant to be together. And what do you do? You take my love and throw it back at me!"

He lifted his head abruptly, arching his neck to sniff the air and cursed in a language I didn't know. He gripped my neck and pulled a Hjördis from his pocket. "They're coming for you," he muttered angrily.

It was a struggle to concentrate, the force of his blow had done some serious damage to my cheekbone and sharp pain was lancing the area. "I don't love you, Archangelo," I muttered. "Let me go, please."

"No! If I can't have you, Charlotte, nobody will have you," he bellowed. He marked sigils on the soil and I couldn't comprehend them. In the distance, I could hear approaching growls and shouts, the sounds of people racing towards us. I turned my head, ignoring the excruciating pain in my cheek and tried to see past Archangelo. As he created the sigils, his grip on my neck tightened and I struggled to inhale air, gasping and coughing. In the distance I recognized Lucas approaching with supernatural speed, the Tines close behind. Harley Fitzgerald and his friends, Thut and the three woman from his Kiss were also approaching at a remarkable speed. Behind them, werewolves and shape shifters followed, barking, roaring and howling as they drew closer.

Archangelo finished the sigils and watched in grim satisfaction as a circular barrier appeared, sheer white light encircling us like a mesh fence. He released my neck without warning, hauling himself to his feet and watching Lucas come into view on the other side of the barrier.

"Let her go!" Lucas demanded grimly, his eyes flashing silver and his fangs out. His entire body was tensed like a spring and he eyed the barrier surrounding us before he touched it.

The effect was instantaneous, energy from the barrier hurled him backwards in a similar effect to what had happened to Nick and Conal when they touched Zaen's walls. I screamed as he slammed heavily to the ground, nearly thirty feet away. Archangelo merely laughed, watching Lucas pull himself to his feet and return to the barrier. Lucas's hand was blackened and blistered where he'd touched Archangelo's barrier and I could have sworn I could smell burning flesh.

"Idiots!" Archangelo declared, watching my friends circling the barrier. "You cannot pass my shield, it's impenetrable! The Consiliului are right about one thing - you all deserve to die." He paced along the barrier, jeering at the crowd outside. "You stand there like imbeciles, unable to stop me. All to save this miserable, pathetic scrap of humanity." He glanced towards me, changing his direction to stand beside my body. With no forewarning, he kicked out, the fierce blow slamming my ribs. I screamed and the vampires, werewolves and shifters roared their fury. Archangelo laughed, surveying the crowd around the cage. "You all want to save this fucking bitch, yet none of you can reach her. How pathetic you are!"

My vision was blurring but I saw Striker and Holden working together at one side of the barrier. Striker held his hands together and Holden launched towards him, stepping into Striker's clasped hands. With a massive show of strength, Striker lifted his brother high into the air and Holden flew towards the top the barrier. For long, hopeful seconds, I watched and thought he was going to make it, would get inside the barrier and help me. Those hopes were dashed as Holden reached the top of the barrier and it reacted, lengthening until it hit him in the chest with the full force of energy. Similarly to Lucas, he was thrown backwards and slumped to the ground.

Archangelo watched and laughed, before striding across to Lucas, standing only inches apart from him. "You," Archangelo said. "I should kill you for what you did. It's because of you that she doesn't love me!"

"She was never going to love you!" Lucas snarled.

"She would have, if you hadn't got in the way! She would have done if you and these pathetic beings hadn't tainted her, convinced her you were worth saving. You're all idiots! You can't win this war! *I* will win this war!" He turned away from Lucas, his attention drawn back to me as I lay helplessly on the dirt. I coughed spasmodically and the coppery taste of blood filled my mouth.

Conal ran along the edge of the barrier, howling despondently. He ran a few steps away from the barrier then turned and pelted at full speed towards it. Hitting the shining white light, he was launched through the air, yelping piteously as he crashed in a crumpled heap on the grass and the scent of burning flesh and fur wafted across me. My eyes blurred with tears and I curled into a ball, aware of the blood pooling in my mouth and terrified Archangelo would smell it.

Archangelo tipped his head back, sniffing the air in delight. "Mmmm, blood. Delicious." He turned his attention to Lucas who appeared homicidal in his intensity, pacing back and forth beside the barrier. His arm hung limply at his side, the skin blackened hideously. "How have you screwed her and not wanted to taste her? You're pathetic, vampire! You should have devoured her, created her to our kind while you had the chance. Or at least, *your* kind," he sneered. "I certainly don't consider myself as worthless as you so obviously are. I could kill you with my bare hands."

"Bring it on," Lucas demanded. "Let her go and kill me, if that's what you want. I'll gladly die for her."

"Oh, how *noble*. You would *die* for her," Archangelo sneered. "That's too easy, vampire." He leaned closer to the barrier, his fangs bared. "No. *You* took her away from me and now I'm going to take her away from *you*."

He dropped onto one knee beside me, yanking my head to one side. "You can watch me achieve what you were too weak to do. If I'd had the option, I would have created her, compelled myself to only taste her sweet blood. But now I'm left with only one alternative." He glared at Lucas, hatred visible in every aspect of his countenance. "I'll savor her blood and drain her of every last drop. And you, vampire, get to watch as I do it."

With a spine-chilling growl he lowered his head and his teeth - not just his fangs - tore into the skin on my neck. I screamed, the sound echoing as Archangelo bit deeply, the pain unendurable.

The pressure on my neck eased and with pain-filled eyes I saw Archangelo straighten, his lips and chin drenched in blood. My blood. I could hear the outcry from all around us, the baying from the other side of the barrier and the sound of bodies repeatedly slamming into Archangelo's shield. "Scrumptious," Archangelo gloated. "Heavenly, in fact. You don't know what you've missed out on, vampire." He dropped his head again, ripping at my neck and the dizziness became overwhelming. I squeezed my eyes shut, unable to concentrate on anything except the indescribable torture of Archangelo sucking vigorously at my neck.

Dizziness was engulfing me but I had to do something, had to think of a way to stop him before he killed me. Drawing on every last scrap of strength I could muster, I raised one hand and pitched a spirit orb. It was feeble, far weaker than usual, but enough to thrust him away and he fell. He shouted his anger, his face drenched in blood. It dripped onto his shirt, the crimson stains providing stark contrast to the white fabric. Warm blood pumped from my neck and I was going to lose consciousness before long. I hurled a second orb at him, in the exact instant he threw one aimed at me.

The forced of Archangelo's orb thrust me across the ground, plowing my body into the dirt. I groaned feebly, agony washing over every inch of my body.

I'd retreated into a pain-filled haze when I heard Epi. He was chanting repetitively, his voice strong and loud, intoning words in a language I didn't comprehend. It didn't matter anymore, my life was pumping away by the second.

Blood flowed from my shredded neck, soaking my clothes and pooling on the dirt beside me. I knew nothing and nobody could help me now.

Over the sound of Epi's chanting, I heard a shout and blurred movement caught my attention. A flash of golden light appeared and I wondered vaguely if this was the gateway to death. My life was ending and there was nothing I could do to prevent the inevitable.

Chapter 31

Aftermath

Strange fragments of conversation reached my mind through the darkness.
"Where did he go?"
"Should we go after him?"
"Charlotte! Charlotte? Look at me!"
"Nick, press your hands against the wound, she's bleeding out."
"Sugar! Don't you die on me, Charlotte!"
"Jerome, you've got to save her. I'm begging you..."
"Rowena, give me that jacket, press it against the wound."
"We have to get her to Zaen."
"Christ, I can't stop the blood! Jerome, what should we do?"
"I can portal her directly into the city, it's the fastest way."
"The vampires can help. Use the Hjördis."
"Lottie, if you die, I'm gonna kick your ass, I swear to God."
"Doc, you've got to do something. You have to save her."
"She'll need blood. I'll need to run tests, see who's compatible."
"Move back! Give us some room!"
"That bastard, I'm going to kill him."
"Pick her up, Conal. Lucas, keep pressure on that wound."
"Jerome! She's stopped breathing..."

Strangely enough, I had the distinct impression I was breathing. Which couldn't be possible. I was meant to be dead, I should be dead. Once again, I was absolutely crippled with pain, a sure sign from past history that I wasn't dead. My eyelids were heavy and despite every effort, I couldn't compel them to open. I retreated back into the darkness.

When I glided into consciousness again, the cool pressure of a hand holding mine caught my fractured attention. Lucas.

His aroma was tantalizingly close and this time opening my eyes was a success. I blinked cautiously, adjusting to the room's brightness before I turned my head at a snail's pace, every movement excruciating. Lucas was beside me, his head bowed. Incredible effort was required to squeeze his fingers and he glanced up, surprise registering in his eyes.

"Charlotte, my love, thank God." He stood up, kissing my forehead tenderly before he called Jerome's name.

I blinked owlishly and swallowed with difficulty. My neck throbbed, my cheek was painful and my ribs burned. I wished I was dead.

Jerome appeared, brushing his fingers across my forehead. "Charlotte, are you in pain?"

I swallowed again and managed an incremental nod, my head pounding with the movement.

"I'll get you some morphine." His footsteps moved away from the bed, limping slowly from the room.

Lucas's cool fingers brushed my cheek, the touch whisper-like on my skin. "I love you." It was the last thing I heard as I drifted back to blessed oblivion.

"Are you sure she's going to be okay?" A voice I didn't recognize, male and gravelly.

"Now she's received the blood transfusion, she will be fine. Thank you again for your assistance. This must be very... difficult for you to come to terms with." Ben's voice, sounding much calmer than when I'd last heard him.

"I've read about this sort of stuff. Never believed in it." The strange man spoke again. I couldn't place him, didn't have a clue what this conversation was about. *"Wouldn't have believed it now, if it wasn't for you showing me the evidence."*

"We understood her psychic abilities came from her maternal grandmother," Epi was somewhere in the room. *"Her grandmother had some psychic aptitude?"*

"Never something we spoke about much," the stranger answered. *"Her mother and I were only married for a couple of years, I didn't spend a lot of time with her folks."*

"What will you do now? Will you stay here in Zaen? She's been through so much, I believe she would benefit from your support. It would certainly be safer

for you, unless you intend to leave before she recovers," Lucas said, his voice low. *"The vampires we spoke to you about - the Drâghici - once Charlotte's aware you're in Zaen it will be difficult to keep your existence from them. They will pick up knowledge of you from Charlotte's thoughts and actions."*

There was a long silence, in which I assumed the man was thinking over Lucas's advice. *"I've missed nineteen years of her life, I don't want to abandon her now. You say my wife and son - they're safe here inside this city?"*

"As safe as any of us can be," Conal answered, his voice deep and husky.

The stranger inhaled heavily. *"Look, while I appreciate how much you seem to... care about her, I intend to take Charlotte away from here. I want to take her home with me. Seems to me she's stuck in a situation which isn't really her problem."*

There was a sudden burst of awareness in my mind, tinged with substantial amounts of disbelief. I knew who this was. I wondered if this was a bizarre, post-traumatic stress induced hallucination, although the voices certainly sounded real and not a figment of my imagination. "Dad?" The word sounded strange as I voiced it hoarsely, it was a word I was not familiar with using. I'd never had much reason to say it in the past.

"Charlotte?"

I forced my eyelids to rise and scanned the room. It was darker now, but soft light filtered into the room from an open doorway. Lucas sat beside me, my hand clasped in his and Ben stood at his shoulder. I swallowed, discovering the pain in my throat wasn't as severe as it had been. Epi stood at the foot of the bed, anxiously gripping the bed rail.

He was standing next to Conal. A strange man, yet familiar in so many ways. His hair was the same color as mine, chocolate brown with a prominent wave and neatly trimmed. He was smooth faced - standing erect at the side of the bed, his bearing suggestive of a man with a military background. His russet hued eyes filled with compassion as he gazed down at me and tears welled against dark eyelashes. "Charlotte," he repeated again and Conal stepped back to allow him to reach me. "It's me, your Dad."

"Dad," I repeated quietly. "Matt?" During our email exchanges we'd discussed that I might find it strange to call him Dad when I barely knew him - now I was truly confused regarding *what* to call him.

"Whatever you want to call me, baby. Matt's fine for now."

Aftermath

It felt comfortable to use his first name. Dad seemed entirely too personal for someone I didn't really know. With a frown, I studied his face, still trying to come to terms with his appearance. "What…" I cleared my throat, trying to get rid of the hoarseness. "What are you doing here?"

He smiled, exchanging a glance with Lucas before he looked back at me. "These… people found me, told me you needed my help." He reached for my hand, clasping it hesitantly in his own. His hand was warm and smooth, with hard calluses on the palm - a working man's hand. "They explained you'd lost a lot of blood and apparently," he smiled again, "my blood and yours are the same."

I closed my eyes, struggling to comprehend what he was saying. "I don't understand."

"Charlotte, you lost an enormous amount of blood, far more than you could possibly survive," Lucas explained. "We attempted to match your blood with every single adult in the city and couldn't find an equivalent. Conal proposed we contact your father, see if he could help as he's your only living relative." Lucas rubbed his cool hand over mine. "It was a long shot, but it was successful. Your father agreed to come to Zaen and provide you with the blood you so desperately needed."

Ben offered me a glass of water, holding the straw near my mouth so I could take careful sips. I drank a little, licking my dry lips as I struggled to grasp what was happening. Looking up at my father, I spoke cautiously. "You… you've got angel blood?"

His eyes were somber when he shrugged. "Apparently. Your Doctor Harding, he can explain it better than I will."

As if he'd overheard his name being mentioned, Jerome appeared in the doorway and stepped inside, leaning over to brush a quick kiss against my forehead. "What is *your* Doctor Harding explaining?" He patted my shoulder gently. "You look like crap, by the way."

Ben stifled a smile. "We were discussing the relationship between Charlotte's blood and her fathers. Charlotte wondered if his blood and hers were the same."

Jerome raised his eyebrows. "We tested your blood when we got you back into Zaen. Essentially it's almost precisely AB Negative, except for a tiny marker which is almost impossible to detect if you weren't specifically searching for it."

"Why couldn't I have someone else's blood?" I asked. "Wouldn't that have worked?"

Jerome smirked. "It would have, if we'd have anyone with AB Negative blood in the city. It's not as common as other blood types. When we tested your father, his blood was a perfect match, including the marker."

"The marker? That's what distinguishes my blood as being different?" I asked huskily.

"Yes. But knowing what we do now, we can have a supply of AB Negative on hand. Although," Jerome added gruffly, "I'm hoping we won't have a repeat of this situation. There's only so many times I can bring you back from the brink, Lottie."

I inclined my head towards Matt. "Can he use the weapons? The Hjördis?"

"No, apparently that is still unique to you, my love," Lucas responded. "Your father can hold the weapons, but the Hjördis doesn't operate."

"Archangelo? What happened?"

Lucas squeezed my fingers. "He got away. Portalled out, presumably went back to Sfantu Drâghici. We've heard nothing else from him."

Squeezing my eyes shut, I recalled the agony of Archangelo biting my throat. "Why did he give up before he killed me?"

"Epi managed to dismantle the barrier he'd created and we're guessing when you threw those orbs at him, he figured you weren't giving up without a fight," Conal responded, his eyes filled with pride. "Nice going, Sugar."

I managed a feeble smile. "I nearly did give up," I admitted quietly.

"But you didn't," Lucas asserted softly. "You managed to get a message through to Ripley, despite his difficulties with the loss of his ability, he heard you, Charlotte. I only wish we'd gotten there sooner."

"I wish you did, too," I admitted quietly.

"Guess Archangelo makes it to number one on our list of priorities, Sugar," Conal added. "Seems he'd a couple of fries short of a Happy Meal."

"Which is all the more reason for Charlotte to leave with me and I'll keep her somewhere safe," Matt announced determinedly. He reached out, tentatively brushing my hair back from my forehead. "Charlotte. This isn't your war. These aren't your people."

Chapter 32

Home Truths

For a couple of seconds I was speechless, frowning at my father. My attention was diverted by a commotion from the hallway before I could respond. Marianne and William, Ripley and Acenith, Rowena, Gwynn, Striker and Holden strolled through the door, laughing and joyful.

"Ripley told us you were awake," Marianne announced, squeezing past Lucas with a delighted grin to kiss my forehead.

"About time too, Lott. Nobody can defeat the demons while you're out of action," Striker teased.

Gwynn kissed my cheek, looking anxious. "Are you feeling better?"

"A little," I agreed.

Rowena leaned over to hug me, but hesitated, a worried frown creasing her forehead. "I don't know how to hug you when you're so badly hurt," she admitted.

"Try anyway. Please?" I needed the comfort desperately, and hadn't realized how desperately until Rowena's appearance. Whether it was the sudden appearance of my father, Archangelo's attack - I didn't know, but I wanted Rowena's comfort.

She hugged me awkwardly, movements exceedingly gentle. Over her shoulder, I caught the expression on Matt's face and struggled to comprehend what he was thinking. He looked... repulsed? Or possibly disgusted? Perhaps I was misreading his reaction, I barely knew him and couldn't even begin to suggest that I could read his thoughts from a facial expression.

"Charlotte... baby," Matt said, squeezing my arm lightly when Rowena released me. "I think you should come back to San Diego with Misaki and me. You don't belong with these people."

Staring at him, I drew my arm away from his touch, eyeing him coldly. "Don't call me baby, Matt. I'm *not* your baby. That was nineteen years ago when you ditched out on me and Mom."

"Charlotte," he began again, trying to take my hand in his. "I told you I was sorry about that. But these people - they've, well, they've *brainwashed* you. They aren't your family. They aren't even people, for Christ's sake! They're making you fight a war that involves their kind - not yours." His voice rose a little, his brown eyes penetrating as he gazed at me.

"Matt, Charlotte is still extremely unwell, this isn't the best time for this discussion," Jerome said firmly.

My father raised his hand, cautioning Jerome to stop. "No offence, Doctor Harding, but this is important. My little girl is fighting your war, for your people and nearly getting herself killed in the process. I think this is exactly the right time for this discussion. She needs to get out of this, before she gets herself killed."

I struggled to sit up, pain blazing through my upper body. "Your little girl," I repeated, my eyebrows raised in disbelief. "I was your little girl *nineteen* years ago. I haven't been your little girl for a very long time. You want me to come and play happy families with you and your new wife and kid?" Shaking my head, I stared at Matt angrily. "Sorry. You've left it about nineteen years too late."

"Baby," he began, then saw my scowl and rephrased hastily. "Charlotte, you don't belong here. You belong with me and your family. We want to support you and look after you."

I gripped Lucas's hand firmly, conscious of the compassion in his dark blue eyes. "You want to be there to support me? That's pretty self-righteous after you vanished out of my life," I announced incredulously. "Where were you, Matt? Where were *you* when I was starting my first day at preschool? Where were you when it was career day and every other father turned up to tell the kids about their jobs? Where were *you* when the other kids were teasing me because I didn't have a father?" Tears stung my eyes and I brushed them away impatiently. "Where were you when I fell off my bike in fourth grade and broke my wrist? What about when I got accepted to Art School and couldn't go because we couldn't afford it? Where were you when I was wearing second hand clothes and worn out shoes?"

"Charlotte, I told you I was so very sorry..."

I shook my head firmly. "Sorry doesn't cut it, *Dad*. You missed out on every important event which happened in nineteen years. My senior prom, my first crush on a boy, graduation from high school. Learning to drive. Nineteen birthdays, nineteen Christmases." I was aware of the sympathetic looks from those around me and my father's face was ashen. "Where were you when Mom met that bastard she married? Where were you when I needed someone, *anyone* who could give me advice when Pete was beating the crap out of her night after night after night!" I gasped down a breath, feeling the all-too familiar shattering pain in my ribs. "And where were you - when I found them dead in the house? What were you doing when I was being accused of murder?"

"I didn't know, Charlotte! I swear to God, I didn't know!" he cried, his face filled with anguish.

For a long time I watched him, my own face ravaged with tears. "No, you didn't know. You didn't know how I felt, the nightmares I endured. You didn't stand in the rain, watching four coffins being lowered into the ground. Do you have *any* idea how small the coffin needs to be for a four month old baby?" I shook my head dejectedly, overwhelmed with a disappointment and pain I didn't know I'd held. "You wouldn't know. You couldn't know because you weren't there." I looked around the stricken faces surrounding me and took a steadying breath before I could continue. "You weren't there when I was trying to figure out how to pay for their funerals. You weren't there when I left my home for the last time. You weren't there when I had nowhere to go, no money, *nothing*! You weren't with me when I was scratching out an existence, eating canned beans seven nights a week because I had to choose between a roof over my head and having something to eat!"

"Charlotte, I want to make it up to you. Baby, *please*?" he begged huskily.

"*Don't... call... me... Baby!*" I gritted my teeth, pain shooting through my cheek. Shutting my eyes, the bitterness which had built up over nineteen years overwhelmed me. "My name is Charlotte and I *am* Nememiah's Child. For better or worse - that's who I am. You can't make up for what I lost when you walked out. You can't walk in here and declare you're taking me away with you. I'm not a child, I'm an adult - and I'll make my own decisions."

I glanced around, at the people I regarded as family. "These people, Matt - these people *are* my family. They love me and nurture and support me. Ben and Rowena treat me like a daughter. Lucas loves me unconditionally, no matter how badly I screw up sometimes. Conal is my best friend in the whole world." I met Marianne's eyes and she smiled sympathetically. "They've fed and clothed me and supported me every step of the way. *That's* what family does, they don't run away from trouble. They don't run out when things are tough."

My father stood indecisively, his distress written on his face. "Charlotte. *Please.* You could get killed. I don't want to lose you, not when I've just found you again."

I chewed on my lip, attempting to compose myself before I answered. "Yeah," I said at last. "You're right, I could get killed. But if I die, I'll know it's because I chose my path and stuck to it, because I've accepted the truth of what I am and why I'm here." I wanted to reach out to him, touch his arm, but I couldn't bring myself to do it. I didn't know this man... not really. I wasn't sure I could console him, nor even if I wanted to at this stage. "Maybe one day, you'll be able to accept the truth of what I am. I really do hope so. You see werewolves, vampires, shape shifters - things you obviously don't understand and can't comprehend. And you look at me and see a human. That's not what I am, Matt. In many ways, I find I belong in this world more than I ever did in yours." Glancing towards Epi, I squeezed Lucas's hand, drawing strength from him. "Epi, take him back to wherever he's staying."

"I'm not leaving," Matt protested. "I want to stay with you, Charlotte."

"Matt, I need you to go," I insisted tiredly. "For now, at least. Talk to your wife, think it over. If you can accept me for who I am and what I'm here to do, I could use your support. But if you can't; well, you need to go back home to San Diego."

Epi put his hand at the small of Matt's back, intent on steering him away from the bed. For a couple of seconds, Matt resisted, gazing down at me, his face contorted with strain. Then he sighed, leaning over to kiss my forehead. "I want to make it up to you, Charlotte. I have to make this right," he announced fervently.

The breath I inhaled was painful. "You already have, Matt. I touched your hand, and even now, I can hear your parents, your grandparents. And you saved my life. It's enough, for now."

He touched my cheek with the palm of his hand, holding it against me for a long moment, before allowing himself to be led from the room.

Chapter 33

Discovery

The silence was like a heavy weight after Matt and Epi left, the only sound breaking up the quiet was the soft murmur of voices in my head. My adopted family encircled me, providing an unspoken empathy.

Lucas spoke first, clasping my hand between his and I realized his arm and forearm were heavily bandaged. "I'm so very sorry, Charlotte, we shouldn't have brought him to Zaen. The situation had reached desperation point, we had no way of saving you..."

I smiled weakly. "It's okay." I indicated the bandage. "Are you alright?"

Lucas returned my smile. "Healing. Archangelo's barrier was highly effective at burning. We have a number of people carrying injuries from trying to breach it."

"I'm sorry."

"Least of our worries, Sugar," Conal responded. "Don't even think about it."

A glance at Conal confirmed he was also injured, the bandage wrapped around his upper arm disappeared beneath the sleeve of his black t-shirt.

"How bad is it?" I questioned, inclining my head towards his arm.

He touched the bandage self-consciously. "It's nothing, Sugar. Healing up nicely."

Rowena slipped past Conal and sat carefully on the edge of the mattress. "Perhaps your father will learn to accept us, Charlotte." She glanced at the group surrounding the bed. "Meeting our kind - it was bound to be a shock for him."

Ripley was standing behind Acenith, his hands resting on her waist and his eyes on me.

"Ripley, can you hear his thoughts?"

"Seems you contacting me from the lake has kick-started my ability," Ripley admitted. "Your father doesn't trust us. His intentions are pure, he genuinely believes you would be safer with him and his family." He met Lucas's eyes and rolled his eyes. "He doesn't like the relationship between you two; it bothers him immensely." Ripley smiled. "Although like most fathers, I don't believe he would like anyone Charlotte was dating. Lucas being vampire isn't the issue - it's the fact that Lucas is a man and you are Matt's daughter."

"Would you like me to speak with him again?" Ben offered. "Perhaps if we can get him to comprehend the situation you find yourself in…"

"No," I said, shaking my head firmly. "It's better this way. He'll be happier in San Diego, not knowing what's going on. It's bad enough that you've all gotten involved in this mess. I don't need to worry about more people getting hurt."

"Hey, Lott - I can't speak for everyone else, but I'm having a damn fine time," Striker grinned broadly. "Life was pretty dull, but since you've appeared in our lives, it's gotten a heck of a lot more interesting."

"Pointing out the obvious, Sugar," Conal added with a twinkle gleaming in his eyes. "You're the one lying in a hospital bed."

Conal's face was tranquil, his eyes warm and I swallowed uncertainly. "You and I - we're okay?"

"We're always going to be okay, Sugar." He rubbed his fingers against my arm. "I blew my cool, and I shouldn't have. And I hear I missed quite a battle with the demon."

"Not as exciting as the battle she had with Epi afterwards," Striker added, with a mischievous twinkle in his eye.

I flushed with mortification. "That wasn't a battle, that was me throwing an immature temper tantrum."

"An immature temper tantrum with *outstanding* use of the English language – including some words that don't even make it into a dictionary," Holden announced enthusiastically.

This time a full-on blush covered my skin and I looked up at Rowena sheepishly. "I'm really sorry, Rowena. The language I used – it was inexcusable."

"Oh, I think under the circumstances it was justifiable," Rowena responded calmly. "A few of those words were ones I was thinking of using myself at the time. I could have quite willingly wrung Epi's neck."

"I…*oh.*" When my eyes widened in surprise, a sharp pain slashed across my cheek.

Lucas chuckled. "I think Epi's under no illusions as to what will happen to him if he puts you in that position again."

"My beloved wife has assured him that once you've 'slit him open, gutted his miserable hide like a fish, ripped his heart out and burnt it', she will be tearing his head and every other conceivable body part from his torso," Ben added with a broad smile.

"I'm never going to live that down, am I?" I asked with a degree of dismay.

"Nope. It's already reached legendary proportions around the city," Striker laughed. "People now think you're a beautiful angel with the mouth of the devil."

"I didn't give a very good impression to our new allies, did I?"

"On the contrary, I think they're under no illusions at all. Not only did you establish exactly what you could do - you also proved that you won't take any nonsense from anyone. Joe Reynolds, in particular, was extremely impressed," Holden responded.

"How's Epi with all this?"

"Epi has agreed he overstepped the mark. From now on, any large demons he wants to test your abilities on will be inside that damn cage he built - you're going to be on the outside," Conal explained.

I screwed up my nose. "How is that going to be helpful? What about when we're training together?"

Conal grinned, his black eyes alight with glee. "Don't think you're getting out of it completely. We still get to train together with the smaller demons, but Epi's seen the error in his ways - no more Naberius for you on your own."

"Well, that's a comfort. I would hate to think I was going to miss out on smelling like rotting carcasses on a permanent basis," I agreed wryly. I attempted a smiled and winced, before I spoke to Jerome. "So, what's the damage? The left side of my face doesn't feel so good."

Jerome shook his head, crossing his arms across his chest. "Fractured cheekbone. Five broken ribs. Bruising over pretty much every available square inch of skin. And a particularly nasty bite on your neck. One of these days, I'd like to have a conversation which doesn't start with you asking what the damage is." He softened the words with a wink.

"Mmmm. Well, at least I'm retaining a high grade point average." A glance showed the vampires were looking deeply troubled, even uncomfortable. "Let me just warn you guys up front - any one of you attempts to bite me and I will kill you, regardless of whether I love you or not." More seriously, I directed my next words to Lucas. "When Archangelo bit me, it was unbearable. I thought you told me there was a paralytic agent which keeps the pain to a minimum when you bite?"

"That's true, but in your case, Archangelo didn't use his fangs alone - he ripped into your neck with his teeth."

"Great," I muttered.

"I don't believe it would have made any difference, Lottie. You're utterly unique. I would imagine the angel blood is likely to make you immune to the vampire's paralytic agent," Jerome suggested.

"You believe so?" Ben questioned, his expression alert. "What makes you say that?"

"It stands to reason. Despite Archangelo using his teeth, his fangs were involved in the process. There should have been some effect from the agent, some relief from the pain."

Hunter pursed his lips, thinking deeply. "Jerome's right. His fangs had to have made contact with Charlotte's bloodstream. There should have been some paralyzing effect."

"O-kay," I said slowly. "In that case, if one of you attempts to bite me, consider yourself dead before you get within ten feet of my throat."

"I would believe that too, having seen you out there with the demon," Lucas agreed.

"So you better keep your fangs and teeth away from her, leech," Conal announced with a contented grin.

"As long as you do the same, dog," Lucas retorted.

I looked from Lucas to Conal. Despite their name calling, there seemed to be no trace of animosity between them. "Are *you* two okay?"

Conal met Lucas's eyes before he returned his gaze to me. "Yeah, Sugar, we're okay."

Before I could reply, Nonny and Epi appeared in the doorway, Nonny balancing a tray in her hands. "Epi told me you were awake and I was sure you'd be hungry." She placed the tray down on a hospital table and Conal wheeled it in front of me. I looked down at the tray and discovered Nonny had brought me one of my favorite meals, chicken enchiladas and an icy cold can of Coca Cola.

"I love you, Nonny," I muttered fervently, inhaling the delicious aroma.

"Of course you do, I know your favorites," Nonny agreed. She eyed my face and muttered something in Spanish which sounded remarkably like cussing. "I'll kill that man myself for what he did to you."

"Get in line, Nonny," Striker said. "There's a queue."

"While I truly appreciate your enthusiasm Nonny, I think he might be a bit much for you to deal with," I added.

"I'll cook enchiladas and fill them with rat poison," she announced triumphantly.

Holden hooted with laughter. "Good idea."

Lucas opened the Coke and dropped a straw into it, while I eyed the enchiladas cautiously. "These look so delicious, Nonny, but I don't think I can eat them." Chewing seemed an impossibility with my face in such sorry shape.

"Lucas, get the Hjördis. Whilst I might be an excellent Doctor, in this case you'll heal yourself much faster than I can," Jerome announced.

Lucas opened a drawer in the cabinet beside the bed and picked up the small wooden box the Hjördis had originally resided in, before I'd begun using it full-time. "After your father attempted to control it, we put it in the box for safe-keeping," he murmured. He handed the box to me and I stared at it for a few moments. The mention of the Hjördis triggered a memory, snippets of the conversations I'd heard in the darkness.

"Charlotte? What's wrong?" Acenith asked.

"Nothing. I..." Shaking my head, I closed my eyes and recalled what I could from the conversations I'd heard. I drew some of the spirits forward, asking questions and clarifying responses. When I opened my eyes, everyone was crowded around the bed, looking at me curiously.

"What was all that about?" Lucas questioned, rubbing my arm.

"When I was... unconscious, or whatever... after Archangelo attacked me and you were trying to get me back to Zaen. I could hear your conversations, or part of them. You and Conal, Epi, Nick - I heard you talking about the best way to get me back to Zaen. You portalled me from the lake directly to here."

"That's right," Conal said with a frown. "You were losing so much blood, Jerome needed to get you back here as soon as possible." He crossed his arms over his broad chest. "But you were out it, Sugar. We thought you'd died."

I shrugged a little, screwing my nose up. "I could still hear your voices. And someone else."

"Who?" Ripley asked immediately.

"I think... I think it was Nememiah. He told me he would be watching, gave me the impression he wasn't taking sides in this war, that every decision and choice would be up to me. But... I think he gave me a clue." Turning the box in my hands, I lifted the lid and offered it towards Lucas. "Take it," I suggested quietly.

His eyes widened and I gazed at him steadily, willing him to have faith in what I believed. "Trust me," I whispered.

He reached for the box and cautiously took the Hjördis in his hands. To everyone's shock but mine, it didn't throw him, hadn't hurt him in any way.

"How did you do that?" Conal breathed, eyeing the Hjördis in Lucas's hand warily.

"I don't know." Lucas's answer was honest and immediate.

"Could it be the wing sigil?" Ripley asked.

"I've never been able to touch it," Epi responded. "It's not the sigil."

"Then - what's allowing him to hold it?" William questioned.

I was watching Lucas. "How does it feel in your hand?"

"Warm. And it's vibrating," Lucas said. His eyes were intense. "Do you think I can operate it?"

"I don't know, let's give it a try," I suggested. "Can you remember the blood sigil?"

Lucas nodded and held the Hjördis towards my neck. I held my breath when he drew a blood sigil near the edge of the bite mark Archangelo had left. When it was complete, everyone watched the wound curiously. My neck tingled and warmed as it usually would whilst healing and I was certain something was happening, but the lack of feedback was disconcerting. "Did it work?" I asked anxiously.

"Perfectly," Rowena assure me. She looked stunned, as did everyone around me.

"Now try the bone sigil," I suggested. Jerome lifted the hospital gown so my ribs were visible, holding it delicately in place so my breasts remained covered. Again the sigil worked, I could feel it in my chest as the bone bonded together and the ache disappeared.

"You need one on your face, Sugar," Conal reminded gently.

I shook my head apprehensively. "No, not on my face. I don't want those marks on my face." Whilst the power sigils left no marks, fading away completely, we'd discovered the healing sigils left a small blemish on the skin. I had dozens of them, one for every injury we'd healed but the thought of having one on my face was more than I could bear.

"It'll heal much faster with the sigil," Jerome urged.

"Put it against her throat. It will work, just not as thoroughly," Epi recommended. Lucas did as he suggested and when he'd finished, I opened and closed my mouth, discovering the pain was greatly diminished.

"How can Lucas use it? Why now?" Gwynn demanded.

"It's my blood," I stated with conviction. "Lucas, you drank my blood. That's the only thing it can be." I recalled the conversation I'd had with Nememiah about the weapons. "Nememiah told me the answer was within me. He was speaking *literally*. Angel blood is needed to operate the Hjördis and the weapons. That's what he told me, when I was dying. *'The vampires. They can help. Use the Hjördis'* - that's what I heard."

"The blood of Angels," Ben murmured, rubbing his fingers over his jaw thoughtfully. He and Lucas's eyes connected and Lucas nodded.

Conal spoke. "It makes sense, except..."

"Except what?" I demanded, pushing up on my arms in the bed, delighted by the absence of pain in my chest.

Conal looked distinctly uncomfortable, his glaze flicking from Lucas and back to me. "Sugar, I drank your blood. Remember? When Reynolds kidnapped us, I licked your wounds."

Striker eyed the Hjördis and held his hand out to Lucas. "Let me try. It'll give us an indication whether it's only you, or if we can all touch it now."

Lucas handed the Hjördis to Striker and he was able to grasp it with no ill effect. After a second or two he grinned. "Warm and vibrating, Lott."

I was positive I was right. "Lucas, where are my weapons?"

"They're in the closet," Jerome answered.

"One of our human friends brought them back and put them in here," Ben added. He opened the door to the small wooden cabinet and handed me the belt.

I pulled the Katchet from the belt and held it against my wrist. "Conal, the amount you had - it wasn't enough. Lucas, Ben, the others, they all drank much more than you did. You licked my wounds after they'd stopped bleeding. You need to drink my blood when it's flowing."

Jerome was alarmed. "Charlotte, this is a terrible idea. Not all the vampires have fed recently and you've lost far too much blood to start giving it away to others. For God's sake, I've just put you back together, don't go causing more injuries already!"

"Jerome's right," Conal captured my wrist, wrapping his hand around it to stop the movement of the blade. "And I'm no bloodsucker."

"You turn into a wolf, don't you?" I demanded. "Are you telling me you don't go out into the woods and eat stuff? There *must* be blood involved."

"That's different, Charlotte." He continued to hold my wrist, his stance resolute. "That's not you."

"This is all hypothetical until we prove it," I snapped. "We're guessing this is the way it is We know it isn't the sigil alone, there's something more and I'm ninety nine percent certain it involves my blood."

"Be that as it may, I'm *not* going to drink your blood," Conal said, his black eyes flashing with anger.

"Yes, you are, because seven people using the weapons isn't enough. Nememiah told me I have to select those I trust the most to give the power of the weapons." I knew my green eyes were flashing with determination. "And I trust you. Next to Lucas, you're the single most important person in my world. We need to know if this is right." I stopped Jerome's argument before he got started. "Only Conal for now. If it works, I'll wait till you tell me I'm ready to give my blood to others. I *promise*. But I need to know, Jerome, I need to confirm what I think is right." Jerome stared at me for a few seconds, his frustration apparent before he nodded his assent curtly. When he did, I turned back to Conal, pleading with him. "Please, Conal. I want you to do this. Please."

Conal stared at the shining silver blade, then raised his gaze to Lucas. "You okay with this?"

Lucas glared back at him, his expression hard. He nodded slowly. "I fed this morning."

"That's not what I meant," Conal snapped.

"I know what you meant. Just drink the damn blood and get it over with," Lucas said, his voice every bit as angry as Conal's.

"Charlotte, I must leave," William announced, an equal mixture of alarm and desire in his face.

"Sure, it's okay William." I glanced around the room. "Maybe you should all get out of here."

"We fed this morning," Ripley said. He exchanged a look with Acenith. "We'll stay."

"I'll go with William and Gwynn," Marianne announced, patting my leg before they left.

"We'd better skip out. Catch you later, kiddo." Striker winked and he and Holden left the room.

"Rowena?" She remained sitting on the bed, looking anguished.

"I'm staying," she replied determinedly. "I'll hold my breath."

"It would be judicious for us all to hold our breath," Ben murmured.

Conal's eyes were wide and focused on the blade. "Please, Conal. I need to know this works."

Conal nodded brusquely, watching as I cut into my skin and winced. The blood welled to the surface and I held my wrist toward him. For long seconds, he wavered, caught in indecision over what I'd asked him to do. In a swift movement he caught my wrist between his hands and lowered his mouth, sucking the blood slowly. For a minute there was complete silence as Conal drank and Lucas stood by my side, his hands clenched into tight fists. The muscle in his jaw was tightly compressed, his chest unmoving which assured me he'd stopped breathing so he wouldn't react to the coppery scent.

When Conal released my wrist, he wiped his sleeve across his mouth. "Is that enough?" he asked huskily.

I nodded, creating a healing sigil against my skin. "I think so."

Conal looked up at Lucas. "Damn. She tastes like heaven."

Lucas looked murderous. "I know!" he snarled.

Holding the Hjördis towards Conal, I watched him as he eyed it uneasily. "I had a headache for days, last time I touched that thing."

"Go ahead. I know I'm right," I encouraged him.

He extended his hand, his fingertips hovering over the Hjördis before he grasped it in one quick motion.

"Well?" Ben questioned anxiously.

"Warm and vibrating," Conal confirmed with a grin.

"Looks like we're in business!" Epi announced happily.

Chapter 34

A Quiet Moment

After the excitement of our discovery, it took a while before my visitors left. Eventually however, the large group dispersed, leaving Jerome with Lucas and I.

"I want one more listen to your chest before I leave you to sleep," Jerome announced, lifting his stethoscope from around his neck.

I lifted the hospital gown agreeably and Jerome probed my ribs carefully. He checked my heartbeat using the stethoscope, then slipped it back around his neck. "Remarkable," he murmured with a warm smile. "Thank God not everybody is an angel, you'd put me out of business."

"I don't think so," I disagreed mildly. "There's a heap of stuff I can't fix and I certainly can't deliver babies." Jerome had earlier announced that the pregnant shape shifter had given birth today, having a healthy baby boy in the converted hospital. It felt like a good omen, the beginning of new life despite the precarious position we currently found ourselves in.

Jerome balanced on the edge of the bed, rubbing his bad leg. "Speaking of babies, Lucas tells me we need to discuss birth control."

I flushed a deep shade of crimson and Lucas rubbed my fingers in an attempt to comfort me. "I guess we should, given that most of Zaen apparently knows about Lucas and I."

"Unfortunately, due to a number of circumstances, your personal life became public. They'll soon forget about it." Jerome smiled. "Lucas and I have spoken about precautions that are available to you. I would strongly suggest the contraceptive pill. I think it's our best chance of avoiding a pregnancy," he explained calmly. "Your menstrual cycles - are they regular?"

The blush crept up over my face again. "Yeah," I muttered.

"Twenty eight days?"

I did a little mental calculation and nodded, mortified at having this conversation with Jerome while Lucas sat beside me.

Jerome seemed satisfied. "Excellent. Lucas and I have discussed the best way to deal with your sexual relationship and we both agree the best we can do is birth control pills. Of course," he shook his head, "I've never been called on to recommend birth control for a vampire and an angel. I can't guarantee anything I can suggest will work."

"We understand," Lucas said.

Jerome patted my leg. "Charlotte, there's no need to be embarrassed. Birds do it, bees do it. This is perfectly natural for a young woman like yourself."

I nodded, still unbearably self-conscious. "We'll talk more later. I'll organize the pills and have them sent up in the morning." He stood up, making a couple of notes on the chart hanging at the end of the bed. "And I want you to take some sleeping pills tonight. Despite your miracle work with the Hjördis, your body still has some recovering to do."

"Jerome…" I began to protest. Sleeping tablets were no doubt a wonderful invention and would definitely make me sleep, but I needed to have a nightmare, had to try and discover what was happening in Sfantu Drâghici.

"No arguments, Lottie," Jerome responded firmly. "While I understand your concerns about what's happening in other parts of the world, you need to regain your strength and recover from the attack. One night of sound sleep and that's Doctor's orders." He disappeared for a few seconds, returning with a small paper cup with two pills and watching like a hawk as I put them in my mouth and swallowed them down with water. "Good girl," he said approvingly. He leaned over and kissed my forehead. "See you in the morning." Straightening up, he turned his attention to Lucas. "I assume you intend on staying here?"

"Of course."

"Make sure she sleeps." Jerome left us alone and I wriggled to the side of the mattress, holding my arms out to Lucas in invitation. With a smile, he settled down beside me, capturing me in his arms and we snuggled together on the narrow bed.

"I swear, I will never allow you out of my sight again," he murmured, brushing his lips against mine.

"It was the last thing I expected," I admitted. "When the portal opened, I expected a demon. Not Archangelo."

"It was unfortunate he was put into the sleep at that particular time, when you were alone."

I rubbed my fingers across his cheek. "I forgot to tell you." I briefly recounted what Archangelo had told me, about stealing the potion and being able to see me for brief moments of time on a regular basis.

Lucas was immediately concerned. "The man is deranged and taking the sleeping potion like that, it may cause him to lose further grip on reality." Lucas ran his fingers through my hair, his eyes distant as he considered the revelation. "Conal believes he's developed an obsession with you and he's obviously enraged about our relationship. He'll be more dangerous now he's failed to kill you." Apprehension was clear in his voice. "And if he's taking that potion as you say, he could reappear at any time if he sleeps and discovers you alone."

"If you're never going to let me out of your sight, he can't get to me," I tried to reassure him, kissing him softly.

"I wish I could believe that," Lucas sounded doubtful. He sighed, pulling me against him. "Maybe your father has the right idea. We should leave, run away somewhere."

"It's funny you should mention that," I admitted. "Before Archangelo came through the portal, I was having exactly the same thoughts."

Lucas flashed a smile. "Believe me, if I thought I could take you somewhere safe, somewhere you couldn't be found - I'd do it in a heartbeat." He leaned his forehead against mine. "I'm terrified of losing you."

"Not as terrified as I am of losing you." Despite the warmth in the room, I shivered. "I wish we could spend all our time together. I hate this, being so busy all the time. Or unconscious." I smiled wryly. "I want to be with you every minute of the day and I resent not being able to do that."

Lucas gazed at me. "I promise you, love. When this is over, we will spend every minute of our lives together." He kissed my forehead and I closed my eyes, relishing the feel of his body against mine. His aroma washed over me, tonight it was a mixture of pine with a hint of something sweet, a comforting smell which made me relax against him despite our worries.

"Lucas... if I had wanted it - would you have tried to create me?"

He pulled away, his expression betraying his answer. "Although I wouldn't wish this existence on another person, the answer is yes. I would have, if you had requested it."

"Because I wouldn't get old?"

He shook his head. "For purely selfish reasons. Not because it would keep you from getting older, I've told you more than once that doesn't matter to me in the slightest. But because I don't want to be without you and when you... die, I intend to find a way of ending my own existence."

Tears brimmed against my eyelashes. "I don't want you to do that, Lucas. You have Rowena and Ben, the rest of your group. If I die, it doesn't mean that you shouldn't live."

"I won't exist without you," he responded quietly. "The five months when you were gone - although I kept my promise to you, it was agonizing to be without you." He ran his fingertips across my bruised cheek, his eyes intense in the darkened room. "I cannot - will not - do it again. My existence has no meaning without you in it." He brushed my tears away with his thumb and watched me curiously. "What brought on this discussion of being created?"

"Being an angel. Before I found out about that, even though I didn't want to be created - I guess it was always an option."

"I see."

Rolling onto my back I stared up at the ceiling. "I feel like I got cheated out of my choices. Maybe later, with time - I might have changed my mind. Decided to be created so we could be together for decades... centuries. Now," I closed my eyes, squeezing back the tears, "now I don't have that choice and I'm going to get old and you'll remain exactly as you are now."

"It doesn't matter, Charlotte. Not to me," he whispered earnestly, pressing his cool lips against my cheek in a kiss so soft, his lips felt like a whisper of air against my skin.

I drew a shuddering breath. "You say that now. If I manage to survive this thing with the Consiliului, and I get old – how do you know you'll still feel the same way? Won't you be embarrassed, when you still look twenty four and I'm in a walking frame?"

He was amused and didn't attempt to hide it, his blue eyes twinkling, the silver in them whirling in slow circles. "I'm having a little trouble visualizing you in a walking frame, love." He saw the troubled look in my expression and continued more seriously. "Charlotte, you're only twenty one. Only *just* twenty one. What you're speaking of, it's years away. Years and years. Can we not concentrate on the present and worry about this later? I love you, you love me and that's all that matters." He leaned forward and captured my lips, stopping any further discussion. I breathed in deeply, aware of the delicious clenching deep in my groin.

"Lucas?"

"Mmmm?" He was distracted, pressing gentle kisses against my cheek, down my throat.

"Make love to me."

His amusement was visible when he glanced up. "Here? In a hospital bed?"

I nodded, beginning to undo the buttons on his shirt. "Yes. Here and now."

He captured my fingers and lifted them to his mouth to kiss. "As much as the thought is delightful," he whispered huskily, "perhaps we should allow you to heal a little more first."

"I don't want to wait to heal."

He sighed, closing his eyes. "Charlotte. There is nothing more that I want on this earth than to make love to you."

"I sense a 'but' coming," I grumbled.

"Having your father in Zaen is affecting my decision-making process. I can't see him being happy with the idea of me making love to you in a hospital bed."

I scowled. "What's that got to do with anything?"

He chuckled, brushing a stray curl from my cheek. "It seems inappropriate to make love to you when he's so close. He doesn't like the idea of you being involved with me as it is, I very much doubt he'll be happy to discover I'm the one responsible for deflowering his daughter."

"I really don't care."

"But I do," Lucas responded gently. "He has enough reasons to dislike me, Charlotte. I don't want to add to the list."

"Why does it matter what he thinks? You're probably four times his age anyway."

"Whilst that may be true, your father sees me as a twenty four year old man who's dating his daughter. His *only* daughter. While you are of age, it's understandable that he's concerned. Particularly because he's aware of what I am."

I rolled my eyes. "It doesn't matter anyway. He'll be gone soon."

Lucas was silent for a minute. And then, "Do you really believe he'll leave?"

I nodded. "I might not know him particularly well, but based on past experience - I'm guessing he'll go."

"How do you feel about that?"

I shrugged, inhaling a sharp breath. "I saw the way he was with you and the others. He can't comprehend what he's seeing. He doesn't understand it and that's only going to make things more difficult for me. It will be better if he leaves."

"When Conal suggested bringing him here - we had grave concerns about whether he could grasp what we were about to introduce him to," Lucas admitted. "Our lifestyle - what we are - there are reasons it's kept secret."

"Well, Matt doesn't get it," I said firmly. "And it doesn't matter anyway."

"Won't you regret it, if he leaves?"

I sighed. "Lucas, he can't fix what's broken. We were attempting a relationship with emails before this happened, but to be honest - he's a stranger to me."

"What you said tonight - I learned more about you in that five minute conversation you had with your father than I've known since I met you."

"That's not true," I protested, "you know a lot about me."

"True, I know a lot about you from our time together," he agreed. "But your life before then - it's like a closed book."

I took a moment to think about what he'd said, thinking back over our time together in Montana. It was a shock to realize he was correct. "I guess I've shut a lot of things away."

"Like your first crush? Who was that, by the way?" he asked with a teasing smile.

I screwed up my nose at the memory. "Alex Petterson. It was in sixth grade. He was the most handsome boy in the class and I worshipped the ground he walked on. At least, until I discovered he was far more interested in himself than any other person on the planet."

Lucas laughed and hugged me close. "And I didn't know you broke your wrist in fourth grade. Although it shouldn't surprise me unduly. Since I've me you, you've had a continual parade of broken bones. Perhaps you really are accident prone."

"Hey, that's not fair," I protested good-naturedly. "The broken wrist was a genuine accident - every other broken bone has been inflicted by someone else."

His expression darkened. "I will stop that from happening to you again, love. I'll protect you."

I snuggled against his chest, safe and happy with him beside me. "I know you will." Despite my intentions of staying awake and savoring this time with Lucas, I yawned loudly.

He wrapped his arms around me, so I lay with my head on his chest. "Sleep now, Charlotte. I'll keep you safe."

"Are you sure we can't make love?" I demanded sleepily.

The smile was clearly recognizable in his voice. "Yes, I'm positive. And stop tempting me. Go to sleep."

Chapter 35

Getting To Know You

Bright sunlight was streaming into the room when I woke up. Rolling towards where Lucas should be, I discovered he was gone. Matt was sitting on the chair beside the bed and he smiled sheepishly, leaning forward in the chair. "Hey, Charlotte."

"Matt?" Scanning the room, I established it was empty other than my father and I. "Where's Lucas?"

"He left a little while ago." Matt paused, eyeing me cautiously. "He seemed to think you and I should talk."

I studied him, seeing him for the first time in daylight. His hair was much like mine, dark with a smattering of grey at his temples and his eyes were chocolate brown. Clearly visible around his eyes were laughter lines and his jaw was strong and wide. He was dressed in blue jeans and a rust-colored golf shirt, his elbows resting on his knees and hands clasped together as he watched me.

"Matt, I meant what I said last night - I'm not leaving. I don't want to go to San Diego with you." There wasn't any point beating around the bush - I wanted my decision to be clear and was intent on ensuring he knew the subject was absolutely and definitely closed.

He surprised me by changing subjects. "This... Lucas - he's your boyfriend?" he asked. "Even though he's a..." he swallowed deeply, "a vampire?"

"Yeah."

He gripped his hands together, clasping them tightly till his knuckles were showing white. "He..." Matt frowned, the shallow lines on his forehead deepening significantly as he composed his question, "he doesn't drink your blood?"

My lips curled into an amused smile. "He doesn't drink human blood, Matt."

For a time he considered this statement, looking puzzled. "I thought they needed to drink human blood."

I pushed myself upright, discovering that overall, I felt much better. Other than a fairly insistent throbbing in my knee. "He can survive as well on animal blood. Lucas and his Kiss have chosen to survive on animal blood."

Matt leaned back in the chair, hooking one leg over the other and he clasped his hands around one knee. "Animal blood?"

"Yeah, animal blood. You know - bears, deer; stuff like that."

Matt rubbed a hand across his chin thoughtfully. "Charlotte, I'm trying to understand this - I really am. Misaki's handling it much better than I am, she's always been a believer in this kind of... stuff." He eyed me doubtfully. "But, you've got to understand that these... these people you're spending your time with, they're meant to be dangerous. And you're my daughter. Despite the mess I've made of this, you're still my only daughter. You can't blame me for wanting to keep you safe."

"They aren't dangerous," I stated calmly. "They do everything they can to keep me safe and protected."

His eyes flickered to the bruising on my face. "They aren't doing a very good job."

I touched my cheek. Although the sigil had healed the bone, the skin was puffy and tender. I hadn't seen a mirror, but I was sure it would be a startling shade of purple after Archangelo's casual slap. "This wasn't their fault, Matt, it was the people we're fighting. Our enemy."

"Our enemy," he echoed. Matt managed a faint smile, shaking his head. "I'm the ex-Marine and my daughter is talking like one."

"Well," I said slowly, "I guess I am. Kind of."

"The Doctor - Jerome - he says this is a recent development with you. Only in the past twelve months or so?"

I dropped my gaze to my hands. "I've heard the voices for years, since I was a kid. It's only when I finally embraced the voices that this other stuff came up."

"And... you have special weapons, like that wooden thing they got me to touch?"

"It's a Hjördis and that isn't a weapon. It's used to create portals, heals wounds. The weapons are different."

"Heal wounds?" he questioned.

"I can heal broken bones, stop bleeding."

His attention focused on my cheek. "The Doc said you had a fractured cheekbone."

"I did," I replied patiently. "I've healed it."

"And your ribs?"

I raised my arms up and forward to demonstrate the amount of movement I had. "Healed."

He took a minute to think this through, his expression thoughtful. "That's impressive," he finally said. "And the weapons?"

I tugged open the drawer and retrieved my weapons belt, laying it on the bed to show him. "This is a Katchet, these are Philaris."

He leaned forward to study the weapons. "How do you - you can kill those creatures with them?"

"Some of them. The weapons are used to kill demons, the werewolves and the shape shifters can handle the others."

He laughed dryly, the sound devoid of any real humor. "It sounds like I've landed in the middle of a horror movie."

I smiled, feeling a little more comfortable in his company. "Nope. It's just... it's my reality, Matt. Welcome to Wonderland."

He was silent, watching me before he managed a smile. "You are so beautiful. You were a pretty baby, but now you're -" He broke off, rubbing a hand over his jaw. "You're so much like Lorraine - your Mom. Exactly the same eyes."

I chewed my lip, composing my words carefully. "Why didn't you ever try and contact us? Why didn't you keep in touch?" It was a question I'd asked myself a million times when I was growing up, wondering why my father didn't want me. The pain it had caused was like an open wound, one I'd carried all my life and I suddenly knew I needed to hear his answer, wanted to know why he'd made the choices he did.

"When I left your Mom, I was a kid. A stupid kid. I wasn't ready for the responsibilities of a wife, a child. My father was an alcoholic, I guess I fell into the same habits," he admitted quietly.

"Do you drink now?"

He scowled, as if recalling a bad patch in his life. "Nope, never touch the stuff. Stopped about three years after I left your Mom. By then I'd joined the Marines and I was working hard. I grew up, I guess. Finally realized I couldn't make a career for myself if I was drunk most of the damn time. And I really did want to make something of myself. I'd screwed up so many things when I was younger." He paused briefly, his eyes lost and filled with misgiving. "And I always regretted leaving Lorraine like I did. She was a good woman."

"Did you love her?"

He sighed deeply, his eyes distant, focused on a time many years ago. "I did. I really did."

I persisted, questioning him despite the pain in his eyes. "You never contacted us, Matt. You never even rang to see how I was doing. You don't realize how much it hurt my feelings."

"I can see that, Charlotte. I can't offer you any excuse which would be good enough. For the first three years after I left, a good proportion was spent in an alcoholic stupor. For the most part I did my job and I did it well, but you see stuff when you're in the Marines - stuff that doesn't help if you're already nursing an addiction. Evenings, weekends - I'd finish up work and go bury myself in a bottle." He looked away to the window, lost in a time of his life that he'd obviously prefer to forget. He sighed deeply, pulling himself from his recollections to continue. "By the time I admitted I had a problem, it took a bit of time to get back on the straight and narrow. Before I knew it, six years had passed, since I'd walked out on you and your Mom. I was overseas most of the time." He shifted uncomfortably in the seat. "In the end, I was too embarrassed to contact you."

"Embarrassed?"

"Charlotte, I'd walked out on your Mom and you, without a word. And I've never forgiven myself for it. But by the time I had my life together and thought about contacting you," he shrugged, a minute rise of his shoulders, "it had gotten too hard. What could I say, after six years? How could I apologize for missing six years of your life? There was no excuse for it and no way of explaining it to you. And then, the time kept passing, and I kept thinking I'd do it soon, I'd do it next week, or when I was next back in the States. I'd decide to contact you for your next birthday, for the next Christmas. I put it off and put it off, waiting for the perfect moment. Until so much time had passed, there was no logical way of doing it, without looking like a complete bastard."

"But you did contact me - after Mom died," I pressed gently.

He squeezed his eyes shut. "When I heard what happened to your Mom, how she died..." His brown eyes filled with tears and it took a minute before he could compose himself. "By then I'd married Misaki, I met her when I was stationed in Japan for two years. She'd been pressing me to make contact." He smiled softly. "She knew why I hadn't stayed in touch with you and she didn't let up, she was determined I needed to make amends. So I started the long process of trying to locate you. It was only then I found out what happened to Lorraine and your family." He met my eyes, his own filled with raw anguish. "I swear, Charlotte. I was going to track you down then, no matter what it took. I had to try and make up for what I'd failed in. Being your dad."

I sat silently, considering things from his point of view when he stopped speaking. What he'd said was understandable, especially when I considered how I'd felt when we'd rescued the Tines from Sfantu Drâghici. I could appreciate his discomfort, how he'd wondered what to say. I'd been in the same situation, trying to find the right way to explain my long absence from my friends' lives. My absence had only been five months, his had been much longer. It was understandable that he'd struggled to find a way to reach out.

"Charlotte?" His voice drew me from my self-assessment and I glanced up to find him watching me curiously. "What are you thinking?"

"I wish I could spend more time with you." The confession slipped from my lips before I'd had a chance to think, but I knew I really meant it. "I want to get to know you better."

"Come back with us to San Diego," he responded and his eyes brightened. "We can get to know one another."

I shook my head. "I can't do that, Matt. And don't start telling me this isn't my war."

He smirked, shaking his head. "Stubborn like your Mom, too." He reached for my hand, clasping it between his. "I want to spend time with you, Charlotte. I really do. Got any suggestions on how we can make this work?"

"Well," I began thoughtfully, "why don't you stay in Zaen, for a couple of days?" Seeing the look on his face, I continued hurriedly. "No pressure. Just see what it's like, spend time with me. We can portal you back home whenever you want to go." I squeezed his fingers. "Please, Matt. Spend a couple of days here. First sign of trouble and I'll get you out of here, I promise."

He stared at me for a second, then a grin slowly spread across his lips. "First sign of trouble, huh? Are we expecting that soon?"

I chuckled. "It depends on what day it is. I don't even know how long it is since I was attacked."

He glanced at his watch. "It's Wednesday."

"Oh good," I announced brightly. "That gives us at least two or three days."

Dad pursed his lips and I saw a twinkle in his eye. "Great. Two or three days. Should be able to make up for nineteen years with no trouble at all in that sort of timeframe."

I laughed out loud and he grinned. "So it's a deal?" I asked, holding my breath.

"Okay. It's a deal."

Chapter 36

Round Two

"You sound happy." Lucas strode through the doorway, a little boy perched high on his shoulders. Lucas took my breath away, absolutely perfect in blue jeans and a grey sweater which clung in exactly the right places. He ducked coming through the doorway, ensuring the little boy didn't hit his head on the jamb. Behind him, a woman wearing jeans and a black sweater followed, smiling shyly.

Lucas lifted the boy from his shoulders and he squealed with delight. He was bright eyed and adorable, with shiny black hair that brushed his collar and huge chocolate brown eyes. He peered at me curiously from Lucas's arms.

Matt stood up, eyeing Lucas warily before turning to the woman and smiling affectionately at her. "Charlotte, this is my wife, Misaki and this here is your little brother, Kazuki."

"Hello, Charlotte. I can't tell you how wonderful it is to meet you, finally," Misaki announced with a charming smile. She was about thirty years old, with a slender figure and wore her long hair pulled into silky black braids. Matt caught her around the waist and stood watching me cautiously for my reaction.

I smiled shyly. "Hi." I thought for a second. "I guess that makes you... my stepmom?"

Misaki smiled. "I guess it does, but I think I'd feel really strange having you call me anything but Misaki. Is that okay with you?"

"That sounds fine." Already I liked her.

"So you two had a better second meeting than the first one?" Misaki asked, her eyes bright as she watched Lucas tickling Kazuki. The little boy dissolved into a fit of uncontrolled giggles, wriggling in Lucas's arms and Misaki smiled warmly at them.

Matt nodded tersely and I realized his body language had changed since Lucas's arrival. Where he'd been relaxed and happy a minute ago, now he was tense, edgy. "Charlotte's convinced me we should stay for a few days longer."

"Fabulous," Misaki said approvingly. She bore only the slightest trace of accent despite her Japanese heritage, her voice lilting and happy. "It'll give you two a chance to get to know one another better. And Kazuki is having a marvelous time, he thinks Conal is awesome - he transforms into his wolf shape and takes Kazuki for rides." She smiled up at Lucas. "And as for Lucas, he'll never rest - Kazuki thinks he's his own personal entertainer."

"You seem to be taking this... exceptionally well," I pointed out, wondering how this woman could so easily accept my reality without qualms.

"I told you Misaki was okay," Dad said. "She's a believer in all this stuff." He eyed Lucas suspiciously. "Maybe I should take Kazuki."

I rolled my eyes with impatience as Lucas handed the little boy to his father. "He won't hurt him, Matt."

"It's okay, Charlotte," Lucas responded evenly. "It's understandable that you father is nervous."

"Do I have reason to be?" Matt retorted sharply.

"Sir, I can assure you - I would never hurt a child. I like children, as a matter of fact," Lucas's voice was composed, but he was clenching his fists, keeping a tight rein on his temper.

"For breakfast?"

"*Matt!*" My temper flared at the outrageous comment. Lucas's jaw tensed as he stared at my father, the silver in his eyes swirling wildly.

"Matt, that was completely uncalled for," Misaki said sharply. "You owe Lucas an apology."

Matt straightened his shoulders, taking a deep breath. "I apologize," he said stiffly.

"Apology accepted," Luke responded tersely.

"No, the apology is *not* accepted," I said angrily. "You just got through telling me you were going to try and understand this, and straight away you go and blow it!"

"Charlotte, please, don't argue with your father over this," Lucas requested quietly.

"I'm trying, Charlotte," Matt said edgily. "But you bring me here, introduce me to these…" he rubbed his hand roughly across his jaw, "he's a vampire, for Christ's sake! And he's too damn old for you! He's what, like twenty four, twenty five?"

"Yeah, Matt. He's like twenty four, and while we're on the subject, how old is Misaki? Not too much older than me, I imagine. This is so hypocritical!" I fumed heatedly. "You've known me for five minutes and you're already trying to tell me what to do!"

"I'm your father, Charlotte. I want what's best for you…" he began, but I interrupted before he could continue.

"What's best for me is Lucas. He loves me."

"Maybe we should talk about this later," Misaki suggested tentatively.

"No, we need to talk about this now." Matt handed Kazuki to his mother and turned to Lucas, his eyes cold. "I don't trust you with her. You're too old for her and you're a God-damn vampire! You'll kill her!"

Lucas's eyes were equally cold and angry, but when he spoke his voice was calm. "Mr. Duncan, I appreciate how difficult this is for you to understand, but I would never intentionally harm Charlotte in any way…"

"What about unintentionally?" Matt countered, his voice tight. "Charlotte tells me you don't drink the blood of humans, but what if you're hungry and there isn't some wild animal handy to suck on?"

"Matt!" I shrieked angrily.

"Keep out of this, Charlotte. This is between me and the vampire."

For a split second, I couldn't believe I'd heard him correctly. *"Keep out of this?* Are you kidding me? You're telling me to keep out of something that is completely my business and absolutely none of yours!" I yelled.

Little Kazuki reacted to the tension in the room and began to cry in his mother's arms, lifting his chubby hands to pull at her sweater. "Matt, that is *enough*," Misaki said determinedly.

"Like hell it's enough!" Matt stepped closer to Lucas, staring at him angrily. "You've got no right to date my daughter. You should be with someone of your own kind!"

Lucas's eyes flared, the silver flashing dangerously and I pulled back the covers, intent on getting out of bed and standing between them before things got out of control. "Lucas…"

"Charlotte, it's okay." Lucas took a deep breath and stepped away from Matt, whose face was ruddy with anger. "I'll leave you to talk this through."

"*No!*" I jumped from the bed, stumbling as I discovered my knee was much more painful than I'd anticipated. Lucas rapidly covered the distance, catching me against him before I could fall. I clung to him, tears flowing down my face. "Don't leave, please!"

Lucas pressed a kiss to my forehead. "Alright," he murmured quietly. "Alright, my love. I won't leave." He gripped my hand, intertwining his fingers through mine.

The sound of voices drifted from the hallway and Ben stepped into my room, followed by Acenith and Clinton Davis.

"Good morning, Charlotte. You're looking much better this morning," Ben announced, his gaze taking in Lucas's protective stance before he turned his attention to my father and his family. "I'm not sure you should be out of bed yet."

"You most certainly should *not* be out of bed," Jerome growled as he walked in behind Clinton. "What the hell are you doing, Lucas, letting her get up?"

"It wasn't his idea," I muttered.

"I don't care whose idea it was, it was a bad one. Get back in that bed right now, young lady."

The tension could be sliced in the room. Misaki was gripping Matt's shirt sleeve, as though expecting him to take a swing at Lucas. The eye contact she was making with her husband left no doubt about her mood - she was utterly furious with him. Perhaps I liked her better than my own father.

While Lucas and Jerome settled me back into bed, Acenith stepped forward, shooting me a worried frown. "Mr. and Mrs. Duncan, this is Clinton Davis. He only recently arrived in Zaen also. Clinton, this is Charlotte's father, Matt Duncan and her step-mother, Misaki. And this is Charlotte's little brother, Kazuki."

"Please, Acenith - call us Matt and Misaki. We don't need to stand on ceremony," Misaki insisted, as Matt and Clinton shook hands and eyed one another warily.

"Pleasure to meet you," Clinton said. "Guess you're finding all this as weird as I am."

Matt raised an eyebrow. "You - you're a normal guy?"

Clinton smiled, the skin around his eyes creasing. "Yep, didn't know about any of this. First I knew about it was when young Charlotte here was attacking a couple of demons and I stumbled into the fight." He shrugged. "Before I knew it, she was tattooing my damn shoulder and I was transported through that freaking whirlpool thing into the city."

"And you've stayed here? With them?"

To give Clinton due respect, he kept his cool. On the other hand, I was ready to punch my father in the nose. "Yeah. I knew Lucas and his friends before I discovered what they were. They were good people then, they're still good people now." Clinton shrugged amicably. "They're vampires, I guess that's a huge thing to get your head around, but I consider them friends. I guess it's a bit like the difference between us and some of the other people on the planet. We all have our own ways, our own lifestyles." He glanced at Lucas and grinned. "While I certainly don't want to drink blood, what Lucas and his friends have to do to survive is their business. Not mine. They don't try to eat me, I mind my own business." He glanced down at Acenith when she nudged him discreetly. "Anyway, I understand you're having your own difficulties getting your head around all this - seems you and I are in a similar situation. How about I take you and Misaki on a bit of a tour around the town? We can stop in at the Mess, grab a coffee and have a chat. I'll introduce you to some of the good folk who live here."

I sighed deeply, glaring at my father. "Clinton, thanks for the offer - but Matt and Misaki are leaving."

Misaki's eyes widened and she pinched Matt's arm, her eyes fierce. "Matt?"

Matt's brown eyes still simmered with unresolved anger. "Misaki, she's right. We can't make this work."

Clinton put a hand out towards Matt and he glanced from my father to me. "Look, Matt. I know this is tough to comprehend. I've been here for a couple of weeks, you've only had a couple of days. Why don't we go and have that coffee, have a talk? Won't do any harm to take another hour or two to think it through." Clinton put all his self-assurance as a former Police Chief into his voice and manner and I hid a smile. He'd been a wonderful addition to Zaen, his quiet authority and sheer size made him a force to be reckoned with and he'd quickly gained the respect of the city's inhabitants.

Matt stood uncertainly for nearly a full minute, finally taking a deep breath and shrugging. "Sure. Why not?" There was pain in his eyes when he looked at me, but he managed a faint smile. "I'll see you before we leave. Misaki, are you coming?"

"I'll be there in just a minute," Misaki agreed.

Clinton led Matt towards the door and Misaki watched them leave before turning back to me with Kazuki snuggled in her arms. "Charlotte, I am so sorry about this."

"It's not your fault."

"He really is a great guy when you get to know him," Misaki continued, offering me a warm smile. She reached down to pat my hand. "He doesn't mean to be so... over-protective. I guess that's the word I'd use. I don't want to make excuses for him, but he really doesn't have a clue how to deal with a twenty one year old daughter. Not when he hasn't seen you since you were two."

I frowned despondently, feeling fragile and emotional. "I think it will be better for you to go back to San Diego. He can't deal with," I waved my hand around the room, "all this."

Misaki smiled and I couldn't help but smile back. "That's because he doesn't believe in *'all this'*." Her expression changed, growing serious again. "I'll talk to him some more, try and get him to see sense." She leaned over and kissed my cheek. "He really does love you, Charlotte. When I met him, one of the first things he did was show me a photo of you. He's been carrying it around in his wallet ever since he left your Mom, all those years ago. I know he's really sorry about not being there for you. I know it isn't any consolation, but he really does regret the decisions he made."

There was nothing I could think of to say, nothing which would be suitable in the circumstances. What was there to say? It seemed there was no way of getting Matt to accept the world I lived in and worse still, no way to get him to accept Lucas. As far as I was concerned, the only option was for him go back to San Diego.

"Either way, we'll come and see you once he's made up his mind," Misaki continued. With an apologetic smile, she turned and slipped from the room.

Chapter 37

Requests for Exile

Acenith slumped onto the edge of the bed, rolling her eyes. "Well, *that* was awkward."

Ben settled on the other side of the bed, watching me with unconcealed compassion. He placed his hand on my arm. "Are you alright?"

I groaned, slumping back against the pillows. "Out of all the people in the world, my father turns out to be a vampire redneck."

Lucas was standing by the window, his back rigid and hands still clenched into fists. He'd strode to the window after Matt left, body language oozing hostility.

"Charlotte, it was always going to be risky bringing your father here," Ben suggested in a low voice. "Don't blame him for being unable to accept what we are."

"While I get that he's freaked out by it all, it seems like he isn't even trying. He's determined to take me back to San Diego. Even when he agreed to stay for a few days, ultimately his plan is to take me back to San Diego."

Jerome jerked his thumb at Acenith and she slipped out of his way. "We've tried explaining to him that it wouldn't work - that Archangelo could find you there," Jerome said curtly as he checked my cheek. "The trouble is that he doesn't have any parameters to relate this to."

"Maybe I was always going to be different," I mused. "Ben, I accepted you and what you are straight away."

"This is true," Ben agreed. "However, perhaps that's because you too are different, Charlotte. Perhaps your acceptance came rapidly because you are Nememiah's Child."

"Show me that knee, Lottie. You shouldn't have been out of bed. You've hardly been conscious for five minutes and you're already getting into trouble," Jerome grumbled.

"Hey, that's not fair!" I protested. "Matt started it."

"Oh, very mature. I should put you over my knee for getting up without permission."

I scowled at him. "Put me over your knee?" I repeated. "You're as bad as Epi."

"Do what you're told and you won't have to see how much like Epi I can be when I'm annoyed," he retorted. He drew the covers down my legs and probed the area around my kneecap. It was glaringly obvious why it was painful - the skin was positively indigo with bruising, swollen and aching intensely.

"Good morning." Ripley appeared in the doorway, closely followed by Epi and Rowena. He offered me a warm smile, then leaned down to kiss the top of Acenith's head. "You wanted to see Epi, Charlotte?"

I was startled, until I realized he'd been reading my mind. "Seems like your ability is fully functioning again."

"Indeed. Since you contacted me from the lake, it's back to normal."

"What about the rest of you?" I glanced from him to Rowena.

"No," Rowena admitted. "Only Ripley, so far."

"You can hear my thoughts now?" I questioned Ripley.

"They're coming through loud and clear. I apologize, I try not to listen, but given the current situation..."

"It's okay, Ripley. If you hadn't been listening a few days ago, Archangelo would have killed me."

He smiled, brushing a hand across his neat ponytail. "Charlotte, I wasn't actively listening. Your voice came completely out of the blue, the first voice I'd heard since Sfantu Drâghici."

"Either way, I'm very grateful you heard me."

My attention was captured by Epi, who was holding something which looked remarkably like a funeral wreath. He placed it on my bedside table with a shamefaced smile. "I brought you some flowers, as an apology for my behavior. Rowena tells me I overstepped the mark."

The flowers were a beautiful arrangement of velvety red roses. Nothing too unusual about that, except the arrangement was shaped like a cross. "Did I die?" I asked, bemused. "Seems to me Jerome thinks I'm alive. Why the wreath?"

Acenith giggled and Rowena covered her mouth with her hand, diplomatically concealing a wide smile.

Epi looked chagrined. "I've been procuring so much for our requirements and I wanted red roses." He scratched his nose thoughtfully. "In this case, my procurement went a little haywire."

It seemed like the right time to let him off the hook. "They're lovely, Epi. Thanks."

"So I'm forgiven?"

"For the moment," I agreed guardedly.

"What did you want to see me about?" Epi asked. "Ripley tells me you have something to ask me."

"I want you to send my father back to San Diego."

"Charlotte, why don't you give it some time?" Rowena suggested gently. She caught my hand in hers and rubbed her other hand over the back of it.

Lucas had turned when I announced my decision and came to stand at the end of the bed, gripping the railings. "Is that what you really want?" he questioned.

Swallowing hard, I nodded my head determinedly. "This morning I thought he might be able to come to terms with our situation. Now, I don't think he can."

Epi's expression was solemn. "You can make him forget about this, can't you?"

Epi took a few seconds to answer. "Yes, child, I can. But I've told you once before, I don't like playing with people's emotions."

I crossed my arms. "You're not playing with his emotions, think of it as protecting him. And Misaki and Kazuki. Remove their memories of Zaen, of meeting me - in fact, remove the memory that he even contacted me in the first place. And they'll need enchantments, to keep the Consiliului away from them. Can you do that?"

Epi nodded. "Yes, I can." His wizened features wrinkled when he frowned deeply. "This is not something that should be done lightly, however. What is taken away cannot be put back," he warned.

"I know that. This is what I want. If he's determined to contact me, he'll start again, but this time, he won't find me so easily."

"Charlotte, don't do this," Lucas implored. "Don't break off a relationship with your father because of me." His eyes were intense, his jaw clenched so tightly the tendons in his neck stood out.

"Lucas, it isn't only his reaction to you. He doesn't understand vampires, but he doesn't understand me, either."

Acenith looked anxious. "He's your only relative," she protested softly.

"I know." I sat up straighter, ignoring the pain in my knee. "I'm positive about this. Epi, tell him you're taking him back to San Diego to collect their stuff, make up some sort of excuse - I don't really care what it is. But get him back to San Diego. I don't want him here." Jerome was watching our discussion with a worried expression and I smiled up at him sadly. "It's okay, Jerome. I've managed without him for nineteen years, I can manage again. Now, when can I get out of here?"

"At least two more days."

"Nope," I argued immediately. "There's too much to do." Another thought occurred. "Speaking of which, did Ambrose's group work out where we are?"

"Yes, we're in northern Europe, somewhere on the border between Poland and Germany. We've organized a group of volunteers who are out spreading the word about Zaen, they'll bring anyone to the city who is willing to join us," Epi explained.

"Why hasn't anyone noticed this city?" I demanded. "Isn't it somewhat conspicuous?"

Epi cackled, his mouth open to reveal his distinct shortage of teeth. "Nememiah has abilities above and beyond what you perceive as possible. To all intents and purposes, Zaen and its surrounds do not exist for anyone other than his Children," he smirked, "and of course, those of us who have the mark of Zaen."

"So how is this working? Our people walk to the border and just appear in Poland or Germany?" The idea seemed laughable. "And how are they getting from there to wherever these packs are?"

"Epi escorted them to the border a couple of days ago. He created portals to transport them to where the packs are located," Ben explained. "He's going to rendezvous with them again tomorrow, to bring them back."

It was mind-boggling, almost more than I could cope with. "Okay, enough information. Just send them out and get them back safely. That's enough for me."

Epi looked stunned. "That's *enough*? Charlotte, it's never enough, you usually want a complete and intricate explanation of everything."

"Maybe I'm mellowing," I suggested. "And in some ways, this is pretty cool."

"Pretty cool?" Acenith repeated with a dazzling smile.

"Sure. I've never set foot out of the States in twenty one years. Now all of a sudden, I find myself in Romania one week and then somewhere near Poland and Germany. All without the assistance of a passport, a visa or a plane ticket." I shared a warm smile with Rowena. "Who *wouldn't* think that was cool?"

The last of the tension dissipated in the room - even Lucas's stiff stance relaxed. "Remind me when this is over to take you to Europe. You need to see it the way it's *meant* to be seen."

I smiled happily. "I won't forget you made that offer."

"You won't need to," he promised.

Chapter 38

Fan Club

"How exactly, did you convince Jerome to let you out?" Marianne eyed me suspiciously as I limped slowly down the street, leaning heavily on a cane to support my damaged knee.

"I think I nagged him into submission," I admitted. "Besides, it's only my knee causing issues and Nonny rubbed her ointment into it before lunch. It's already much better."

The weather was cooling rapidly as we approached November and I was grateful Marianne had thought to bring a coat when she'd visited our cottage to collect some clothes. She'd disappeared for literally seconds when I told her I was allowed to leave the hospital, arriving back in record time with my belongings. I was snug and warm in blue jeans and a thick sweater, boots and the thick black coat. It had a faux fur collar in dark grey, which kept the cool wind currently whipping through the narrow streets at bay, plus had the added benefit of hiding most of the bruising on my face.

"Excuse me, Ms. Duncan?"

We turned together to find a teenage boy behind us. He was perhaps sixteen years old, accompanied by a group who stood a few steps behind him. They were clustered together, whispering and grinning.

"Uh, hi." I exchanged a glance with Marianne, saw her eyebrows rise imperceptibly and she shrugged as if to suggest she didn't have a clue what he wanted.

"Hi, I'm Randy, uh, Randy Norton." He was blushing and obviously nervous. "Ms. Duncan... I just wanted to say..."

"Charlotte. Call me Charlotte," I corrected him gently.

If it was possible, he blushed even harder and the acne marks on his pale skin glowed red. "Cool, Charlotte, um..." He took a deep breath, wringing his hands together. "I wanted to tell you, I think... well, I just wanted to say you're awesome. And I was wondering... maybe, if you'd consider... maybe later you might have a soda with me?"

It was my turn to blush and I ignored the sharp prod Marianne gave me with her elbow. The other boys were watching expectantly. I was convinced they would mercilessly tease Randy Norton later, if I wasn't sensitive with my response.

"Well, thanks, Randy. I really appreciate the offer and..." I bit my lip firmly, trying to force back the giggle which was threatening to burst out. "I'd love to have a soda with you." His eyes lit up and he watched me expectantly. "But I really can't. You see, I have a boyfriend and I think he'd be a little jealous if he saw me with you. I'm sorry."

Randy looked dejected, his blue eyes averted as he fidgeted from one foot to the other. "Gee, that's a shame." He brightened suddenly. "But you would have, right? If you didn't have a boyfriend and all?"

His question startled me and I looked to Marianne for help, but she was barely stifling her own giggles. "Um, yeah, I guess so. If I didn't have a boyfriend, I would love to have a soda with you, Randy."

"Wow," Randy glanced back at his friends to confirm they'd heard my answer. "That's... awesome. Charlotte, I want you to know, I think you're... beautiful. And the way you fight the demons, you *rock*."

I cleared my throat. "Uh, thanks." I glanced at Marianne again, giving her an exasperated look. "Um, I have to go now, my boyfriend is training. He'll be waiting for me."

Randy blanched visibly. "Your boyfriend... he's one of the *vamps*?"

"Yeah, he is."

"Oh, okay. Wow."

"See you later, Randy. It was nice to meet you." Marianne and I set off towards the gate and Marianne could barely suppress her amusement as we walked.

"Shut up, Marianne!" I hissed, grinning at her to soften my words. A quick glance confirmed that the group of boys were still walking behind us, chuckling and talking together in hushed tones.

"It's so *sweet*," Marianne said happily. "He must be all of seventeen."

"It is *not* sweet," I grumbled good-naturedly. "And stop laughing."

The gates out of the city were closed and Marianne pushed her hand against the wall to trigger them open. Outside, people were milling around, but not nearly as many as the day I was attacked. Epi had been at work yet again, the cage where we'd been training had been joined by four more, each identical to the other.

Marianne pointed to the cage on the far right where Epi stood. Nick, Conal, Lucas, Striker and William stood with him. Some of the other people who'd joined us were standing around expectantly.

The familiar tendril of desire flared to life as I studied Lucas from a distance. He was talking to Nick and dressed in similar attire to what I wore for training - camouflage pants and a black t-shirt which emphasized his broad shoulders and lean waist. He wore a belt slung low across his hips, with Katchet and Philaris visible. William and Striker were dressed similarly and William saw us approaching and waved. The movement caught Lucas's attention and he turned, spying me. With a dazzling smile, Lucas strode towards me, his eyes filled with delight. "I thought Jerome wanted you to stay in hospital?"

I rolled my eyes. "He did, but I wanted to get out and see you guys train." I glanced back towards the gates, confirming the group of boys were still following us. "Would you do me a favor? Please?"

"Of course." Lucas's gaze followed mine and then he looked back down at me, one eyebrow raised in question.

"Kiss me," I requested huskily.

Lucas inhaled sharply, his eyes filling with undiluted desire. He lifted his hand to capture the back of my neck, dropping his mouth to mine. "That's not a favor, my love. That's a pleasure." His cool lips captured mine and I wrapped my arms around his waist, leaning into him. When he pulled away, he smiled tenderly. "May I ask what that was all about?"

"Charlotte's got a fan club," Marianne announced gleefully, her face bright with unadulterated amusement. "She got asked out on a date."

Lucas's gaze drifted back to the group of teenagers, a bemused smile playing on his lips. "Hmmm. So I've got competition?"

I rolled my eyes, the heat of a blush creeping across my cheeks. "Hardly."

"He seems *very* keen," Marianne added mischievously.

"In that case..." Lucas caught me in his arms, aligning me against his body as he dropped his mouth to mine and kissed me more firmly. My knees buckled as he ran his hands lightly down my back and my heart pounded as I breathed in his luscious aroma. When he released me, he held my arms to steady me. "I'm sure he wouldn't kiss you like that, love," he murmured against my ear, making me shiver with desire, "and if he did kiss you - I would probably have to kill him." With a smug smile he caught my hand in his and we walked to where the others stood.

"Hey Sugar, how's the knee?" Conal grabbed me in a bear hug, kissing my cheek. "Ready to get back into it?"

"Nope. I've got a leave pass for another couple of days. Thought it would be fun to see someone else getting covered in demon blood for a change."

Epi strode across, his eyes magnified enormously behind the thick glasses. "All right, let's have one of you men in with Nick and Conal initially and we'll get an indication of how you work together."

"I'll go," Striker volunteered. In the camouflage pants and black t-shirt he cut an imposing figure, with muscles rippling across his chest and shoulders. His long blond hair was pulled back at the nape of his neck, secured with a leather strap.

The three men slipped through the opening into the cage and we moved closer to watch. Striker approached us, obviously geared up for a fight and looking positively jubilant at being involved in some action. "Any advice, Lott?"

"Keep away from the sharp bits."

The look he threw my way was scornful. "Lott, I'm a vampire. Sharp bits won't worry me in the slightest."

I laughed. "All right, so don't worry about the sharp bits." I leaned against the bars, relieving some of the weight off my knee. "The most important thing to remember is to aim for the chest. You can injure them with the weapons but to send them back to the Otherworld, a wound to the heart is most effective."

"Demons have a heart?"

I shrugged. "I don't have a clue, you'd have to ask Epi about that. But the chest shot always works."

"Cool." Striker bobbed his head in understanding and bounced eagerly from foot to foot, waiting impatiently for Conal and Nick to transform. They were imposing figures in wolf form, Conal was absolutely enormous, standing taller than Striker and broad across the shoulders. Nick was only a head shorter and he barked happily from inside the cage. I would have sworn he winked at me.

"Let's begin with something simple," Epi announced. He dropped to one knee and drew the pentagram on the dark earth. The dirt erupted inside the cage as the fifth sigil was completed and a demon stepped out. Epi had begun with a Valafar, however this demon was perhaps half the size again of the one he'd produced for Conal and I. As it coalesced, Striker sprang forward, his movements quicker than a lightning strike. In a blur he reached the Valafar's side, standing so close he was almost touching it and I thought he was going to kill it before it even had an opportunity to attack.

At the last second, the demon comprehended that Striker was there and represented a danger, swinging its huge claws. It hit Striker's chest, hurling him towards the side of the cage. The sound of the demon hitting Striker was sounded like a crack of thunder and while the noise still reverberated, Conal and Nick pounded across the cage, sinking their teeth into the Valafar's body, snarling as they tore into the oily black flesh.

Striker was on his feet, his form blurring as he hurtled towards the demon, a Katchet clutched in his fist. Intuitively, Conal and Nick dropped back from their assault, allowing Striker to attack the Valafar. They circled, biting and growling while Striker launched himself onto the demon, knocking it off balance. He stabbed it once and thick black blood sprayed in an arc from its body. With a deafening shriek, the Valafar rushed Striker, catching him with another thrashing crack from its claws. Conal and Nick joined in for a second time, gnawing at the Valafar's legs while Striker regained his balance and twisted back toward the demon. This time his aim was accurate and he plunged the knife into the demon's chest repeatedly until it folded in on itself and vanished.

Striker jogged across to where we stood, his face and arms smeared with demon blood and I could see a new respect in his eyes. "They're tougher than I anticipated," he confessed, which was a huge admission from Striker. "The fact that you can kill them, that's pretty astounding, Lott."

Lucas wrapped his arm more tightly around my waist, squeezing me against his side.

"Conal, Nick; remain in wolf form, please," Epi instructed. "We'll go again."

Lucas kissed my forehead. "My turn," he announced.

Striker slipped out of the cage and Lucas entered, straightening up inside the enclosed space he glanced at Epi, watching the ancient Warlock complete a new pentagram.

I anxiously watched the demon forming, it became an Omias, the demon we'd fought in Sfantu Drâghici. When it roared, the tentacles on the jet black head quivered and Lucas leaped at it, throwing a Philaris with stunning precision. The Philaris caught it a heavy blow to the chest, but the toughness of its skin layer guaranteed it wouldn't be enough to return it to the Otherworld.

It did make the Omias howl in agony and succeeded in antagonizing the enormous creature further. It sped towards Lucas, tossing Conal and Nick away as they endeavored to bite its legs. One massive arm swung towards Lucas, throwing him into the air and he smashed into the cage bars with tremendous force. My heart was in my mouth, but Lucas recovered in a second and ran toward the creature again.

The Omias had rotated, focusing its attention on Conal and Nick and I was dismayed when Nick was tossed, hitting the cage heavily. He lay motionless for a few seconds before rolling onto his feed, shaking his head and pounding towards the demon once more. Lucas caught up with the Omias from behind, somersaulting over it and clearing its head by a good foot of free air. Dropping to the ground, he smashed the Katchet into its chest. The force of the blow produced a gush of blood, which quickly soaked Lucas. He remained intent on his task, thrusting the blade into the demon's chest for a second time. The Omias disappeared and I breathed easier, thankful that all three men were safe. Lucas swung out of the cage and I wrinkled my nose in disgust as he approached. "Ew. You reek."

Lucas grimaced, wiping his face with the sleeve of his t-shirt. "It does smell repulsive. Even worse to me, I imagine, as my sense of smell is heightened."

"See, there are some advantages to being human," I responded smugly.

William entered the cage after Lucas and managed to defeat the demon Epi created with little trouble. A natural warrior, William was a product of his past in the Army, with tactical experience in warfare. He destroyed the demon in a shorter time than Striker and Lucas, and appeared quite pleased with himself when he finished. "Certainly a challenge, but now we have the use of the weapons, they'll be no problem to us," he reported.

"That's good news, excellent, in fact," Epi agreed, clearly delighted by this report. "Let's call it a day and we'll organize a training plan at the meeting tomorrow morning."

Lucas grasped my hand. "Let's go home."

"Wait a minute." I turned back to Epi. "Did you do that job for me?"

Epi glanced up from creating a tent for Nick and Conal. "No, I haven't done it yet. Your father was deep in conversation with Clinton when I located him - I preferred not to interrupt."

My displeasure at this news must have been obvious in my expression because he raised a hand towards me. "Now, Child, don't be impatient. I will do this for you, but you must accept that I will do it when I believe it's the right time. I promise you, it will be today."

I flashed him a grateful smile. "Thanks, Epi."

We walked back to Zaen together. Lucas offered to carry me but I refused. Getting demon blood all over my beautiful coat was not something I would consider, regardless of how much my knee hurt. I limped slowly through the gates and we split up at our street, with Marianne still teasing me about my teenage admirers.

Lucas and I strolled leisurely toward our cottage, Lucas matching my dawdling pace. "I think I'll go and shower," he suggested once we were inside.

"Excellent idea," I agreed, wrinkling my nose delicately. "I'm going to make coffee."

Lucas went upstairs and I hobbled into the minuscule kitchen. It was basic and clean - with all meals obtainable at the Mess Hall, all we had was a kettle. I made a strong coffee, limping into the living room to sit down and drink it. Being back in our tiny home was wonderful, even better to be with Lucas. Being separated from him for any period of time was too long nowadays.

The living room was truly tiny, with a petite couch, one chair, a bookcase, a small coffee table and a lamp. Nothing else would fit into the diminutive room. It was pleasantly decorated, with pale yellow walls and white curtains at the windows. The couch was upholstered in a sturdy tan material and the wooden furniture all crafted from light ash. Despite the size, it was comfortable enough for our needs, although the artist in me yearned for something to decorate the walls. With a sense of rueful longing, I considered whether I might get the opportunity to paint again. It had been so long since I'd picked up a brush, sketched anything. There was never enough time.

Lucas came downstairs as I finished my coffee, in faded jeans and a grey t-shirt, a blue shirt hanging unbuttoned over the top. He dropped onto the couch beside me, stretching his long legs out and slipped his arm around my shoulder. "I've missed you," he whispered against my ear.

"I missed you too," I agreed. He wrapped his arms around me and I rested my head against his neck.

We were content to be wrapped in each other's arms, Lucas playing with my hair while I savored his masculine aroma.

"Why didn't you tell your father how old I really am? When he suggested my age, you merely agreed with him," Lucas questioned.

"He was having enough trouble dealing with everything, without me telling him you're one hundred and sixty five."

His mouth rose in a little smile. "Not to split hairs, but I'm one hundred and thirty six."

"When was your birthday?"

His expression darkened. "While we were separated."

"I'm sorry I wasn't there," I admitted, downcast by this news. "I wish we hadn't been separated from each other. It feels like I got cheated out of more time."

"Charlotte, please don't worry about this age business anymore," Lucas requested quietly. "I love you, I will continue to love you, and nothing will change that."

"But..." Before I could continue, Lucas lowered his head, his mouth searching out mine and I draped my arms around his neck, holding him tightly. I moaned softly when he ran his tongue across my lips, seeking entrance. I opened to him, swept away with desire.

For the briefest of moments, he released my lips and murmured against my skin. "No more regrets, my love. Only delight at being together. Let's live for the moment." He kissed me insistently, creating delicious shivers which trembled up my spine. "I want to make love to you," he whispered huskily. "Do you feel up to it?"

I was so completely overwhelmed, I couldn't string words together. As an alternative, I could only nod.

Lucas stood up, running his fingertips down my arms. He scooped me up, holding me against him as he walked upstairs to the bedroom, his mouth never parting from mine. He lowered me carefully onto the floor, reaching for my top and tugging it from my body. I slipped my fingers underneath his t-shirt, his muscled abdomen contracting at my touch. Interspersing our efforts with long kisses, I slipped the shirt from his shoulders and he shrugged it off, dropping it to the floor before he divested himself of the t-shirt in one polished movement.

I gazed at his bare chest, the tight muscles in his abdomen and the tendrils of desire ignited into a white hot flame.

Lucas reached behind me, unclasping the lacy bra and slipping it from my shoulders. I watched him as he undid the button on my jeans, slowly releasing the zipper and dropping to one knee to slide them down my legs. He stood again, supporting me while I stepped out of the denim and then watched me, his breathing heavy as his eyes raked across my body, filled with yearning.

"You are so beautiful," he whispered huskily. And then he pulled me down with him onto the bed, his mouth finding mine and nothing else mattered but being with him, loving him. And I was complete.

Chapter 39

Confrontation

"I wonder how many times we can do that before we'll tire of it," Lucas announced thoughtfully. He was lying on his back, hands tucked behind his head and I lay against his chest, my arm draped over his stomach.

"Well, I don't know about you, but I don't think I'll ever tire of it." I was feeling euphoric, positively glowing with the knowledge of Lucas's insatiable desire for me. And my equally insatiable longing for him. He'd awakened sensations I'd never known existed and a profound sense of well-being was making me positively radiant. I rolled over to study his perfect features, leaning against his chest on my forearms. "Why? Are you telling me you've already had enough? You're bored already?"

His expression implied he thought I was crazy. "Absolutely not. Never. I was merely contemplating whether this glorious expectation I feel when I think about making love to you would fade off, or if every time will be like the most amazing moment of my existence." He lowered his arms and rubbed my shoulders tenderly. "I wasn't suggesting I didn't want to make love. I doubt another minute of my existence will pass without wanting to be with you, loving you."

I entwined my arms around his neck, wanting to feel his skin against mine, to have him loving me and making me forget - if only for a brief time - what my future held. "Lucas, *please*." I drew him towards me, my mouth seeking his and he rolled until he I lay beneath him, his eyes dark with lust.

"I think you're right, love. We'll never tire of this..."

≈†◊◊†◊◊†◊◊†≈

Confrontation

Much later, Lucas kissed my forehead and slipped from the bed. "I'm going downstairs. Why don't you indulge in a nice long nap? You look exhausted."

"That's because you exhaust me," I mumbled drowsily.

He smiled, pushing my hair back from my face with a tender movement. "I believe that last time was at your insistence, love."

"I've waited a long time. I don't want to miss any opportunities," I muttered. I closed my eyes, listening sleepily as he dressed and slipped from the room. It took only seconds to fall into a deep sleep, curled against the pillow which was infused with his scent.

≈†◇◇†◇◇†◇◇†≈

The sound of persistent knocking woke me - snuggled against Lucas's pillow I'd slept soundly until the noise drew me back to alertness. I rolled onto my back and sat up, drawing the sheet over my naked breasts. Darkness had fallen and the room was bathed in shadows from moonlight reaching through the open curtains.

Lucas's voice floated up the stairwell, his words lost to me. I wondered if it was the Tines coming to visit, but when I heard the other voice I slipped out of bed, scouting around for fresh underwear before pulling on my robe and tying it securely at my waist. In the few seconds it took to get dressed, the volume of voices increased and I swiftly limped downstairs.

Lucas stood at the open door, with Matt standing on the doorstep. Misaki was on the steps behind Matt, Kazuki snuggled in her arms.

Lucas heard me approach and glanced up, his eyes hard. "Charlotte, your father would like to speak with you." His eyes grazed over my skimpy attire and a tiny smile played on his lips.

Pushing my hair behind my ears, I stopped at Lucas's side. He slipped his arm around my waist protectively. "Hi Matt, Misaki," I greeted them cautiously.

Matt inhaled deeply before he spoke. "Charlotte, I... *we* don't want to leave."

I looked at Lucas and he met my gaze evenly. His eyes were impassive, clearly allowing me to make up my own mind about what to do. "Come in," I invited begrudgingly.

Lucas indicated the couch, waiting for Matt and Misaki to sit down. He offered me the chair but I settled awkwardly onto the floor in front of it. Lucas sat down and I leaned back between his legs, his hands reassuring on my shoulders. For a few seconds there was an awkward silence.

"Charlotte, I know what you were planning - having Epi send us back through that portal thing." Matt's voice was calm, perhaps sounded a little defeated. He smiled faintly as he shook his head. "I'm not an idiot. Being in the Marines for sixteen years, you have to get up pretty early in the morning to fool me." His eyes met mine and sadness was clearly visible in his. "I know I've made a mess of this, but I'm a little disappointed that you were going to have us leave without even saying goodbye. And worse still, making us forget this ever happened."

Lucas's touch against my shoulders was reassuring, his presence giving me confidence. "Matt," I began, crossing my legs at the ankle and clasping my hands in my lap. "It's been great to meet you, it really has. But the only way this could work is if you accept what I am. What Lucas is. Because he's the most important person in my life and he's a vampire. If you can't accept him and my friends, understand that this is what I am and what I do, a relationship between you and I is impossible."

Matt's gaze went from mine to Lucas's and back. "You didn't give me a lot of time, Charlotte."

Kazuki was stirring restlessly in his mother's arms, his eyes firmly trained on Lucas. "Wucas! Wucas!" The little boy wriggled to get off Masuki's lap and she released her hold on him, setting him down. He ambled across the floor, bypassing me to get to the object of his desire. "Wucas!" The little boy raised his arms to Lucas, smiling with delight.

Lucas rubbed his hand over the boy's silky black hair, but made no attempt to pick him up. His focus remained on Matt, a silent question in his eyes.

"Go ahead, I don't mind," Matt said quietly. I scrutinized my father's face suspiciously, watching for any reaction when Lucas lifted Kazuki into his arms. Kazuki shrieked with delight and settled happily in Lucas's lap. I was surprised when Matt's face remained composed and calm. Either he'd suddenly come to terms with my situation, or, more likely, was deliberately keeping his expression composed to stop me from losing my temper before we'd had a chance to talk this through. I was betting on the latter scenario.

Sighing deeply, I turned my attention to the matter at hand. "Matt, I have to be honest with you - I just don't have a lot of spare time to deal with this. Sometime in the next couple of days we'll be attacked. We're fighting a war here and everyone has to work together, whether they like it or not. I thought it would be better if you didn't have to be involved. Sending you home to San Diego, letting you go back to your normal life - it seemed like the kindest thing to do," I admitted. "Particularly when there seemed to be no way to get you to accept my choices and my life."

"But you were going to make us forget about meeting you, Charlotte," Misaki said. "And that's something neither Matt, nor I would want to lose."

I shrugged, uncomfortable with what I'd asked Epi to do. "It isn't what I wanted - but Matt, you painted me into a corner. I cannot and will not leave Zaen. Even if I did, Archangelo can use his abilities to locate me. He sees me in his potion-induced sleep, just as surely as I see him when I have the nightmares. There is nowhere safe for me to hide." For a second I wondered if Matt and Misaki knew about my bizarre psychic link with Archangelo, but they appeared to understand what I was talking about, so obviously someone had taken the opportunity to fill them in. "And at the moment, I'm the primary target." Lucas squeezed my shoulder in a gentle grip and I knew he worried about his capability to keep me safe. "It seemed easier for everyone if you didn't remember coming here, didn't know what I'm doing."

"Let me try to help, Charlotte," Matt responded, leaning forward on the couch. "I've got sixteen years experience as a Marine. I've seen active service in Afghanistan, Iraq, Somalia. My experience could be put to good use, I'm sure of it. I want to help."

I turned to Lucas, wanting his guidance on this decision. He smiled warmly and nodded imperceptibly, squeezing my shoulder. Turning back to Matt, I took a deep breath. "You can live amongst my friends? With *total* acceptance of what they are?"

He squared his shoulders, his determination apparent. "I will."

"You'll accept Lucas?" Narrowing my eyes, I waited for the response.

Matt glanced at Lucas, his eyes clear and honest. "Yes."

I bit my lip nervously. "We're living together."

Matt chuckled, the skin around his eyes creasing. "You're running around in a bathrobe at seven o'clock at night, Charlotte. I'd figured that one out for myself."

His reaction startled me for a couple of seconds, then I smiled sheepishly. "And there's something else you should know."

"Okay," he responded evenly.

"Lucas isn't twenty four. Vampires are immortal."

Matt frowned, his head tilting to one side. "So that means?"

It was hard to keep the smile from blossoming on my face, imagining the reaction I was about to get. "Lucas is one hundred and sixty six. He was born in 1842."

It was Misaki who responded, brown eyes twinkling with mischief. "Guess that redefines dating an older man, Charlotte. My parents worried about *us* dating - and I'm only a decade younger than Matt."

Matt's chest heaved, but he surprised me by controlling his reaction. "Charlotte, that's okay." He met Lucas's gaze, saw the hand Lucas held protective on my shoulder. "I'll admit it isn't what I would have expected - but he seems to have your best interests at heart. If you care for him, and he cares for you - if he treats you well and cherishes you - that's good enough for me."

"I love your daughter, Mr. Duncan. There's nothing in this world that would stop me from loving her and I'll do everything within my power to protect her from the dangers she faces," Lucas responded gravely.

For a minute, Matt was silent and when he spoke again, his attention was on Lucas, scrutinizing him, sizing him up. "Given that I've just found out you're four times my age - maybe you should call me Matt."

"All right, Matt," Lucas agreed easily and Misaki and I shared a joyful smile.

Someone knocked at the door and Lucas stood to answer it. "It's Epi," he announced, lowering the now-sleeping Kazuki carefully onto my lap. "Hold your brother."

I was captivated by the little boy nestled against my arm and marveled at the sudden swell of emotion. The knowledge that he was my brother warmed my heart, something I wouldn't have believed possible just a year ago.

In a burst of supernatural speed, Lucas was at the door. I knew he'd done it deliberately, to see how Matt would react. Matt looked stunned and I giggled, amused by the wealth of emotions that flickered across his face. "Vampires can move quickly," I confirmed.

"So I see," he responded weakly. "Anything else I should know about?"

My shrug was deceptively casual. "Heightened senses - he knew it was Epi because his sense of smell, hearing and eyesight are far superior to ours. And incredible strength."

"Strength?" Misaki repeated happily. Judging by the delight in her eyes, she was fascinated by the whole concept and excited to come to the realization that the myths were true. "I've read about that."

I shook my head ruefully. "Speaking as a person relatively new to the supernatural word, I can tell you the majority of what you've read isn't true. But strength is."

"How strong is he?" Matt asked, scratching his eyebrow.

"Strong enough to lift a car, throw a tree. His body is like granite. He can't be injured by conventional methods."

"I guess I've got a lot to learn," Matt admitted, watching as Lucas stepped past him to sit down.

"Epi was checking if everything was alright," Lucas explained, dropping his hands onto my shoulders. "And he's pleased you've chosen to join us, Matt. He asked if you would attend our meeting tomorrow morning."

"Absolutely. I'd appreciate the opportunity to find a way I can help." He looked at Kazuki sleeping peacefully in my arms and smiled tenderly. "It sure is good to see you with your little brother, Charlotte."

I smiled with genuine warmth. "He's really cute."

"And completely besotted with 'Wucas'," Misaki grinned and stood up. "Matt, we should go back to our cottage and leave Lucas and Charlotte in peace."

"Sure, yeah." Matt drew himself up and Misaki leaned over to scoop Kazuki from my arms. "He looks very comfortable with his big sister," she said softly.

"He's adorable," I admitted. "I hope I can spend more time with him."

"Of course you can," Misaki responded. "He's your brother." She straightened up and I pulled myself onto my feet, favoring my leg only a little now the Tremaine ointment was having its desired effect. "And besides, he's devoted to 'Wucas'," Misaki continued with a devilish look. "We can hardly keep him away from his favorite plaything."

Lucas and I shared a warm smile. "Well hopefully, he'll get to adore his big sister as much as he adores 'Wucas'," I suggested. Lucas rolled his eyes, but they were filled with amusement.

Matt bridged the small distance between us. "Thanks - for giving me another chance." He stood awkwardly and I reached for him, hugging him.

"Thanks for wanting to have another chance," I agreed.

He held me close and I shut my eyes, strangely comforted by being held by this man, who'd been missing from my life for so long. When he released me, he extended a hand to Lucas. "And thank you for caring for her. I appreciate it."

Lucas accepted his handshake. "It's an honor, Matt. Charlotte gives me far more than I ever felt worthy of receiving. She's a remarkable woman."

Matt nodded thoughtfully, hugging me briefly once more before Misaki kissed my cheek. "We'll see you tomorrow?"

"Absolutely," I agreed.

Lucas followed them to the door and they said their goodbyes before he closed the door behind them. In a swift movement he was in front of me, taking me in his arms. "That went well," he murmured.

"Better than I expected," I admitted.

"I'm glad you told him the truth."

"Well, I figure he'd already freaked out. Finding out we're living together and how old you are wasn't going to make too much difference."

Lucas smiled. "I suppose that's true." He kissed my nose. "But I'd like to make an honest woman of you."

I frowned, scrutinizing his face carefully. "What?"

Lucas gazed down at me, his expression solemn. "I come from an era where a man and a woman married before they made love. Perhaps it's old-fashioned, but it seems to me I have... stolen your virtue."

For a few seconds I gaped at him - then burst into laughter. When I recovered my composure it was to find Lucas looking somewhat perturbed. "I'm sorry..." I bit my lip, trying to find the right words. "I understand you come from a different era, but I'm a modern girl. You're a modern man. I'm not all that concerned about my... virtue.

Lucas drew a deep breath. "So you're not concerned about living in sin?"

I giggled, unable to suppress my amusement. "Um, no." I studied him for a few seconds. "Why on earth would this be worrying you? You've slept with lots of women before now."

"No-one I've intended spending my existence with. I feel I should make our union legal between us and before God."

I raised an eyebrow. "Really?"

Lucas smiled. "You don't worry that you'll go to hell?"

"Definitely not. Besides, I'm an angel, I think that gives me a free pass to heaven." I narrowed my eyes suspiciously. "Why? Are you?"

Confrontation

"I come from Irish stock, Charlotte. I was raised a Catholic. Yes, I have doubts about my passage to the afterlife." Observing my startled expression, he explained further. "Charlotte, we're vampires. Our belief system suggests we have no souls. Without a soul, you can't be admitted to heaven."

"I don't believe that," I scoffed lightly. The very idea seemed absurd. Lucas, Ben - all of them - the very idea they could be seen as soulless creatures was implausible. Vampires they may be, but their inherent goodness was beyond reproach in my eyes.

Lucas looked uncertain, his dark blue eyes filled with some emotion I couldn't fathom. Not quite worry, but certainly some vacillation. I had to remind myself that he came from a different era, a different century. He was a thoroughly modern man in so many ways, but his belief in religion was likely to be completely different from my own modern thoughts on the subject. "Even so, perhaps I should be pushing my luck," he commented quietly.

Shaking my head, I held his gaze steadily. "I'm not sure what you're saying."

He inhaled deeply before he spoke, almost as though he were frightened. For a moment, I caught an emotion I'd never seen in Lucas before. He was... *nervous*. "I'm saying - I want you to marry me."

My breath caught in my throat for a few seconds, then released with a quiet whoosh. "Marry you," I repeated slowly.

"Yes."

A tiny smile played on my lips. "You're proposing?"

He sighed heavily, arching one eyebrow. "Yes. That's what I'm doing."

I bit my lip, composing a careful answer. It had obviously been important to him, his concern about my... *virtue* paramount, to make him ask me this question. It was based on a belief system from more than a century ago and I didn't want to hurt him or dismiss his offer out of hand. "Lucas, I love you. I adore you. I can't imagine my life without you, but I'm only twenty one. I'm... well, I'm not sure I'm ready to get married."

"I see," Lucas responded softly. The silver highlights in his eyes were rotating slowly, his expression calm. "So, you aren't saying no?"

"I'm saying... I'm happy with the way things are."

"You will marry me though - at a later date?" he pressed quietly.

I touched his cheek, caressing his cool skin as I smiled. "Yes. Later, when the time is right - I'll marry you."

He reached into the pocket of his jeans and when he drew his hand out, he was holding the ring I'd abandoned in Puckhaber Falls. "I've been carrying this with me since you left, hoping that one day you would wear it again." He reached for my left hand. "Will you do me the honor of wearing it again?"

"Like... an engagement ring?" I asked warily.

He smiled softly. "I've got the impression you may be a little cagey about a marriage proposal. Shall we call it - a promise ring?" He slipped the delicate gold band onto my finger and I stared at it, watching the light overhead catching the brilliant gold and making it gleam. "When you feel ready to accept my proposal, I will replace this with a ring of your choice."

I shook my head resolutely. "Lucas, I won't ever want another ring, I love this one. It's... well, it's special to me, because it's special to you." I looked up into his eyes. "It's as though this ring carries a piece of your heart. When I took it off - before I left Puckhaber - I felt as if I'd lost your heart." My eyes filled with tears, remembering the awful night when I'd left Lucas, thinking I would never see him again.

Lucas drew me against him, holding me firmly to his chest. "You'll never lose my heart, Charlotte. I will love you, with every fiber of my being, for eternity." He leaned down, catching my lips with his own and I clung to him, savoring the love he embraced me with.

Chapter 40

Into the Valley of the Shadow…

Acenith and I were standing atop the huge battlements two days later, when the first of the new groups arrived. Portalled to the outskirts of Zaen, they were walking in from the border, protected by a group of shape shifters and werewolves.

"They look scared," I remarked quietly. The group were straggling along, carrying their worldly possessions in rucksacks and duffel bags. Some of the men carried babies and toddlers, other children were holding the women's hands, clinging to what or who they knew.

"It's hardly surprising. Being isolated here, we don't know how many have been attacked, other than what you learn from the nightmares. Perhaps these groups had already been attacked," Acenith suggested. Her long hair was braided, hanging across her breast as she leaned on the wall watching the new arrivals.

"Better get down there." We walked down the steps, arriving at the gates just as the first of our new residents arrived.

Nat Finton was already there, dressed in blue jeans and a checked shirt he greeted us with a warm smile. "Hey Charlotte, Acenith."

"Do we know where they're from?"

"Bray and Tom brought them in from the States. They're a group of werewolves from Minnesota, attacked three weeks ago. They gladly agreed to join us, their houses were destroyed, they had nowhere to go." Nat watched the group approach, hands perched on his hips.

I'd learned from Nick that his pack could speak telepathically with one another when they were in their other form and as other groups joined us, we'd discovered they had the same ability. The fact that Nat already knew information about the newcomers wasn't surprising as his men were on the retrieval team.

Ripley came up beside me, his expression sober. "I'll read them as they come through, ensure we haven't got anyone with issues," he suggested quietly.

"You're ability is still working?"

He nodded, his gazed fixed on the incoming group. "It's working fine. And some of us are beginning to regain the telepathy between us."

"We can be thankful for some small mercies, then," I suggested.

Acenith drew the Hjördis she'd been issued from her pocket. "I'm a little nervous about this." She and Rowena had volunteered to mark the new arrivals with the wing sigil and my own presence was two-fold - to greet the new arrivals and physically touch each person. It would build up the group of spirits that Epi assured me were my best weapon. It would also allow us to double-check that we weren't allowing anyone into Zaen who had ulterior motives. Despite my belief that anyone willing to have the mark of Nememiah could be trusted, Epi, Lucas and Ben insisted we needed to keep up our guard.

"There's no choice, Acenith. It must be done," Ripley reminded her gently.

Rowena joined us and we spent an hour or so greeting and marking the latest allies. As I'd suspected they were frightened, having been attacked by the Consiliului, they'd been in hiding the past three weeks, struggling to stay alive. All were willing to be marked if it gave them an opportunity for safety and security. Although only a small group, perhaps sixty people - by the time I'd made contact with the spirits released from their touch, I had a headache coming on. Once inside the gates, a second group of volunteers were assisting the newcomers to settle in to their allocated accommodations.

To a certain extent, we were developing a cohesive unit. Each inhabitant of Zaen had their responsibilities, overseen by their own leaders. Jerome was in charge of medical facilities, but we'd been incredibly fortunate in having another doctor join us, which took some of the pressure from Jerome's shoulders. Nonny was presiding over the Mess and next week we planned to commence school lessons for the children. A group of women had volunteered to handle the washing for the city and another small group of women, who had younger children, were providing childcare in one of the large houses in the central courtyard, allowing parents to work in their designated roles.

Archangelo remained my biggest concern and as I stood greeting new arrivals, I mulled over the perpetual fear I carried - Nememiah's warning about Archangelo. He'd almost killed me once and I doubted I could defeat him. Despite my abilities, he was so much stronger and I had no idea how to kill him. Nememiah's words haunted me - his warning about only one of us surviving was a heavy burden to bear. It was something I tried not to think about, but the thought constantly niggled at the back of my mind. There must be a way of killing him, but if he could regenerate, what could it be? The spirits were non-committal with regards to defeating him, much to my continual irritation.

I was mulling this question when a cacophony of sounds filled my head without warning and I clamped my hands to my temples.

"Charlotte?" Acenith questioned, abandoning the man she'd been marking when she saw what I assumed could only be abject panic in my expression.

"What's wrong?" Ripley demanded. It was clear from his face that he'd guessed.

I looked around, aghast at the sight of forty or more people still waiting to be marked. "Demons. They're sending demons!" I stared up at Ripley, panic bubbling in my chest. "Go and sound the alarm. Get anyone inside who can go." I glanced around frantically, expecting to see the demons coalescing as I spoke. "Ripley, get Epi. We need some way to shield these people until they can go in."

Ripley nodded tersely and ran towards the gate in a burst of superhuman speed. The group waiting to gain entrance to Zaen swarmed forward in terror and I held up my hands. "Stop! *Stop!*"

"We have to get inside - you said demons are coming!" one man shouted.

"You can't go in without the mark," I stated. "We will keep you safe!"

The warning siren sounded over Zaen, further alarming the already panicked group outside. Nat held up his hands. "We'll get you in safely! Remain calm, please!" he roared, his voice filled with authority.

I shut my eyes briefly, forming a barrier of spirits around the newcomers and from the corner of my eye, I caught the first eruption from the ground. People started to scream, and Nat and one of his men forcefully held them back from the gates.

"Charlotte, what can we do?" Matt appeared, along with Ben and Epi.

"Matt, get as many of these children through the gates as you can. They don't need the mark. Check for any humans, they can go through now and be marked later."

Matt looked at me blankly and Ben spoke, simplifying my garbled explanation. "Matt, shape shifters, werewolves and anyone with mixed blood can't enter. Anyone purely human and those under sixteen can."

"Right." Matt turned to speak to the group, his voice commanding. Despite panic overwhelming me, it was encouraging to see my father use his military experience to control the crowd. He was good at it.

"How many, Charlotte?" Epi questioned.

"More than we can handle," I responded grimly. "Probably one hundred demons. Or more. And younglings."

Epi swallowed nervously, then straightened his shoulders doggedly. "Charlotte, you can do this. Concentrate on the demons, child. I will do what I can to help from the turrets."

"Not yet," I responded. "I need you to provide these people with some sort of shield." There was no doubt that he could do it. Epi had proven more than once that he had abilities beyond my imagination.

"As you wish, child."

Lucas appeared in the gateway, wearing a weapons belt and carrying mine. I took it gratefully, wrapping it around my waist and clutching the Hjördis in the palm of my hand.

"What's our plan?" Holden asked with a grin when he arrived with William and Conal.

Misaki had appeared and along with Clinton Davis she was escorting the children through the gates, her demeanor calm despite the panic surrounding her. "I'm going out to deal with the demons. You guys need to get these people marked."

"Charlotte, that's a crazy idea," Conal argued immediately. "The vamps can fight the demons."

"Not like I can," I responded. "And these people need the mark before we can get them in." I turned to Lucas and Ben. "They're helpless without the mark. I've got spirits in a protective barrier around them until Epi can take over. You need to finish marking them. Once that's done and they're safely inside, I might need a hand."

Into the Valley of the Shadow...

"Might?" Conal smirked, but the twinkle in his black eyes confirmed his respect for my courage. Or insanity.

"I'm not letting you out there without me," Lucas stated.

I watched as werewolves and shape shifters hurried out through the gates, already transformed and prepared to fight. "I'm not on my own, Lucas. This is important, *please*. I can't let these people die," I begged quietly.

"I'll be with her, leech." Conal spoke up. "I'll make sure she's safe."

For long seconds, Lucas studied Conal, his eyes filled with disquiet. "You'll stay with her? No matter what happens?"

"Absolutely. I'll protect her with my life," Conal responded somberly. "You know that," he added with a growl.

"I know." Lucas glanced down at me and nodded. "I'll be there as soon as I can." He pressed his cool lips against my forehead and turned away.

I rapidly applied sigils to my arms, horribly aware that the werewolves and shape shifters were fighting out there without them. There just wasn't time to get everyone marked and I cursed again, the lack of people able to use the weapons and Hjördis.

In front of us, in the open fields surrounding Zaen, the ground erupted as demons starting to coalesce before us. The noise was horrendous as the newcomers screamed in terror, shape shifters howled, werewolves snarled and the demons shrieked above it all, an unearthly and eerie sound which echoed across the plain.

"Alright, Charlotte. I have them secured," Epi announced. He'd taken up a position on the outskirts of the new group and had created a number of markings on the dirt surrounding them.

I released the spirits, watching them dissipate and return to my mind. Finishing the last sigils hastily on my skin, I was relieved to discover Conal had already marked himself and Nick with a couple of hastily drawn marks. "Ready?"

Conal nodded grimly before he and Nick stepped away to transform, tearing off their t-shirts and throwing them to the ground before they shifted into wolf shape. With one last glance towards Lucas, I ran into the fray.

Chapter 41

...of Death and Destruction

It was worse, far worse than I'd ever anticipated. Even in my most terrible and darkest imaginings, I'd never dreamed it would be so horrific. This was nothing like training with Epi, nor was it like taking on a couple of demons and vampires, as we'd done only a few days ago.

This was terrifying.

Demons and youngling vampires were appearing everywhere on the ground and the noise was deafening. Shrieks, screams and yells sliced through the air, along with other sounds which I struggled to comprehend. The sounds of ripping, tearing - bodies slamming into bodies as we faced the enemy head on.

No matter where I turned there was an adversary. And they continued to arrive, demons appearing through erupted fissures in the ground and the younglings from portals, their eyes crazed. Instinct kicked in and I utilized my powers, throwing spirit orbs at everything in line of sight, pulling the Katchet out to attack demons. There was no time to think, no way of selectively choosing who best to attack first. The only way of dealing with this massacre was to take on the enemy as they appeared.

Epi's magic had already removed the huge metal cages and as I fought my way across the battlefield, the ground was awash in blood both black and red. I witnessed one of the werewolves eviscerated by a demon and there was nothing I could do. There was no time to tend to the wounded. I hurled a Philaris at one demon, hitting the massive creature's chest and then launched myself at it, sinking a Katchet into its broad torso.

...of Death and Destruction

Jumping from the demon, I found Conal and Nick attacking a youngling as it headed towards me. With careful aim, I threw a spirit orb and the vampire crashed backwards, eyes lifeless when he hit the ground.

There was no time to consider stopping for breath. Minutes passed rapidly - or was it hours? I was drenched with sweat, my clothing and skin soaked in demon blood. All I could do was attack, with little regard to what I was attacking, or what might be coming next. It was impossible to think further ahead than the next split-second. I hardened my heart against those of our own I saw killed, there was no time to mourn in this cacophony of battle.

A huge vampire trapped me while I was dispatching a demon and gripped my neck. Judging by the sheer size of his body, the human had been a weightlifter before his creation. He squeezed my neck and I thrashed about trying to suck air into my lungs. Nick and Conal took a second to realize I was in trouble, they'd been attacking yet another vampire. The weightlifter holding on to me was tightening his grip and whilst he remained at my back, I could do little to save myself.

Conal and Nick catapulted across the ground but before they could reach me, a blur of orange and black flew past and I heard a bloodcurdling roar. The grip around my neck abruptly loosened when the huge tiger ripped the weightlifter's head from his body. I stumbled forward, gasping air into my lungs as I indicated towards one of the more intimidating demons to Conal and Nick.

We were losing. We were seriously outnumbered and although our side was battling valiantly, the ground was littered with the dead and injured. Anger was building in my heart, anger at the injustice of it all, fury at the loss of innocent lives. For just a moment, I stopped moving, realizing that fighting as we were was just not proving effective. Epi's words echoed through my mind and I knew I had to try a different tack.

I slipped the Katchet onto my belt and centered on the spirits, requesting their aid. Concentrating hard, I drew the spirits one by one from my mind, watching as they formed before me and without delay, entered the battle. It took intense concentration to bring this many into our world, the exertion leaving me weak at the knees. Conal and Nick stopped fighting, sensing what I was attempting and began running interference around me, keeping the enemy at bay. I increased the number of spirits fighting on the battlefield one by one, my limbs trembling with exertion. I had no idea what they were doing, how they might be aiding in the fight - I couldn't risk losing concentration for even a second. All I was certain of was their presence - I knew they were attacking the enemy, standing side by side with our allies in this seemingly never-ending mêlée.

I was relieved to glimpse Lucas and Ben, Ripley and William joining the circle of protection surrounding me and I closed my eyes, centering my efforts still further to keep the corporeal spirits fighting. Gently, and with infinite care, I created a mental divider in my mind.

Satisfied that I still had control of the spirits who were fighting, I used the divided section of my mind to call additional spirits to my aid. I visualized the demons, watching their images form in my head and when I had them clearly pictured, I created a spirit orb and envisaged the demons captured inside it. I raised my arms shakily, straining with the effort and clenched my hands into fists. The fetid stench of demon wafted over me and my skin was awash with their blood.

I repeated the same procedure for a second time. The noise and sounds dissipated, retreating from my mind as I intensified my efforts. The noise of the battlefield disappeared entirely until all I heard was the soft murmuring of voices in my mind. Encouraging me, those remaining in my head offered support and encouragement, providing details of the battle around me and counsel. My head ached colossally, but I kept my breathing steady, my concentration paramount to defeating the enemy.

"Charlotte, Charlotte! It's over!" Lucas stood in front of me, his clothing and skin covered in dripping demon blood. Taking a deep breath, I watched as dozens of spirits disappeared in a swirl of white mist and my knees gave way. Lucas caught me in his arms, holding me tightly against him as I trembled uncontrollably.

Conal sat on his haunches at my side and yelped, licking my cheek with his rough tongue. He looked relatively unharmed, other than a few cuts and scratches, there were no signs of major injury. Similarly, Nick had come through in good health, a minor gash on his front leg and his fur matted with demon blood the only signs of his involvement.

"Are you alright?" Lucas was examining me carefully, searching for signs of injury. "Are you hurt?"

I shook my head, incapable of forcing words from my lips. There was chaos all around us, bodies littered the ground, the soil dripping with blood. The Tines were walking around the battlefield, using Hjördis to treat the wounded. In the distance, people ran out through the gates, intent on finding their loved ones. Jerome limped out, his small staff carrying all manner of medical equipment whilst still more people brought stretchers to carry the injured inside.

It was with sadness that I realized how easy it was to tell who'd lived and who'd died amongst the werewolves and shape-shifters. Those injured remained in animal form - either unconscious or yelping piteously. The deceased had reverted to human form, crumpled and naked on the hard dirt. The sounds of battle were replaced by a noise even worse - the sound of grief. Tears welled in my eyes and I inhaled a shuddering breath.

I pushed away from Lucas and walked off, unable to comprehend what I'd witnessed - unwilling to face it for a minute longer. Stumbling blindly, I left Lucas and the others, heading back to Zaen.

Chapter 42

Cold, Hard Reality

With my back resting against the wall, I watched the sun set on the horizon, casting long shadows across the wooden floor. I'd sat here for ages, thinking of everything and nothing, wishing I could remove the memories from my head.

Peaceful and quiet, this room was one of the few places I'd found where I could relax and listen to the spirits without constant bombardment from the people surrounding me. I'd found it by accident, investigating the assembly hall one day, I'd followed a set of stairs which led to the chance discovery of this small area above the main rooms. There was no furniture, no indication of its past use - but it was ideal for me.

When I'd first escaped up here after the battle, I'd curled into a fetal position on the floor, wrapping my arms tightly around my body to stop the shaking. Every nerve ending was screaming, every muscle trembling with terror. I couldn't do this. The recollection of what I'd seen filled me with abhorrence, my heart racing and sweat beading on my forehead as I recalled the images of the battlefield. Today I'd run on instinct. Now I'd seen what we were facing - the *reality* of our situation - I knew I couldn't do it again. Worse still, seeing people dying before my eyes. What if that happened to Lucas? Or Conal?

The trembling gradually reduced and I pulled myself into a sitting position. I'd been staring off into space for hours, wondering how I could face anybody again. The thought of their pain, their anguish at losing loved ones - how could I possibly face them when I'd failed so miserably? Naïve and foolish, I'd promised I would protect them, thinking I could fight and win against the Consiliului. Today had exposed the impossibility of our mission. Their forces were too physically powerful, there were too many of them and they were going to annihilate us.

And I was frightened of dying. Seeing the deaths of those people today - the thought of dying as they had made me nauseous. After trying so many times to commit suicide in my past, it seemed ridiculous to fear dying. But that had been different. Death at my own hand would have been a release, a way of ending the pain I endured. Peaceful.

I studied my left arm, which still bore the faint scar from slicing it open, first to feed the Tines and again for Conal to drink my blood, to give him the abilities of Nememiah. Despite my upset, I smirked. For someone who'd found it impossible to slit her wrists, I'd grown to ignore the pain of cutting into my own skin.

The smile died as the images of today's fight overwhelmed my thoughts again. Dying like those people today, surrounded by enemies - it had been violent and terrifying. How long had they lived, knowing there was no help coming? How long had they lain there, knowing they would die but unable to do anything to prevent it? How painful was that death?

The sound of footsteps alerted me to their arrival. Lucas appeared first, followed by Conal, Ben, Epi and Matt. Lucas slid down the wall to sit on the floor beside me and Conal took the other side. Belying his age, Epi dropped nimbly onto the floor, sitting cross-legged and he was joined by Ben and Matt.

"How did you find me?"

Conal smirked. "I'm a werewolf and Lucas and Ben are vampires. It wasn't difficult. We followed the charming scent of demon blood."

I glanced down at my clothes, still completely soaked with drying blood. In comparison, they'd all showered and dressed in clean clothes and I wrinkled my nose in distaste. "Should have had a shower."

Conal grinned wryly. "Wouldn't have made any difference, Sugar. We would have followed your own scent instead."

I lapsed into silence, vaguely wondering what they were doing here. I wanted to be left alone, to wallow in depression and shock. Pulling my legs up, I wrapped my arms around them and rested my chin on my knees. I focused on the floor, hoping they would get the hint and leave me alone.

"What you did, Child, it was remarkable," Epi began sincerely. "You defeated an army of demons and younglings. We knew your skills were considerable, but you astounded even me."

"It wasn't enough." And it hadn't been. People had died and I felt personally responsible for each and every person who'd lost their lives.

"You did what you could. What you did do, saved many lives," Ben responded.

"How many died?" I snapped.

"Fifty six," Conal responded, catching my hand in his. "Sugar... Phelan Walker was one of them."

"I know," I remarked quietly. "He's been giving me a pep talk for the past hour."

The pain in my heart amplified, thinking about Phelan's death. Despite our initially rocky start, we'd developed a strong friendship based on mutual respect. Phelan had accepted his death without misgiving, with no regret. He'd accepted it far better than I had. The incredible loss was overwhelming.

"He was a good man, Sugar. He'll keep helping you through this."

"Through what? Watching you all die, one by one?" I shook my head dismally. "This is unwinnable. This time it was a hundred demons - what happens next time when it's a thousand? We lost fifty six people in our first battle. Twenty percent of our people are gone, instantly. It's impossible for us to win this."

Lucas slipped an arm around my shoulder. "Charlotte, it would have been much worse if you hadn't done what you did." He caught the startled look in my eyes and seemed stunned. "You don't even *know* what you did, do you?"

I shrugged. The entire events of the battle were a blur and when I'd been working with the spirits, all I'd been able to concentrate on was the effort taken to keep them cohesive.

"You were incredible, Charlotte." Matt spoke, his eyes filled with respect when he gazed at me.

I looked up at him, confused, then glanced towards Epi with a frown creasing my forehead.

"Charlotte, you fought the demons for over six hours. Not only did you bring dozens of the spirits into our world to fight our enemies, but you also simultaneously created spirit orbs that decimated the demons, sometimes three or four at a time." Epi reached toward me, rubbing a hand awkwardly against my knee. "Child, you exceeded what I imagined you would be capable of."

"But people still died. We lost fifty six people, trying to get sixty people into Zaen," I said dully. "I couldn't save them."

"We all know what we're facing, Charlotte. Nobody expected to get through this without casualties," Ben responded softly. "And everyone out there today knew the risk they were taking, the possibility that people would die. You aren't responsible for their deaths – they chose to fight, knowing that what they were doing was for the good of their families, their Packs. Nobody expects you to be responsible for keeping everyone alive."

"Charlotte, this is a war. Death goes with the territory," Matt stated matter-of-factly. "That doesn't make it easy – one of the toughest things anyone has to do is watch their friends die. And from what your friends here tell me, this is the first time you've gone into battle. It's understandable that you're feeling shell-shocked, doubting your abilities. Anyone who's ever had to fight in combat feels the same way, it's a natural reaction to the stresses of fighting a war." A ghost of a smile lifted his lips. "I know it's no consolation, but I'm terrifically proud of you. You did a great job out there."

"You saw me?" I asked quietly.

"Watched the whole thing. With my heart in my mouth, admittedly," Matt said with a tight smile. "Clinton and I watched from the battlements. Thought maybe we could figure out some ways that we can help."

"Come up with anything?" I asked curiously.

Matt nodded slowly, his voice cautious. "A couple of things. They're a work in progress."

"Charlotte, we have more people coming which will boost our numbers. This attack today, it was twenty four hours earlier than we'd expected," Conal added. "Considering we had about five minutes warning, we did a pretty good job in difficult circumstances."

"How do you know that they aren't going to attack over and over again?" I demanded. "This could happen every day. How are we going to get the new people into the city?"

"We made a grave error in judgment by choosing to bring people to Zaen before they're marked," Epi admitted. "We'll portal to them henceforth, do the markings and then portal directly into the city itself."

"We can't hide in here forever," I argued.

"No, we can't," Lucas agreed gently. "But we can increase our numbers for next time. And today has given us the opportunity to locate our weaknesses, get a handle on exactly what the demons are capable of. Everything we have learned from today can be used to ensure we're better prepared for the next time." He kissed my forehead. "We've all had to fight before, in one theatre of war or another. The very nature of what we are, means there are situations in which we've had to fight. Whether in a battle amongst our own kind or in a human war because we've got caught up in it, we've had to fight. You haven't. I know it's a terrible shock to see what a battle is like - and God knows I wish you hadn't needed to. But we can win this, Charlotte. I promise you, we *will* win."

I turned to Matt, regarding him seriously before I spoke. "You're the ex-marine, Matt. Do you think we can win?"

Matt eyed me calmly. "Well, admittedly, this is a new type of warfare to what I'm used to. But yeah, I think we can. It's going to take a lot of work and I'm not going to lie to you, Charlotte. Other people are gonna die. But from what I've seen, these people are all dedicated to this cause. Your cause. Lucas is right - the first battle was always going to be the toughest. Now we've seen what the enemy are like, seen how they operate, we can work on finding their weaknesses. We have to ensure our people are trained to best handle the way the enemy fights. Work on strategies and tactics to find effective ways of defeating them." He stood up, holding out his hand. "Now how about you come down with us and get cleaned up? And I've heard a few rumors about your perpetual appetite - seems to me after that, you must be starving."

I took his hand and he pulled me gently to my feet, warm fingers clenching my own. "I'm proud of you, Charlotte. Really proud." He pulled me into an awkward hug and I wrapped my arms around his waist, feeling oddly secure with this man I barely knew.

Chapter 43

Learning to Cope

The funeral pyres burned constantly for the next forty eight hours as our city honored its dead. The heavy pall of smoke coincided with a change in the weather, the skies overcast and heavy rain falling as I stood with the other mourners outside the gates.

Lucas, Conal and Nick attended every funeral with me, after I announced it was my duty to attend. Listening as tributes were delivered for each of our dead, I sorrowfully realized that I'd learned more about these people after their deaths than I'd been given the opportunity to do in life.

The three men were resplendent in suits, the muted colors soaked to a darker hue by the constant rain. In contrast, I'd elected to wear white, with Marianne providing a knitted cashmere skirt and jacket. I stood beneath the umbrella Lucas held over us, listening mutely as the deceased were given their final rights.

Every funeral was overseen by a company of guards, watching vigilantly for signs of further attack. The spirits were in continuous contact, ensuring I'd have warning if the Consiliului sent more assailants. Whether by accident or good timing, there were no attacks during the funerals and we cremated the dead without any further incident.

Finally, the last of the funerals concluded and we walked back into Zaen, splashing through muddy puddles created by the incessant rain.

"Let's go and have a drink," Conal suggested as we entered the gates, following behind other mourners. His eyes raked over my pale skin, dark shadowed and dull eyes. "I think you need one."

It was probably true - the effect of attending fifty six funerals was depressing and as I'd watched the fires being ignited beneath the bodies, I couldn't help but feel liable for their deaths. Lucas had his arm wrapped around my waist and Conal and Nick walked close to my other side, providing support through their proximity.

"I'm going to go home and get into bed," I replied. My feet were aching, my head thumping and the last thing I needed was the company of other people.

"Charlotte, Conal's right. You should have a drink, relax a little. You've endured a number of difficult days."

I narrowed my eyes at Lucas. "It disturbs me when you two agree with one another."

"Sometimes the dog is right," Lucas admitted, his tone suggesting he hated to confess it. In recent days, Lucas and Conal had presented a united front, getting along with each other, but I was aware of the tension simmering just beneath the surface.

"Gee, thanks for the vote of confidence, leech," Conal grinned.

"Oh, stop it, both of you," I grumbled. "Fine. I'll go home and shower, then I'll come down to the mess for one drink. That's it."

We parted ways at the street where our cottage was situated and Lucas and I walked slowly to our home. Other than a brief couple of hours sleep, I'd barely been there since the attack and I craved a long, hot shower to try and wash away the memory of the funerals.

Lucas followed me upstairs and sat on the edge of the bed as I hunted for clean clothes. "You've barely spoken in the past few days," he announced.

"I've had a lot on my mind." I rummaged through the drawers, searching for a sweater. Everything seemed so complicated right now, even the search for something suitable to wear, and I sighed, pushing clothing haphazardly out of the way as my frustration grew.

Lucas came to stand beside me. "I wish you would talk to me, my love. I'm worried about you."

Pulling my hair from the tight chignon I'd pulled it into, I shook my head a little until the curls fell around my shoulders. Then I returned to the search of the drawer, my tension increasing. "There's nothing I want to talk about."

Lucas sighed, gripping my hand in his. "Charlotte, stop throwing clothes about and talk to me. I want to help you through this, if only you'll let me."

Learning to Cope

I shut my eyes, a torrent of pain pouring through my heart. "You want to know what's wrong with me?" I asked, wrenching away from his hold. My eyes blazed with anger and shame. "You all seem to think I'm noble and wonderful because of what I did out there. But I'm not! I'm frightened and I'm a terrible person. I've been attending funerals for the past two days and all I could think about, standing out there in the rain was the fact that it wasn't you! Or Conal, or Nick! And I feel so guilty about that! Guilty and terrible, and I wish… I wish…" I sobbed brokenly, unable to continue speaking as everything overwhelmed me.

Lucas pulled me into his arms, holding me close. "It's a natural reaction, Charlotte, to feel this way." He brushed his fingers across my damp curls, the motion exquisitely tender. "We all feel the same way - the desire to keep those you love safe, is a powerful sensation."

I drew a shuddering breath, leaning against Lucas and clinging to his jacket. "I don't want you to die," I whispered.

Lucas kissed the top of my head. "We all feel that way, Charlotte. Everyone one of us fears for the people we love and feels relieved that death came to someone else, not our own loved ones. It's a normal response. We can feel sympathy for those who lost their own, but it's natural to feel relief that it wasn't someone you love who was killed." He rubbed his hands soothingly down my back. "Imagine how you feel, my love, and increase it a hundred fold. Despite your abilities, you are still very much human - when you ran out into the battle - the pain of thinking I might never see you alive again was excruciating." He held me closer still, his arms wrapped around me as though he was attempting to cocoon us from the world. "Charlotte, you must try not to worry about others around you when you are battling these creatures - all your concentration must be on keeping yourself safe. Conal, Nick - the others - we're different. The very fact of what we are gives us stronger abilities when fighting the demons and vampires. And there's not one person who fights with you, who hasn't had battle experience, who hasn't fought something or someone before." He kissed my forehead. "But you - while the sigils you draw on your skin amplify your physical abilities, the fact remains that you are a human woman. The thought of you battling those demons - knowing that one mistake could see you killed. It's more than I can bear. More than any of us can bear."

I wished again that I could leave this place, run away from here and find somewhere safe to hide. My confidence had taken a beating in the battle on the fields outside and doubts filled my mind.

"I'm frightened," I admitted quietly.

Lucas caught my face between his hands, searching my eyes. "You *should* be frightened. In many ways, I prefer you being frightened to being courageous. It makes me feel as though you might be a little more aware of your own mortality." He bent forward, briefly catching my lips with his own. "Fear is a healthy emotion - it isn't something you should avoid. These past couple of days, when you've been so silent, not discussing your feelings... Charlotte, promise me, that you will discuss these things with me? I'm here for you and I want to support you. But it's difficult when you aren't allowing me to know what you're thinking."

I nodded mutely and threw myself back into his arms, holding him tightly against my body as tears began to roll down my cheeks. The pent-up emotions of the past two days had burst across the top of the dam I'd built up and I sobbed as Lucas whispered soothing words against my ear and rubbed his hands lovingly across my back. When I'd cried myself out, I pulled away from his grip and smiled weakly. "I love you."

"And I love you, Charlotte. I will always love you." He rubbed his thumb across my cheek, wiping the tears away. "You are the most important thing in my world."

"Even though I'm a mess?"

Lucas smiled. "You're not a mess, my love. Stronger people would buckle under the pressure in your position. But please, don't hide your feelings from me anymore, all right?"

I nodded. "I promise."

Lucas kissed me, his lips brushing gently across mine and released me. "You're still soaking wet. Go and have a shower, warm up a little."

I flicked my fingers across his wet suit jacket. "You're soaking wet, too."

"Unlike you, I don't feel the cold."

"Still," I said insistently, raising my hands to push the jacket from his broad shoulders, "wouldn't it be a good idea for you to have a shower too?"

Lucas arched one eyebrow, gazing down at me I saw the desire spark in his eyes. "Are you suggesting we share the shower?"

Tugging at the neat tie around his neck, I grinned. "Yes, I think that's exactly what I'm suggesting."

Lucas reached for his tie and in one swift movement had it undone, throwing it to the floor. "Maybe I should be worrying about my own virtue," he suggested with a smile, leaning forward to capture my mouth with his.

≈†◇◇†◇◇†◇◇†≈

The central courtyard was overflowing with people, lights glowing brightly from every window in the Mess. Lucas and I walked hand-in-hand across the grass and he squeezed my fingers reassuringly. I wasn't sure how the people of Zaen were going to react. Were they angry that I'd been unable to keep everyone safe? Did they blame me for the attack? I'd had little opportunity to speak with anyone in the past forty eight hours and my knowledge of the community's mindset was limited.

All apprehension evaporated as people approached us to talk, to offer a welcoming hug and incredibly, to thank us for providing sanctuary in the city.

Lucas and I walked slowly through the crowds milling around outside, our pace reduced by the continual procession of people greeting us. It was the precise opposite of what I'd expected. I'd assumed they would hate me, would blame me for what happened. Instead, they treated me with respect and thanks for providing safety for their wives and husbands, children, grandparents. Despite my misgivings, they accepted the deaths we'd suffered as a natural part of battle, exactly as Lucas had predicted.

We reached the Mess and Lucas held the door open, allowing me to enter before him. Linking his fingers through mine, we strolled across the room. Again, people seemed eager to talk and I spotted Conal sitting with some of his pack. He grinned, winking and raising his beer in salute. I flushed with embarrassment and glanced away.

Epi sat with Ben, Rowena, Nat Finton, Matt and Misaki. Ben located two chairs in the crowded room and I sank down into one thankfully, whilst Lucas went to the makeshift bar to get a drink.

Misaki sat by my side and enveloped me in a warm hug. "How are you?"

I shrugged. "Okay. Where's Kazuki?"

Misaki grinned, her brown eyes filled with delight. "He's playing with Katie and some of the other kids. Gwynn is keeping an eye on them."

I smiled brightly, the first time I'd done so in days. "I bet she's loving that."

"That woman was born to be a Mom," Misaki agreed. "She loves those kids."

Lucas placed a glass on the table and slipped into the empty chair at my side. "Drink this, my Charlotte. It'll help you to relax."

I lifted the glass and sniffed at it, recognizing the familiar odor of scotch. Tears filled my eyes as I recalled Phelan giving me a scotch only a few weeks ago, when he'd been so determined to get me to drink. Now it seemed like a lifetime ago.

I bit my lip and inhaled deeply, straightening my shoulders. If these people could celebrate being alive, I could too. I gulped down some of the drink, feeling it warm my throat as I swallowed.

Epi leaned across the table. He was wearing a bright blue tunic, which matched the color of his eyes. "Are you feeling calmer now, child?"

"I am." To my surprise, it was the truth. I did feel better. Releasing pent up emotion had been a panacea to my shattered nerves. I still felt an indelible sadness in my psyche for those we'd lost, but it was countered by happiness for those we'd saved. And with that happiness came a belief that perhaps we would find better ways of fighting, discover the secret to winning this war and defeating the Consiliului.

Marianne and Striker approached, locating another two chairs and they sat down with us. Marianne smiled elatedly. "Charlotte, it is *wonderful* to see you dressed in something other than camouflage pants and a tank top!"

I returned her smile. "Well, I could hardly wear this to fight demons, could I?"

Lucas let his eyes roam over my clothing and his gaze heated my skin. I'd selected a red cashmere sweater, with a low cut neckline, teaming it with tight black jeans and boots. He looked up, meeting my eyes again and winked. "Definitely not," he agreed huskily.

"Charlotte?" Nat caught my attention from across the table. "Your father has some good ideas which I think you should hear."

I sipped a little more scotch and glanced at my father. "Funnily enough, I've heard a few rumors, Matt. What's the grand plan?"

"What rumors have your heard?" Matt countered coyly. I noticed he was drinking a soda, nursing the can between his hands.

"Something to do with the humans being able to help out during a fight." I stirred my drink thoughtfully with the straw. "Although I'm hoping it doesn't involve any of you being out there." The thought of putting humans in the field of battle, with no increased abilities was something I wasn't going to consider, democracy or not. The little I knew about my father confirmed without doubt he was a brave man, honest and strong. But this was a different type of war to what he was used to and I would never consider him being out there with us. Never.

"Your father and I have already discussed that, child. He agrees our human allies would not be safe in the field itself, due to the very nature of our enemies. Rather, he has some other, quite good ideas," Epi said.

I studied Matt for a moment, seeing the determined set to his jaw, the strong features. Every single characteristic spoke of a military man who was brave and proud, but also intelligent and well-spoken. "So? Spill it."

Matt sipped his soda, scanning the crowd. "Hey! Clinton!"

Clinton Davis came over to join us. Matt greeted him like they were old buddies and brought him up to speed on our discussion, before turning to me again. "Clinton has been helping me with these ideas, so he should be here to add his input."

"Hey Clinton," I greeted the former Chief of Police warmly.

"Charlotte." Clinton grinned.

I narrowed my eyes, eyeing both men suspiciously. "So?"

Matt twisted the soda between his fingers. "We've been talking with Epi and Ben about these demons your fighting. They've already convinced me that humans can't do much about the young vampires, they're too strong for us to have much impact. But the demons, they might be a different matter. Epi tells me the only way to return them to this Otherworld place is to attack them with the weapons. But Clinton and I have been discussing whether with modern technology, there might be other ways to fight them."

"Such as?" I was curious now, obviously Matt had been doing his homework and he'd apparently thought about this long and hard. I found myself warming further to him.

"We can't be certain until we run some tests, but we're wondering if we can use modern technology, set up on the ramparts, to attack the demons."

"What sort of modern technology?" Lucas queried.

"Machine guns. Rocket launchers," Matt explained. "Epi reckons he can procure some equipment for us and we'll test out the theory, see if it's workable."

"Do we have any idea if those sort of weapons would work on the demons?" Striker questioned. "We know there's something specific about the weapons which causes the injuries to the demons. None of us can injure them enough to return them to the Otherworld without the weapons. What makes you think we could use machine guns and rocket launchers and have any success?"

"We don't know for sure," Clinton admitted, "but Matt and I think it's worth experimenting, see if we can find a way to MacGyver the ammunition to injure or kill the demons."

"What? Bullets made out of the same material the weapons contain?" I wondered aloud.

"That would be impossible, child. The weapons were created by Nememiah himself and I doubt their construction is something we could replicate," Epi contradicted immediately. "However, your father and Clinton have some other ideas which we would like to try."

"We want to set up some weapons on the ramparts, have Epi create some demons to practice on. Your Dad and I have got a list of things we'd like to attempt, see if anything is useful," Clinton continued. He ran a hand across his stubbled jaw. "We're thinking at the very least we might be able to injure them. If we can come up with something to disable them, stop them in the midst of an attack and allow our people to gain an advantage, it would be beneficial."

Matt leaned across the table, clasping my hand in his. "What do you think, Charlotte? Should we give it a try?" He regarded me earnestly and squeezed my fingers. "If we can find some way of making this work, it would add another forty people to our group who can fight..."

I wrenched my fingers from his grip and raised my hands to my head as the spirits clamored for attention.

"What's wrong?" Matt demanded.

"Sound the alarm," I gasped. "We've got incoming."

Chapter 44

Madness

Outside the walls, utter chaos reigned. The entire horizon was filled with demons and vampires, our little band making a valiant effort against them. The skies over the city were pitch black, it was a moonless night and I was grateful when huge bonfires flared to life on the ground around us. Epi was lighting our way.

There hadn't been time to change, I still wore the sweater and black jeans, my sleeves rolled up where I'd marked sigils swiftly as we made for the gates.

Our little group poured out through the gates of Zaen to meet the enemy head on, and the sounds and images were a repeat performance of the attack four days ago. Remaining inside, Marianne and Rowena were marking people, giving them a few rapid marks to increase their strength and agility.

Lucas, Conal and Nick were in close proximity to my side, not only attacking the enemy and defending themselves, but keeping a close eye on me as I fought everything which approached our position.

The reverberating sound of a weapon rang out from the ramparts and I risked a quick glance. Matt and Clinton were up there, high above the battleground, operating a rocket launcher and machine gun. Their efforts were inhibited by our people mixed amongst the enemy, but Matt was firing the rocket launcher further out, towards the demons as they coalesced.

The noise was deafening, a constant barrage of sound which assaulted me as I dipped and whirled, throwing orbs and attacking. For every demon which arrived and was dispatched, two more erupted from the ground to replace them. The portals remained open as dozen upon dozen younglings poured through them. Ambrose Wilkes and his pack were doing an outstanding job in this regard, Ambrose had his men positioned at the portals. As quickly as the vampires appeared, the tigers pounced, tearing limbs from the vampires and immobilizing them. They weren't able to impede every vampire, but they were disabling at least one out of three. It was reducing the numbers we had to deal with, but barely making a dent in our overall situation - there were too many demons, hundreds of them in all shapes and sizes and they steadfastly ambled towards the city.

"Form a barrier!" William ordered, dispatching a Valafar with the Katchet and throwing a Philaris towards an Omias which was lumbering towards him. "Keep them back from the gates!"

The demons were making a concerted approach towards the walls and I couldn't understand their determination, as they had no way of passing the barriers guarding the city. Yet they continued to pound their way towards the massive walls, forcing us into a slow retreat.

The gates swept open, and light shone through the entrance, creating a shaft of illumination over us. I stole a fleeting glance to see Clinton and another couple of human men running towards us, boxes in their arms. The gates slammed shut again and Clinton dropped to the ground behind us, handing me a new Philaris. I was grateful as I'd lost both of mine and now relied on the Katchet alone, but the thought of them being outside terrified me.

"Get back inside!" I shrieked, grunting as a demon swiped at me with claws as long as my arm.

"You need rearming - I can help by doing that. The machine gun wasn't having any effect," Clinton argued loudly.

"Clint, you'll get yourselves killed!" He was a good man, but human, with the fragility that would take seconds to destroy out in this hellhole. "Get back inside, for God's sake!"

"No," he repeated stubbornly. "There are few enough of you who can use the weapons. I'm staying here to help."

"Leave it, Charlotte!" Ben ordered as he swung past me and threw a Philaris towards the demon who'd approached while I dealt with Clint. He dispatched the demon seconds before it would have sliced through me with its razor-like fangs. "We need the replacement weapons!"

Clint handed me a second Philaris. "Don't worry about me, just fight the damn demons!"

With no further debate, Clinton continued to work valiantly, replacing our weapons as needed. We needed them desperately. The onslaught seemed never-ending, as fast as we dispatched demons, killed vampires - more arrived to take their places. The fires burnt themselves out as night receded and daylight filtered over the horizon.

Exhaustion was beginning to overtake me, along with the terrible apprehension that this would never end. They would never stop sending demons, we would be fighting here until we dropped. The stark reality when daylight crept over was clear - we weren't winning. A glance at my arms confirmed the sigils had nearly burnt themselves out, the marks faded to almost nothing, explaining my weakened condition. The potency of the orbs was waning, although managing to dispatch the demons in small groups, it was becoming more difficult to sustain the orbs in which to crush them.

The most bizarre thing happened - the majority of the demons vanished, their forms turning to mist and floating away in the cool breeze which blew over the plains. As they disappeared, I realized the vampires had also drastically reduced in numbers. They'd ceased coming through the portals and we were battling perhaps thirty or forty who remained.

Which was when I saw him.

Archangelo stood near the edge of the battleground. He was watching me over the heads of those fighting, his handsome face impassive.

When he saw he'd captured my attention, he took off at a run towards the woods, his speed dizzying as he made a beeline for the trees.

"Archangelo!" Without a thought, I ran through the battlefield, evading both demons and vampires, steeling my heart to the number of bodies lying motionless on the soil. We'd lost more people during this battle and I would grieve for them, but not now - now I needed to stop Archangelo before he reached the small group of fifteen who still insisted on camping in the woods.

"Charlotte, wait!" Lucas roared, but I was sprinting with a burst of adrenaline-induced speed. Anger swamped me, a murderous rage directed at the vampire who'd disappeared into the woods. This man had tried to kill me, he was my enemy. This man was the reason these people lay dead and dying around me. I had to stop him. I had to confront him and try to kill him. And I still had no idea how.

I heard Lucas shouting, but I couldn't stop, wouldn't wait. Archangelo might be intending to make his escape, or would kill the fifteen innocent people residing out in the woods. A sliver of fear had me wondering if this was an opportunity he was creating to kill me.

I narrowly avoided a youngling who reached towards me, but he was cut off by one of the panthers who leaped onto him, knocking him to the ground. Skirting around the last of the demons, I hurtled towards the woods.

The sky progressively darkened as I entered the tree line. The sounds of the battle began to fade, the silence in the woods all-encompassing. Having never entered the forest before, I was disorientated, uncertain where the small group were camping and how to locate them.

"It's a trap, Charlotte! Go back!"

Mom's voice rang through my mind, making me jump. *"I don't have a choice. I have to follow him, try and stop him."*

"Go back! Wait for the others!" Mom sounded determined.

"I can't, Mom." I didn't have a choice, Archangelo had to be stopped. Somehow.

The trees were thick around me, the ancient limbs gnarly and their branches reached out, catching my skin and clothes. The darkness of the woods deepened still further.

Pulling the Hjördis from my pocket, I stopped for a short time to mark fresh sigils on my arms. I'd need every scrap of strength I could muster if I had to fight Archangelo and I knew that was what this would come to. He had to be stopped - he was responsible for the deaths of those I considered friends. Without him, the Council would lose their greatest strength. Niggling in my mind was the memory of Nememiah's words - only one of us could survive. It was going to be me.

I almost fell over the first body, staggering back in horror, bile rising in my throat. It was a young girl, perhaps nine years old. A little girl with silky blond hair and pale blue eyes which stared lifelessly upwards, no longer seeing the leaves on the trees above her.

Stumbling through the trees I came across others, the people who'd been living out here. Every single one was dead. I couldn't tell if they'd been murdered in the past few minutes or if their deaths had come before the battle had begun.

Shaking with a combination of shock and revulsion, I knelt beside the next body I discovered and touched it gingerly. His skin was cold, the man had evidently been dead for hours. Wrenching myself to my feet, I yelled, the words echoing through the trees. "Archangelo! *Archangelo!* Where are you? If you want me so badly, show yourself."

"Over here." His voice drifted through the woods, coming from somewhere on my left. I turned towards the sound, lurching through the darkened forest until I arrived in a clearing, evidently the former campsite of those murdered. It was a shambles, belongs and tents strewn everywhere, the ground littered with the detritus of people who'd called this home.

I stopped at the edge of the clearing, sucking air into my oxygen starved lungs. Cautiously, I drew a Katchet from my belt and scanned the tree line.

"I'm here."

Twirling towards the sound, I found him leaning against a large oak tree, arms crossed casually over his chest. He wore a weapons belt and pushed himself away from the tree, approaching me leisurely.

"I knew you'd come." He sounded smug, his voice calm and assured. "You couldn't resist, could you?"

"Archangelo." I stepped towards him cautiously.

"I'm pleased you survived our last encounter."

This comment was so far out of left field, I stopped moving, wondering exactly what his plan was. "Only just," I admitted. "But I don't see why you'd be pleased. You *want* me dead."

"Charlotte, I only wanted you dead because you were with the bloodsucker. But now you're here, with me."

I stared at him, hardly able to believe what I was hearing. "I'm only here because I want to kill you, you God-forsaken piece of shit."

Archangelo circled warily, fingering the Katchet on his belt. He wore a white shirt and blue jeans, his startling green eyes never leaving my face. "I don't think you do," he announced quietly.

"You're delusional," I spat. "Besides, my friends will be here soon and we're going to ensure you die."

"No, they won't. The minute you raced off, there was a surge of demons arriving. You're on your own, Charlotte."

A trickle of fear wrapped itself around my heart. "What do you want from me? Why drag me out here?"

He looked smug. "I believe you followed me, Charlotte. I wanted to talk to you, get you to see reason."

We were pacing the outskirts of the clearing, eyes focused on one another, resembling lions preparing to attack. "I will never see things from your point of view, Archangelo. You're killing innocent people back there!"

He sighed, fingers caressing the Katchet's engraved handle. "Why must you be so stubborn? Why can't you see that they're worthless? It is you and I who are important."

"Like I said - delusional!"

"You have to admit - we are the only two of our kind. That makes us more important than any other being on the planet," he continued calmly.

"No, I think *I'm* the only one of my kind on the planet. You're a vampire, remember?" My senses were on high alert and I was listening anxiously for any sound of assistance, but the woods remained intensely silent.

"I like you dressed like this," Archangelo said, scanning my attire. "Red suits you. Pity it's covered in demon blood."

"I don't really care what you like me dressed in or not dressed in, quite frankly."

Without any warning, he was in front of me, only inches away. "Mmmm. Not dressed would be a much better option."

I stepped back. "You're crazy."

He remained motionless, eyeing me thoughtfully. "You may be right. Perhaps I am. It's crazy to be in love with you, when you act so foolishly."

I laughed nervously. "You *are* crazy. You don't even know me."

"Ah, but you forget. I've seen you, Charlotte. I've been watching you for weeks now and I still want you as much as I did the first time I saw you."

"Keep dreaming, buster," I stated angrily. "It's never going to happen."

He was in front of me again, squeezing my wrist until the Katchet dropped from my fingers. "I think you're here because you want me. Sure, you've been sleeping with him, but you came straight out here when you saw me. *To me.*" He dragged me roughly into his arms and dropped his mouth over mind, forcing his tongue into my mouth.

"Let her go!" Lucas's voice reached my ears and I used the opportunity to pummel Archangelo's chest with my fists until he released me. Before I could make an escape, he grabbed me, the Katchet pressing firmly against my jugular vein.

"Vampire, you've tried my patience once too many times," Archangelo snarled. He threw his free arm forward and a spirit orb erupted from his fingertips, flowing swiftly towards Lucas.

Lucas lunged, narrowly avoiding the orb as it swung past him and hit one of the ancient oaks surrounding the clearing. The power of the orb cracked the trunk of the tree and it crashed to the ground. Lucas ran towards Archangelo, barely visible to my eyes and slammed into him, throwing him off balance. The sound of their bodies colliding echoed loudly through the forest.

They battled against each other, Lucas's natural fighting ability keeping him one step ahead of Archangelo's youngling strength. Their movements were incredibly swift and there was nothing I could do but stand and watch.

Despite his superior fighting skills, Lucas didn't have Archangelo's angel abilities and I was horrified when Archangelo flung Lucas away. Lucas crashed onto the ground, the force of his landing creating a deep furrow through the dirt. Lucas got to his feet almost instantly, but it was too late. Archangelo had created a second orb and hurled it with unswerving accuracy towards Lucas.

I screamed as Lucas was blasted backwards, his back slamming into a tree. The sound of bone crunching reached my ears and Lucas slumped to the ground, his body laying at an awkward angle.

Before I could react, Conal hurtled through the woods in his wolf form. He ran towards Archangelo, the look in his eyes crazed as he launched at the vampire. Archangelo slipped a Katchet from his belt and when Conal landed over him, the vampire stabbed the Katchet deep into Conal's chest. Conal collapsed on top of Archangelo and I screamed as Archangelo plunged the knife into Conal's body over and over again.

"*Stop!* You're killing him!" I shrieked, throwing myself at Archangelo to try and get between Conal and the blade.

He shoved me, throwing me through the air to land some ten feet away, before returning to his vicious attack. Conal yelped helplessly and blood flowed in streams from his battered body.

Again I stood and ran towards Archangelo, pitching an orb at him. It blew him away from Conal's battered form and slammed him back through the dirt.

"You bitch!" Archangelo snarled, getting to his feet. "I'll have you, whether you want to be had, or not!"

Reaching me with preternatural speed, he held me against him, the blood soaked Katchet pushed tight against my spine. He ground his hips against me as he sought my mouth again, the blade of the Katchet slicing into my back.

I twisted and clenched at the Katchet, ignoring the agony as it sliced through my fingers. "I hate you! I hate you!"

"You're lying." His eyes were cloudy with the desire for both blood and sex. "You want me. Just as much as I want you." He dropped his mouth to mine again and mauled me. I lowered my hand and focused creating an orb. I centered all my energy on it, trying to entrap as much power as possible into the small sphere.

Archangelo groaned and his lips trailed a path down my neck, licking salt from my skin. It was only a matter of seconds before he'd bite and I focused on the orb growing against my fingertips.

"Archangelo - look at me," I demanded.

He raised his head and stared into my eyes, his own crazed with lust. "What?"

"You've killed both the men I love," I stated coldly. "I hope you're going to enjoy life as a eunuch, you sick son of a bitch." I swung my arm with all the strength I could muster and slammed it into his groin, the orb leaving my fingertips and exploding against his body.

He screamed, shrieking in agony as he hit the ground, clutching his groin with both hands. The orb didn't have the strength to kill him, but I hoped I'd done the next best thing. He'd killed Conal and Lucas and I wanted revenge with every cell in my body.

Snatching up the discarded Katchet I ran to him. I wanted to stab him, kill him and see his dead body lying on the ground before me. He was rolling around in the dirt and I leaped on to him, prepared to pound the Katchet through his chest and into his heart as many times as it took to stop it beating. He would never take another breath.

As I plunged the Katchet towards his chest, Archangelo caught my wrist, squeezing until I heard the snap of breaking bones and the knife dropped uselessly to the ground. Sobbing with frustration, I scrambled to grab it with my other hand.

The sound of people crashing through the undergrowth reached my ears as I groped helplessly for the Katchet. Gunfire reached my ears as I was again tossed through the air. I hit the ground hard, all breath squeezed from my lungs by the impact.

There was yelling and shouting all around, as more of our people arrived in the clearing. Archangelo was gone, vanished into the woods.

The scene before me was horrifying - Conal, lying in a pool of blood and Lucas, motionless on the ground.

"Charlotte!" Matt dropped the gun he'd been wielding and dragged me into his arms. "Baby! Are you okay?"

Numbness crept over me incrementally and I sagged against him.

I'd lost the two most important people in my life.

And I'd failed to kill Archangelo.

Dear reader,

We hope you enjoyed reading *Knowledge Hurts*. Please take a moment to leave a review in Amazon, even if it's a short one. Your opinion is important to us.

The story continues in *The Knowledge of Love*

Discover more books by D.S. Williams at
https://www.nextchapter.pub/authors/ds-williams

Want to know when one of our books is free or discounted for Kindle? Join the newsletter at http://eepurl.com/bqqB3H

Best regards,

D.S. Williams and the Next Chapter Team

ABOUT THE AUTHOR

Wife and mother to four demanding young adults, D.S. Williams started writing at the age of five, when life was simpler and her stories really didn't need to make sense. When you're five, 'happily ever after' always ends the story and how you got there? Well, that didn't matter so much.

An extreme introvert, D.S. Williams has created her own worlds to exist in, found friends among her characters and traveled the Earth from the safety of her laptop keyboard.

D.S. Williams enjoys writing (obviously), reading (voraciously) and making lists (obsessively). She's enjoyed a lifelong addiction to foods starting with 'ch' - cheesecake, chocolate and chips - and when it comes to books, she loves a multitude of genres and authors.

She shares her life with her beloved husband of twenty nine years, the Gang of Four and the current furry residents, Tuppence the Groodle and Angus the Bull Mastiff.